JUST CALL ME
GATSBY

GARY GOLDSTICK

JUST CALL ME GATSBY

CITIOFBOOKS, INC.
3736 Eubank NE Suite A1
Albuquerque, NM 87111-3579
www.citiofbooks.com
Hotline: 1 (877) 389-2759
Fax: 1 (505) 930-7244

Ordering Information:
Quantity sales. Special discounts are available on quantity purchases by corporations, associations, and others. For details, contact the publisher at the address above.

Printed in the United States of America.

ISBN-13:   Softcover   979-8-89391-929-5
              eBook   979-8-89391-930-1

Library of Congress Control Number: 2025920141

TABLE OF CONTENTS

PROLOGUE

GATSBY

March 13, 2003

Five-foot-ten, blond, muscular Christopher Gatsby Brooks stood at a window in his partner's foyer in the Mellon Bank Center, looking at the late afternoon skyline.

Philadelphia had been good to him, thanks to the three hundred thousand potential investors the city housed. He knew many of them; they were his clients.

Gatsby's friend and best investor, Moe Shultz, sat in a chair next to him, reading a magazine. And listening to his pocket radio. Moe looked up at Gatsby.

"Do you have any idea why Bill wants to see us?" He kept the radio on and the magazine open in his lap.

Gatsby continued to look out the window. "No idea."

"He sounded pretty upset when he talked to me," said Moe.

Gatsby turned from the window. "He sounded quite calm when I talked with him. What are you listening to?"

Moe shut the magazine and tossed it on the table. "Two commentators speculating whether Bush will push the button and invade Iraq."

Gatsby shook his head. "Insanity! The only bright spot for me is that I'm no longer in uniform," he said. Bill's office door opened, and he stuck out his head. His white hair had thinned, and he wore horn-rimmed glasses. Prominent age spots mottled his face.

"Gatsby, could you come in? Moe, I'll speak with you after my meeting with Gatsby. Is that okay?"

"Sure." Moe looked to the magazines on the table.

Gatsby followed Bill into the office. It was well decorated in a manner befitting a business executive with a long-distinguished career in Pennsylvania. The office walls were covered with diplomas, documents evidencing his membership in various organizations, and photos of Bill with several Pennsylvania governors and US presidents.

Bill sat behind his desk, his back to the window.

Gatsby was surprised to see Bill's niece, Shirley, already seated in one of the chairs in front of Bill's desk. Calmly, Gatsby said, "Hello, Shirley," and he sat down in the chair on her left, making himself ignore the large birthmark on the right side of her face.

"Shirley has shared this interesting document with me and related the substance of your conversation at the Continental Midtown Restaurant." Bill took a document from the pile of papers on the right side of his desk and slid it toward Gatsby.

Gatsby picked it up looked briefly at the front page, turned a few pages, and placed it back on the table.

"I'd appreciate your explaining this document to me," Bill said, with only a slight hardening of his voice.

Gatsby didn't mind the man's annoyance. "It's a convertible promissory note for $25,000. It pays eight percent interest. I'm sure Shirley has explained that to you."

"She has. But what I'm interested in is your explanation. Bear with me. And as I understand it, you are the borrower?" Bill picked the document back up and rifled through its pages. "The lender, General Sam Walters, didn't receive any security when he made this loan to you, did he?"

From the corner of his eye, Gatsby could see Shirley had turned to face him. "Nope. None requested, none offered."

Bill looked directly at Gatsby. "What did you use the money for?"

"I have no idea. That was four months ago. Why does it matter to you?" He sat back in his chair and stared at Bill.

Shirley uncrossed and re-crossed her legs.

It was a good sign Bill had begun to perspire. He took off his glasses, pulled a handkerchief from his pants pocket and mopped his brow. He said, "Come on, Gatsby. Don't bullshit me! Did you use it to invest in a deal, pay off a creditor, or use it to cover living expenses?"

Gatsby feigned intense thinking for a minute and then flashed a big smile.

"Probably all three."

"This note, Gatsby…" Bill waved the document in the air. "Under what conditions is it convertible and what does it convert into?"

Gatsby continued to smile, then talking slowly and precisely, as if he were addressing a roomful of second graders, he said, "It's all described in the note, Bill. It is convertible if and when the company identified in the note—in this case, FVG—has a liquidity event that permits the holder of the stock options, namely me, to exercise my options. In that event, I would exercise my options and transfer shares of stock to the lender to pay off the principal and accrued interest of the note. It's simple."

"And what if the company fails, never has a public offering, and isn't sold? What does General Walters do under those circumstances?"

"He asks me for his money back and I pay him his principal and every cent of interest he's earned. He has no risk." Gatsby adjusted his shirt cuffs. "I'm good for it."

Bill leaned back in his chair and looked up at the ceiling. Gatsby continued to stare at him. Bill sat up and picked up another document and tossed it across the desk to Gatsby. "I see you sold one of these to Moe for $250,000."

"Yes," said Gatsby.

"Probably several more than this one?"

"Probably."

"How much of this shit have you sold? What do you owe?"

Gatsby found that holding his smile in place suddenly required effort. The questions startled him, and he didn't want to answer. He felt a cool skiff of air on his forehead from the vent and realized he, too, had begun to perspire.

Finally, he said, "Maybe a few million."

"A few million?" Bill shouted, his face reddening. "What's *a few*? Three? Four? Five? Where the hell will you get the money to pay General Walters and Moe in the event EVG fails and the options become worthless?" He stood up and put his hand on his desk and leaned toward Gatsby. "The general and Moe and all the others to whom you've sold this crap will want their money back—and with the interest you promised to pay. You don't have the net worth to pay those off. I don't have the net worth to pay those off. Your wife doesn't have the net worth to pay those off. Moe and his cronies will want their money back. Those guys will drive you into bankruptcy." He slapped his leather chair. "This is a disaster!"

Gatsby sat up in the chair. He narrowed his eyes and clenched his jaw, performing indignation and meanwhile forcing himself to consider his words before speaking. "I've always paid my debts, Bill. Always. You and Shirley—" he turned to his right and glared— "are taking this whole thing out of context. I'm an honorable businessman. I wouldn't borrow money I couldn't pay back. I'm good for it."

Bill jabbed his finger at Gatsby. "Don't you realize you're selling unregistered securities? What you're doing is illegal. Shit, we're supposed to be partners. When this gets out, we're both going to be toast." Bill began pacing behind his desk. "You should have your head examined. This is insane. You've put us both at risk." He looked at Shirley, shook his head and collapsed back in his chair, exhausted.

Shirley scowled at Gatsby and stood up, walked around the desk to her uncle. "Bill, I'm concerned you're working yourself up to a point that it's going to affect your health. Let me—"

Bill waved her away. "Sit down, Shirley. I'm fine. I've got to get to the bottom of this, for all of our sakes."

His composure restored, Gatsby spoke coolly. "I have an opinion from the Parsons firm it is perfectly legal for me to sell convertible notes like the ones on your desk. I don't see why you're going hyper on this. This is all on the up and up. All the lenders are wealthy, sophisticated investors."

"Okay," said Bill. "Let's see what the securities guys in the attorney general's office have to say." He reached for the telephone on the left side of his desk and was about to lift the receiver when Gatsby jumped up, leaned across the desk, and pressed on Bill's hand with all his weight, preventing him from lifting the receiver.

Shirley sputtered something and started to get up.

"I can't let you do that, Bill," said Gatsby through gritted teeth.

Bill strained against Gatsby's pressure but couldn't lift the receiver. He gave up and allowed his hand to go limp. The pained expression on his face was directed inward now, rather than at Gatsby. Yet the thought that his intention was to immediately call the attorney general locked Gatsby's hand in place like a vise.

Shirley yelled, "Gatsby, stop. You're killing him."

Bill gasped and fell back in his chair. He clutched his chest with his right hand.

Gatsby backed off and stared at Bill's ashen face.

"I think I'm having an attack. Shirley, quick, bring me my pills." He nodded in the direction of the credenza. "They're over there next to the TV. There is a water bottle there, too."

Shirley rushed to the credenza get the pills and water. "For Christ's sake, Gatsby, you did this. Help him!" She brought her uncle his medication and yelled, "Call 9-1-1!"

Something in Gatsby unfroze, and he dialed 9-1-1 and told the operator the situation.

Bill's eyes were closed, his mouth was open, and he clutched his chest. Shirley bent down beside his chair. "Bill," she called to him. "Uncle Bill..."

Gatsby pushed Shirley out of the way, lifted Bill out of the chair, and laid him down on the floor. He took off his jacket and started administering CPR.

"Shirley," he said, "tell Moe to go downstairs and make sure the paramedics know where to go."

CHAPTER 1

JERRY

February 5, 2003, Five Weeks Earlier

Jerry Bascomb eased his five-nine frame into the chair at the head of the table in the spartan Endovascular Group conference room. To his left sat Philadelphia venture capitalist Christopher Gatsby Brooks, who preferred to be called Gatsby, and to his right sat Gatsby's consultant, an ex-McKinsey partner, Shirley Frazier. Shirley was dressed in a business suit and had long black hair which she frequently touched, twisted, and tossed. Her most distinguishing facial feature was a one- to two-inch-wide birthmark that extended from the right side of her mouth to the middle of her cheek.

Across the table sat Dr. Verne Ragan, vascular surgeon, who had founded EVG with Gatsby. To his left was Oliver Kessel, the EVG chief engineer. Standing in front of the room next to an easel full of presentation charts was Harry Driscoll, CEO of the Endovascular Group and a protégé of Gatsby's.

Jerry's managing partner, Birney Schwartz, had been asked by his close friend, Philadelphia's most prominent investor and philanthropist, Moe Shultz, to send out his "best man" to evaluate Endovascular Group—EVG—for a potential merger. Moe had explained he had made a large investment in EVG, and although the company had been founded over ten years ago, he was becoming concerned it didn't seem to be going anywhere.

Jerry and his wife Helen had arrived in Philadelphia late the previous night on a train from New York City, and they were staying at the Bellevue Stratford Hotel on South Broad Street. At Gatsby's request, Shirley had sent Jerry the company's February 2003 private placement memorandum to raise $15 million; she'd also taken the liberty of sending him the PPM for November 1993.

Jerry had met Shirley for breakfast. She expressed her delight over the fact that Moe had pushed Gatsby to seek help from Jerry's firm, Bricker and Weldon, an investment bank she knew and respected. She had been telling Gatsby for the last year she thought Driscoll was in over his head, but Gatsby had repeatedly brushed her off.

They discussed the basic elements of the private placement memorandum pitch: the proprietary technology, the health care benefits it could provide, the challenges that needed to be overcome and the large market potential. She'd said, "Gatsby needs to know whether this dog can hunt, to use his words."

Gatsby was dressed like a Wall Street banker—dark gray Gucci suit, a Hermes tie, a tapered white shirt with French cuffs, and Prada loafers. He stood in front of his conference room chair. "I want to thank all of you for making time in your schedules to attend this meeting. I asked Moe Shultz to help identify a firm to evaluate the draft of our private placement memorandum, and he selected Bricker and Weldon. Therefore, we are all happy to welcome Jerry Bascomb to Philadelphia to hear the EVG story. Our agenda this morning includes: one, an overview of the EVG history and technology; two, the status of the EVG technology and current plans to begin human trials; and three, a period for questions, answers and comments, led by Jerry Bascomb. We'll conclude with a tour of our facility. I anticipate we will be able to wrap up by noon. And now I'll turn the meeting over to Harry."

Harry Driscoll was the tallest person in the room, six-six at least. He was casually dressed in an open-collared, tapered shirt and khaki slacks. "Good morning, lady and gentlemen. I'm going to employ the charts on the easel for my presentation and will use the whiteboard to elaborate where necessary.

"The Endovascular Group, EVG, has developed and manufactured in limited quantities surgical tools for addressing the buildup of plaque in the interior walls of the superficial femoral artery, or SFA. The SFA runs from the top of the thigh to the knee. It is the main artery that supplies blood to the lower portion of the legs. In approximately 50 percent of the cases of SFA blockage, the patient is treated via bypass grafting in which the surgeon routes blood from the groin to the knee through an artificial graft or through a vein, bypassing the blocked artery. In the other 50 percent of the cases, the patient is treated via balloon angioplasty. If the procedure is not successful, the leg is amputated.

"EVG has developed a much less invasive procedure which will enable the SFA bypass procedure to be performed in one hour instead of the three to four hours required by the current bypass technique." Driscoll described the procedure and the patented EVG tools. "The major advantages of the EVG procedure over the current bypass procedure are lower cost, shorter hospital stays, and a drastic reduction in the patient's discomfort, owing to the endoscopic procedure. Furthermore, it appears, based on trials performed to date, these advantages are achieved at no greater rate of restenosis, i.e., recurring blockage, which haunts the current techniques."

He passed around several photographs and diagrams showing the various stages of a typical surgery.

"If the financing set forth in the current private placement memorandum is accomplished within the next two months, we would expect to start clinical trials in Europe by the end of this year. Good initial clinical trials will result in heightened enthusiasm on the part of our vascular surgeon investigators. When clinical results are available in the 2004-to-2005 timeframe, we believe that EVG will become an attractive acquisition candidate.

"This concludes my presentation," said Driscoll, as he took his seat at the front of the table.

"Thank you, Harry," said Gatsby, standing. "And now, Jerry, I'm sure you have lots of questions. Why don't you state the question and I'll ask Oliver, our chief engineer, or Dr. Ragan to address it? And Shirley if you believe we've not addressed an important issue, please speak up." Gatsby sat down, and all eyes were on Jerry.

Jerry scanned his notes, looked up and asked, "How many patients have been treated using the EVG technology and when and where did the treatment occur?"

Gatsby nodded to Driscoll. "About 160. The trials were performed by our investigators in Germany, Belgium, and France in the 1999–2000 period."

"Okay," said Jerry. "And I assume the limited manufacturing you referred to was to provide instruments for those procedures?"

"Correct," said Harry.

"And what further trials are necessary to secure FDA approval in the US, and when are those trials scheduled?"

Harry did not immediately respond. He looked over toward Gatsby. "In order to achieve FDA approval," said Gatsby, "it is likely we will have to study at least a hundred additional patients distributed over ten clinical test facilities and the patients will have to be monitored for one to two years to determine the average patency, that is the amount of plaque that returns to the treated artery. Unfortunately, we can't even begin to arrange the trials until we're producing the new graft and have had an opportunity to test it."

"New graft?" Jerry asked. "Why do you need a new graft?"

"Because the graft we used in the trials was pulled off the market by the manufacturer, and there is no other commercially available graft that is adequate. That's why we've developed our own manufacturing process. You'll see the equipment during our tour."

"When do you expect to start producing the graft?" Jerry asked.

"I'll let Oliver address that," Gatsby said.

"We are still running tests on the equipment," said Oliver. "My best guess is we'll have usable grafts in three months."

"I see," said Jerry. "So, I guess that means you're going to run a number of company-controlled trials to test the new graft and wait the twelve-to-eighteen-month period to prove out the new graft before you can even begin to structure the clinical trials you need for FDA approval. Am I correct?"

Dr. Ragan spoke up. "Unfortunately, you are. In my opinion, we are at least five years away from the possibility of receiving FDA approval. Do you agree, Harry, Oliver?" They both nodded.

Jerry was astonished. He had been told the company was within a year of being able to market their tools and procedures worldwide. He looked over to Shirley. She was slumped in her seat, unmistakably discouraged. He looked at Gatsby. Completely unfazed. It was clear he had been aware of the time frame for FDA approval.

Jerry referred to his notes. "I noticed in both the 1993 and the 2002 private placement memoranda you received a number of patents. Could you elaborate about how effective they are in raising the bar to discourage competitors? The reason I'm asking is there appears to be several competitors active in the market."

Gatsby asked Dr. Ragan to weigh in.

Ragan got to his feet with the typical brisk energy of a surgeon. He was wiry and quick, and in no time had hurried around the table, handing out a one-page document to each of the participants. "This matrix identifies the specific patents our competitors are infringing upon," he said. "I've talked a length to Harry about this, but he's repeatedly advised me we do not have the resources to defend them against infringement."

The room was silent as a meat locker for at least a minute. Jerry noted the only person in the room who still evidenced enthusiasm was Dr. Ragan. What had been a dirty little secret—competitors were using EVG's technology before EVG was even out of the starting gate—was out in the open.

Jerry said, "Thank you, Harry and Dr. Ragan, for your succinct presentations of what is usually a dull slog in the weeds." Then he turned to Gatsby. "I'm ready to see the hardware."

Oliver Kessel, the chief engineer, guided the tour. As they stopped at the various stations containing instruments, grafts, and the other items used in the EVG procedure, he explained in detail how the surgeon used each item in the operation. The final stop was the new production equipment to manufacture the graft. It took up an entire twelve-foot-square room. Oliver explained it had been designed and constructed by a vendor and cost north of two million dollars. This was the highlight of the day for Jerry. His education and engineering career at National Technology surfaced as he followed Kessel's detailed explanation of the apparatus's operation, and even as he was immersed in the machine's workings, he thought of himself and the energetic engineer as the duo in Kafka's "In the Penal Colony," tracing the details of what already seemed to be a doomed project.

When it was all over, Gatsby and Shirley drove Jerry back to the Bellevue and reconfirmed they would meet with Jerry at seven o'clock for drinks and his briefing. Gatsby arranged for a conference room to ensure the privacy of their conversations.

~ ~ ~ ~ ~ ~

Jerry went up to his room. It was spacious, with a large king bed, huge TV, and city views. His wife, Helen, had gone out to explore the apparel shops in the Old City and she'd promised to be back around five. He dropped his jacket and briefcase on the bed, picked up the ice bucket, walked down the hall to the ice machine and filled it. He returned to the room, opened the minibar refrigerator, and withdrew two bottles of Grey Goose vodka. He filled a glass half full of ice and then poured in the two mini-bottles of vodka, took a large swallow, and lay down on the bed.

The information about EVG conveyed at today's meeting was not what he expected, and he imagined it was a far cry from what Moe would have wanted. What a disaster! Driscoll was incompetent, and Gatsby hadn't been involved enough, or else he would have known the private placement memorandum was a lousy piece of fiction.

He took another large swallow of vodka. He checked his watch. He had four hours to complete his report to Moe so he could share the conclusions with Gatsby and Shirley. He drained the glass, got out of bed, set up his computer on the desk, and went to work.

~ ~ ~ ~ ~ ~

At seven o'clock Jerry, Gatsby and Shirley assembled in a meeting room. Gatsby called the restaurant and ordered drinks and snacks. He turned to Jerry and said, "It's your show."

"I'm still working on my memorandum for Moe," said Jerry. "However, I've formulated my opinion. I'll share it with you, and then you and Shirley are free to ask me any questions. I've prepared a table that presents the facts supporting my opinion." He opened a folder and removed three sheets, passing one each to Gatsby and Shirley and retaining one or himself.

Jerry looked over to Gatsby as he stared at the document. His expression revealed nothing.

"It is evident," Jerry said, "Dr. Ragan and EVG have created important technology that addresses a large market opportunity. And the company has demonstrated the products can deliver the results forecasted in the 1993 private placement memorandum. That said, the table also shows that progress has been achieved at a far slower rate than predicted, to the extent that success may prove to be elusive."

Jerry noticed Shirley was twirling a strand of her hair and had sunk into her chair. He recognized something about the way she failed to hide her body language. She was not reacting as an independent consultant. From his long years in finance, Jerry saw she was acting like an investor who had skin in the game.

Gatsby looked up from the sheet, his face suddenly drawn and slightly reddened. "What makes you say that?" he said.

"Look at the table, Gatsby. Ten years ago, EVG told the investors if they gave EVG $6.5 million, EVG would secure FDA approval for their tools and procedure and would achieve $50 million in sales by 1998. EVG raised $11.4 million. Agreed, it made progress regarding human trials. But here we are, ten years later, asking for an additional $15 million and predicting FDA approval and $60 million sales in four years, nine years later than the original date. And you're facing a hurdle that you did not have nine years ago, namely, you must prove the viability of your new graft.

"Also, EVG has three direct competitors, all of which are public companies. They are recruiting vascular surgeon apostles and building market share. EVG is not even out of the starting gate. The fact that three competitors got FDA approval for their devices and technology while EVG was puttering along is evidence the technology was not the impediment. EVG's failure to compete can only be attributed to lack of money or lack of competent management."

Gatsby's face was flushed. EVG was his baby. He was its founder and chief fundraiser. He had handpicked the management. He had promoted EVG as one of the brightest stars in his constellation of companies. Jerry knew all of this already and noted Shirley had sunk even farther down in her chair and appeared despondent.

The room was quiet for several minutes. Gatsby managed to master himself, and the flush went out of his cheeks and neck. "The vascular surgeons who are most familiar with EVG and all of the competitors," he said, "have told us the EVG technology is safer for the patient and achieves greater patency."

"That may be true," said Jerry, "but that is likely to have a minimum effect on EVG's ability to penetrate what will be a mature market, if and when it acquires FDA approval."

There was more silence. Shirley sat up, took a sip of wine, and forced a smile that verged on a challenge. "Given your analysis, Jerry, what course of action would you recommend? I'm sure you've thought about that."

"Of course," said Jerry. "I have three specific recommendations. First, the new private placement memorandum values EVG at $79.2 million. That is way out of line for a company twelve years past startup with no sales and no earnings and at least five years away from market viability. I think it would be a stretch to value the company at over the $12-to-$15-

million range. Also, under the circumstances, I'd try a rights offering in the range of $0.75 to $0.80 per share and hope for the best.

"Second, hire the best patent defense litigator you can find. File suit against any competitor Dr. Ragan feels is encroaching, and make sure you raise enough money to support the litigation.

"And finally, assuming the rights offering is successful, and you get to take another bite of the apple, I suggest you replace the CEO. He is in way over his head." Jerry paused and looked over to Gatsby and Shirley. "Any questions?"

"You appear to feel strongly we can attack the folks infringing on our patents," said Gatsby.

"Absolutely. If you don't, you can't assign any value to the patents because you're not protecting them and its open season on EVG's technology. You should have done this the first time you detected the infringement."

"I see." Gatsby looked like he'd taken a swig of vinegar. He turned to Shirley, whose expression was grim. "Any questions?"

"No. I think Jerry's hit the nail on the head as to the key issues. Now it's up to us."

"I agree," said Gatsby. He stood up and walked over to Jerry, carrying his glass of wine. He extended his hand, which Jerry took. "You've been a great help. Let's toast to the success of EVG." All three lifted their glasses and said, "To the success of EVG."

They drained their glasses, picked up their belongings and turned out the light as they exited the room.

~~~~~

At four o'clock the following afternoon, Shirley and Gatsby were at a table in the bar of the prestigious Union League of Philadelphia enjoying their drinks when Jerry and Helen entered. Gatsby seemed to fully inhabit himself at the prospect of meeting an elegant woman, and he stood up to greet them.

"I'd like to introduce you to my wife, Helen."

Gatsby extended his hand and said, "I'm so pleased to meet you."
~~~~~

Jerry was not surprised Gatsby lost no time visually devouring Helen. He was used to it. He had the very same experience when he'd seen her at his brother's dinner party thirteen years ago. She was magnetizing.

Gatsby smiled at her and gently shook her hand. "Come, I'll introduce you to my associate, Shirley Frazier."

They sat around the table in the bar and the waiter took their orders. Shortly after the obligatory small talk regarding the previous day's meetings, Gatsby and Helen dominated the table. Gatsby was smitten. He drilled down, asking questions about her interests, her children, her life in France.

Jerry listened to their conversation, a smile pasted on his face. He considered another double Jameson but turned to his water. Shirley played with the silverware.

Even Helen grew tired of the flattery. She turned to Jerry and said, "Hon, why don't you explain to Mr. Brooks why we wanted to meet him?"

Gatsby interrupted. "Please, Helen, call me Gatsby." He turned to Jerry and said, "I apologize for giving your wife the third degree. It's one of my many foibles. When I first meet a stunning woman, like Helen, I'm immediately driven to learn everything about her. I apologize." Jerry laughed to distract from the look of boredom that flickered across his wife's face. "No need to apologize. I admire your skill. It took me months to wheedle out of Helen the information you were able to harvest in twenty minutes."

"Oh, come on, Jerry. I was not *that* inscrutable."

Jerry let the comment pass and turned to Gatsby. "Helen and I are seriously considering moving to one of the suburbs of Philadelphia, like Lower Merion. We believe it would be a better environment in which to raise our boys, would provide us with more living space and still be close to the business and cultural center of Philadelphia. I have a great position at Bricker and Weldon in Manhattan, but since commuting to New York every day would get old quite quickly, I need to explore the opportunities available in Philadelphia. Moe tells me you are the go-to guy here, at least with respect to finance and venture capital."

Gatsby laughed. "I do have a pretty good contacts file." He turned to Helen. "And what about you, Helen? Do you have career objectives you'd like to pursue in Philly?"

Helen gave him a practiced, beaming smile. "Absolutely! I have a first-rate education in fine art from De Montfort University in Leicester, England, and gallery experience in Paris, Los Angeles, and New York. I expect to go back to work when our youngest son starts middle school."

"You know Moe's sister is in the gallery business," said Gatsby.

"I'm meeting with her tomorrow."

"How long do you plan to stay in town, Jerry?"

"We leave Monday morning."

"Do you have any prior commitments I need to consider?"

"Not really. I'm flexible."

"I'll make a few calls and set up some meetings for you over the next few days. I'll leave a message for you at the Bellevue by 9 a.m. tomorrow. See, easy!"

The waiter came over to the table and handed Gatsby a note. He smiled as he read the note and slipped it inside his coat.

"I hope you won't mind, Jerry, Helen, but Shirley and I need to excuse ourselves. We have a previously scheduled meeting with a recent immigrant to Philly, retired Admiral Jesse Hartford. Admiral Hartford is leaving on a trip tonight and we need to meet with him before he leaves town." He stood up and turned to Helen. "I can't tell you how much I enjoyed meeting you and your husband. Please stay if you'd like. Have another round of drinks and perhaps eat an early dinner—my treat! The food here is fabulous."

He shook Jerry's hand. Shirley stood up and she and Gatsby headed to the foyer to meet the admiral.

CHAPTER 2

SHIRLEY

Admiral Hartford was six feet tall, still had broad shoulders, and still wore a buzz cut. He, Gatsby, and Shirley were seated at a table across the room from Jerry and Helen, sipping wine.

"Admiral," said Gatsby, "what brings you to Philadelphia?"

"Pardon me, Mr. Brooks, but let's dispense with the *admiral* business. Just call me Jesse."

Gatsby laughed. "That's my line. And you can just call me Gatsby. Okay?"

"*D'accord.*"

"You speak French?" said Gatsby.

"*Je parle un peu de français.* A little."

"Don't let him bullshit you," said Shirley. "He is as fluent as a native Parisian. I studied French for four years in college and he speaks rings around me."

"Don't oversell me, Shirley. I'm not looking for any assignments in France. *J'ai roulé ma bosse!*"

"So, what *are* you looking for, Jesse?"

"Let me be direct. I need to make some money. A lot of money. I've got five grandkids to put through college. None of the parents has a pot to piss in. And my pension won't buy a cuspidor of warm spit. I've been told by several people, including Shirley here, you might be able to help me."

Over the following half hour, Gatsby briefed the admiral on his business and status of the nine companies he was working with, including EVG, describing in detail the investment and board opportunities, and told him he would send over documents, and they would talk in a few days. When the meeting broke up, Gatsby said goodbye to Admiral Hartford, turned to Shirley, and asked her to stay a few minutes.

They sat back down at the table and Gatsby ordered another round of drinks. They chatted about the admiral for several minutes. Gatsby inquired about the status of Klamathgold, a company out in Oregon he was promoting. He had asked Shirley to look at it. Shirley responded with a succinct summary identifying the current challenges of each aspect of the company and how they might be addressed.

When the waiter came with the drinks, Gatsby picked up his glass and said, "You're doing a terrific job, Shirley. Here is to continued success in both our business and personal relationships."

Shirley lifted her glass and clinked Gatsby's. "I appreciate that. I've enjoyed the time we've worked together, and I am excited about these deals in the works. I think we make a great team."

"So do I, Shirley." He put his hand inside his jacket and pulled out an envelope. "In recognition of both your efforts and your successes, please accept a token of my appreciation."

He handed her the envelope. She put down her wine glass and opened it. Her face lit up.

"Wow," she said.

"I've had a timeshare condo on Saint Martin for years. It's our number one vacation spot for warm weather. The weather will be great during the Thanksgiving week I've given you. Enjoy!"

She got out of her chair and went around the table and kissed Gatsby on the cheek.

"Thank you so much. What a surprise!"

Gatsby stood up, put his arms around her and hugged her. "You deserve it, Shirley." He glanced at his watch. "It's almost six. What about dinner? We need to talk about Klamathgold. What about Butcher and Singer? Yes?"

"I'd love to," she said. "Absolutely."

Chapter 3

HELEN

The next morning when Helen was in the shower, the telephone rang. She turned off the water, grabbed a towel and picked up the receiver.

"Hello?"

"Helen, it's Gatsby. How are you doing?"

"Fine." Instinctively, she tugged the towel higher on her body. "I'm reading a book about Philadelphia's rich history. It's fascinating."

"When do you plan to meet with Moe's sister?"

"Not until three."

"How about having lunch with me? Say 11:30?"

"Well, I—"

Cutting her off, Gatsby said, "I'm sure you'll find me a lot more interesting than reading a book about Philadelphia, even the X-rated parts."

Helen felt a catch of alarm. But she didn't feel she could refuse him, considering what he was doing for Jerry. She put the smile back into her voice and responded, "I'm sure I will. When should I be ready?"

"I'll pick you up at 11:20."

Helen replaced the receiver and immediately regretted having accepted Gatsby's invitation. She picked up a towel and began to dry herself in front of the full-length mirror. She shook her head and grumbled at her image in the mirror. Having a private lunch with

Philadelphia's most prominent Casanova, she thought. Am I crazy? This is not going to be pretty. As she walked toward the closet she looked back toward the mirror. Idiot! She selected a beige pants suit, a high-necked crème-colored blouse and a matronly set of pearls.

Gatsby pulled up to the Bellevue 11:20 in an XK8 Jaguar convertible. Helen was standing just outside the entrance to the left of the revolving door. As she walked toward the car, the doorman reached for the handle and let her slide into the passenger seat.

She smiled at Gatsby. "Nice car," she said, knowing it would be rude not to comment on such a spectacle.

He smiled back. "It's my special-occasion car. I usually drive an old BMW."

"I should be flattered," she said.

"That was my intention." He released the brake, pulled away from the curb and drove north on Broad Street.

"It's very kind of you to interrupt your busy schedule to take me to lunch."

Any uncertainty about Gatsby's purpose in inviting her to lunch soon fell apart. He looked straight ahead at the road but moved his hand toward Helen. His fingers brushed over her thigh, found her left hand, and squeezed it ever so gently. Continuing to smile he said, "I can always find time for a beautiful woman." At Center City he turned right and drove east on Market Street.

Just as gently she extracted her hand from his grip, moved his hand off her thigh and said, "That's sweet of you to say." She turned toward him, softening her words with a hint of humor. "So, where do you take beautiful women to lunch?"

"I thought we'd go to La Veranda. It is light, airy, and has great views of the Delaware. And the Italian food is excellent."

"Sounds great," said Helen.

The rest of the fifteen-minute drive to the restaurant was uneventful. Gatsby asked her how she had spent her day yesterday and she described the several galleries she had visited and the various people she had met. Gatsby was familiar with the galleries and their proprietors and was well-informed about the artists each of them represented. Helen was impressed at his knowledge and was relieved he could converse without groping. She hoped the combination of her conservative dress and her decisiveness in deflecting his advances had put a full stop to it.

They entered the modern restaurant. The wall facing east was solid glass and overlooked the Delaware River. They were seated at a raised booth facing the water. Gatsby sat on the right, awkwardly close to Helen. She felt his body pressing on her. As they both perused the menu, she crossed her legs and used the movement as an excuse to shift away from the pressure. Shit, she thought. This is what I was afraid would happen.

"How about a glass of wine," said Gatsby, "to fortify you for your meeting with Moe's sister, Alicia?"

"And why would I need fortification?"

"She's a pistol. Loud, opinionated, aggressive. She dominates every space she occupies," said Gatsby. "She can be very nice and sweet, but she often comes on strong. If I had to grow up with a sister like Alicia, I would have put myself up for adoption."

"Thanks for warning me."

"Just don't challenge her about anything. If she says the Sistine Chapel was painted by Leonardo da Vinci, don't correct her."

"I get it," said Helen. "And I will take your suggestion and have some wine. A chardonnay."

Gatsby motioned for the waiter, who came quickly to the table. He ordered the drinks.

The waiter recited the list of specials and left.

"Helen, how are your plans to leave the Big Apple progressing?"

"Slow, real slow. Jerry's dragging his heels. He simply can't accept the idea of leaving New York. But at least he's going through the motions. That's something."

"You're the driving force for the move?"

"Absolutely. It's too damn hard to raise kids in the City and Jerry doesn't want to live in the New York suburbs and fight the daily commute, either by train or car."

Gatsby smiled at her and moved a little closer, so she again felt the pressure of his body against her. At this rate, she'd be clinging to the edge of the booth by the time lunch was over. The waiter brought their drinks. She ordered the blackened salmon and Gatsby ordered the lasagna. The waiter wrote down their orders, turned and left the table. As he walked away, Helen felt Gatsby's hand, ever so gently, begin to explore her right thigh.

Helen grabbed the napkin from the table and held it up to her mouth and began to gag. She slid out of the booth and took the napkin away from her face only long enough to ask Gatsby the directions to the restroom. She gagged into the napkin again and headed toward the restroom. She sat on the toilet for about ten minutes, performing a complex calculation of her pride, her vanity, and Gatsby's probing hands. Finally, she exited the restroom and quickly walked back to the table.

"I'm sorry, Gatsby, I'm sick. I just threw up my breakfast and am still terribly nauseated. Please take me back to the hotel. I apologize."

"Don't be silly," said Gatsby, sliding out of the booth. He tossed a few bills on the table, and undeterred by the specter of vomit, quickly led her by her arm back to his car. On the way he told one of the waiters his guest was ill and to cancel their order.

Gatsby ignored the speed limits and stop signs during the drive back to the Bellevue.

Helen maintained the charade of being nauseated and felt guilty Gatsby's reckless driving was motivated by his belief she was in distress. It could end badly. She crossed her fingers and said a silent prayer. She kept her face buried in the napkin, groaning, and coughing occasionally. When they reached the Bellevue, Helen took the napkin away from her face long enough to apologize again to Gatsby, then quickly headed to the entrance.

When Helen entered her hotel room, she stripped off her clothes and threw herself on the bed. She was furious—primarily at herself. She was only as angry with Gatsby as the frog could be at the scorpion: in the fable, the frog, having agreed to carry the scorpion across the river on the condition that the scorpion would not sting him, demanded an explanation from the scorpion after he was stung. The scorpion replied, "Hey, I'm a scorpion—that's what we scorpions do— we sting things." Gatsby's routine had clearly worked on enough women that Helen couldn't expect anything better.

Scorpions sting, Gatsby chases women. Q. E. D. What do I tell Jerry? Answer. As little as possible. Gatsby invited me to lunch. We went to the La Veranda. Beautiful restaurant on the water. We ordered drinks. I got sick. He drove me home. Case closed!

She got up from the bed, retrieved her purse and pulled out her phone book, and picked up the receiver.

"Alicia? It's Helen. I'm fine. I'm calling to confirm our meeting at three."

"Yes, I have the address. I am so looking forward to this."

She replaced the receiver and fell back into bed—where Jerry found her when he returned.

CHAPTER 4

SHIRLEY

Following her dinner meeting at the Butcher and Singer with Gatsby about Klamathgold, Shirley had thrown herself into the crucible of problems dogging the company. In preparation for her trip to their facility, Shirley had spent several hours on her computer and in the library researching the supposed attributes and claimed benefits of the health supplements manufactured from the algae harvested from a far-West body of water called Klamath Lake. She also studied the information available on the harvesting methods and manufacturing processes Klamathgold's competitors were currently employing.

She was, therefore able to formulate tentative hypotheses prior to boarding the plane, namely (1) there was a large and growing market for supplements produced from the blue-green algae, called AFA, that grew on Klamath Lake; (2) the amount of algae that grew and was available for harvest varied from year to year and was unpredictable; (3) there had been several studies that revealed AFA contained toxins that can damage the liver, nervous system, and kidneys, a problem that required expensive systems to extract those toxins and make the product safe; and (4) it appeared the capital invested in Klamathgold was woefully inadequate.

For the sake of utter thoroughness, via a chain of ever-smaller connecting flights, she cleared her schedule for several days and flew out to Klamath Falls, an Oregon city of 20,000 that lay 280 miles south of Portland on the southeastern shore of Upper Klamath Lake. She booked herself into a motel room, and for the next week, she worked eight to ten hours a day at the company's site investigating operations, talking with staff and suppliers and reviewing documents.

She updated the accounting records, including verifying checkbook balances of the five accounts; audited year-to-date transactions, reviewed, and verified all the contracts for services that had been provided to the company; and in several cases where there was no contract for services that had been provided, she determined the terms and conditions of the services with the vendor and the responsible operations personnel. She assembled all notes and reviewed accounts payable and reconciled everything with the amounts carried on the company balance sheet. She identified and assigned market values to the machinery and equipment the company owned; drafted the winter season plan to secure the site, reviewed insurance coverage, and revised the quality assurance manual. She reviewed the order processing procedures and negotiated with the Division of State Lands for the terms and conditions that would allow the company to operate commercial facilities on the Upper Klamath Lake. She determined the algae yield numbers and equipment capacity projections to be used in the financial projections. Finally, she returned calls from Klamathgold's creditors, many of whom were close to sending the accounts to their legal departments.

And after she had completed her long days, she grabbed a bite at the restaurant next to the motel and got to work on the revised business plan, which required her to change entire sections of the current one, including a summary of the business risks, the review of the competition, the marketing strategy, and the financial and cash flow projections.

Every night she would fall into bed, exhausted. And she would be up by seven the next morning. After gulping down a continental breakfast, she would drive to the site to deal with a new set of problems.

When she flew back to Philadelphia on Friday night, she was exhausted but exhilarated over what she had accomplished. She thoroughly understood the company and knew what was required to fix it, even from thousands of miles away.

She loved the challenge of walking cold turkey into a company that was on the ropes and being able to analyze how it operated, what did and didn't work, and whether it was worthwhile to save it. She had been doing turnarounds, sales, and liquidations of distressed companies for fifteen years, ever since she joined McKinsey after earning her MBA from Harvard. When she was involved in a complex deal, working ten to twelve hours a day, nothing could distract her. The few times she was involved in a relationship that had marital possibilities, a big deal would come along and consume her time, energy and focus to the extent that the suitor would become discouraged and drift away. It was unfortunate. She would have liked to get married and have a family. But, deep down, she knew she could not change her priorities. Either she would meet someone who understood, or she wouldn't, and she accepted the high probability of the latter.

Her work revealed Klamathgold could not survive without a significant infusion of capital. And she was skeptical as to whether even a smooth promoter like Gatsby could charm the current investors or could attract new investors to throw the company a life ring. But fortunately, that was not her problem.

The trip back to Philadelphia provided her the first opportunity in a week to think about the EVG situation and her investment of $25,000. She needed to talk to Gatsby about that. She also needed to talk to Gatsby about the call she received from General Walters, who was suddenly unhappy about his investment in EVG. It nettled her because she had introduced them.

Her mind was so stuffed with Klamathgold problems and issues she didn't feel she had the brain capacity for anymore. She was looking forward to the meeting with Gatsby, Bill, and Jim Jenkins, the Klamathgold president on Thursday—that would get Klamathgold off her plate and onto Gatsby's. She smiled. Then she could think about how she'd celebrate.

~ ~ ~ ~ ~ ~

On the Monday following her week at Klamath Falls, Shirley entered the foyer of Gatsby's office, on the fiftieth floor of the Mellon Bank Center, said hello to Cissy, and sat down. Cissy was tall, slender, and wore her straight red hair down to her shoulders. The combination of her wide smile, bright blue eyes and body language exuded friendliness. And Shirley had worked with Gatsby long enough to know appearance was very much a job skill in his office.

"He's on a conference call with Bill Dewyne and Jim Jenkins. I think they're talking about Klamathgold."

Shirley laughed. "I'm not surprised."

"How did it go last week?"

"I got everything done I had to do. But it was exhausting."

"I bet. What did you do with your evenings?"

"Worked. It was just as well. There is nothing to do at night out there. And I didn't have the energy for social interaction." She paused. "Hey, didn't you have a date with Phil Glass last night?"

Cissy put on her broad smile. "Yes, and it went very, very well."

"That's great," said Shirley. "He's a catch."

"Don't I know it," said Cissy.

The door to Gatsby's office opened and Gatsby stuck his head out and said, "Hi, Shirley, come on in and sit down. I just got off the phone with Bill and Jim. We're all anxious to get your report."

Shirley planted herself in front of the desk. "Gatsby, I'll be frank. Klamathgold is a mess, and it will take a lot of work and a lot of money before it has any prospect of being a success. There is a huge gap between Jim's offering memorandum and the reality on the ground, and several statements in the offering memorandum are either misleading or just plain wrong. The cash flow assumes a harvest this year, which is iffy. There is more than $50,000 of past-due payables, and we've already received demands from two attorneys. Several pieces of harvest equipment have never been tested. And it seems we are operating on a portion of the lake that requires a permit from the county. I've laid out all the problems in my report. Are we still on for Thursday?"

"Yes, ten o'clock in Bill's office. Frankly, I'm surprised. Jim, the president, gave both Bill and me the impression Klamathgold was going great guns. Based on Jim's offering memorandum, Bill and I signed a contract to raise $800,000 for the company, and $250,000 has already been raised and invested."

"That will be a problem," said Shirley.

"What are you recommending?" said Gatsby. He seemed dismayed, but mostly energized by the quality of her work. She was glad to know the answer without glancing at her notes.

"That the company either gets an immediate cash infusion of $1.8 million, or it liquidates."

"That much?" said Gatsby.

"There are a lot of uncertainties, and I don't think you can poor mouth this deal."

"Assuming the money is available," said Gatsby, "can the deal provide a return more than twenty percent?"

"Definitely. You'll see my numbers on Thursday."

"Any chance you can get it out before the meeting?"

"I'll try. I have everybody's email and I'll shoot for Wednesday afternoon."

<center>~~~~~~</center>

Three days later the four attendees sat at Bill Dewyne's round conference table. Gatsby started the meeting, stating Klamathgold was in a crisis and the company's survival was not at all certain. "Shirley has prepared a report, which she will send to the board of managers this afternoon.

"Bill and I have a contract to raise $800,000 based on Jim's offering memorandum. We've already raised $250,000, which the company has received. However, based on Shirley's preliminary calculation, which includes some significant modifications to the offering memorandum, the company needs a total of $1.8 million to have any possibility of succeeding. I assume we've all read it?" Bill and Jim nodded.

"Then I'll turn the meeting over to Shirley."

"Thank you, Gatsby." She looked at Bill and Jim. "As you probably know, I spent a week at the company's operations on the lake and reviewed every aspect. I've prepared a projection of next year's potential sales and earnings and I've identified the major marketing and operational challenges and risks. I've incorporated my analysis into a revised business plan and a cash flow projection to determine the new investment required to achieve self-sustaining operations."

Over the next forty-five minutes she revealed the details of her findings, analysis, and conclusions. When she completed her presentation, she looked over to Gatsby, Bill, and Jim, hoping to solicit some combination of praise and constructive criticism of her work. Gatsby and Bill were inscrutable, but Jim's reddening face revealed his suppressed anger.

Bill spoke up. "I have not been nearly as involved in this project as Gatsby, but it seems to me, based on Shirley's presentation, we have a huge can of worms on our hands." He turned to Jim and said, "How do you feel about Shirley's assessment and her suggestions?"

"I don't feel good at all," said Jim. "I think the criticisms are overstated and overblown and fail to consider the fact we've been starved for cash during the entire eighteen months I've been president. Frankly, I'm shocked and disappointed in the tone of this woman's report."

Shirley was annoyed, but unsurprised by Jim's response. Her report could and would be seen as a negative critique of his management of Klamathgold. But there was no way to put lipstick on this pig, and that wasn't her job, anyway.

Jim was about to continue, but Bill raised his hand with his palm toward him and said, "I understand how you could view Shirley's assessment as a personal attack. I, for one, don't see it that way. It is crystal clear Klamathgold has serious operational and financial problems, and the board of managers is going to be very unhappy when they review our analyst's report. Even if the report were only 75 percent accurate, Klamathgold is still a can of worms. What we need to talk about are the options for saving the company and as much of the investment as we can. Don't you agree?"

Jim's face had recovered its normal hue, and he said, "I agree. Let's move on."

Shirley handed out a five-page summary of her revised business plan. She led Gatsby, Bill and Jim through the plan, pointing out the assumptions, risks, and limitations of the current operational methodology. "In summary, providing the company can immediately raise the capital required, and assuming algae growth is normal next year, and sales materialize as anticipated, the company could achieve a gross profit of $2.5 million on sales of $5.5 million within eighteen months. That said, product sales will be limited to about $6 million owing to the physical limitations of the screens that can be placed in the waterways."

She continued, "Like any crop farming business, production is limited to the amount of dirt under cultivation and the number of crops per year. If you could grow the algae in a controlled environment and achieve the quality equal to that of the lake grown algae you might replicate the process and expand production to meet a higher demand. But that would require an R&D process, and I haven't budgeted any funds for that."

"What's the total invested capital to date, Shirley," said Bill, "counting the recent investment of $250,000?"

"$1.4 million," said Shirley.

"So," said Bill, "assuming a net profit of approximately $1 million, an additional investment of $1.8 million for total invested capital of $3.2 million, the investor's return would be 31.2 percent—but with no growth. That is not much of a venture capital play. Would investors put in another $1.8 million, Gatsby?"

"I don't see why not," said Gatsby. "It's an attractive return—if it all works. I suggest we send out Shirley's restructure plan, mark it as a draft, and arrange a conference call among the investors for next Tuesday to take their pulse. I think we need to hear enthusiastic support and financial commitments to go further. If we don't get it, we should probably liquidate."

"I agree," said Bill. "What about you, Jim?"

"I'm tapped out. My opinion doesn't matter. I can't spare another dime."

"I understand," said Bill. "Gatsby, let's get all the emails out to the investors and set the conference call for Tuesday." He rattled off the rest of the meeting's details, and they agreed to meet up again next week to see whether the investors were willing to save Jim's company.

As they were filing out of Bill's office, Gatsby invited Shirley for a drink. They walked the two blocks to the Continental Mid-town and seated themselves at a table in the bar.

Shirley ordered a margarita and Gatsby ordered a martini. When the waiter left the table, Gatsby said, "Shirley, you are doing a fantastic job on the Klamathgold project. I'm amazed you were able to complete your assessment and draft the guts of a new plan in such a short time. And I know Bill was also impressed."

Shirley smiled. "Thanks. I will tell you it wasn't easy." She took a sip of her drink and wiped her lips. They were both silent for a minute. Then she said, "Gatsby, can I change the subject?"

"Sure."

Shirley took a deep breath and said, "General Walters called me when I was in Oregon to express concern. He's never received any acknowledgment from EVG regarding the $25,000 he gave you for an investment in the company. He asked me to look into it."

"Why didn't he call me directly?" said Gatsby. "I'm the one he gave the money to."

Shirley laughed. "I'm sure you'll find this strange, but even though he's a four-star general, he is new to the business environment, and he probably feels intimidated by you. Since he is depending on you to open some doors so he can build up his net worth, he probably wanted to side-step the possibility of a confrontation."

"I see," said Gatsby, his voice flat.

"I called Driscoll, and he said he had no knowledge of the company receiving any investment funds from a General Walters. I asked him to check with the CFO. He called me back and reiterated the fact there was no record. I called the general and told him EVG had no record of his investment, and I would talk with you. He went ballistic. I tried to calm him down and suggested we meet when I returned to Philly at his home in Chestnut Hill, which we did. He's anxiously waiting to hear from you."

The smile had disappeared from Gatsby's face, replaced by a sour expression of concern. "I see," he said, as carefully as if he'd watched her make a particularly tricky chess move.

Shirley's curiosity was piqued—she'd seen him take much worse news in stride. The waiter came to the table to inquire whether there was anything else they wanted. Gatsby shook his head, but Shirley ordered an espresso to ensure he had a reason to stay and listen to the rest of what she had to say.

She continued, "He gave me this convertible promissory note, stating as he did so, 'This is the piece of shit Gatsby gave me for my $25,000.'" She slid the document over to Gatsby. "I read the document neutrally, given how surprised I was that the paper you gave him was a note incorporating an option on 10,000 shares of EVG—which you own—and not evidence of an investment in EVG. When I explained the document to him, he became furious and stated he'd been duped—he clearly understood that the funds would be going into EVG and not, and I quote, 'into Gatsby's pocket.'"

Gatsby continued to stare at her.

"You have some fence-mending to do, my friend. I suggest that you call him ASAP." The waiter brought Shirley's espresso.

"Well," he said, a smile returning to his face, "I certainly did not expect that." He took another sip of his martini. "I'll call and arrange to meet with the general and explain the transaction to him." He looked at his watch. "Anything else?"

Shirley took another deep breath. "Okay, I'll be plainer. I'm confused about these promissory notes. I don't understand what you're doing."

Gatsby started to respond, took a sip from his drink while focusing his gaze on Shirley.

"The form of these notes should be of no concern to you. They evidence private transactions with sophisticated investors. Pennsylvania security lawyers have vetted the documents. I'm simply borrowing money at an interest rate that should be very attractive to the lender. Plus, I'm providing an incentive to the lender in the form of a call on stock or options that I own in promising companies I have helped or am helping to finance. And the lender pays nothing for the option. That's it. Look at it as a bonus. My lender gets to participate in the potential upside of one of the companies I'm helping, and he hasn't paid a dime for the opportunity. And if the company fails, which, as you well know, is the fate of many startups, the lender doesn't lose a dime because he or she still has my note. Why the hell would anyone complain?"

"Well," said Shirley, hesitating, "the general was obviously confused. And—"

Gatsby cut her off. Still smiling, he said in a firm voice, "It's not your concern. I'll speak to him. I'm surprised he did not understand the transaction, but if he wants his money back, I'll be prepared to give it to him when we meet." He started to rise.

"Are you certain that you don't need to register these notes? My lawyer advised me that these notes are securities and they needed to be registered with the State. He strongly advised me against introducing any other investors to you."

Gatsby's expression hardened. He pushed his chair back and stood up. "That's unfortunate," he said, "but I've been advised by a securities attorney that these notes do not have to be registered as long as they are being sold to sophisticated investors." He turned abruptly, and headed toward the door, not bothering to say goodbye.

Shirley remained at the table, nursing her espresso. She had upset a colleague, which was not her intention. She regretted having challenged him about the securities registration issue. But it was clear that her comments and questions had hit a nerve. She drained her espresso and left the restaurant.

CHAPTER 5

SHIRLEY

On the following Tuesday, Gatsby, Shirley, and Jim convened in Bill Dewyne's office for the scheduled conference call with the Klamathgold investors. Shirley had not talked with Gatsby since their meeting at the Continental Mid-town, so she was surprised and relieved when he greeted her as though the conversation had never happened.

Jim had prepared a document that listed the name of each of the investors, the number of shares held and their investment. He distributed copies to Gatsby, Shirley, and Bill.

"I've talked with the five top investors after they received Shirley's package," said Jim.

"The vibes are not promising. None of them expressed enthusiasm for Shirley's plan."

"What were their main concerns?" said Gatsby. "Shirley's analysis shows that a 30 percent return is possible. They certainly can't get that from a bank."

"Unfortunately, they've focused on both the operational risks and the marketing risks Shirley outlined in her report. Even though the potential return is attractive, they feel that the management is going to have to slay too many dragons to achieve it. Also, the fact that the upside is limited is a big negative."

Bill shook his head. "Well, let's get on with it. I suggest that Jim welcome the investors, take attendance, and immediately open the meeting to questions and comments. Jim, Shirley, and Gatsby will field the questions and respond to comments, and I'll take notes." Bill buzzed his secretary and asked her to call into the conference line and record the names of the investors as they came on the line. He turned to Jim. "Have you given any thought to the next step if the investors are not going the support the revised plan?"

"Quite a bit," said Jim. "I'll propose a resolution we appoint Shirley CEO, assuming she's willing, and have her liquidate Klamathgold. The investors will guarantee her compensation, and that of any staff she requires in the event the proceeds of the liquidation do not cover the fees and costs."

The room grew silent. "Are you willing to do it, Shirley?" said Gatsby.

Shirley was glad to see how much Jim's tone toward her had changed. She quickly reviewed the pros and cons of taking on the assignment. The fact that Gatsby supported her appointment was a pro; the fact that the investors would guarantee her fees and those of the staff was a pro. She could see no downside as long as Jim wasn't a pill to work with, given it was his company on the block.

"Sure," she said, "assuming a written guarantee signed by all the investors. I'll give Jim a document tomorrow he can distribute to the investors. When the investors representing at least 80 percent of Klamathgold's invested capital sign up I'll go to work."

"Eight investors account for eighty percent of the invested capital," said Jim.

"Great," said Shirley. "We should be able to put the deal together by the end of the week. We need to staunch Klamathgold's bleeding ASAP."

Bill's phone buzzed. He picked it up. "I think we have a quorum. Let's go live." He pushed the button on the speakerphone and pointed to Jim. Jim called the roll and confirmed the presence of a quorum and confirmed that everyone on the line had received Shirley's report. He then opened the meeting to questions.

Silence.

After half a minute, which seemed to Shirley to have been three eternities, Jim said, "I take it that no one has any questions or comments. Is there any support for the revised plan?"

Silence.

Finally, Herman Stevens, one of the major investors, spoke up. "During the past few days, several of us have chatted about the situation and compared notes. The feeling is pretty much universal, that while algae harvesting and processing was an intriguing concept, and you have all given it your best shot, the risk–reward numbers don't pencil. We were all impressed by Shirley's report. It's incredible how she put that together so quickly. But we think it prudent we fold our tent and leave the field."

"Does anyone disagree with Herman?" said Jim.

Silence.

Then Jim offered his resolution to hire Shirley to liquidate Klamathgold and guarantee her compensation and expenses and that of her staff. That resolution carried unanimously.

As Shirley was leaving the office with Jim, Gatsby put his arm on her shoulder and said, "I appreciate your doing this, Shirley. I know it's a thankless task. Bill and I will owe you."

Shirley smiled at him. "I'm happy to do it," she said, thinking, *it's in my best interests to save your butt, you bastard.*

Bill announced he needed to have a private meeting with Gatsby. Shirley and Jim got up, said their goodbyes, and exited Bill's office.

~ ~ ~ ~ ~

After Shirley and Jim had gone, Bill sat back in his chair. "What are we going to do about the four guys who invested the $250K based on Jim's memorandum—which was obviously defective? They are going to be pissed and come knocking at our door. We need to be proactive."

"I agree," said Gatsby. "I think we should give them some of our EVG options. I think that will make them happy."

"I should say so," said Bill. "How many options do you have in mind?"

"EVG's last transaction was at two dollars a share. They invested $250,0000 in Klamathgold, so we should give them 125,000 shares, 62,500 from me and 62,500 from you."

Bill thought about Gatsby's suggestion briefly. "I agree. Will you approach them and sell them on the deal? And have McKnight prepare a release which each of them will sign and will become effective once the options transfer."

"I'll handle it," said Gatsby.

CHAPTER 6

GATSBY

Friday, February 28, 2003.

The weather was still exceptional for February: sunny skies with few clouds, temperature between 60 and 65 degrees, winds below 10 miles per hour. It was the kind of day that you should be skiing, snowboarding, or hiking on Blue Mountain. The thought depressed Gatsby as he stepped past the doorman of the Bellevue Restaurant.

A distinguished gentleman of about sixty waited in front of the Palm Restaurant's maître d' station. His coat was draped across his lap and there was a briefcase next to the chair on his left side. Gatsby walked over to him and said, "Mr. Larsen?"

Larsen stood, turned to Gatsby, and smiled. "Nils Larsen." He thrust out his hand. "I'm so happy to meet you, Mr. Brooks. I've heard so much about you."

Gatsby took his hand and shook it. "Just call me Gatsby, Nils. Everyone does."

He turned to the hostess and handed her a $10 bill. "Let us have one of the large tables along the windows. We're going to need some space to lay out documents."

"Of course, Mr. Brooks." She gathered up the menus and the wine list and led them over to a window table and took their drink order—

Tito's vodka over ice for Gatsby and a European-style chardonnay for Larsen.

"How long have you lived in Philly, Nils?"

"We moved back East just after the first of the year to be near our daughter's family. It was chaotic. We sold a rather large house in Pacific Palisades, in the Los Angeles area, and were on a forty-five-day escrow. My wife and I worked nonstop for thirty days clearing out our place—packing, setting up garage sales, donating—and then finding a place to rent in Philadelphia. A huge hassle. Now we're just trying to get used to the cold."

Indeed, the man was bundled up as if he were about to sail the Bering Sea. Gatsby opted not to contradict him.

"What do you do?" he said instead.

"What *did* I do is a better question. I was a partner in the LA office of Price Waterhouse and retired at the end of the summer. Thirty-five years were enough. Time to move on."

"So, you're retired?"

"Absolutely not. I'm healthy, and I'd like to do something different. Fortunately, we've got enough money that I don't have to punch a clock to put bread on the table. And I don't want to spend four to five days a week following a little white ball on the grass. If that was my goal I would have stayed in California or moved to Florida. That's why I wanted to get together with you. Your colleague Shirley Frazier and I have been friends for many years. We both served on the board of the Institute of Management Consultants. She mentioned that you were working on an exciting investment, and I'd like to hear about it. I'm looking for investment opportunities as well as a situation that could use my talents. Anyway, enough about me. Tell me just exactly what it is that you do, and why does everyone I meet tell me that you are the go-to guy in Philadelphia."

Before Gatsby could start with his spiel, the waiter came by, described the specials, and asked whether they needed more time. While Nils waffled, Gatsby sifted through what he'd just heard. So, he's operating on some outdated advice from Shirley, Gatsby thought. He trusted her but knew her well enough she wouldn't send this guy to him until she knew what had happened with her friend, the general. Or maybe she truly had let it go? Gatsby debated this possibility, framing it in light of her new workload with the Klamathgold liquidation. Hard to know for sure, but he'd find out.

When the waiter had carried off their orders for the duck special and a plate of salmon, Gatsby resumed. "You asked me what it is I do and why I've got such a high profile in town. The short answer is startups, politics, and philanthropy. I raise money for and serve in the management of startups and emerging companies in the computer technology and biotechnology areas. I'm active in the Republican Party, at both the state and national levels, and I serve on boards and raise money for charities. My professional life keeps bread on the table, but my political and philanthropic activities are my passion. These three core activities bring me in contact with many lawyers, accountants, business executives, politicians, and wealthy individuals."

"Fascinating," said Nils. "Have you ever run for office?"

"I ran for state treasurer many years ago, but I'm no longer interested in getting elected. The time and energy required to run a campaign would drain my ability to raise money for the deals that I'm involved in—and that would be unfair to the investors who previously committed resources. I'm happy with the role I play in the Republican Party. I just wish there were more of us so that Harrisburg stays on our side of the fence."

"Hear, hear," said Nils. The waiter brought their order and filled their water glasses. Gatsby picked up his fork and was about to start eating when Nils said, "This is where I'd like to hear about the 'exciting investment opportunity.'"

Gatsby replaced his fork, and took a sip of water, wiped his lips and leaned forward in his chair. "Nils, several years ago, a Philly surgeon and I co-founded a biotechnology company, Endovascular Group, which is the pioneer of remote endarterectomy, a surgical technique for removing plaque in the superior femoral artery. Occlusion in the SFA is a serious health problem for the elderly, especially those who smoke.

The number of patients a year who are afflicted is about 300,000 in the US and 500,000 worldwide."

"Wow," said Nils. "I haven't heard about this before, but I don't follow the biotechnology market."

"Our company," said Gatsby, "has a technology that beats the current treatment methods both in cost and patient discomfort. It could be a billion-dollar firm."

"Impressive," said Nils. "How far advanced is the company? Do you have FDA approval?"

"Not yet," said Gatsby, "but we are on track. We're projecting FDA approval in about eighteen months to two years. Things are ramping up, and investors who buy in now are getting a great deal. The current round of investment that I'm working on will carry the company for two years and will position it for an IPO by February 2005." He paused, adjusted his chair, and placed the napkin on his lap, picked up his fork and said, "Hey, let's not let this great food go to waste."

Fifteen minutes later, the waiter had picked up their plates and brought them coffee. Gatsby looked at his watch. He reached into his briefcase and pulled out a document and handed it to Nils.

"Here is the offering memorandum for the EVG deal. I'm raising $15 million in a hundred units of $150,000. I need to make a brief call. Could you excuse me for a minute?"

Without waiting for an answer, Gatsby stood and left the table and headed toward the Bellevue lobby. When he returned to the table, fifteen minutes later, Nils was still reading the memorandum. Gatsby sat down, motioned to the waiter to bring fresh coffee, and said, "Well, what do you think? Are you interested?"

Nils looked up from the memorandum. "I'm interested, but I need to do some due diligence on my own before I'm ready to make a commitment. Plus, I need to talk with my wife. This would be a significant investment for us."

Gatsby hid his disappointment. He drew a smile on his face. "I can appreciate that, Nils. How long will you need to decide? I'd like to get you into this deal, but I need to tell you, the units are going to move quickly. Many of the original investors have already made commitments."

"Look, Gatsby," said Nils, "I'm an accountant. I'm cautious. I don't make $1,500 decisions without serious thought, let alone $150,000 decisions."

Gatsby struggled to hide his agitation. The smile faded ever so slightly, and he forced some more energy into it. "Nils, would it help if you could get into the deal for $75,000, a half unit? I have a few current investors who are not able to purchase an entire unit. I plan to make a few half units available." Gatsby tried to read Nils's body language and expression to determine whether he appeared to be motivated. He decided to be quiet and let Nils make the next move.

"That is somewhat more attractive, but I still must think about it, then talk with my wife. You know the way spouses are. They want to be involved, especially when we're talking about committing five to six figures."

"I understand," said Gatsby. "If you give me a check for $10,000 by noon tomorrow, I'll reserve at least a half unit for you. It's just a placeholder. If you decide against going forward, I'll promptly return your money. This is a huge opportunity, Nils. I don't want you to miss out on it." Gatsby stood up. "I need to run. Stay and have one of their excellent desserts. I've handled the check." He turned and headed toward the door.

~ ~ ~ ~ ~

At 4 p.m., Gatsby entered the intimate private dining room in XIX Restaurant on the nineteenth floor of the Bellevue. General Walters, tall and graying, was standing at the window, holding a martini, and taking in the view.

"I'm delighted that you could make it," said Gatsby. He extended his hand to the general.

The general, displaying the visage that had once sent whole generations of junior officers shrinking from his presence, took Gatsby's hand in a firm grasp and shook it once.

"No problem, Mr. Brooks. I'm anxious to get this matter resolved."

"Good," said Gatsby, "So am I. Just give me a minute to order a drink and we'll get started. Please sit here so the sun is not in your eyes." He pointed to a specific chair. He picked up the phone, ordered his drink, and sat down opposite the general and placed his briefcase on an adjacent chair. He opened the briefcase, removed a white envelope, and placed it by his side. He turned toward the general and said, "General, this envelope contains a $25,000 certified check payable to you. I'm going to put in in the breast pocket of my jacket. If at the end of this meeting you still want your investment returned, I will hand you the check. You can mail me the convertible promissory note at your convenience. Is that agreeable?"

The general's eyes opened a little wider. It was obvious he had not expected this. His stern expression softened into a more casual, relaxed, and slightly bemused one. "Well, yes," he said. "Of course."

"Good," said Gatsby. "Now let's see if we can resolve this misunderstanding about the note."

The general nodded. "Fine."

"Please do not view what I'm going to say as the least bit critical of you, Shirley, or anyone at EVG. This was simply a misunderstanding. Had you first called me rather than Shirley at the instant that you became concerned over the fact that EVG had not received your investment, you would have avoided the several days of anxiety. Unfortunately, I could not meet with you prior to today. Shirley and I were tied up dealing with another matter."

He picked up the copy of the convertible promissory note he had given the general.

"You agree, don't you, that this document states quite clearly that you, General Walters, are lending me, Christopher Gatsby Brooks, $25,000; and in return, I am agreeing to pay you eight percent interest and I am giving you an option to purchase 12,500 shares of my EVG stock at $2 a share, if and when you want to—correct?"

The general nodded. "Yes, I understand that now. But that was not my understanding at the time I agreed to make the investment. I understood that the money would go into EVG, to help EVG grow."

"Yes, General, I acknowledge that. But you understand, don't you, that the offer I made to you could not be made by EVG?"

The general looked perplexed. "Why not?"

"General," said Gatsby, struggling not to appear condescending, "EVG is a small, emerging company. It spends every dollar it can get its hands on—and then some. It stretches its payables to the breaking point, and then stretches them some more. EVG can't give you a note at any interest because the management knows that, more likely than not, they would be unable to pay you back. The failure rate of startup companies is in the 90 percent range. If you wanted to purchase shares in EVG, you would give EVG the money, and if EVG failed, your money is gone. In my deal, if EVG fails, you ask me for the money, and I'll pay it back to you with interest. You have no risk."

The general picked up the convertible promissory note and looked at it again. It was evident to Gatsby that the other man was buying time to absorb what was for him a revelation.

He shook his head slightly, set down the note, and looked straight at Gatsby.

"Gatsby, I'm embarrassed. I confess, that until just now, I did not appreciate the benefits of your deal. This just shows my lack of sophistication in the world of finance. I'm deeply sorry. I should have called you immediately."

"You need not apologize to me. It was a simple misunderstanding." He looked at his watch. "Do you have any other questions? Are there any other issues you want to discuss?"

The man obviously had something else on his mind, but he appeared reluctant to bring it up.

"General, please take the time to think this through. I need to use the john. Can I order you anything else? Would you like something to eat, another drink?"

"No, I'm fine. You go ahead. I need a few minutes of quiet time to think this through."

Gatsby returned fifteen minutes later. The general had made notes on the tablet provided by the restaurant. "Where are we?" asked Gatsby as he took his seat. The general pushed his chair back from the table and stood up and walked over to the window. He stared at the view and then turned toward Gatsby. "When I discussed the promissory note with my attorney and my accountant, both of whom are aware of your activities and reputation, they both raised the issue of your capacity to repay the note if I made a demand—which I would only do if EVG failed."

Gatsby laughed. "Are they aware of something I don't know? Is anyone claiming that I'm a deadbeat? That I don't pay my bills? That I've stiffed some creditors?"

"No, no," said the general. "On the contrary, they both say that you have a stellar reputation. It's unblemished. They both raised it as a due diligence issue and suggested that I discuss it with you."

"Well," said Gatsby, "I'm delighted to see that you are being well served by your professional advisors. It *is* a due diligence issue." He opened his briefcase and removed a two-page document and handed it to the general. "This is a copy of my personal financial statement that I used to open a brokerage account at Smith Barney. It is extremely confidential, and I cannot allow you to keep it. However, I am prepared to answer all questions you may have about it. Take your time."

The general scanned the financial statement and let out a low whistle. He looked over at Gatsby, his eyes wide and a broad smile covering his face. "You have certainly done well for yourself," he said.

"Thank you," said Gatsby.

The general looked over the financial statement for several more minutes and then slid it back to Gatsby. "I have no further questions."

"You are certain?" said Gatsby.

"Absolutely. And" he said, pointing to Gatsby's jacket that held the white envelope containing the $25,000 check, "you can cancel the check. I'll keep the convertible promissory note."

Gatsby smiled and held out his hand to the general. "I think you've made an excellent business decision."

CHAPTER 7

SHIRLEY

Friday, March 8, 2003

The following Monday, Shirley received the written guarantee for her salary and expenses to liquidate Klamathgold. She also received the certificate from Gatsby's timeshare in Saint Martin, confirming she would be occupying the condo there for the week of November 23 through November 29, which included Thanksgiving. She also received the email confirming her business-class, round-trip flight. As she filed the email and the reservation in her filing cabinet, she thought, *the bastard really does have some blood flowing through his arteries.*

The following day, she flew back out to Klamath Falls to meet the operations manager who would be working with her during her project. For the next five days, she spent ten to twelve hours a day addressing the myriad activities required to liquidate a business. But during the time she was not focused on her Klamathgold tasks, she thought about Gatsby. She thought about him during her solitary evening meals, during the drives between her motel and the plant, and during the time she lay in bed prior to dropping off into an exhausted sleep. Gatsby and his damn convertible promissory notes—she couldn't stop ruminating about them.

The $25,000 she had given him was directly invested in EVG. So, until General Walters called her, she was completely unaware of Gatsby's CPN scheme. She had plenty of concerns about her investment which looked a hell of a lot less secure after the meeting with Jerry and the EVG staff.

Then, there was the fact that came out of the EVG meeting when Jerry asked about EVG's lack of progress with the Food and Drug Administration's approval. Driscoll's explanation was they were always starved for cash. So how did Gatsby reconcile diverting cash from General Walters, who wanted to invest in EVG, into his own pocket? And, apparently, although Driscoll had hired Gatsby to raise money for the company, he was unaware that Gatsby was using his EVG options to motivate investors to loan the money to him rather than invest in the company directly.

Did Gatsby have the right to sell CPNs? A prominent Philadelphia attorney had advised him he could rely on certain exemptions to the Pennsylvania securities laws—or was that just one more lie? How many investors had Gatsby persuaded or duped? How much money had he borrowed? How much could he pay back if the notes were all called? How many of the investors she had introduced to Gatsby have bought his CPNs? Besides her reputation and the goodwill of her friends and colleagues, what liability might she have if those friends and colleagues lost their investments? And then there was the conversation she overheard when she was in the foyer of Gatsby's office and Cissy was on the phone. It was apparent that Cissy was talking with a vendor who had provided the flowers for Gatsby's daughter's wedding. The florist hadn't been paid. The wedding had occurred more than a month ago. Cissy was apologizing for the delay and said she would talk to Gatsby about it, and when Cissy got off the phone, she'd commented she didn't understand why Gatsby always strung vendors out. It made her job so much more difficult. Was it possible that Gatsby is not the millionaire he claimed to be?

The incremental accretion of facts and the myriad questions swirled around in her head. When she awoke on Tuesday morning, she recognized she had to put the ruminations on hold until she returned to Philadelphia, when she could consult with an attorney. Her priority was to liquidate Klamathgold to minimize the investors' loss.

On Friday, she arrived at the Klamath Falls airport at 2 p.m. Her flight to Philadelphia was running two hours late. She decided to use the time to contact Brad Lester, a securities attorney who had worked for Duane Morris and since moved to San Francisco.

Fortunately, Brad was still in his office. She related the Gatsby/CPN situation in detail. She told him her primary concern was whether she was liable for losses of CPN investors whom she had introduced to Gatsby. Brad agreed to research the issue and get back to her the following week. When she hung up, she felt a sense of relief. At least she was going to have some help coping with this mess.

The following Monday morning, after a sleepless night, Shirley dragged herself into her kitchen, opened the refrigerator and scanned the shelves. She had a hangover. She had gulped down about four ounces of vodka at around 3:30 a.m. in a last-ditch effort to drive herself into sleep. It had worked—but now she felt terrible. Nothing in the refrigerator appealed to her. She decided to have tea and toast and shuffled between the sink the stove and the cupboard to assemble the ingredients. While the water was heating, she called Brad Lester.

"How are you this morning, Shirley?"

"I'm not doing very well, Brad. I can't sleep. I ruminated half the night about this Gatsby business. I have to put the phone down for a minute. I've got water boiling." She poured the water into a sixteen-ounce cup, dropped in a teabag, a lump of sugar, and a wedge of lemon, picked up her phone and sat down at the table. "Okay, I'm back. So, is it too soon to ask what the verdict is?"

"Not at all. I've thoroughly researched the issue as to what legal duties you've incurred because of what you've learned about Gatsby's selling of convertible promissory notes. It's over four pages long and it'll cost you $3,500. I'll send it by email later today."

"What's your conclusion?"

"You don't have any liability, nor do you have any obligation to tell anyone anything— and I strongly suggest that you don't volunteer any information to anyone unless you're asked."

"Why not?"

Brad did not answer immediately. Shirley could almost feel him agonizing over his choice of words. "Listen carefully, Shirley. I know that you've been consumed by this Gatsby situation. And I know that you're unhappy over the way he's used you and several of your friends. But you need to let it go. Gatsby has developed a unique way to achieve liquidity from his options in the startup companies he sponsors. That is apparently how he finances himself and maintains a lavish lifestyle. Even if the sale of CPNs doesn't violate any Pennsylvania securities laws, he is probably breaching the covenant of good faith and fair dealing in that there is an inherent conflict in his using his options in Company X as an incentive for his lenders when he's signed an agreement to raise capital for Company X.

"Selling CPNs is obviously essential to maintaining his lifestyle, image, and business. Gatsby and the company he purportedly is raising money for are competing for the same resources, namely investments from individuals and institutions. So, if the company needs cash and Gatsby is taking that cash for himself rather than encouraging the investor to invest in the company, he is breaching the fiduciary duty he owes to the company. Frankly I'm astonished he's gotten away with it for so many years."

"That's what I was afraid of," said Shirley. "And I am pissed to high heaven he's used me and my contacts to further his scheme. God *damn* him."

"I can understand your outrage, Shirley, but you need to be prudent about this. You don't want to be the one to question his activities or call attention to them or discuss them with your friends and colleagues. You may just want to get your money back from your investment in EVG and move on. Gatsby is a powerful and influential Philadelphia entrepreneur, and if he sees you as an adversary threatening to undermine his reputation, he can get dangerous. He is a successful counterpuncher.

This is a losing proposition for you. As both your friend and your lawyer, I strongly advise you to stand down."

"Do you think he's running a Ponzi scheme?"

"I have no idea. I would need to know how many dollars of these CPNs are outstanding and his approximate net worth. If he is unable to pay off all the outstanding notes in accordance with their terms, he'd be running a Ponzi scheme, yes. But you're not listening, Shirley. It doesn't make any difference to you whether he is running a Ponzi scheme. If you start to play detective and delve into his operation, you'll ruin your career. Give it up. Walk away. The authorities will eventually catch up to him."

"I'll think about it, Brad. Thanks for the quick response."

Shirley hung up the phone and sat, drinking her tea. Intellectually, she could see the wisdom in Brad's advice. If she became identified with a get-Gatsby effort, her income and her career would take a hit. But she couldn't be a potted plant and do nothing and allow Gatsby to deceive her friends, colleagues, and even strangers. It would be like being wrongly diagnosed by a doctor, surviving a near-death medical situation which the doctor had exacerbated, and then failing to report the doctor to the state medical board, thus allowing that doctor to put other lives at risk. That would be immoral. And doing nothing about Gatsby would also be immoral.

She lifted herself out of the chair, walked over to the stove, refilled her cup, dropped in another tea bag and another slice of lemon, and tasted the tea to ensure it was hot. As she was walking back to the kitchen table she suddenly stopped, smiled. She'd take the problem to her Uncle Bill. He was Gatsby's partner. He'd know what to do.

CHAPTER 8

GATSBY

March 13, 2003

When the paramedics arrived at Bill Dewyne's office, Bill was on the floor, Gatsby was performing CPR, and Shirley was sitting on the floor holding Bill's left hand and stroking his brow. The paramedics took over and put Bill on a gurney and took him down the elevator to the ambulance. They put on the siren and headed to Jefferson Hospital.

"I hope he'll be all right," said Moe as he entered the elevator.

"He'll be fine. He's as strong as an ox," said Gatsby. He re-tucked a shirttail back into his belt and deliberately smoothed his hair in the elevator's mirrored wall.

Moe took the handkerchief from his breast pocket and wiped his brow. He pushed it back into the side pocket of his jacket. He hesitated. "I'm worried, Gatsby. He's got heart issues. He takes a blood thinner, Coumadin, I think. We should go to the hospital and check up on him."

Gatsby laughed as the elevator came to a stop. "Moe, you're being an old lady. Shirley's staying within him. She'll call Ono. The last thing he needs is a crowd hovering around his bed, wringing their hands. There's no role for us. We'll check in with the hospital later and see how he's doing. Besides, I need to talk with you. Let's go walk over to the Capital One 360 Café on Walnut. I need a large cappuccino."

Gatsby took Moe's arm and steered him out of the elevator. They walked through the front door of the office building, crossed, and walked south on Seventeenth Street.

"Can you believe this weather, Moe? Not a cloud. God, we're lucky on this side of the state!"

"Yeah," said Moe. "When it's not muggy or freezing."

They ordered their drinks from the barista in the open-air bistro and seated themselves at a small metal table. Gatsby adjusted his cuffs, swept a napkin across the edge of the table, and lightly rested his elbows there. He held Moe in a placid, unblinking gaze at odds with the emergency they'd both just endured.

"Moe, why didn't you tell me that you sent over a copy of a convertible promissory note to Bill?"

"Why? It wasn't any big deal. He asked, and I sent it. So what?"

Gatsby's mouth shifted into a smile, but no other muscle on his face moved. "No, it's not a big deal, Moe. But you're my friend. I think you should have told me, that's all."

"Christ, Gatsby, I've got a banker's box chock full of your notes. I would have told you if he asked for all of them—which he did not."

"Okay, let's drop it. I've made my point. Let's move on." He leaned forward. "Moe, I need your help on one of our deals. We've got a problem and I've racked my brains looking for a solution. I can't come up with one. That's why I need your help."

"Which deal?" said Moe.

"EVG."

"What's the problem?"

"The problem is Driscoll, the CEO."

"You're kidding, I hope? I thought you loved Driscoll. The last time we talked about Driscoll—a few weeks ago, at most—you said he was doing a great job."

"I know," said Gatsby, "but that's old news. He's fucking up, and we can't tolerate it because we're raising another round of financing from some heavy hitters on Wall Street. You've read Jerry Bascomb's report. He said Driscoll is just not up to the job. We need someone in that slot who can show some leadership and be part of the team while I'm raising the money. Driscoll's not that guy."

Moe shook his head. "Damn! What are you going to do?"

Gatsby shrugged lightly. "Between your direct investment and your options in the convertible promissory notes, you have almost twenty percent of this deal. That's why I'm talking to you."

"Okay," said Moe, shrugging his shoulders, "what are we going to do?"

"I think the drinks are ready," said Gatsby. "I'll get them."

He walked over to the barista stand, scooped up the drinks and brought them back to the table. "Here's your mocha," he said, and sat down. He leaned into the table and waited until Moe took his first sip. Then he tasted his own, pushed the cup back, and looked directly into Moe's eyes.

"EVG will be out of cash in three months. The company has enough potential that I think I can get some big guns on Wall Street to participate in another round. I have a Columbia doctor who has looked at the technology and likes it. He's a consultant to several firms—Goldman, KKR, and so on. The money raising should be smooth, but I need to shore up the EVG executive team. Driscoll doesn't have it. And I've got no one else to put in there. I need you to take over as CEO for a while, maybe until I get the money in the door, start the trials for the new graft, and find a permanent CEO." Gatsby sat back in his chair and picked up his cappuccino.

Beads of sweat started to form on Moe's forehead. His seat was uncomfortable. As he reached for the handkerchief in his pocket, he sloshed his mocha on the table and on to his trousers.

"Fuck!" he shouted and quickly stood to avoid the mocha that continued to drip through the slatted table. "Fuck! Fuck!"

Gatsby hurried to the barista's window and asked for a wet towel and another mocha for Moe. While he was waiting, he reviewed the events leading up to Bill's passing out and the calling of the paramedics. The tinge of relief he had felt when the paramedics had wheeled Bill out of the office, still breathing, had dissipated. Shirley's witnessing of the entire drama presented a real problem, depending upon whether Bill survived, how much she might choose to reveal, and to whom. Damn! And then there was the chaos she was creating over the promissory notes.

He looked over toward Moe who was rubbing the mocha from his trousers. Gatsby returned to the table with the towel.

"I ordered you another drink," he said, and sat down in his chair. An agitated Moe continued to stand and wipe. "Sit down, Moe, and calm down. You can afford to throw away the damn suit. You've got fifty more in your closet."

Moe picked up the towel and wiped his trousers and then his hands.

Gatsby clapped his hands to get Moe's attention and said again, "Moe, SIT DOWN!"

"After I get my mocha," said Moe. He went to the barista window, retrieved his new drink, sat down, and faced Gatsby. "Come one, Gatsby, you know that job requires someone who is really good at details and follow-up. Those are definitely not my skill sets. You've got to find someone else."

"I don't have any other options. EVG is out of time and will soon be out of money. I have investors in the wings who want to throw money at the deal. I need an executive who can catch the money and who has the pedigree, education, position in the community to make the investors comfortable. You are that guy. You need to take it on. Just for six months. By that time, I'll have corralled your replacement."

Moe stared at his mocha. He shook his head. He picked up the mocha and took a long sip. He replaced the cup on the table. All during this time Gatsby continued to stare at him, willing him to agree.

Finally, Moe muttered, "Okay, I'll do it. I don't like it, but I'll do it."

Gatsby patted him on the shoulder as he stood. "Great," he said. "I'll call you later today and we can work out the details. Meanwhile, mum's the word until I talk with Driscoll."

Moe pushed back his chair and stood. He clasped Gatsby's extended hand and muttered some more agreements. "I think I'll call Jefferson and see how Bill is doing."

"Good idea. And I'll call you later today." He turned away and quickly walked off.

CHAPTER 9

GATSBY

The following Monday, March 17

Wearing an Augusta-green jacket, green cap, and pale-green slacks, Gatsby pushed open the door to the foyer of his office carrying a walking stick and strolled over to Cissy's desk. He placed a bottle of crème de menthe on her desk and handed her a bouquet consisting of bells of Ireland, gladiolas, zinnias, daylilies, and chrysanthemums.

He said, "The top of the mornin' to you, lassie. As the Irish say:

"Tis better to buy a small bouquet and give
it to your friend this very day than a bushel of
roses, white and red To lay on her coffin after
she's dead."

Cissy, puzzled, looked up from her computer. "But I'd hardly call this a small bouquet."

"It's March 17, darlin', St. Patrick's Day, so I've taken some liberties. This is the day for the wearin' of the green, the day the…the day when our pot of gold may appear."

He stood back from the desk and spread his arms wide. "You see—I'm ready for it."

"You certainly are!" She turned back to her computer. "I'd love to celebrate with you, but I've got to get out these invoices so we can get some money in here. Our balance is under $1,000."

"Not to worry! Just remember the Irish blessing: *May your pockets be heavy, and your heart be light, may good luck pursue you each morning and night.*"

"Okay, already. Please let me get back to work! Oh, Barbara—Mr. McKnight's secretary—called and asked me to tell you he needs to see you and the matter was urgent."

Taking the hint, Gatsby briskly walked the three blocks west to One Commerce Square and passed through the revolving door. He waved to the security guard and took the elevator to the thirty-first floor offices of his attorneys, McKnight and Collingswood. He entered the reception area and greeted the receptionist with more of his Irish capering.

Barbara smiled at him "Well, Mr. Brooks, you certainly are dressed for the occasion."

"Thank ye, lassie, and Happy St. Patrick's Day to you. As we Irish say, 'May the best day of your past be the worst day in your future.'"

"I'll tell George you're here."

Gatsby sat down in the reception area and picked up the *Wall Street Journal* and scanned the front page.

"Mr. Brooks, you can go on to his office."

Gatsby entered George McKnight's spacious corner office with its striking view of the Philadelphia West Hills. The two outside walls were composed of floor-to-ceiling windows that gave the illusion of stepping into space. George McKnight, an aging college lineman, was an imposing presence in any courtroom. Yet his gray beard somewhat softened the image and created an avuncular impression.

"I forgot what a great office you have," said Gatsby.

"Ah," said George, "the proceeds of plunder!"

"Of your adversaries or your clients?"

George didn't respond. Instead he said, "I didn't know you were Irish!"

"Yes, I am, and proud to be a son of the Emerald Isle. It is the only legacy from my father, who disappeared when I was a wee one in my sainted mother's womb."

"Well," said George, "that explains why you're such an excellent raconteur. It's in your blood."

"Barbara called and said it was urgent," said Gatsby.

"This letter was hand-delivered this morning." He handed Gatsby a two-page document. "In substance, it alleges that by selling your convertible promissory notes, or CPNs, you have been and are committing securities fraud. By introducing you to several investors who purchased CPNs, Shirley has unwittingly put herself at risk for both her financial situation and her reputation. She demands that you cease and desist selling CPNs to her contacts and unwind all the transactions that have been completed with clients she introduced you to and return all the money you've been paid for those CPNs. The letter also threatens to report the matter to the Pennsylvania Attorney General."

Gatsby quickly read the letter. He felt a blank in his chest where anger should be, and he tossed the sheet of paper back on the desk.

"I'm not surprised. I met with Shirley a week and a half ago and she was quite upset about my selling a $25,000 convertible promissory note to General Walters, a professional colleague of hers. I met with him about two weeks ago and offered to give him back his money—and he chose to keep the note."

George poked his glasses higher on his nose and gave Gatsby a steady look. "Are you illegally selling securities?"

Gatsby gave him a relaxed smile. "I obtained an opinion from Parsons, advising me that if I limit my sales of CPNs to accredited investors or ten purchasers in any twelve-month period, that under Pennsylvania law, the notes need not be registered. And I've scrupulously adhered to that limitation."

"That's helpful. Can you send me a copy of the opinion?"

"Unfortunately, I can't. They wouldn't put in it writing for less than $20,000, which I couldn't afford at the time. I always planned to buy the damn opinion but never got around to it."

George fiddled around with a pen and highlighter on his desk, obviously mulling over this response. "Do you think Parsons will sign an affidavit he provided you the opinion orally? Although I'm not sure it will be of much help."

"Why wouldn't it?"

"Because the attorney general will refer the matter to the securities guys who will conduct their own investigation, examine the paper you've been selling, and decide whether these are securities that should have been registered. If they decide they're not kosher, they'll issue a cease-and-desist order and assess some fine. I'm assuming, a cease-and-desist may cause you some problems and subject Parsons to some uncomfortable publicity."

Gatsby stood up and started pacing around the room, trying to let the sudden burst of annoyance burn off. He looked over to George. He could feel his face becoming warm. "You bet it will. My cash flow will dry up. I will be out of business. And I'd have no way to pay the investors who ask to be paid pack. That cunt will destroy my business and my life. *Damn* her!"

Gatsby perched on his seat and looked over to George, who was leaning back in his chair with his eyes closed. Suddenly, George moved forward and buzzed his secretary.

"Hi, Barbara, please bring us in some fresh coffee. Thanks." George stood up and headed toward the door. "I need to use the head." He pointed to a document on the credenza, the *SEC News Digest*. "You might be interested in reading about the Dowdell case on page five."

Gatsby thought that coffee was the last thing he needed. He jerked the document off the credenza, rattled it open to page five, and began to read. When he had completed the article, he re-scanned the other pages of the document, all of which set forth summaries of meeting notices and enforcement actions of the SEC for the week.

George returned to the office twenty minutes later and sat down behind his desk.

"Did you read the case?"

"I did," said Gatsby. "I don't see what it has it do with me. I'm certainly not selling fictitious 'prime-backed securities' and offering returns of four percent per week up to 160 percent per year."

"I agree," said George. "You are offering a legitimate note at an above-market interest rate with an inducement of a legitimate option to purchase stock in a legitimate startup or early-stage business."

"So, what's the damn problem? Why should the Department of Securities have a beef with me?"

George picked up the article from the credenza. "Let me read you the last line of the third paragraph. 'As Dowdell admitted in his Consent and Stipulation, he was operating a classic Ponzi scheme in which *old* investors were being paid with *new* investor money.' Gatsby, that is precisely what your CPN business requires and which you have been doing. Your inducement to investors to lend you money is the option that you give them in a startup or an emerging company. However, since many of these companies will either fail or never have a liquidity event to generate the cash to pay off the underlying note, the investors will look to you to pay them back and you do not and will not have the assets to satisfy them—unless you sell new CPNs and pay the old investors off with the money you collect from new investors. Q. E. D.! You *are* operating a Ponzi scheme."

George leaned forward against his desk and looked intently at his client. "Gatsby, when the Pennsylvania Banking and Securities Department completes their investigation and issues their cease-and-desist order and fines you, they will likely make a referral to the Pennsylvania Attorney General or the US Attorney's office. It will only be a matter of time before you are the subject of a *Wall Street Journal* article like the one you've just read. You can take that to the bank!"

Gatsby sat, silently absorbing George's analysis. He was composed and outwardly calm despite the pounding of his heart, which was making him a little nauseated. He had never considered the possibility that the cops might come after him for borrowing this money. He had been doing this for years and no one had complained.

After a few breaths that slowed his heart, he looked George full in the face. "What are my options?"

"You've got two. I will refer to them as the *Mea Culpa Option* and the *Stealth Option*. The major advantage of the Mea Culpa Option is that it will resolve all your problems immediately, be relatively inexpensive and, in my opinion, there will be a low risk of your being subject to a criminal prosecution. On the other hand, the Stealth Option will drag out your problems over a long period, will be very expensive, will expose you to substantial risk of a criminal prosecution, and, in my opinion, has a very low probability of a Hollywood ending."

"Go on," said Gatsby.

"If you select the Mea Culpa Option, I'd talk with my wife, the US Attorney for the Eastern District of Pennsylvania, and explain the problem to her. I'll ask she assign one of the more empathetic Assistant US Attorneys to the case. We would lay out our problem to him or her and take the position that any violation of Pennsylvania securities laws was unintentional. We haven't defrauded anyone, but the issue has been raised and you need to get it resolved. Because until it is, you are unable to conduct business."

Gatsby had slumped down in his chair. He could not have felt worse if an oncologist were telling him he had cancer and there were two options for treating him, both of which were unattractive.

George continued, "They will initiate an investigation in conjunction with the Pennsylvania Department of Banking and Securities, conclude that you have been selling unregistered securities, advise you they intend to issue a cease-and-desist order precluding your selling any more convertible promissory notes. You will be out of business. And then you will file a Chapter 7 bankruptcy, which will discharge all the promissory notes. You will be able to start a new business with a clean, debt-free slate. I expect that there will be some backlash from your investor-creditors who will receive little from the several million dollars in CPNs they invested in you. But you've got a big enough reputation in this town and with all your contacts in the Republican Party across the country, you'll be fine. You just will have to find a new business model, one that doesn't rely on a Ponzi scheme."

"How will I pay my living expenses until I can start my new gig?"

"Your wife has plenty of money. I'm sure she'll support you until you can get something else going."

Gatsby sat, thinking. He shook his head. "I don't know about this mea culpa business. It seems risky to me."

"Okay," said George, not suppressing his exasperation, "let's look at the alternative Stealth Option. You would continue business as usual, perpetuating the Ponzi scheme to keep the business going. But simultaneously, you would set up a new business model. You'd form an LLC and start to raise venture capital to invest in startups—the same thing you've been doing—but under an appropriate legal umbrella. When the Pennsylvania securities attorneys, prodded by Shirley, start to investigate you, you'll be cooperative but be slow to respond. You'll play for time in order to raise the money for the new venture capital operation. You'll reluctantly turn over documents and force them to jump through a lot of hoops when they ask for sensitive information. Eventually they will piece together sufficient information to make their findings and will issue their cease-and-desist order."

"How long?"

"You may be able to stretch it out over a year, maybe more. It depends."

"On what?"

"How aggressive they are, how creative your attorneys are. I can't predict. But when they issue their order, you are out of the CPN business. And there could be serious fallout and unintended consequences."

"Like what?" said Gatsby.

George paused, leaned back in his chair, took a sip of coffee and said, "There will probably be stories in the newspapers that will be less than flattering. The stories may spook some of your CPN investors and they may demand their money back. Some of your well-heeled investors from out of state may initiate complaints with their securities department. You won't control the process, so you can never tell what may happen next. There is a substantial probability that the Pennsylvania AG or my wife's office will get involved and file a criminal complaint. That is why the Stealth Option is risky. Also, there is the problem of finding money to pay off all the CPNs that mature after the Department issues its order. You won't be able to sell any more promissory notes, and moreover, you won't be able to dip into the money that you raise for your new deal, other than for your salary, because you effectively will be operating the venture LLC as a trustee."

"Some of my deals will pay off. Like EVG," said Gatsby.

"Well," said George, "I know that you need to be optimistic. But you and I are having a realistic conversation. You need to know that the Stealth Option carries a huge amount of risk including the real possibility of criminal charges, conviction, and incarceration. Like I said, not a Hollywood ending. You need to think about this carefully. You understand?"

Gatsby, still slouched in his chair, nodded.

"Good," said George. "Think about the alternatives. Call me if you have any questions. You need to decide within the next few days so that you can respond to Shirley's letter. How you respond will reflect what option you've decided on. If you choose stealth, you will have to be aggressive in your response, threaten to sue for defamation, scare the hell out of her, and try to shut her up."

Gatsby sat up in his chair. "You've used the pronoun *you* in describing the actions that need to be taken if I choose the Stealth Option. Don't you mean *we*? I mean, you're going to help me on this, right?"

George smiled and shook his head. "You're perceptive, Gatsby. I chose the pronoun *you* because if you choose stealth, you will be effectively on your own. I cannot represent you. The attorney that does, assuming he is not an absolute idiot with a degree from some online-scam law school, will recognize he is aiding and abetting a Ponzi scheme. You may find an attorney to represent you who can figure out a strategy to stay protected. But, since I'm married to the US Attorney for the Eastern District of Pennsylvania, I can't go there."

He stood up and said, "I have another meeting." He walked to the front of his desk, shook Gatsby's outstretched hand, and said, "You are at a critical crossroads in your career, Gatsby—and your life. You need to think long and hard about your decision." Then he escorted Gatsby to the lobby.

Gatsby used the phone in the foyer to call Miriam. He asked her to cancel whatever she'd had scheduled this afternoon and to meet him at the Inn at the League at 1450 Sansom Street in an hour for lunch. He added that they needed to have a serious conversation that might take several hours. He suggested she bring a change of clothes for the two of them in case they decided to spend the night. Before she could voice any objections, he hung up.

CHAPTER 10

GATSBY

Gatsby arrived at the Inn at noon. He registered and took the elevator up to his room. He grabbed the ice bucket and headed down the hall. He returned to his room, took two mini-bottles of vodka from the minibar, and poured them over a glass of ice. He ordered club sandwiches with fries and a bottle of Kendall Jackson chardonnay for lunch to be delivered at 1 p.m. Then he undressed and stepped into the shower.

He increased the temperature of the stream until it was just below scalding. He slowly turned around so that every square inch of his body was pummeled. As he exited the shower and started to dry himself, Miriam entered the room wheeling her overnight bag. She parked the bag and went to the doorway of the bathroom. She was wearing a pale-green, form-fitting dress whose neckline made the most of her high collarbones and her shapely breasts—which were a site of her unapologetic vanity.

"Hi," she said.

Gatsby dropped the towel and took her in his arms and pressed his body against hers.

"Hey, you're wet," she said, "and this is a new outfit."

"It will dry." As he kissed her, he pulled the zipper of her dress down so that the soft fabric slipped to her feet. "Meet you in bed in three minutes."

Twenty minutes later Gatsby rolled off Miriam and pulled the covers up to his neck. "I'm sorry for raising your expectations and not following through, but I'm distracted by the results of my meeting with George." He looked at his watch. It was 12:30 p.m. "I scheduled lunch at one. Please call room service and tell them to hold the lunch until we call. I need to sleep for an hour then we'll talk. I'm under a lot of stress."

"I can see that." She moved over and kissed him. "No problem, I've got plenty to read."

Over two hours later, Gatsby awoke. He looked at his watch. Miriam was curled next to him, having let him sleep while she'd plowed through half her book. He headed to the bathroom, took another long shower, and emerged a while later wearing a white terrycloth robe provided by the hotel.

"Want a drink?" he asked.

"Scotch on the rocks," she said, still reading.

He took two scotch mini-bottles and two vodka mini-bottles from the bar and made two drinks while she made the call for lunch. He handed the scotch to her.

She took a sip and placed the glass on the nightstand, on top of her closed book, which she'd nearly finished. "Okay, why are we here?"

Gatsby sat down on the chair facing the bed. He drained his drink to the ice cubes. Then he proceeded to tell her the issues he'd been dealing with for the past two months. She listened intently, occasionally asking a question to clarify an issue or an event; she expressed surprise at learning that Bill Dewyne's heart attack occurred during an argument. She asked several questions about Gatsby's meeting with McKnight, especially about the two options McKnight had outlined. As he spoke, she occasionally swirled her drink, taking it in as she took in his story—carefully, deliberately, until she had fully consumed it.

There was a knock at the door. Miriam, still nude, slipped into the bathroom and closed the door. The room service waiter pushed in the trolley with their lunch into the room and Gatsby scribbled his signature on the check. After the waiter left, Miriam emerged from the bathroom wearing the other white terrycloth robe.

"Let's eat. I'm starved." Miriam poured two large glasses of wine and took a sip. "Is there anything else you need to tell me?"

"No," said Gatsby, "that's pretty much the whole shebang."

"And the bottom line?"

"We've got to make a decision, now, tonight. I've run out of time."

"You mean we just need to decide between the Mea Culpa Option and the Stealth Option? That's it?"

"Not quite," said Gatsby. "No matter what option we choose, I'm going to need a couple of hundred thousand dollars for lawyers and to carry the business for a few months—until we can work through the transition."

Miriam took a long gulp of wine, and then refilled her glass. "I see."

They both sat in silence, drinking their wine, suddenly uncomfortable with each other.

Finally, Miriam broke the silence. "I'm going to tell you about an experience from my past. Many years before we met." She placed her wine glass on the table.

"During my first marriage, my first husband and I and the kids spent many weekends and vacations skiing. My husband and the kids became expert skiers. I wasn't as good as they were and often skied alone. One of our favorite spots was Mammoth Lakes in Central California. We owned a condo there for years.

"One year during the mid-eighties, I made a commitment to improving my skills so I could ski with my husband and children. I signed up for a week of ski lessons, a total of thirty hours over six days. There were three other women in the class. The instructor was a fellow named Roger Armstrong. He was in his mid-thirties and perfect for his job—he was gorgeous and had a great personality. As you might expect, while sharing coffee and lunch and after skiing together over several days, we women got to know each other well.

"One of the women, Marylyn, was a recent divorcée who had gotten a five-million-dollar settlement from her investment banker husband. During the lessons it became obvious that Roger was paying the most attention to Marylyn and the rest of us got whatever morsels he had left. Marylyn was attracted to Roger. So, it was no surprise when we returned to Mammoth Lakes the following year and learned that Roger and Marylyn had gotten married. Roger had retired from the ski instruction business.

"I called Marylyn and we met for lunch. She was a starry-eyed newlywed who absolutely would not stop talking about her fantastic sex life—which I didn't want to hear, because mine was a disaster. When I asked her why he was no longer giving ski lessons, she said he had quite a bit of experience in construction, and they were thinking about starting a construction company."

Gatsby stood up and started pacing. Unlike his wife, his talents did not include patience. "What is the point of all of this? I have no idea where you are going."

A high flush appeared on Miriam's cheekbones. She gave him her apex-predator stare and said, "Sit down, dammit. You'll see where I'm going in a minute."

Gatsby sat down, poured some wine in his glass, took a large swallow, and crossed his legs. He hadn't stayed married so long by ignoring danger when he felt it stirring under his own roof.

"When we came back the following year," Miriam continued, "Armstrong Construction Company was developing a thirty-unit condo project, building a shopping center, and buying up empty lots all over town. Their signs were everywhere, and it appeared that many residents of Mammoth Lakes were working for Armstrong Construction.

"The next year, Armstrong Construction filed bankruptcy and was out of business. Roger and Marylyn had literally been driven out of town, leaving thousands of dollars in payroll and payroll taxes unpaid. Their house had been vandalized, their dogs were poisoned, and during the annual Mammoth Lakes Parade, their images were burned in effigy.

"I looked up one of the women who had taken the ski lessons with me, and she said to the best of her knowledge, Roger and Marylyn were living in Southern California. They still were very much in love and Marylyn still bragged about their sex life. But the five million dollars was gone, and they were dead broke."

Gatsby pushed the French fries around his plate and took a sip of wine. "Interesting story, Miriam. What am I missing?"

Making no attempt to conceal her exasperation, Miriam blurted, "Damn it, Gatsby, don't act dumb. Marylyn Armstrong's story is always with me, warning me not to go down that road. I intend to hold on to my divorce settlement like an Ebenezer Scrooge. It is my safety net if I find myself out on my own. I've already lent you over half a million dollars. Don't look to me for any additional money. I will no longer be your banker."

Gatsby hadn't been prepared for this. He had always assumed that if he was about to go over a cliff, Miriam would support him. She would be his safety net. But she was effectively pulling it from under him. He was simply not able to muster a response. He sat silently sipping his wine, willing himself to become drunk enough on it that it softened the stinging of his pride and the blaring of his fear.

She continued, "The decision regarding McKnight's options is yours. But if it involves bankruptcy, I'm gone. I will not stay with you and endure the humiliation, scorn, and belt-tightening that will follow the bankruptcy filing. I'd rather strike out on my own. That's it."

Gatsby picked up the wine bottle and saw it was empty. He dialed room service and requested another bottle and more coffee.

He turned to her and said, "I don't want to lose you, Miriam. I love you. You're the one person on this planet that I totally trust."

"That's nice to hear, Gatsby, but you're facing enormous problems. You need to focus on what is best for you. Take me out of the equation. I don't want to be responsible for your making a decision that is not in your best interest. I'm not concerned about myself. I'll get by. But I'm concerned about you. You can't afford to screw this up. You have too much at stake, and too much risk."

Miriam went to the bathroom. Gatsby leaned back in his chair and closed his eyes. He needed time to work out an alternative plan. His assumption that Miriam would bail him out was obviously wishful thinking. It would take some mettle to deal with this situation.

When Miriam returned from the bathroom, Gatsby was already on the phone canceling the wine and the coffee. He hung up and turned to her, his Cheshire smile returning.

"Let's get dressed, check out, and go over to The Victor Cafe in South Philly for some Italian. Maybe will get lucky and some budding Pavarotti will come buy and serenade us."

CHAPTER 11

SHIRLEY

At six o'clock, the following Friday, Shirley entered her condo on the eighth floor of the Residences at Dockside on the Delaware River. She had completed another long week in Klamath Falls working on the Klamathgold liquidation. She dropped her briefcase on a chair and threw her coat on top of it. Then she went to the refrigerator, took out the bottle of vodka and poured three ounces into a glass. Then she stretched out on the sofa and turned-on Fox News.

Several minutes later, she heard an alert on her computer. She sat up, took the computer out of her briefcase, and checked her emails. She had just received a notification from Ono, Bill's widow, that the funeral would be held on Wednesday, March 28, the following week at the Cathedral Basilica of Saints Peter and Paul downtown. Attached was the program. It listed the pallbearers, the church officials who would conduct the funeral and the various individuals who would speak—Gatsby would deliver the eulogy.

Shirley let out a loud cry. "The sonofabitch! He should be going to jail." She took a large swallow of vodka and closed her computer. *Poor Ono. She has no idea that Gatsby killed her husband. What a travesty. But there is nothing I can do about it but go and keep my mouth shut.*

She checked her watch. Six-thirty. Perhaps she could still catch Brad in the office. She called his private line and he answered.

"Do you have time to talk for a few minutes?" she asked, already pacing her living room.

"Sure. I heard that your Uncle Bill died. I'm sorry. I know that you were close to him."

"He was a wonderful man, caring and loving, as well as being a brilliant executive. His death was unwarranted. Gatsby killed him." And then she described, in detail, the meeting that ended with Bill's heart attack.

After a long pause, Brad said, "I can see why you're angry."

She sat back down on the sofa. "Angry is too weak an adjective. Try furious. I received the notice and the program for the funeral mass. It's next Thursday. Guess who's delivering the eulogy."

"Not Gatsby?"

"The one and only. It will take every vestige of self-restraint to keep from standing up and yelling, 'Murderer, you killed him.'"

"I know you're not serious. But you need to be careful. You are the only person other than Gatsby who knows what went on in Bill's office prior to his heart attack. Combine that with what you've been able to deduce about his CPN business, and you pose a real danger to him. I'm worried about your safety, Shirley. You should seriously consider moving out of Philadelphia. Get out of Gatsby's territory so he is not constantly reminded as to how great a threat you pose. Maybe you should spend more time out in Oregon."

"Aren't you being overly dramatic?"

"I'm counseling caution. Neither of us knows what Gatsby is capable of if he decides you are a serious threat to his reputation and livelihood."

"Speaking of his livelihood, in the meeting with Bill, Gatsby admitted that there are several million dollars of CPNs outstanding."

Brad whistled. "Then I'd have to say that the probability of his running a Ponzi scheme is high. Which is more reason for you to get your butt out of Philly. Your presence is the equivalent of a red flag in front of a raging bull."

Shirley did not respond to Brad's last exhortation. She took a sip of vodka. Over a minute elapsed while she sorted through what he'd told her, and she heard him sorting papers and clicking his mouse at his desk. The noises tapered off, and finally Brad said, "Shirley, are you still there?"

"Yes. I'm processing what you just said. I can't get my arms around the problem."

"Well?"

"I'm not worried about my safety. I don't think Gatsby would do anything to physically harm me. But I do believe he would not hesitate to destroy my reputation if it were in his best interest to do so. What I'm trying to resolve is how to reconcile my civic and moral duty to expose Gatsby for what he's done and what he is, to prevent his doing further harm in the community, and my desire to pursue my career objectives in Philadelphia. I love this city and I love my work as a turnaround consultant."

"You know, Shirley, that those two objectives are incompatible," said Brad.

"I realize that I might be buying a lot of grief, and it might damage my career, but I refuse to accept that Gatsby's so powerful he could bury me—either figuratively or literally."

"All right," said Brad, with a reserve that suggested it was most certainly not all right.

"I want to thank you for working on my problems with such short notice. I appreciate your concern over my safety, but I need to do what I feel is right."

~~~~~

The following Saturday night she was unable to get to sleep. She tossed and turned and dreamed about Gatsby, CPNs, Bill's death, and EVG. Shirley drifted off in the early morning hours and awoke around 10 a.m. Fortunately, it was Sunday, and she could catch up on some domestic projects: gather up the clothes that need to go to the cleaners, wash and change the sheets on her bed, and clean the kitchen and bathrooms.

On Friday night she had bumped into Gatsby and Miriam at Colin Frye's concert.. She had put on her game face and acted as if nothing
~~~~~

had changed in their relationship. Gatsby had inquired about the Klamathgold liquidation, and she had brought him up to date. And Gatsby had told her that Driscoll was gone, and Moe was going to be CEO of EVG for the time being.

On Saturday night she was the guest of a local artist whose work was being exhibited at a benefit for the Philadelphia Art Museum. There were approximately fifty to seventy-five attendees at the event, so it was impossible to avoid chatting with Gatsby and Miriam again.

She had come away from each encounter with Gatsby and Miriam emotionally drained, furious, and humiliated. She assumed Gatsby knew she thought he'd been deceitful; but he also knew that there was nothing she could do about it without risking her own reputation. It was as if Gatsby were privy to the opinion and advice she'd received from Brad. She had no legal risk arising from her relationship with Gatsby, and she was certain she could get her EVG investment back from Gatsby and move on. She had almost been ready to accept Brad's recommendation and get on with her life, but the events of this weekend diminished her resolve. She realized she had to put her consulting hat on and review the situation objectively, as she would do for any client.

She glanced at her watch. Ten thirty. Not too early for a bloody mary. She filled a glass with three-quarters full of tomato juice, added Absolut with a heavy hand, splashed an equally generous dose of Tabasco into the mix, and dropped in four large olives. She carried her drink and a yellow pad and pen to the deck of her condo and sat down in one of the plush chairs, where she could watch the river traffic and think.

She realized that after her encounters with Gatsby this past weekend and several sleepless nights, she would not be able to have peace of mind until finding closure on the situation. Gatsby had been perpetrating this Ponzi scam for several years and no one had called him on it. And it was easy to see why. Most of his marks were high-net-worth individuals— like Moe—such that their investment in CPNs amounted to chump change; they'd been willing to let it ride, hoping that Gatsby could deliver. Others, like herself and her fellow working-stiff colleagues, valued the investment and might, after some time, get nervous and ask for their money back. No problem. Gatsby would simply sell a few more CPNs to a new set of naïve and impressionable investors—and *voila*! The money he needed to pay off the disgruntled investors who couldn't wait or who had lost faith suddenly would appear. He could keep the scam going until either he died, or someone blew the whistle on him. The sonofabitch could win an Olympic gold medal in the dancing on the head of a pin competition.

The view of the Delaware from her deck soothed her anxiety. The weather was warm and sunny, and the river was loaded with boats hauling brightly dressed partiers. She envied them. That's where she wanted to be this morning rather than wrestling with her moral dilemma. She remembered the statement she made in her conversation with Brad: "How to reconcile my civic and moral duty to expose Gatsby for what he's done and prevent his doing further harm to the community." She wrote the sentence at the top of her tablet. Then she started to list the various actions she could take and whether that action could adversely affect her career and her reputation in Philadelphia.

It took her a half hour to formulate her list. She reviewed it carefully and was satisfied it was complete. She continued to enjoy the weather, the view, and her bloody mary. At noon, she decided to put the list aside until she had completed her domestic duties. She got up from her chair and headed to her bedroom to strip the bed.

After she completed her chores, she took a nap and awoke around 5 p.m. She debated whether to take herself out to dinner, but she decided she needed to get back to her list. So, she put a frozen spaghetti dinner in the microwave and poured herself a large glass of pinot noir. When the spaghetti was ready, she poured it into a large bowl, retrieved her notepad and sat down at the kitchen table with her glass of wine.

She reviewed the schedule she had created that morning. It consisted of two columns. In the first, she had listed the names of every one of Gatsby's contacts whom she knew; in the second, she estimated the effect that telling each person what she knew about Gatsby's nefarious activities would have on her career.

As she reviewed the entries on the chart, she felt something was missing. The chart was incomplete. Then she hit her forehead with the heel of her hand when she realized she had failed to take into consideration the potential unintended consequences of speaking with Gatsby's clients and friends. And suddenly she felt nauseated and realized she was about to throw up the mushy microwave spaghetti she was eating. She headed to the bathroom and did indeed throw up, and as she was throwing up, she knew what had made her sick. When she took her CPN concerns to her uncle, Bill had confronted Gatsby, and the unintended consequence was that her uncle had had a heart attack and died.

She left the bathroom, picked up her notepad from the kitchen table and sat down in the living room. It was crystal clear that talking with Gatsby's clients, friends, and investors was way too risky. The list had been a waste of time. The only feasible strategy left was to take the Gatsby problem to those who could do something about it, the authorities like the US Attorney. And that was precisely what she would do.

CHAPTER 12

SHIRLEY

March 26, 2003

The following Wednesday at 1:30 p.m. Shirley entered the offices of the United States Department of Justice, Eastern District of Pennsylvania, carrying a large briefcase. She told the receptionist she had an appointment with Frank Foster, Assistant US Attorney.

She took a seat in the foyer, picked up a copy of the *Inquirer* and made herself comfortable. Frank had told her he would try to squeeze her in between 1:30 and 3 p.m.—but he couldn't give her a specific time.

"Ms. Frazier," said the receptionist. "I've advised Mr. Foster that you have arrived. Would you like some coffee?"

"I'd love some," said Shirley. "Black, and some water, please." She turned her attention back to the paper and continued reading.

Shirley read the paper until shortly after two o'clock when Frank Foster came into the lobby. He was a slim but imposing figure. A feathering of gray touched his dark hair at the temples, and he had the bearing of a career military officer.

"Shirley," he said, as he approached her. "It's good to see you. It's been way too long!"

Shirley put down the newspaper and rose from the chair to greet him. Before she could say anything, Foster engulfed her in his arms. "You look great! This is a wonderful surprise." He released her, noticed the briefcase, and smiled. "Heavy matter to discuss?"

Shirley laughed. "I probably over-packed. I tend to do that whether I'm going to Singapore for a week or Vermont for a weekend. I hope I haven't scared you."

"I want to express my sincere condolences over the death of your Uncle Bill. Unfortunately, I won't be able to attend his funeral on Friday. I need to be at a conference in New York. Please convey my condolences to Ono."

"Sure," said Shirley. "I expect it to be huge."

"I'm not surprised. To say he was a pillar of the community would be a gross understatement. Philly's lost an important asset."

The reception area was empty, and they stood far enough away from the receptionist's desk that Shirley felt an envelope of privacy around them. She lowered her voice. "You know, I was present when he had his heart attack."

"No, I hadn't heard that." Mingled with the obligatory notes of condolence, Frank's expression registered the change in her tone with a flicker of puzzlement.

"I'll tell you more about that when we talk about the issue I mentioned on the phone."

Foster picked up the briefcase and said, "This is the big leagues, Shirley; we're not easily intimidated." He turned to the receptionist. "Sally, please hold all my calls."

When they were settled at the conference table in Foster's office, he said, "Before we get to the business part of the meeting, fill me in what's been happening in your life. The last time I saw you, you were at your father's funeral. When was that?"

"About eight years ago. January 15, 1995."

"How's your mom?"

"Amazingly well. She's adapted to widowhood a lot better than I expected. She plays a lot of bridge and is an active member of the

Philadelphia Orchestra Association and a Kimmel Center member. She's busy. Her calendar is denser than mine."

"When we talked at your dad's funeral, I recall that you were disenchanted with McKinsey Consulting and were looking at other options."

"I left McKinsey in early '99 when I moved to Philly. I worked solo on several assignments. Several months after I arrived, I worked on a project that Gatsby was involved in and it appeared we were *simpatico*. He was the big-picture Mr. Outside who could generate quality assignments, and I was Ms. Inside who could make the trains run on time. A match made in heaven—or so it seemed. But that's why I'm here."

"When we talked on the phone yesterday, you sounded a bit distraught."

Shirley laughed. "Shortly before I called you, I had drunk a bloody mary with three ounces of vodka. I'm gratified to learn that I was sufficiently coherent that you could discern anything I said at all. I'm beyond distraught. I'm angry, depressed, and confused as to what to do. I'm hoping that by talking with you I can get some clarity and decide how to move forward."

"Okay, Shirley," said Foster, "so tell me about it."

"How much time do we have?"

Foster checked his watch. "It's 2:15. I have a briefing scheduled with my boss at 3 p.m., so we have forty-five minutes."

"That will do," said Shirley. "I'll tell you what I know about Gatsby's activities.

"Several months ago, Gatsby told me he had something 'special' for me. He offered a no-lose investment in EVG, a company he is sponsoring. He told me he anticipated EVG to be sold soon, and I would make a lot of money. I recall he said my investment would help carry the company to an IPO. Then he asked me if I could invest $25,000, and he offered me a copy of an EVG business plan. I thought about it for several days and decided to invest. I wrote a check made out to the company, as he had asked.

"In early February, I attended a meeting where an investment banker hired by Gatsby reviewed the EVG business plan and opined that the company was at least five years away from being able to put any products on the market. Gatsby had out-and-out lied to me."

Shirley then related the details of the events starting on March 13 when she received the call from General Walters, her follow-on meeting with Gatsby at the Continental Mid-town, and the meeting in Bill Dewyne's office which ended in a heart attack. She concluded with copies of the CPNs that Moe Shultz and General Walters had signed.

Foster reviewed the three CPNs and then placed them on the table. He looked at Shirley with an open expression and said, "I think I get the gist of your concerns, but it would help if you articulated them."

"Okay," said Shirley. "I think that Gatsby is engaged in a criminal enterprise. He sells investors on the proposition that he's going to let the investor participate in the potential growth of a company he's sponsoring, but without being exposed to the risk of loss in the event the company fails or is not successful. In the process of promoting the investment, He structures the deal as follows: He sells the investor a personal note, and the provides the investor with an option on stock that he owns in the subject company. In the process Gatsby makes two representations, both of which are false. One, the investor's money will be used to build the company, and he'll have an option on the company's stock; and two, if the company fails and the option is worthless, Gatsby can pay off the note along with the accumulated interest. I don't think Gatsby is anywhere as wealthy as he would have everyone believe. Nor does he have the resources to pay off all the notes he's sold. Cissy, his assistant, is a good friend of mine. She told me they are always operating with checkbook balances close to zero, and they are often months late in paying suppliers."

Shirley had talked for twenty straight minutes. She was tired, and her throat was dry.

"Could I get some water, Frank?"

Foster picked up the phone. "Sally, please bring us a pitcher of cold water and two glasses." He turned back to Shirley and said, "Is that it?"

Shirley was surprised. "Isn't that enough?"

"It depends on what your objective is, Shirley. You have some evidence of possible unethical behavior by one of our leading citizens—but even that is not at all solid. Have you asked Gatsby to arrange to get your money back from EVG?"

Sally came into the office with the water. Frank poured water into two glasses and handed one to Shirley. She took a long swallow, draining the glass. She wiped her lips with a tissue and turned to Frank.

"No. I haven't decided whether I want out of the investment."

"How does Moe feel about Gatsby—you know, generally? Does he have a significant investment in Gatsby's deals?

I estimate Moe's invested at least a million dollars, Moe has great respect for Gatsby and trusts him implicitly."

"So, is Moe, Philadelphia's prominent billionaire, a dupe, a patsy?"

"Moe is an astute and intelligent businessman, but when it comes to Gatsby, his judgment is clouded.

Foster checked his watch. "We have ten minutes left. Want my opinion?"

"Absolutely."

"On the basis of your own description of the events and situations involving Gatsby's CPNs, there is no evidence of criminal behavior. Gatsby may indeed be operating a Ponzi scheme, but you have no evidence of one.

"Gatsby may be implying that your invested money will be used to build the company in which you will hold an option on Gatsby's stock, but the agreement that the investors—like Moe and General Walters—signed doesn't say that. Gatsby can do anything he wants to with the money. And for your second point—that Gatsby will not be able to pay off all the CPNs he has issued—the evidence you provided proves the opposite: he can pay off the note when there is a demand.

"Based on what occurred in the meeting in Bill Dewyne's office, there is a possibility he is selling unregistered securities, which may be illegal, but that determination will be up to the regulators at the Pennsylvania Department of Banking and Securities."

"Is that the best government agency to address this issue?" said Shirley. "I was thinking about bringing this to the attention of the Pennsylvania Attorney General."

"He'd just kick it over to Kyle Rowan at the Department of Securities. If Rowan believes that Gatsby may be violating Pennsylvania securities law, he will be a pit bull. That's where you need to go."

He emptied his water glass and moved it aside, clearing the space between them completely. "Shirley, I value your friendship and have enormous respect for you. If you feel compelled to take this matter further, you should drop this on the desk of Kyle Rowan, chief compliance officer at the Department of Securities in Harrisburg. Cooperate with them if they decide to investigate further. But don't do anything else. Don't become an Inspector Javert, where your life's purpose becomes pursuing Gatsby. He is an influential and powerful individual, independent of what you may personally think, and you do not want him to see you as an adversary who is trying to put him out of business."

He glanced at his watch, stood up and said, "I've got to run."

Shirley quickly got up from her chair and hugged Foster. "Thanks. You've been a great help."

"I hope so," said Foster. "Do you want me to call Rowan and give him a heads-up that you'll be contacting him?"

"I'd appreciate that."

Frank picked up Shirley's briefcase. "Come, I'll walk you out."

Shirley was feeling upbeat as she exited Frank Foster's building. She had a plan to deal with the Gatsby issue, namely, drop it on the Pennsylvania Securities Department and let them deal with him. Frank told her that the Department was careful about preserving the anonymity of complainants, so she didn't have to worry about word getting back to Gatsby.

She checked her cell and saw she had a voicemail from the devil himself. She listened to the voicemail: Gatsby asking whether she could meet him for a drink at the Bellevue Lounge at 9:30 p.m. He added it had been several weeks since they last met, and it was important they clear the air.

~~~~~~

Shirley arrived at the Bellevue early, selected a quiet corner of the lounge and ordered a glass of the house white. Gatsby arrived at the appointed time. He was wearing a tuxedo. He explained he came directly from a Republican committee dinner. He ordered a vodka tonic and settled into a lounge chair opposite Shirley.

He inquired as to the progress of the Klamathgold liquidation, and she described the status and the various major tasks that were pending. It was mindless talk, and as she answered the question, she took the temperature of their rapport. Now she was in possession of a plan to have this man investigated without jeopardizing her career, she felt a sense of power. She was curious about what he had to say.

"You're doing a great job, Shirley," he said when she'd finished talking. He raised his glass. "Here's to a successful burial of Klamathgold."

She clinked his glass and said, "Amen."

"So, Shirley, what exactly do you hope to accomplish by harassing me over the CPN issue?"

"I've asked you via email and letter to tell me whether you've sold any CPNs involving Klamathgold options. As the CEO of Klamathgold, I need to know. You haven't answered me. I wouldn't call that harassment."

"Shirley, you have all the records of Klamathgold. You must know that since no stock options were ever issued to me, there can be no CPNs involving Klamathgold options."

"The records of Klamathgold are in disarray. I can't rely on them. Will you send me a letter that you've never issued a CPN involving Klamathgold options?"

"Of course. I'll email it to you tomorrow. I can understand why, in your CEO role, you might want to talk to the recent investors in Klamathgold about my CPN business. But what possible reason could there be for you to call Admiral Hartford?"

Shirley didn't answer. Gatsby smiled at her.
~~~~~~

"Let's cut to the chase, Shirley. Let's stop bullshitting each other. You are upset with me. You do not approve of my selling CPNs. You question whether they're legal. You perceive that I've sullied your reputation. I accept that. But every time you talk to someone about the CPNs or my business practices, or insinuate that I've done something illegal, you are raising questions in people's mind as to *my* ethics, competence, and reliability, all of which can damage my reputation and affect my ability to earn a living. You're operating on a double standard."

He leaned forward and looked directly into Shirley's eyes. "I will not allow you to destroy what took me thirty years to build. I've talked with an attorney about your activities, and I have ample resources to crush you. If you continue this crusade, you do so at your peril."

He stood and picked up his jacket. "Goodnight." He turned and walked out of the lounge.

Shirley remained at the table sipping her wine, which was still cold. It helped her get her bearings. The meeting with Gatsby provided validation for the strategy she selected, namely, give the problem to the authorities to resolve. If she got a letter from Gatsby's attorney, she would have her attorney respond she agreed to refrain from talking about Gatsby or his CPNs. Easy.

She finished her wine and left the Bellevue with a bounce in her step and a burden off her conscience.

CHAPTER 13

SHIRLEY

March 31, 2003

Four days after Bill's funeral, Shirley drove to Harrisburg to meet with executives in the Pennsylvania Department of Securities. She was ushered to a conference room where she met Kyle Rowan, chief of securities compliance, Nathan Mitchell, chief of enforcement, and Sid Campbell, securities investigator.

The austere conference room was devoid of windows, pictures, or accessories. Shirley was seated at the head of a steel four-by-eight-foot conference table. The table was bare except for a pitcher of water and four glasses. The room had all the ambiance of an interrogation box at the police station. Rowan sat to her left side and Mitchell and Campbell sat to her right.

"I want to express my appreciation, Kyle, for your organizing this meeting on such short notice. I was pleasantly surprised."

"Frank Foster called me after his meeting with you and said you would be contacting us and that the information that you wanted to provide was important. So, we rearranged our schedule to expedite matters." He filled their water glasses.

Shirley launched into the same presentation she had made to Frank Foster including her reasons she thought that Gatsby was involved in a criminal enterprise. She paused and said, "In the interests of providing you full disclosure, Foster doesn't think there is any evidence that could lead to a criminal complaint."

"Thank you, Shirley," said Kyle. "I appreciate your taking the time to share that information with us. I don't think Frank overstated the significance of the information. Do you have copies of the convertible promissory notes that you showed to him?"

"Of course," said Shirley. She opened her briefcase and removed several documents and distributed them to Kyle, Nathan and Sid. "There are three notes. It is my understanding that Moe Shultz has purchased at least one million dollars' worth of CPNs."

The three executives read each of the notes carefully. When all three of them had placed their copies on the table, Kyle said, "Do you happen to have a copy of Mr. Brooks' financial statement?"

"No," she said, "but I know one exists."

"How so?" said Kyle.

"General Walters told me that Gatsby showed him his financial statement during their meeting several weeks ago, but Gatsby would not let him keep it. The general said his financial statement was 'impressive.'"

"Do you think you can get a copy?" asked Kyle.

"I doubt it," said Shirley. "Gatsby is secretive."

"Do you have any idea as to how many CPN investors there are or how many dollars' worth of CPNs Mr. Brooks has outstanding?"

"I don't know how many investors there are; but in the meeting with my uncle, Bill Dewyne, he said he sold 'a few million.' He refused to be more specific."

"Who else have you talked with regarding the CPN issue?" asked Nathan.

"I talked with EVG's president, EVG's auditor, my attorney, Frank Foster, and retired Rear Admiral Hartford, a friend whom I introduced to Gatsby."

"Why did you talk with the admiral?"

"He's a friend of Gatsby's and he is considering investing in Gatsby's projects."

"Could you generate a list of all the companies and other enterprises that Mr. Brooks may have been involved with over the past several years?"

"Yes," said Shirley, "I'd be happy to do that if it would help."

"It will definitely help," said Nathan.

"Shirley, have you told anyone else that you are talking with us?"

"The only person who knows is Frank."

"Good," said Kyle. "We need to keep it that way. It is essential for any investigation that may arise from this meeting to remain confidential. Also, we will be happy to review any information that you can provide on this matter, but we are barred from advising you on the status of any investigation—or if there is an investigation."

Shirley's felt her face becoming flushed. There was a knot in her throat. Struggling to stay calm, she said, "I thought I just provided sufficient information to warrant an investigation of Gatsby and his CPN scheme."

"You very well may have," said Kyle, "however, we must do a lot more work to ensure that an investigation is warranted and there is a reasonable probability that an enforcement order will result. You've given us a lot to chew on." He stood, and the two other executives of the Department followed suit. Shirley closed her briefcase and lifted herself out of the chair. She suddenly felt tired. Each of the executives shook hands with her, expressed their appreciation, and Kyle led her out to the department's foyer and said goodbye.

Shirley sat in her car for twenty minutes before she began her drive back to Philadelphia. She felt somewhat deflated because Kyle would not say they would start an investigation. But then she was reminded of the fact he had stated at the beginning of their meeting that they do not tell anyone whether they are investigating at all. It was how they preserved their confidentiality.

A bright spot in the meeting was Kyle's request she prepare a list of all the companies and enterprises Gatsby had been involved with over the past several years. That certainly indicated interest.

After she had ruminated sufficiently, she concluded that the meeting went as well as she could expect. It was likely to be a long slog before Gatsby got his comeuppance—an outcome she didn't think of in strictly putative terms. Rather, imagining the congruity of wrongdoing and punishment satisfied the same urge she felt when sifting through years of a company's mismanaged records. Something was wrong, and she would fix it. She'd built her career on finding order in a mess.

CHAPTER 14

HELEN

Saturday, April 26, 2003

Birney, Jerry, Helen, and Jeff were seated in the family room of Birney's apartment drinking wine and snacking on hors d'oeuvres. The room was decorated with mid-nineteenth-century paintings and antiques in the style of an exclusive London club. The aroma of Jewish cooking seeped into the dining room.

The phone rang. Birney's wife, Sarah, who was in the kitchen preparing the dinner with her live-in maid, answered the phone. She emerged from the kitchen and announced, "That was Ze'vie. He's locked in a traffic jam and estimates he'll be here in fifteen minutes."

"Thanks, hon," said Birney. "Why don't you let Carmella complete preparations so you can join the party?"

"In a few minutes," said Sarah, and then disappeared into the kitchen.

"So," said Helen, turning to Birney, "how did Ze'vie get to be a national hero? What's the story?"

Birney smiled. "What makes you think he's a national hero?"

"Come on, Birney. You knew that I'd research him when you invited us to dinner. I know what's been published—which is not much. Tell us what isn't published—you know, the backstory."

"I can only give you the G-rated stuff. If you want the R- and X-rated parts, you'll have to get that directly from him. Mossad members operate under strict confidentiality rules, and frankly, I have no idea what he will be able to tell you."

"This is a rare opportunity for us," said Jerry. "Anything you can tell us will be a delight."

"Absolutely," said Jeff. "Come on, spit it out!"

"Okay, okay," said Birney. He took a sip of wine. "Ze'vie was the baby of my grandfather's family. My grandfather was a Professor of Economics at the University of Berlin in the 1920s and 1930s. He decided to leave Europe in 1930, when the Nazi Party became the second largest in the German government. He arranged to send my father, his eldest son, to live with a colleague in the US, and he, his wife, and the other children emigrated to Tunisia, where his fluency in Arabic and French got him a position at a university.

"He and his family emigrated to Israel in 1948, after the War of Independence. Ze'vie was six when they arrived in Israel, and when he graduated from high school in 1960, he joined the Israeli Defense Forces for his three years of obligatory military service.

"Ze'vie came to the attention of the intelligence services during his IDF service—for three major reasons. He was fluent in French, Arabic, German, English and of course Hebrew; second, he had volunteered for an elite commando unit and impressed his commanders with his creativity and daring; and finally, he was strong as an ox. He lifted weights and could bench press 300 pounds.

"When he was discharged from the IDF, he joined Mossad—or you can say, he *married* Mossad. Unlike many other agents, he decided not to begin a family because he did not ever want to be in a position where he would hesitate to take a risk because of the fear of creating a widow and orphans. He intended to dedicate his life to the State of Israel. And that is what he's done. He is a true patriot."

"One of the articles that I read," said Helen, "implied he was the leader of the team that tracked down and assassinated the PLO terrorists that murdered the Israeli athletes at the Munich Olympics."

"Mossad would never confirm that," said Birney, "and I doubt that Ze'vie would admit it, either. But you could ask him. It is common knowledge he served in the Kidon Unit which carries out operations involving kidnapping, sabotage, and assassination."

The doorbell rang. Sarah came out of the kitchen and opened the door of the apartment. Helen saw her throw her arms around a six-foot, barrel-chested hulk with arms as thick as piano legs. They spoke in French.

"Ze'vie, *ma cherie, je suis tres heureux de te voir. C'est trop horrible, le massacre!*"

Helen heard Ze'vie start to cry. "*Beaucoup d'amis sont morts. Je suis désolé. Je ne peux pas contrôler mes émotions.*"

Helen turned to Birney and asked, "What massacre are they talking about?"

"There was a suicide bombing about two weeks ago at a popular fast-food restaurant in Tel Aviv. Eleven people were killed and more than seventy were injured. Ze'vie has lived in Netanya most of his adult life, which is thirty miles north of Tel Aviv and several of the victims were his friends. He has spent the last week and a half attending funerals and memorial services and visiting victims in hospitals."

"Oh, my God," said Helen. "How horrible."

"I read about the attack in the *Journal*," said Jerry. "The article said it was the worst suicide bombing in a year."

"What's amazing," said Jeff, "is that despite all the terrorist attacks and the hundreds of victims they generate every month, the Israelis manage to maintain a democratic civilized society. In many ways it's more dangerous to live in Israel than it was to serve in South Vietnam."

The diminutive Sarah led Ze'vie into the family room. Everyone stood. Sarah said, "Let me present Birney's uncle, and my dearest friend, the pride of Israel, Colonel Ze'vie Goldblatt of Mossad."

"Oh, shush, Sarah. This is not a political rally. A simple Ze'vie Goldblatt would suffice. You know how much I hate pomposity."

"In my home, Ze'vie, heroes are properly introduced. Besides, you're the only hero I know."

Ze'vie smiled at the group. "Don't pay any attention to Sarah; she always acted somewhat like a star-struck teenager." Ignoring Ze'vie's last remark, Sarah introduced Ze'vie to Helen, Jerry and Jeff. She glanced at her watch and announced, "It's getting late. I suggest we go into dinner."

The dining table was rectangular, and Sarah had arranged the seating so that Birney would be at the head of the table, Sarah at the foot. Helen sat to Birney's right and Ze'vie would sit between Helen and Sarah. Jerry and Jeff sat opposite Helen and Ze'vie.

Carmella brought in the gefilte fish, and Birney walked around the table filling everyone's wineglass.

Birney announced he wanted to make a toast. "Please lift your glasses. I want to toast Uncle Ze'vie and all the brave men of Mossad for the work they do to preserve the independence of the great state of Israel. *L'chaim!*"

When they began to eat the fish, Jeff said, "Ze'vie, I had the opportunity to meet and work with Nahum Adomoni during the 1982–1983 timeframe."

"The Chief? Under what circumstances?"

"I was working in the Defense Intelligence Agency."

"You were in the military?"

"From 1969 to 1989."

"Did you serve in Vietnam?"

"Unfortunately, yes."

"What a nightmare that was," said Ze'vie. "An unforced error that turned into a tar baby."

"No kidding," said Jeff.

"When I was in the IDF, I had my fill of the infantry—living in filth, eating K rations, pooping in the bush, and always wondering whether the next crack you hear will result in a bullet coming your way."

"That sums up my time in Vietnam, but I also had to worry about the bullets that would come behind me," said Jeff.

"How so?" said Ze'vie.

"Fragging, i.e., disgruntled and stoned troops killing their superior officers, especially lieutenants and captains. It was all too common in Vietnam."

Ze'vie shook his head. "I jumped at the chance to join Mossad when they offered me a position. When we were on assignment, we stayed in the best hotels, ate at terrific restaurants, and often flew first class."

"But" said Jerry, "you do most of your work in hostile environments, where virtually every person you meet might blow your cover and put your life at risk."

"Very true," said Ze'vie, smiling. "But every profession has its risks. I'd choose a covert operation in Lebanon or Syria over being a battalion commander in Vietnam."

"I would have, too," said Jeff, "but I didn't have the choice."

Carmella circled the table collecting the fish plates and Sarah followed her, placing a bowl of gazpacho in front of each guest.

"What brings you to the US?" said Jerry.

"Mossad and Shin Bet, Israel's homeland security service, have a contract with your Central Intelligence Agency. That is all that I'm authorized to say. Sorry."

"No need to apologize," said Jerry. "We understand." He took a sip of wine. "I have another question, that I believe you will definitely be able to answer."

"Shoot," said Ze'vie.

"What's your opinion about Spielberg's film, *Munich*, and to what extent did he capture the events and the personalities of Mossad assassins?"

"My God," said Ze'vie. "How could you know to ask me about *Munich*?"

"Why?" said Jerry.

"Because" said Ze'vie, "that film exhibits a totally false narrative that many American Jews promulgate to unfairly judge Israel's God-given right to defend itself and its population. It's total garbage. Spielberg should be ashamed of himself for making it. If *Schindler's List* is one of the high points in his career, *Munich* is definitely the low point."

He looked over to Sarah. "Perhaps you want to serve the main course before I launch my rant."

"An excellent idea," said Sarah. "Birney, please make sure everyone's wine glass is full."

After everyone had the brisket entree in front of them, Sarah signaled Ze'vie.

"First," said Ze'vie, "Mossad is not in the revenge business. The Israeli government would never risk Mossad's human assets in a tit-for-tat strategy. Israel wanted their enemies neutralized. Since Europe would not jail them, Israel was determined to eliminate them any way they could. Which they did. A dead terrorist cannot carry out another terror attack. We disrupted the PLO's operational structure, and after approximately ten assassinations, we achieved a certain level of deterrence. Israel was perceived as a country that would exact a high price from those that would trifle with it."

Jeff laughed and said, "I get your gist, Ze'vie."

"You know, Uncle," said Birney, "it is rare we find a topic that you can let loose on without worrying about security clearances and censors. I, for one, find this refreshing."

"I could go on about the damn film for another hour—but, as Jeff said, I'm sure you all get my gist."

Helen had glanced over at Jerry while Ze'vie was talking about the film and she thought that, although he appeared to be listening carefully to Ze'vie, he appeared depressed.

Ze'vie's passionate comments about the Spielberg film had the effect humanizing him to Jerry, Jeff, and Helen. The atmosphere at the dinner table became more casual and devolved into three groups: Birney and Jerry, Sarah and Jeff, and Helen and Ze'vie. Sarah excused herself and went into the kitchen to prepare the dessert. When Carmella came out to pick up the dinner plates the conversation hit a lull.

As Carmella entered the kitchen, Jerry said, "You know, Ze'vie, the violence in Israel that developed since the collapse of the Camp David talks in late 2000 has been covered extensively in the media; but living in the US, and not being Jewish, it all seems so remote—almost like a war videogame. Helen and I would love to visit Israel, but I'm concerned about the violence. What it is like for an Israeli living under the unrelenting threat of a terror attack or a suicide bomb?"

Sarah came into the dining room followed by Carmella carrying a tray of blueberry tarts which she proceeded to pass to the guests. Other than for the clinking of the spoons against the dishes, the room was silent.

Ze'vie looked around the table and began to speak. "You know, what it is like living under the unrelenting threat of terror depends upon who you are, what you do, and the structure of your family. For example, as a single man in the military, it is a situation you learn to cope with. In many ways, my day-to-day life in an Israel under siege becomes another mission to be carried out—namely to stay alive and train in the event I am deployed. On the other hand, if you have a family, a wife, and kids of various ages, it is tantamount to living in a nightmare. You are on the front lines of a battlefield. Guards are in front of every restaurant, store, or any building that is open to strangers. You are constantly being searched. There is no place that is truly safe. You are surrounded by people who want nothing more than to kill you and your loved ones, and you recognize and accept that there is little you can do to guarantee that when you send your children off to school, they will return.

"The newspapers and TV report continuously on attacks and victims who are killed and those who are injured. Since Israel is a small country, it is likely that you will recognize the names of victims. Since the failure of the Camp David talks and the start of the intifada, there have been 75 terrorist attacks that have resulted in 350 dead and 2,000 maimed and wounded. The current atmosphere is ugly, and the conflict with the Palestinians shows no real signs of subsiding. For the civilian population, the only options are to endure it or leave the country. Many people have emigrated during this period. But for those citizens who believe it is their duty to preserve and protect the State of Israel for the benefit of the current population, and the Jews of future generations, leaving is not an option. And they remain, all the while maintaining the pretense they are living a normal life."

The room remained silent. Helen's eyes glistened. She took a Kleenex from her purse and dabbed her eyes. "How dreadful," she said, turning to Ze'vie. "But the situation as experienced by Palestinians living in Israel or in the occupied territories, is no picnic either."

"Now Helen," said Birney, "how can you compare—"

"Birney," interrupted Ze'vie, "I want to hear what Helen has to say. Please continue, Helen."

"When I was working at an art gallery in Paris in the 1980s, I represented a Palestinian artist who grew up in the West Bank, and we chatted extensively about his life. He said children as young as eleven are routinely rousted out of bed and incarcerated until they confess to whatever crimes they've been accused of. He told me that his family emigrated to France because Jewish settlers occupied his house when they were on vacation and the Israeli courts would not force the settlers to leave. So, they lost their house. And the system of passes that the IDF has devised to control the movement of Palestinians virtually precludes any Palestinian family from leading a normal life. I could go on, Ze'vie, but as Jeff said, I'm sure you get my gist. I hope I haven't offended you."

The room was silent, and all eyes turned to Ze'vie.

"Helen," said Ze'vie, "why would I be offended by the truth? I have several Palestinian friends who frequently bombard me with similar stories. Unfortunately, Israel has been in control of the Palestinian territory for almost forty-five years and has created laws, agencies, military procedures, and systems to protect the Israeli population. The IDF troops and the civilians who are on the front lines do the best they can. It's just an ugly situation."

"When will this end?" said Helen. "When will the Israeli and Palestinian populations be able to live in peace?"

Ze'vie smiled. "Study the histories of the Cold War that resolved the conflict between the Soviet Union and the West, and the Good Friday agreement that ended the decades-long conflict between Northern Ireland and the Irish Republic. These conflicts ended when the combatants had competent leaders who both saw the advantage of a resolution and could avoid being assassinated long enough to make and implement a deal. We can only hope and pray that the Israeli–Palestinian conflict will be similarly blessed."

~~~~~

During the drive back to their apartment, Helen could sense that there was something amiss. Jerry had not uttered a word. "Penny for your thoughts, hon?"

"I can't get my arms around them. What is your impression of Ze'vie? You spent quite a bit of time huddled with him."

Helen felt her ire building. "Christ, Jerry, that's not true. When there was a lull in the general conversation, we chatted briefly in French. He's a fascinating and charming man and I was just being cordial. You have no reason to be jealous."

"I'm sorry," said Jerry. "That remark was uncalled for. I can understand why you found him so charming. He is a national hero, and he has had a starring role in building a country. I'm just reeling from the epiphany that I experienced during the dinner."

"What epiphany?"

"The realization that I've wasted my life. It came upon me like a ton of bricks. I couldn't help comparing what Ze'vie has done with his life with what I've done with mine. And I came up wanting—big time."

"I don't understand you, Jerry. You've had a good life. You've been successful; you have a good marriage and two wonderful sons. And our retirement is assured. In my book, that is a successful life."

"I won't argue the fact we've lived the American Dream. But five years after I die, the only people who will remember what little I've accomplished are Jeff, you, and the boys. Fifty to a hundred years after Ze'vie dies, Israeli children and members of the military will be studying how and what Ze'vie did and the impact he had on the State of Israel. That, my dear, is a life that would be worth living!"

Helen shrugged, trying to modulate his self-recrimination. "But he also committed himself to a life full of risks and eschewed having a family and having to cope with situations rife with moral gray areas and questions. That's not you, Jerry. That's not the man I married."
~~~~~

Jerry fell silent.

"Perhaps," said Helen, "you're just bored with your job and your career."

Jerry shook his head. "It's not that. The fact is that until the dinner we just enjoyed, I've never questioned whether my life had meaning beyond having a successful career and a happy home life." He took his eyes off the road for a minute and looked at Helen and smiled. "I know I'm a lucky guy to have my career and you and the two boys. I'll get over it."

Chapter 15

GATSBY

May 5, 2003

"Good morning, Mr. Brooks," said Cissy. "Did you have a good weekend?"

"Not bad. Actually, I spent most of my time in front of the television set watching the news from Iraq."

"I have a nephew over there. Our entire family is praying he comes out of it unscathed."

He turned to Cissy and said, "I'm sorry to hear that. This war is not worth dying for. I'll also pray for your nephew."

As he turned to walk into his office Cissy said, "Oh, here's your mail."

Gatsby carried the mail to his desk and thumbed through it. He came across a letter from the State of Pennsylvania, Department of Banking and Securities. He dropped all the other letters on his desk and ripped open the envelope and read the one-page document. It stated the Department had received a complaint relating to securities he sold, and they were initiating an investigation. They requested all documents relating to the sales of notes, options, and warrants over the past ten years and wanted to schedule a meeting within the next month.

He yelled: "That fucking cunt! She did it! She really did it. She threw me under the fucking bus!"

Cissy opened the office door. "What's wrong?"

"Close the door and leave me alone," he shouted.

She quickly retreated.

Gatsby sat down in his chair, leaned back, and closed his eyes and began to breathe deeply. He needed to think. He knew he was in an absolute heap of trouble and he needed help—and a lot of it—and immediately.

He jumped from his chair, stuffed the letter in his pocket and pushed open the door to his office. As he walked past Cissy's desk he said, "I'm going for a walk, I'm not sure when I'll be back."

He exited the building and turned to the left and walked briskly the five and a half blocks to George McKnight's building. He entered the office complex and approached the reception desk.

"Hello, Mr. Brooks," said Barbara. "What can I do for you?"

"I need about a half hour with George—just as soon as you can arrange it. It is an urgent matter."

"Please sit down and I'll see what I can do."

Gatsby sauntered over to a chair and picked up the *Wall Street Journal*, struggling to conceal the anxiety that was coursing through his body.

The receptionist came over to his chair, speaking to him in a low voice a nurse might use with a sick patient. "He can see you," she said. He nodded and told himself to stop wearing his panic on his sleeve. With a fortifying breath, he entered George's office.

Gatsby dug the letter from the Department of Securities out of the breast pocket of his jacket and tossed it onto George's desk and sat back in his chair. After reading the letter George looked up at Gatsby.

"Are you surprised?"

"Somewhat. I didn't think that Shirley would follow through with her threat."

"Well then, you better get busy." He handed Gatsby back his letter. "You know that I can't help you with this."

"I understand," said Gatsby, "but you can recommend an attorney who can."

"Sure," said George. "Why don't you retain Duane Morris? They'd be ideal."

"Several partners own about $100,000 of CPNs," said Gatsby. "They're conflicted. And so are Dickie McCamey and Chilcote, Erp Cohn, Braverman Kaskey, and Schnader Harrison, all of which are probably also on your shortlist."

George leaned back in his chair. "That's unfortunate. You just named the cream of the Philadelphia Securities Bar."

"I know that" said Gatsby. "That's why I'm here. I need your brilliant counsel to help me dig out of this mess that the cunt's put me in."

George McKnight sat way back in his chair and stared at the ceiling. Several minutes passed. Suddenly he sat up and said, "I think I have just the guy you need. You probably know him from the Philly GOP. He's worked on Rick Santorum's reelection campaign. Colin Frye."

"Yeah," said Gatsby. "I've met him and seen him at some meetings. I didn't know he was a securities attorney. Isn't he a jazz pianist? I recall attending one of his concerts with Miriam.

George laughed. "Yeah. That's his passion. He sheepishly admitted to me that he practices an average of fifteen hours a week. I personally think he works at law to support his music addiction. But he's damn smart. Prior to his stint with Costello in DC, he was an assistant US Attorney in Manhattan and worked for Mary Jo White. The guy must work twelve to fourteen hours a day. I don't know how the hell he finds the time for his music obsession. The key fact here is he's just made partner at Grant & Taylor, and he will work his ass off for you. You'll be his highest-profile client and he will not want to disappoint."

Gatsby thought for a few minutes. "Other than the music stuff, are there any other issues I should be aware of?"

"Not that I know of. He's got a great wife and a couple of kids. He's got to keep the heat to the seat. He'll do well by you. I'm confident. And don't let his music obsession turn you off. We all have our crazy passions."

Gatsby laughed. "What are yours, George?"

Ignoring Gatsby's question, George scrawled Frye's telephone number off the back of his card and slid it over to Gatsby. "Call him. I think you'll be impressed. And you *know* my obsession. I marry strong women and let them dominate me. Three to date."

Gatsby took the card and stood up. "Thanks. This is a big help."

He rose and took Gatsby's hand, held it tight and stared into Gatsby's eyes. "Go talk to Frye, get his opinion, talk to your wife, and seriously consider the Mea Culpa Option *before* you respond to the DoBS. I can help you get out of this mess if you choose to let me. In either event, good luck to you, Gatsby." He released his grip on Gatsby's hand and turned away.

~~~~~

Later that evening while they were savoring their glasses of Courvoisier, Gatsby told Miriam about his meeting with George McKnight, and that if Gatsby was going to pursue the Stealth Option, George recommended Colin Frye. He did not mention receiving the letter from the Pennsylvania DoBS.

"Do you know Frye?"

"Yes," said Miriam. "He's on the board of Big Brothers Big Sisters. I see him once or twice a month."

"And he's a jazz pianist?"

"He's a complex personality," said Miriam. "Tightly wound and taciturn. He is undoubtedly driven to become a Philly poohbah—like you. Other than the fact you're extroverted, and he's introverted, you have a lot in common."

"McKnight recommended him to help me structure a venture capital company and fight off the Pennsylvania Department of Banking and Securities. What do you think?"

"I haven't heard much about his legal skills. He went to Stanford and worked for the justice department prior to emigrating to Philly. But what I do know is he is smart and intense. You just need to accept the fact he is quirky."
~~~~~

~~~~~~

The next morning Gatsby met Colin Frye in his office at One Liberty Plaza. He was a short middleweight who, with his excellent posture, projected an image of being a few inches taller than he was. He exuded confidence, intensity, and competence. He greeted Gatsby with a wide smile and a two-handed handshake. They walked into Frye's office and sat at his round conference table. Frye had a pot of coffee, a pitcher of water, cups and glasses laid out on the table.

"Coffee?" he asked.

Gatsby nodded, and Frye poured two cups and handed one to Gatsby.

Gatsby had asked George McKnight to call Frye and brief him so that Frye would know he was being handed a client who could be a healthy meal ticket for years to come. Normally, in this type of situation, Gatsby would spend a considerable amount of time chatting with the prospective attorney, exploring connections and mutual friends and acquaintances, school ties, sports interests, and so on. However, Gatsby realized he was in no position to be choosy. McKnight had done the groundwork. Frye was the only viable candidate, so he might just as well dispense with the small talk and get down to business.

Gatsby handed Frye his financial statement—the real one—and a spreadsheet showing the CPN schedule and the number of shares of the various companies to which the notes could convert.

"George explained my problem?"

"Thoroughly."

"And you understand that both my wife and I have rejected George's mea culpa strategy?"

"I do."

There was a brief silence. Gatsby shifted in his chair. "So?"

Frye's entire response to the conversation so far seemed to be buried behind his quick, dark eyes, leaving his face maddeningly blank. It was unusual for someone to make such a little effort to establish a rapport with Gatsby, and Gatsby found himself annoyed.
~~~~~~

Finally, Frye asked, "How long have you been selling these convertible promissory notes? I mean, when did you start?"

"About ten years ago," replied Gatsby.

"And, during this period, how many companies have you sponsored, received options from, and assigned these options in a CPN transaction?"

Gatsby thought about the question for several minutes. "My best guess without reviewing all my records is seventeen."

"How many are currently operating?" said Frye.

"Nine."

"What happened to the other eight?"

He's asking all the right questions, thought Gatsby. "Three were huge successes returning between three times and thirteen times their initial invested capital; one was sold for the approximate amount of the capital invested. The remaining four failed and the options became worthless. I paid off most of the notes. Some are still outstanding."

"Even though the options are worthless?"

"Yes," said Gatsby. "The investors obviously like the interest rate."

"So," said Frye, "to summarize, during the past ten years you've sponsored and raised money for about seventeen companies, received stock options from these companies, and have sold convertible promissory notes. You have offered some of your options to investors as an inducement to lend you unsecured funds at eight percent interest. Of these seventeen, nine companies are currently operating, four have been sold or gone public, events which extinguished the notes, and four have failed, and you have satisfied investors who have demanded repayment?"

"Yes," said Gatsby.

"And some of the money that paid off the notes where the companies failed came from the sale of convertible promissory notes to new investors using options you received from new startup companies that you've sponsored."

"Yes," said Gatsby. "That is correct."

Frye leaned back in his chair. "Amazing! And you've never run out of startup companies that want to hire you to raise money, nor investors who are willing and able to lend you money?"

"Not so far."

"And" said Frye, "all the investors have met the definition of a 'sophisticated investor?'"

"Most of them, but not all," said Gatsby.

"Have any of the prospective investors asked you for a financial statement?"

"Rarely."

"And what did you show them?"

"I presented them a pro-forma balance sheet, which showed all the assets and liabilities."

"What do you mean by *pro-forma*?"

"It wasn't prepared by a CPA."

"And where are these investors located?"

"Mostly in Philly and the suburbs, probably ten to fifteen percent in the rest of Pennsylvania, New York, Delaware and other states."

Frye stood up and picked up the two coffee cups. "I'm going to get some fresh coffee."

As Frye exited the conference room, Gatsby stood and inspected the large wall photographs of early-twentieth-century Philadelphia. He paced. He was unaccustomed to being grilled, but then again, he didn't have any options.

Frye returned with the coffees and sat down at the conference table. "I may have a plan that might get you out of the Rubik's cube in which you're currently trapped." Frye leaned back in his chair, twirling a pen between his fingers. "But—"

"But what?" said Gatsby. "What the hell is the *but*?" he said, showing some slight irritation. "I'm here to hire you and get your help. I'm not here to listen to conditions or beg."

"*But*," Frye said, still playing the part of the aloof interlocutor, "you, along with your CPA, are going to have to persuade me and my partners that you have a firm handle on the extent of the shortfall between the debts you are carrying and the 'realistic' value of the options you're holding. This information, along with the assets and options that you own, will provide the foundation of a business plan for a new enterprise which we'll name the Gatsby Venture Fund—the GVF. It will replace your current business of selling convertible promissory notes which will probably be shut down by the state's DoBS. That shortfall needs to be reduced to an estimate we can both agree on. This is the Stealth Option you've chosen to pursue."

Gatsby leaned forward and spoke softly. "I don't have a clue as to what the options are worth! No one has a clue! One of these companies could turn out to be another Microsoft—which would solve all my problems. Or they could all wind up in the toilet."

"I know," said Frye. "But you believe they have value, don't you? Otherwise, you would not have taken money from your investors and offered them an option as an incentive for their providing a loan. Correct? And you can cite at least four examples where they did prove to be valuable." He stared intently at Gatsby, who was trying to decide whether this was actually a question, or if Frye was already practicing the backbone of his argument to anyone who might say otherwise.

Gatsby sat back in his chair, paused. "Of course, I did—and I still do."

"Good," said Frye. "Get your CPA and write up your assumptions and analysis and when you're done send it over. Incidentally, who is your CPA?"

"Everett Hawking."

"Excellent accountant," said Frye. "My partners and I will review the material and advise you whether we'll represent you." He stood, indicating that the meeting was over.

Gatsby was shocked. It was a total diss. But he held his tongue. Miriam had said he was quirky, and if Gatsby came home having told Frye not to waste his time, he'd have to start the whole process all over again with someone else. He stood, forced a smile, and extended his hand to Frye.

"I understand," he said. "I'll contact you in a few days." He quickly exited Frye's office before he lost his temper.

Gatsby walked back to his building, willing himself to calm down. As he entered the foyer of his office, he asked Cissy to get Everett Hawking on the phone. He plopped into his chair leaned back, put his feet on his desk and closed his eyes. Five minutes later Cissy buzzed him on the intercom to tell him that Everett was on the line.

"Everett?"

"Yes."

"Can you rip yourself away from KPMG for several hours to help me with a project? I am under the gun."

"Does it have to be today?"

"It would be better if it were today. Can you do it?"

"I'll clear my calendar and come over around noon. Ask Cissy to order lunch. Would you care to give me some inkling as to what this is all about, so I can start thinking about it?"

"I'd prefer to do that when you get here. Thanks, Everett."

Gatsby buzzed Cissy. "Hold all my calls for the rest of the day and go get some sandwiches from the Continental. I think we're okay on the drinks."

Everett arrived shortly after noon. He kept himself in good shape, and he was so fair that his eyelashes were nearly white, and his face flushed easily when he laughed. He oozed self-confidence and had a no-bullshit demeanor that Gatsby especially appreciated. They chatted for a few minutes, primarily about Iraq and the friends who had kids in the service.

Everett changed the subject and said, "What is so important that caused me to piss off half of the office to make time for you?"

"Okay," said Gatsby, "so here you go." And he described in detail his two meetings with George McKnight, his meeting with Colin Frye, and the project that Frye would require to implement his plan for digging Gatsby out of his financial morass.

When Gatsby completed his briefing, Everett sat in almost total stillness for several minutes, his head down and his large bony fingers forming a steeple. "George McKnight is smart, competent, and has excellent judgment. He makes a strong case for the mea culpa route. It would get a lot of problems off your back. You've been operating on the edge of a precipice for a long, long time."

"I know," said Gatsby, "but Miriam will not hear of it. She doesn't feel she could withstand the social stigma of a bankruptcy. And I'm not about to put my marriage on the block, too."

"I'm not surprised she feels that way," said Everett, "but to strip this problem down to the basics, it may be the only way that you can ensure that you're not indicted, fined and sent to prison for several years. I could talk with her—to make sure she understands the risks you're assuming if you don't take George's advice."

Gatsby shook his head. "She won't listen. She's adamant. And she'd see it as your interfering in a part of this matter that is solely between spouses. So, we're committed to McKnight's stealth strategy—assuming the numbers pencil. I need your help to present my current situation to Frye, so he has the tools to pitch me to his partners."

"And give him and his partners some cover."

"What do you mean by that?"

"His partners," said Everett, "will need a document that presents a credible argument that you are a successful entrepreneur who has formulated a feasible, although perhaps risky, business plan, and that the Gatsby Venture Fund is not merely a scheme to cover up a Ponzi scam that is about to crater. I expect that all of his partners will scrutinize the plan carefully."

"He said as much," said Gatsby. "You know my situation as well as anyone, Everett. Can we make the argument?"

The morning sun had suddenly engulfed the office, and Everett was squinting into the sun. His eyebrows and eyelashes were arcs of light around his pale eyes, rendering his expression entirely impossible to read. Gatsby got up and went over to the window and closed the blinds. As he returned to his chair, Everett said, "We are not going to make the argument. You are. But I'll help you put the pieces together, so it reflects what you believe. And then I'll participate in the meeting with

Frye so that there is no miscommunication. If you opt for stealth, you need to believe that you have the tools to defend yourself if you are ever investigated."

After a long silence, Gatsby said, "Okay, what do you need?"

"You and Cissy need to prepare a spreadsheet showing for each company for which you've pledged your options, the notes and accrued interest that are attributable to that category of options. And then you must estimate what your total investment in stock, notes and options is worth today and what it is likely to be worth in three years. And you also need to provide some rationale for each of your estimates. Next you must generate a spreadsheet scheduling your professional fees and expenses for the next three years. When you have everything completed, call me, and I'll bring over one of my associates, and the three of us will go over the numbers— carefully to make sure that you are on solid ground. When we are satisfied, I'll generate a professional-looking presentation for you to give to Frye."

Everett stood up. "I want you to understand, Gatsby, that this is not an easy road you've chosen. There are going to be many bumps. It's a high-wire act. And, as George told you, the whole thing could turn out badly."

"I understand," said Gatsby. "I'm fine with the risk—and I appreciate your help."

After Everett left the office, Gatsby asked Cissy to come in and take a seat at the conference table. "Cissy," he said, "Everett has asked me to prepare extensive schedules on our convertible promissory note obligations. Those schedules will be part of a report we'll submit to Colin Frye's firm which hopefully will persuade them to help us raise a hundred million dollars for a Gatsby Venture Fund. I can't do this myself. I need to lean on you. Do you have commitments through the weekend that you can't cancel?"

"We're going to raise a hundred million dollars? Wow." She smiled. "I'm scheduled to go to Atlantic City with Shirley and two other friends. But they'll just have to go without me. I'll do whatever it takes."

Gatsby got up from his chair, took Cissy's hand and lifted her out of her chair, and hugged her. "You're a wonder," he said, while also wondering exactly how close she was to Shirley.

Chapter 16

GATSBY

May 11, 2003

After five days of intense effort by Everett, two KPMG associates and Cissy deciphering, analyzing, and organizing Gatsby's financial records, Gatsby messengered Frye a document entitled "Three Year Forecast of the Gatsby Convertible Promissory Note Portfolio." Frye called Gatsby approximately a week later to set up a meeting in Frye's office.

As Gatsby entered Frye's office, he was surprised to see another man sitting at the conference table opposite Everett. As Gatsby approached, the man stood and extended his hand. "Hello, Mr. Brooks. My name is Art Fallon. I'm new to Philadelphia and the firm. Colin asked me to sit in on the discussion."

Gatsby took Fallon's hand and smiled at him.

"Welcome to Philly, Art. Where are you from?"

"New York City," said Fallon. "Colin and I met when I was with the US Attorney's office. He's been singing the praises of Philadelphia since he arrived here, and I finally succumbed to his entreaties to join the firm."

"You guys certainly get great press," said Gatsby. "There doesn't seem to be any shortage of bad guys to prosecute."

"Mary Jo White gets the great press," said Fallon. "We peons just work our asses off to make her look good in the hope she'll get a presidential appointment or run for office, like Giuliani, and clear the way for one of us. We're like a pack of rabid dogs."

"Well," smiled Gatsby, "I hope your training will help keep me from becoming prey."

"We'll do our best," said Frye. "So, let's get to it."

Frye took the seat at the head of the table with Gatsby and Everett to his right and Fallon to his left. He handed each of them a spiral bound booklet.

"Rather than go over my detailed analysis, which you can review later, I'll provide the big picture, as I see it. Are you okay with that, Mr. Brooks?"

"Sure. But please, no need to stand on formality. *Gatsby* is fine."

Frye opened his booklet to the first page. "The first-page spreadsheet summarizes the status of your convertible promissory notes. The key numbers are as follows."

Gatsby reviewed the bullet points:

1. *Notes outstanding: $5,650,000 comprising 230 CPNs, all at 8.0 percent simple interest.*

2. *Yearly interest on the notes: approximately $448,000.*

3. *Accumulated interest, obligation: $860,000.*

4. *Total obligation, assuming no further CPNs are sold: $6,510,000 which increases at $112,000 per quarter.*

5. *Finally, based on the valuations placed on the investments for which Mr. Brooks owns stock or holds unassigned options, the value of his portfolio could be as high as $12 million, resulting in a net value of $5,510,000.*

He'd had time to assimilate these numbers, laid out starkly, since putting together the spreadsheet for Everett. Now he tried to gauge the reaction of Frye and Fallon; but his lingering tension over Frye's commitment to the job blurred his instincts. He really couldn't tell.

"Are you following me, Gatsby?"

"Right," said Gatsby.

"Note, that I've used the word *could* in describing the value of your portfolio. Not *is* and not *will be*. The valuations are speculative because of all the hazards startups must navigate before there is a liquidity event."

Everett was nodding. "We understand that," said Gatsby. Fallon was still expressionless.

"So," continued Frye, "given the status of your CPN portfolio, and the likelihood that the DoBS will issue a cease-and-desist order within the next year, and assuming no additional CPN sales, page ten of your booklet summarizes our suggestions as to how to move forward."

Gatsby, Hawking and Fallon opened the booklet and read the plan summary. "We," said Frye, "are proposing that Gatsby form a new LLC, the Gatsby Venture Fund, called GVF for short, to invest in the technology startups and emerging companies, a business in which he has been successful. The firm would be capitalized at $100 million. Gatsby would have contributed his portfolio of stocks and options which he would discount to $5 million and would raise $95 million in capital. His company, Gatsby and Associates, would act as general partner of the new LLC and be compensated in accordance with the 2 percent–20 percent customary formula for hedge funds. Namely, he'd receive a yearly income of 2 percent of the invested capital, or $2 million a year and 20 percent carried interest in the profits of each successful deal—paid when that deal achieves a liquidity event. He would create a three-person investor advisory board that would provide advice on new investments and address conflicts of interest between you and the investors."

Frye turned to Gatsby. "You would conduct your CPN business in parallel, but since you would not be selling any new CPNs, it would slowly wind down." He then went over the calculation showing that if the current nine companies represented by his current portfolio of CPNs performed similarly to the eight no longer operating, half of Gatsby's current CPN debt would self-liquidate—the debt would be paid off through mergers, IPOs or liquidations, leaving about $2.5 to $3 million plus interest that would need to be handled from Gatsby's

$2 million in yearly income and 20 percent carried interest from the Gatsby Venture Fund.

Gatsby and Everett huddled and whispered as they reviewed the plan. Fallon, who was obviously familiar with it, had closed his brochure and was reading from his Blackberry device.

Hawking spoke up. "I assume that the GVF private placement memorandum will be replete with disclosures about the CPN portfolio and the potential conflicts if Gatsby wants to invest GVF assets in some of the current firms he's sponsoring."

"Absolutely. The current CPN portfolio would be disclosed—but of course, not the investors in those companies."

Art Fallon finally spoke up. "This deal is not a slam dunk by any stretch of the imagination. Even if Gatsby can raise the $100 million needed to fund it, a lot of stars need to align for it to be successful. Gatsby will have to carefully manage the money he receives from the GVF to ensure he has adequate reserves to pay off the CPN investors who demand repayment in the event the options they're holding become worthless. Also, we are assuming that the financial performance of the eight firms that are no longer in play are indicative of the nine that compose the current CPN portfolio. Anyone who has spent time on Wall Street knows it is hazardous to base predictions of future success rates on prior success rates."

Everett turned to Gatsby and said, "Do you understand what Art is saying?"

"I do," said Gatsby. "He's saying that the plan looks feasible on paper, but even if I raise the $100 million and launch the GVF, there is no guarantee the income from the GVF that will be available to service the CPN portfolio will be adequate to meet the noteholder demands."

"And," continued Everett, "if you cannot satisfy the demands, and the notes go into default, you might wind up having to file bankruptcy to protect yourself from creditors."

"I understand that," said Gatsby.

Everett turned to Frye. "What is your estimate to prepare the GVF private placement memorandum and what kind of retainer will your firm require?"

"About $40,000 to do the PPM and file the required documents with the DoBS. We'll need a $25,000 retainer."

"Let's mull over this for a day or so," said Everett to Gatsby. "I'd like to do my own analysis, formulate a recommendation, and then talk with you and Miriam."

"Good idea," said Gatsby. He stood and said to Frye. "I appreciate the effort that you and the firm have invested in developing a solution to my problem. I'm damn impressed. And I am comforted to know that a former member of Mary Jo White's posse is looking out for me." He shook hands with Frye and Fallon. His mood was rising—almost ebullient. He could hear the theme from the movie *Chariots of Fire* filling the room. He could feel the hot sun hitting his upturned face, even though he was still in an office. The only concern that dampened the volume of the *Chariots of Fire* was Shirley.

Chapter 17

GATSBY

The following Saturday found Gatsby in bed, reading the *Wall Street Journal*. He glanced at the clock on the end table—9:30 a.m. He tried to recall the last time he luxuriated like this, enjoying the taste of a deep brewed Kona coffee, the Saturday paper, and the gentle aroma of his beautiful, naked wife sleeping next to him. He was trying to ignore his growing tumescence because he wanted to preserve the exquisite feeling.

Suddenly, he felt a hand stroke his penis. He looked over to Miriam. She was wearing a broad smile.

"Oh, that feels good, very good. Do you want to—?"

"Mm, one sec." She slid out from the sheets and headed into the bathroom.

"Be quick, please," he called, laughing.

Later, while they were cuddling, Gatsby said, "What's your schedule for today?"

"I'm meeting Joyce for lunch at La Veranda at noon and then we're going to shop in Old City."

"Okay. Will you give me a half hour to bring you up to date on the Shirley problem and that plan Frye and Hawking were working on?" She nodded against his chest. "Then let's meet at eleven on the deck for coffee. That should give you enough time to get coiffed and dressed so that the guys you encounter in Old City have to adjust their pants to avoid embarrassing themselves."

"I have a reputation to maintain."

"How does Joyce feel about your ability to turn heads in almost any venue? Is she at all jealous?"

"No, she is content to be a hausfrau and a mom with a billionaire husband. That's the reason she and I can remain friends. We don't compete."

When Miriam came out to the deck a while later, Gatsby had the table set with a pot of coffee and scones. He put down his paper and looked up at her. "Wow, you are smashing. Are you sure you have a date with Joyce?"

She laughed and raised her right hand in the three-finger Girl Scout salute. "Scout's honor." She sat down and poured herself a cup of coffee and cut off a piece of the blueberry scone. "I'm listening. Shoot."

Gatsby picked up a spiral notebook from the adjacent chair. "Let's start with the strategic plan to create the Gatsby Venture Fund and how it might dig me out of the CPN problem. Frye, his partner Art Fallon, Everett, Cissy, and I have been working nonstop for a week to draft a financial plan and supporting documentation that would pass muster with Frye's partners so they would agree to represent me. We got the final approval yesterday, so the ball is in my court to raise $100 million to fund the GVF. I'll be going to New York to meet with several groups that may be interested in investing. I'm cautiously optimistic we can pull this off."

Miriam put down her cup and wiped her face with the cloth napkin. "That sounds encouraging. But how are you going to handle the CPN problem and Shirley's nonstop effort to destroy us?"

"Okay, first let me tell you what I know about Shirley's latest antics." He pulled out a copy of the letter he had received from the Pennsylvania Department of Banking and Securities and waited while she read it. Several minutes later she handed it back to him "You expected this?"

"Yes, and so did McKnight."

"I assume that this is Shirley's work. She is going to continue to be a huge problem."

"I know. That's why I need to get busy on Plan B."

Miriam glanced at her watch. "I need to go in a few minutes, but I can't resist saying I told you so. She is bad news and needs to be stopped."

"I remember what you said. Notwithstanding this latest revelation, my position is still the same: 'Leave her to heaven.'"

"How long do you expect to be in New York?"

"I'm still working out the schedule, but as of now, I'm flying out on Tuesday the twenty-third. I've already scheduled several meetings that will keep me busy for a week."

"Then I'm going to use the opportunity to go on a girl's trip to Europe with Joyce. We've been looking at various river cruises in Europe. I'll talk to her to see if she can go when you're gone."

"If you and Joyce do go on a cruise, how about I fly to wherever you end up and we have a holiday?"

Miriam put down her cup, stood and said, "I need to go. If Joyce says yes, I want to spend a few days shopping in Geneva, and then I'll be free to party. I'll let you know what she says." As she was turning to leave, she said, "You can fill me in on how your new plan will deal with the CPN issue tonight."

"Fine," said Gatsby. "Have a good time."

CHAPTER 18

SHIRLEY

The following Monday, Shirley called Everett Hawking and asked to meet with him at his office at KPMG. She arrived exactly on time and was ushered into his office. Everett greeted her, showed her to her seat at his small round conference table and asked whether she would like water and coffee. She nodded. Everett buzzed his assistant and asked her to bring in two cups of coffee and two glasses of water. The basic hospitality put her at ease.

He sat down opposite Shirley and said, "So why did you want to meet with me?"

She smiled and said she wanted to talk with him because she was seeking clarity regarding the business practices of KPMG.

Everett laughed. "Well, I've never been asked that before. What aspects of our business practices can I shed light on?"

Before Shirley could answer, the assistant brought in the coffee and water and napkins and placed the cups and glasses in front of each of them.

"I know KPMG to be a fine company. I've hired KPMG to work on several of my projects both in New York and in Philly. They've never disappointed me. That's why I can't understand why you would have Gatsby Brooks for a client."

Everett sat up straight. He took a sip of his coffee, wiped his lips with his napkin and said, "What do you mean by that?"

"You're familiar with the convertible promissory notes Gatsby's been selling?"

"Yes."

"Do you know how many he's sold and the total dollars outstanding?"

"I have a good idea."

"You do know that Gatsby's running a Ponzi scheme? He pays off old notes by selling new notes. He could never pay them all off. That's why I'm surprised that you would have him for a client, and by doing so, you indicate that you are comfortable with his business practices."

Everett took a sip of water and waited several, considered moments before he answered. "Shirley, you should be more careful. You're making outlandish accusations against a prominent businessman. That isn't smart. You do not know what Gatsby's resources are nor what his financial situation is. I recommend that you consider the risk you're taking by making these reckless charges." He stood up. "I don't think there is any purpose in continuing this conversation."

Shirley remained in her chair. She was inwardly seething. It was clear to her that Everett was covering for his client. It was that simple. She stood up and said, "Gatsby is a liar and a swindler, and you're full of shit." Then she picked up her glass of water and threw it in Everett's face.

As Shirley observed Everett's shocked expression and his efforts to wipe the water out of his eyes, she put her hand up to her mouth and gasped. Everett's secretary rushed into the room.

"What happened?" she said.

Shirley started to cry. "I'm so sorry," she said. She backed away from the chair, looked at Everett, who still seemed to be in a state of shock, and ran past the secretary, out the office door, and didn't stop running until she was safely inside her car. She folded her arms on the steering wheel, placed her head on them, and sobbed for five minutes.

She found some Kleenex in her purse and wiped her eyes and blew her nose. She realized she had humiliated herself and done irreparable damage to her reputation. She had snapped, and all the thinking and planning about how she was going to turn over the Gatsby problem to the authorities and stand down had been flushed down the toilet. She was completely out of control, and she needed to get back in control before she did any more damage. She would write Everett a letter of apology and send it along with a large bottle of Jameson—the good kind. She would stop volunteering at Colin Frye's concerts. She would avoid any interaction with anyone who was in Gatsby's network, except Cissy.

~ ~ ~ ~ ~ ~

The following Saturday evening, Shirley was in the office of the theater in which Colin Frye had just completed a concert, totaling the receipts from the performance.. Being a volunteer for Colin gave her access to an eclectic group of people whose variety was refreshing after so much time in the company of conservative businessmen. Here she befriended musicians, sponsors, and executives of charitable organizations who frequently used Frye's concerts for fundraising events. Her involvement made her happier, less lonely. It was what made what she was about to do so difficult.

Normally, totaling the receipts and preparing the deposits would be a happy occasion because the after-concert party would soon begin. But not tonight. Tonight, she was just fulfilling her commitment despite the fury that was coursing through her body.

She checked her watch. The concert would be over in fifteen minutes and Colin would be coming into the office to ask about the take. She'd usually ask him about the audience and how the concert went. But tonight, she wanted to finish up her work and leave before he arrived. She wanted to avoid a confrontation. She knew from her recent meeting with Everett she could not control her anger over Colin's agreeing to represent Gatsby. On one hand, she understood that the buzzing outrage in her mind was irrational—she'd done what she felt was right, was making the list for the Department, and at this point, should have resumed minding her own business. But the scene with Everett had shocked her as much as it had angered him. She'd tried reflecting on it afterward, but it only fanned the flames. Her whole life she'd worked harder and kept her nose cleaner than her classmates and her colleagues to build her success—and at times, it truly had felt like the bar was higher for her because she was a woman. Higher still because, even well into adulthood, she still saw how people's gazes went first to her facial birthmark and how they struggled to see past it—or, in some cases, didn't bother to try. Thinking about her real achievements in such binary terms was reductive and usually it annoyed her when she noticed these thoughts in herself or heard other women mention them; but there was something inside her that had snapped when she saw Everett come to Gatsby's defense. Gatsby would skate. He'd always skated. And maybe it was the fatigue of working her ass off for Klamathgold—thanks to a set of inept, overly optimistic, aging frat boys who'd made such a mess of it in the first place—but she was tired of it all. She was exhausted on some unfathomable level that was as moralistic as it was intemperate. And before she could make another scene, she just wanted to square the receipts and leave the theater. She intended to process her thoughts in peace so as to exorcize them.

She planned to put the cash and credit card receipts in an envelope along with a note explaining that because of business commitments she would not be able to volunteer for a while, and just leave the envelope on his desk.

As she was inserting the documents into the envelope, Colin walked in.

Surprised, Shirley said, "You're early."

"I know. I wanted to find out about the take. I think we may have broken $5,000!"

"You're brilliant, Colin. We're just north of $5,300. Congratulations." Shirley completed stuffing the envelope. "Everything is in the envelope. I need to leave."

"You're not staying for the party?"

She got out of her chair. "I'm sorry. Something came up last minute." The unbearable awkwardness of the moment made her tear up. She turned away from Colin and left the office.

~ ~ ~ ~ ~ ~

Armed with the information she received from Cissy over the weekend, the first thing Shirley did on Monday was to call Kyle Rowan at the Pennsylvania Department of Banking and Securities.

"Kyle, this is Shirley Frazier." When he asked how she was doing, she said, "I'm not doing so well. I just learned that Gatsby has hired a new attorney to help him raise a lot of money for a new fund."

"Are you certain?" said Kyle.

"I have a reliable source."

"I don't understand why you're unhappy about this. It could be a positive development, assuming he does it properly. It may provide the resources to service his existing CPN debt."

"I'm unhappy because I know that Gatsby is a liar and if he is raising money, it will be another swindle. I'm calling you so that you can stop him."

There was a long pause.

"Shirley," said Kyle, "first, it appears that you do not know enough about the proposed transaction that Gatsby and his attorneys are working on to determine whether it is illegitimate. And second, even if you had reliable evidence he was planning an illegitimate transaction, and you presented the evidence to us, I doubt whether our office would be able to prevent it."

"You couldn't?"

"I don't think so."

"Do you think I should report Gatsby to the attorney general or the FBI?"

"Sorry, we don't offer advice like that. Surely you understand."

She was so angry—at the situation, at herself for being unable to let it go—that her eyes clouded with tears. "I'm so frustrated, Kyle."

Kyle did not respond.

Finally, she blurted out, "Thanks for listening. I'm working on the list you requested. I'll keep in touch." Then she hung up, having humiliated herself yet again.

PART II

CHAPTER 19

JERRY

On the evening of June 6, the Spectrum in South Philadelphia was packed. The basketball floor was empty, but the sounds of stomping, clapping, and shrieking drowned out the organ. Above the din came the strained voice of the announcer, Lars Larson, a well-known conservative radio talk show host with a deep, sonorous voice.

"Laa-dees and gentlemen and basketball fans everywhere—the moment has arrived! The moment, 18,168 of you've paid to see. The Houston Rocket's Eddie Griffin, is about to take up the challenge of Philadelphia's own Christopher Gatsby Brooks, known affectionately by all as Gatsby and especially by me as an old friend. Gatsby has challenged...."

The roar of the crowd drowned out Larson. The sounds of stomping and screaming segued into "Ed-die, Ed-die, Ed-die".

Helen and Jerry were seated in the third row up from the floor. Jerry was next to Moe and Helen was next to Joyce.

Lars Larson's voice boomed. "Ladies and gentlemen, I have never seen anything like the pandemonium in this or any arena in the country, and I've seen one helluva lot of games. This crowd is wild! Philadelphia, listen to yourselves!"

The packed arena continued to chant, "Eddie! Eddie! Eddie!"

"Gatsby, a five-foot-ten-inch, amateur scrub league player has offered to contribute $100,000 to the Children's Hospital of Philadelphia if Eddie Griffin defeats him in a one-on-one contest. He has agreed to contribute $50,000 if he wins. Eddie Griffin has taken on the challenge and agreed to contribute $100,000 if he loses. Eddie has also agreed to contribute $50,000 if he wins.

"In addition, Comcast Spectator, owner, and operator of this arena, has agreed to donate all the profits from ticket and food sales to the Children's Hospital. I'll explain the rules after we get these guys on the court. And in the meantime, I thank Gatsby for his kind invitation to come out tonight as your host and get acquainted with all of you!

"And now, here is the moment you've been waiting for. I give you the pride of the Roman Catholic High School of Philadelphia, … EDDIE GRIFFIN!"

The stadium erupted. Helen and Jerry stood up with the rest of the crowd, clapping, screaming, and stomping. Eddie Griffin came on to the floor waving, smiling, laughing, and soaking up the affection from his fans. He was wearing the red, black, and silver colors of the Houston Rockets.

"And now, ladies and gentlemen, citizens of Philadelphia, basketball fans everywhere… It is my great privilege to introduce to you a Philadelphian who needs no introduction. He is an entrepreneur, a venture capitalist, a philanthropist, a veteran of the United States Army, an accomplished singer, and most important, an avid basketball fan and player. And if you were ever introduced to this man, this man of so many accomplishments, he would undoubtedly ask you to 'just call him Gatsby.' And here he is!"

As Gatsby jogged onto the side of the court opposite Eddie Griffin, the crowd rose to its feet and started chanting, "Gatsby! Gatsby! Gatsby!" Gatsby, a graduate of Wharton, was wearing the red and blue colors of the University of Pennsylvania. He walked around the court, waving and smiling. He stopped at the courtside seats to shake hands and say hello to several friends. Helen caught his eye and he waved at her and Jerry. He walked across the centerline to shake hands with

Eddie Griffin who at six foot, ten inches, towered over him. Several teenage boys wearing warmup suits brought basketballs to each side of the court. Eddie Griffin and Gatsby took practice shots, and the teenage boys retrieved the balls and returned them to the respective players.

Helen was still trying to chat with Joyce when Lars Larson's voice drowned out their conversation again.

"Here are the rules that Eddie Griffin and Gatsby have agreed to. They will play ten fifteen-point, one-on-one games with a seven-minute break between each game. Each game will begin when the player, Eddie, or Gatsby, receives the ball from his coach at the half court line. For each possession, the player will get one shot at the basket, so rebounding skills will be moot. Griffin has agreed to spot Gatsby ten points in each game, so Gatsby only must make five points to win a game. It is fifteen minutes to game time, so get your hotdogs, Cokes, and beers and relax. The money is going for a good cause.

"I want to bring in Matt Cord, whom all of you know. Matt has been calling the play by play for the 76ers for seven years. I think his insights will add to your enjoyment of the contest. Welcome to the Children's Hospital Challenge!"

"Thanks, Lars. I'm happy to be here. What an exciting night. The crowd is as big as we get for a 76'ers game."

"And a tad more exuberant," said Lars. "It's a sellout, Matt. You and I have talked about this challenge over the past several months and we both agreed that by taking on Eddie Griffin, Gatsby has shown what my Jewish friends call an amazing level of *chutzpah*."

"I think you've understated the situation, Lars. My Hispanic friends would say that Gatsby has brass *cojones*."

Lars laughed. "In the interests of full disclosure, Gatsby is my friend. I met him over ten years ago at a political function. But I know zip about his basketball skills and whether he will offer any competition to Eddie. Can you help us, Matt?"

"I think I can. When the news of the Children's Hospital Challenge broke, I decided to investigate Gatsby's basketball skills. I observed several of his pickup games at the Northeast Racquet and Fitness Center in Philadelphia and talked with several people he competes with. I can say that among his peers, he's much respected. He's quick, handles the ball well, and shoots at about 45 percent. He's devastating in the three-point zone, shooting about a 35 percent rate. Eddie will not find him to be a pushover—especially with a ten-point spot."

"I'm happy to hear that, Matt. What do you think his chances are?"

"I'd say they are pretty good. Eddie's shooting average is about 40 percent, so it might take him twenty shots to make the eight baskets he needs to win a game. Gatsby only needs one two-pointer and one three-pointer to win. I think Gatsby might do well."

"Thanks, Matt I know that Gatsby's friends are happy to hear that. Matt will chat with us after each of the ten games and will be here for a post-game wrap-up. The refs are meeting with Eddie and Gatsby at center court. Scott Padgett will be taking the ball out for Eddie and acting as his coach. 76'ers star Allen Iverson will be taking the ball out for Gatsby and coaching him. Gatsby has won the coin toss, so he will get first possession."

During the next two hours, the screaming fans who filled the Spectrum were treated to a panoply of visions rarely seen in the basketball world. Set in the realm bounded between NBA professionalism and collegiate varsity, two players, mismatched in height and experience but well matched in energy, motivation, and thespian skills, succeeded in maintaining the enthusiasm of the crowd at a fever pitch for the entire length of the match.

On the first play of the first game, Gatsby received the ball from Alan Iverson, turned toward the basket and immediately made a three-point goal. Griffin received the ball from Scott Padgett, faking a three-point shot and driving the basket for a layup, leaving Gatsby standing flatfooted. And so, it went. These were the visions that that photographers captured that made up the special spread in the following day's *Inquirer*: Eddie Griffin blocking a Gatsby two-point attempt; Eddie Griffin making a fifteen-foot jump shot from the side; Gatsby losing the ball as he tried to dribble around Griffin; Griffin making a three-point shot; Gatsby making an attempt to get off a three-pointer over Griffin's close defense; Gatsby and Griffin each handing a check to the president of the Children's Hospital of Philadelphia (CHOP). The headline of the *Inquirer* was: GATSBY:4, GRIFFIN:6, CHOP: $975,826.57.

132

CHAPTER 20

HELEN

The next evening just before six o'clock, Jerry and Helen exited the elevator in the lobby of the Bellevue Hotel. The lobby was crowded. There was a bar on the north side of the lobby and there were several waiters carrying drinks and hors d'oeuvres. All the women were elegantly dressed. Jerry went to the reception desk to find out where the event for Moe was being held.

Helen was wearing a plain black sheath. "I feel so under-dressed," she said. "Did you see all the jewelry?"

"Don't worry about it. You'll be the best-looking woman in the place—you always are. You can explain we're traveling from New York and we're last-minute invitees." He took her hand and they walked in the direction of the grand ballroom.

They located the registration desk. Jerry gave their names to the smartly dressed young woman at the table. She looked at the list of guests and located their names. She retrieved their seat assignments and name tags from a large box, and as she handed them to Jerry, she said, "You and Mrs. Bascomb are seated at table one with Mr. Shultz and Mr. Brooks. Have a wonderful time."

"Thank you," he said, and then he and Helen walked to the door behind the registration desk. They entered the large ballroom which was teeming with men in dark suits and expensively bejeweled women in gowns. Waiters scurried around with trays of champagne flutes.

Helen asked Jerry if he recognized anyone. Jerry looked over the crowd.

"I know a total of ten people in Philadelphia, and only five of them might be at this affair." Out of the assemblage of tightly packed bodies, about fifty feet away, Gatsby emerged hand in hand with a stunning blonde woman, each carrying a flute of champagne. He had apparently noticed Jerry and Helen and headed in their direction, leading what appeared to be either an escort or a trophy wife. Either way, Helen thought, any wife would have to be blind and dumb as a brick to put up with a many-tentacled cad like Gatsby.

"Jerry! Helen!" He bellowed from forty feet away as he approached. "I am so happy to see you." He shook Jerry's hand and nodded to Helen. "I'd like to introduce my wife, Miriam."

As Helen shook the other woman's hand, she met a blade of chilly intelligence in Miriam's eyes. Helen stifled her earlier judgment before it could register on her face as surprise.

After the introductions, Gatsby turned to Helen and Jerry. "I'm delighted that you had the time to travel to Philly to see the game and attend Moe's birthday party. Both Moe and I appreciate your being here. You are sitting at our table, along with Moe and Joyce, Miriam and myself, and Shirley and Alicia, Moe's sister."

"I met Alicia and toured her gallery when we were in Philadelphia in February," said Helen. "I'm looking forward to seeing her again."

"Ah, that's right. And I also see that you don't have drinks." Gatsby approached a waiter who was carrying a tray of champagne flutes and directed him to Helen and Jerry.

"That's my Gatsby," said Miriam, "ever the impresario."

"And he seems so good at it," said Helen.

"Oh, yes," said Miriam, "whatever the venue."

After Jerry and Helen had taken their glasses, Gatsby suggested they move in the direction of their table. "They will be sounding the gong in less than five minutes."

There had been much jockeying over seating arrangements, with no one willing to be the first to sit down and stake out a place at the table. Gatsby took charge—he saw that everyone had been introduced to everyone else, accompanied by a handshake, peck on the cheek, or hug to seal the introduction. Then he dictated the seating arrangement clockwise: Gatsby, Miriam, Jerry, Helen, Alicia, Shirley, Moe and Joyce.

Alicia was a muscular middle-aged woman who towered over her brother. Her face was smooth and unblemished. She wore reading glasses around her neck on a gold chain. She spoke in an alto voice. Next to Gatsby, she was the most dominating presence at the table.

Helen was also struck by how similar Miriam and Joyce appeared. Both were stunning, but on closer look, Miriam's beauty was in her bone structure, and Joyce's was in the considerable but subtle care she put into her appearance. The result could have marked them as sisters or cousins. They both had donned evening gowns that must have cost upwards of $5,000. She noticed that Jerry was also having trouble keeping his eyes off their breasts.

A dinner of tomato bisque tossed salad, salmon, green vegetables, baked potato, and a chocolate mousse dessert was served. Although the food was delicious, Helen's attention was consumed by Alicia who battered her with direct questions about her education and gallery experience in France, Los Angeles and New York.

"Have you ever been to the Philadelphia Art Museum?" said Alicia.

Helen shook her head.

"If you are staying over until Monday, I would be happy to take you and show you the major pieces in the collection. Would one o'clock work?"

"Yes, that will be great. Where is the museum?"

"It's on Franklin Parkway, a short cab ride from the hotel. You'll recognize it as soon as you get there. It has a huge staircase in front—the one that Sylvester Stallone ran up in *Rocky*."

The noise level was high, and Helen could not hear any part of the conversation at the opposite side of the table. Moe's attention was dominated by an unending parade of well-wishers who stopped by to congratulate him on his fiftieth birthday.

Gatsby left his seat, moved toward the stage, and motioned to the conductor of the ten-piece orchestra. They chatted for a minute, and Gatsby came back to his seat and announced that the program would be starting momentarily.

The orchestra struck up "Stars and Stripes Forever," the doors opened at the back of the room and a four-person color guard emerged carrying the flags of the United States and the State of Pennsylvania. As the color guard moved down the center aisle, everyone rose to their feet and placed their hands on their hearts. The color guard stopped in front of the stage, turned, and faced the audience.

The conductor announced that Philadelphia native Patti Labelle would lead in the singing of "The Star-Spangled Banner." Ms. Labelle, wearing a red gown, came onto the stage, and backed by the orchestra, filled the ballroom with her strong soprano voice.

The color guard receded, and the audience took their seats. The priest of the church that Moe and Joyce attended delivered the invocation. Gatsby followed the priest to the podium.

"Ladies and gentlemen, we are gathered here this evening to honor one of our most outstanding citizens. An individual who for years has given unflinchingly of his time and his wealth to the Philadelphia and Pennsylvania and there can be no question in the mind of anyone in this ballroom that Moe Shultz has earned, and deserves our affection and respect on this, his fiftieth birthday." Loud applause interspersed with whoops and screams followed.

"Moe and I have been close friends since 1980 when we were both at Wharton, and I've never known Moe to refuse to help someone, or some institution, when they were in need. Who will ever forget what Moe did when Hurricane Floyd wreaked devastation on Philadelphia in September 16, 1999? He deposited one million dollars in a special checking account and placed an ad in the *Inquirer* announcing he was ready to help any family that was in extremis due to Floyd's devastation. Then for the next ten days he sat in his office listening to people's problems and writing checks. He had to be on the scene, meeting with folks whose lives had been turned upside down by the storm. And that's why, ladies and gentlemen, I love him, and we all love him." The audience jumped to their feet and clapped for several minutes.

Moe stood, a slight smile on his face, and nodded his appreciation for the adulation being heaped on him.

Gatsby quieted the audience and asked everyone to sit down. "Mr. Daniel L. Lombardo, president and chief executive officer of the Volunteers of America, Delaware Valley, will soon take this podium and show an excellent film that will describe Moe's history of service to the Philadelphia region. I've seen the film, and I guarantee that no one will leave this hall without being teary-eyed. But first I wanted to tell Moe how we all feel about him in the best way I know."

The orchestra played the introduction to "You're the Tops," and Gatsby spoke into the mike. "Mr. Moe Shultz, please stand up, straight up, so every one of the two hundred and fifty people assembled here can see you. Good. Okay, Maestro, from the top."

The orchestra started up, and, looking directly at Moe, Gatsby filled the ballroom with his mellow baritone.

At words poetic, I'm so pathetic
That I always found it best,
Instead of getting 'em off my chest,
To let 'em rest unexpressed.
I hate parading, serenading
As I'll probably miss a bar,
But if this ditty is not so pretty
At least it'll tell you how great you are.
You're the top! You're the Colosseum,
You're the top! You're the Louvre Museum,
You're a melody from a symphony by Strauss...

After Gatsby completed his song, Moe smiled, clapped, and waved. There was no question he enjoyed the adulation. Helen was happy for him and grateful he had invited Jerry and herself to share in his big evening. Alicia beamed.

The applause went on for five minutes. Gatsby called Moe to the stage, and they stood there, side by side, waving to the guests, like newly anointed presidential and vice-presidential candidates at the end of a political convention.

CHAPTER 21

JERRY

The next morning, Jerry and Moe were in the Famous 4th Street Delicatessen having a late breakfast. The waitress has just placed the plates on the table and asked whether the men would be ordering anything else. Jerry shook his head. "After I eat this sandwich I won't eat for a week."

Moe laughed. "I guess I should have warned you. The large portions are one of the things that makes this place famous."

"I appreciate your meeting me for breakfast, Moe. You must be exhausted from all the festivities."

"We didn't get to bed until two. Gatsby insisted on keeping the party going. Several of our friends came over to our house and we were drinking, dancing, and singing until 1:30 a.m. Then I threw everybody out and Joyce and I went to bed. What a night!"

"Birney never told me that you were a celebrity. He only told me that you were rich and ran several auto dealerships."

"Celebrity is overstating it. I do a lot of charity and volunteer work because I have the means and the time, and my parents instilled me with enough guilt over being born rich that I need to work my ass off to assuage it." He laughed. "It's a burden. There are so many needy people and I try to do as much as I can."

"Well, Helen and I feel fortunate to have shared in your celebration." He lifted his coffee cup. "Here's to you, Moe. May you enjoy many more years of being able to serve."

Moe lifted his cup and clicked Jerry's.

They ate in silence for several minutes. "As Helen and I were talking last evening and revisiting the various folks whom we'd met, we realized we were not sure how Shirley fits into your world."

Moe put his fork down and wiped his face with the cloth napkin. "I apologize for that, Jerry, it was my oversight. I had assumed that Gatsby had filled you in on all your tablemates. My father and Shirley's uncle, both of whom are deceased, were business associates and were close friends. They both served as officers in the University of Pennsylvania's alumni society, sat on each other's boards, participated in the activities of many of the same charities, played golf together and often vacationed together with their spouses. Shirley has a Harvard degree and worked for McKinsey and Bain Capital in New York. After her father died, she returned to Philly to be close to her mother. I introduced her to Gatsby, and they've worked on several deals together."

"That certainly helps," said Jerry. "But tell me, Moe, how did Gatsby get to be Gatsby?"

Moe laughed. "I was waiting for you to ask."

"The only Gatsby I know," said Jerry, "is Jay Gatsby of F. Scott Fitzgerald's imagination."

"That's the origin," said Moe. "Gatsby's mother came up with the name when she was in the hospital in the final stages of labor. She wanted to give her son a name that would inspire him to do great things, one that would tell the world he was destined to do great things."

Jerry was stunned. "But the original Gatsby character is a swindler and dies disgraced."

"Right," said Moe. "His mother obviously never read the whole book." Moe took a sip of coffee. "Her husband abandoned her while she was pregnant. She was all alone, in despair, and had to name her new baby. That's the story."

"It's obvious that Gatsby is proud of his name," said Jerry. "I mean he wants everyone to use it. I don't get it. I would think he would want to avoid using it, especially after he'd read the book."

Moe laughed and drank some water. "You don't understand Gatsby. His overarching objective is to live down his name. To prove to the world he is a brilliant financier, an astute politician, a generous philanthropist, and has unquestioned integrity—even though his name is Gatsby. The guy is the consummate Energizer Bunny. He goes and goes. I can't keep up with him. He is a truly remarkable guy and I'm fortunate he considers me his best friend."

Jerry nodded. "He is that. He has certainly been gracious to Helen and me." He sipped some coffee. "Based on my limited observations last night, he and Miriam seem to have a unique relationship. His wife doesn't hesitate to take shots at him."

"You noticed that?" Moe smiled. "This is a second marriage for both, and they are devoted to each other. But she doesn't put up with Gatsby's bullshit. If she thinks he's climbed too high on his horse, she brings him down to earth. She's one hell of a tough lady."

"A tough, attractive lady," said Jerry.

"And an intelligent one." Moe said it softly but didn't look up from his plate, and something about the odd tilt of his smile carried a hint of warning.

They finished their breakfasts. The waitress removed the dishes and handed Jerry the check. He handed the waitress his credit card. While he was signing, Moe said, "So what do you think? Can you see yourself moving to Philly?"

Jerry looked up. "Both Helen and I like what we've seen. She would move tomorrow. But we have a high-six-figure income that will be difficult to replicate in Philadelphia. I just don't know."

They got up from their chairs. "I hope you decide to move here. I think you'd be surprised at the opportunities. Feel free to call me if you'd like to talk about it. And give my love to Helen. You hit the jackpot when you captured her."

"Don't I know it!" said Jerry.

They shook hands and headed toward the exit.

CHAPTER 22

MIRIAM

As Jerry and Moe were finishing their breakfast Miriam and Joyce were being seated at the Bellevue. They were both wearing dark glasses and headscarves.

"That was one helluva party," said Miriam. "I assume that Moe was pleased?" The waitress stopped at the table to hand out menus.

"Bloody mary, spicy," said Joyce.

"Ditto," said Miriam.

"Will you be ordering brunch?" said the waitress.

"Eventually," said Joyce. "Just hurry up with the bloody marys." Joyce turned to Miriam. "You were saying?"

"I assume Moe was pleased with the way the party went."

"He was ecstatic! He was so moved by Gatsby's song. Your husband was brilliant."

"He certainly has his moments," said Miriam.

The waitress brought the two bloody marys to the table.

"Now that's what I call fast," said Joyce. "Thanks." They took long sips of their drinks.

"I needed that," said Miriam as she dabbed her lips with a napkin.

"Me too," said Joyce. She took another sip, set down her glass and sat back in her chair. "Are you packed?"

Miriam laughed. "I've been packed for several days. I am *really* ready to go."

"I'm going to start this afternoon," said Joyce. She looked quizzically at Miriam. "Let's have it, Miriam. What's bothering you?"

"Am I that transparent?" said Miriam.

"To your good friends only, I promise."

"Okay,'" said Miriam. "Gatsby and I had an argument last night. I told him he really embarrassed me—the way he was fawning over Helen. The only time he took his eyes off her was when he went to the stage to perform. I couldn't enjoy the party. I was so furious."

"She is attractive," said Joyce. "And Gatsby loves attractive women. I wasn't surprised at his behavior. It was just Gatsby being true to form."

"No, I wasn't surprised he was fascinated by her. I just didn't expect him to be so obvious—especially at Moe's party." She took a sip of her drink. "Gatsby can fuck any woman he wants to just so long as he doesn't embarrass me. That's our contract—and he broke the contract last night."

"Do you think he's slept with her?"

Miriam stabbed at the ice in her drink a few times, thinking. "I don't believe he's had the opportunity, and I don't get the impression she's available. If he did, he would not have been looking at her as he did. But there is no question he would if he could. No, it is a mission that was not accomplished."

They sat quietly for several minutes, draining their drinks. Joyce broke the silence. "You know that when she was here in February, Gatsby took her to lunch at La Veranda and she apparently became ill, and Gatsby had to take her back to the Bellevue. At least that's what she told my sister-in-law."

"Gatsby told me about it. Helen probably figured out where things were going and played sick to cut him off without a confrontation. She's clever."

"You are a saint, Miriam, for putting up with philandering. I couldn't do it. Not for a minute. If Moe cheated on me, I'd be out the door in a flash. That would be the end of it."

"Come off it, Joyce," said Miriam. "That $50 million prenuptial agreement that you got Moe to sign gives you a lot of options. I'm not in your league. If I walked out on Gatsby, my lifestyle would deteriorate by several notches. I am not a saint. I'm a businesswoman. When Gatsby's not screwing some tart, he's a good husband, a great father, a good provider—and he's terrific in the sack. I wish he wouldn't screw around so much, but considering everything, it's a small price to pay."

She lifted her glass. "Here's to my husband—warts and all." She drained her glass, set it down on the table and spoke. "These are spicy! I think I'll order another."

CHAPTER 23

SHIRLEY

June 13, 2003

The following Friday night at 11:30 p.m., Shirley was returning from a four-day trip to Klamath Falls. She picked up her car at the Philadelphia Airport and was driving toward downtown Philadelphia. She struggled to keep her mind focused on driving, but thoughts about Gatsby and her recent encounters with Everett, Colin, and Kyle Rowan at the DoBS continued to distract her.

"God*damn* it!" she yelled. There had to be some way to stop the sonofabitch. The driver of a car in an adjacent lane leaned on his horn. She was startled out of her reverie and realized that her car had drifted over the line. She corrected and waved to the driver. She needed to concentrate, or she'd kill herself and maybe some other innocents. She smirked. That would make Gatsby happy.

She negotiated her Subaru into the parking garage of the Residences at Dockside, carefully pulled into her assigned parking space and got out of the car. She shut the door, pulled her briefcase out of the back seat and locked the car with her remote. As she turned toward the exit, she saw Miriam.

She realized that there was no way to avoid her, so she steeled herself for what she knew would be an unpleasant confrontation. She began walking.

"Hello, Shirley," said Miriam. "You're certainly not keeping banker's hours."

"Unfortunately, I'm not. I've been working my ass off 24/7 trying to save something for the Klamathgold investors."

"I'm sorry to hear that," said Miriam. "Could we chat for a few minutes?"

"Sure, but we'll have to keep it brief. I'm totally bushed."

She placed her briefcase on the floor of the garage.

"I understand," said Miriam. Her expression was warm, but her eyes had the fixedness of a stalking lion's. "Shirley," she began, "frankly, I don't understand what is happening. Gatsby and I are getting calls from many of our mutual friends expressing their shock over the outlandish statements you have been making about his ethics, business practices, and financial situation." She glanced around the garage as if taking in a fine view, then returned that gaze to Shirley. There was something rehearsed in her demeanor, but it was only in the smoothness with which she delivered her threat. "The statements that have been attributed to you are both false and libelous and cannot have any other purpose than to ruin Gatsby's reputation. Neither I nor any of our mutual friends have any idea why you are doing this. Gatsby is an honorable and successful businessman, a philanthropist. You are hurting both Gatsby and yourself, and diminishing the prospect that you will ever again find work in Philadelphia."

Shirley could feel her throat constrict and her muscles tighten. Her defenses were down, owing to her grueling schedule. She was determined to avoid becoming emotional, though, and took a deep breath. She listened calmly to Miriam. After all, part of her knew this had been coming.

"Miriam, I know you love your husband and feel obligated to defend him. But I have ample evidence that Gatsby has been running a Ponzi scheme for many years and a significant percentage of money he receives selling his convertible promissory notes winds up in his pocket, even though the companies he is sponsoring are starving for cash.

"I know of several investors who wanted to redeem their notes and have waited months for their money. I doubt that Gatsby is anywhere near as wealthy as he claims to be. In short, Miriam, notwithstanding my respect and affection for you, there is no doubt in my mind that your husband, Christopher Gatsby Brooks, is an evil fraud. And frankly, I don't understand why you are so willing to overlook it. You and I both know that if the places were reversed, and one of us had been running this cavalier scheme, we'd probably have been crucified for it long ago."

Shirley picked up her briefcase and walked past a stunned Miriam toward her condo.

CHAPTER 24

MIRIAM

When Miriam entered her condo, Gatsby was dozing on the recliner. The fireplace was on, the *Wall Street Journal* was on his chest opened to the story about the war. She gently kissed him on his lips.

He opened his eyes and smiled at her. "What a great way to wake up." He glanced at his watch. "Jeez, the ballet meeting was long."

"Moe was there. He went on and on about expenses not being under control. He simply would not shut up."

Gatsby laughed. "It's a small price to pay for the million a year he donates. Big bucks buy bloviation."

She kicked off her shoes and headed toward the kitchen. "I'll get a glass of wine and we'll talk." She returned to the living room and fell into the recliner opposite Gatsby.

"I just had an unsettling conversation with your least favorite consultant."

He sat up and folded the newspaper and took a sip from the half-full glass of wine next to the chair. "When?"

Miriam pushed herself deep into the recliner and sighed. "As I was coming in from the garage. I saw her car enter and I waited for her at the exit."

"Why?"

"I thought I might be able to talk some sense into her."

"Good luck," said Gatsby. "How did it go?"

"Not well. No, that's an understatement. How about 'terrible?'"

"What did you say? What did she say?"

"I merely told her about the calls we've received from friends and investors reporting on how she is trashing you and your ethics, and how she's saying that the CPNs are illegal. And she appears to be obsessed with destroying you—and me by proxy."

"I bet that went over well. What was her response?"

"She says she has evidence that you are running a Ponzi scheme and a significant percentage of money that you receive from selling the CPNs—and I quote— winds up in your pocket even though those companies are starving for cash.'"

"What else?"

"She says she knows several investors have waited months for their money after they asked you to redeem their investment, and therefore, she doubts that you are as wealthy you claim to be."

"Is that it?"

"No, the last thing she said was, quote, 'Your husband, Christopher Gatsby Brooks is an evil fraud.'"

Gatsby let out a laugh. He took another sip of wine. "I can't say I'm surprised. In addition to being smart, I've found her to be highly motivated in pursuing whatever objective she selects. Unfortunately, her current objective is to pillory me. I don't think we'll invite her for Thanksgiving dinner."

"You're not taking this seriously. That woman is determined to destroy you and me along with you."

Gatsby smiled. "What the hell would you have me do? Throw stuff against the wall? Rant and rave? Write a letter to the editor of the *Inquirer* claiming she is deranged?"

"Well, no, but—"

"I had a come-to-Jesus meeting with her. I tried to reason with her. I offered her incentives to back off. I had McKnight send her a cease-and-desist that threatened a libel suit. There has been no change. She is behaving as if she has absolutely nothing to lose. She's an obsessive person, and unfortunately, we just have to wait until she gets her teeth into something else. In the meantime, we just have to work on getting the Gatsby Venture Fund launched."

"You didn't tell me about your meeting with Shirley and the cease-and-desist letter."

"I didn't want to burden you. I have no options to affect her behavior. My venture business, which is based on selling convertible promissory notes, is struggling, primarily because of the dotcom bust. I had three deals that were either at the IPO stage or acquisition stage that could have provided the liquidity to guarantee solvency. But the bottom fell out of the tech market, the investors scurried for cover, and all three companies failed. As of now, the business is insolvent and struggling. Shirley is in the process of driving a stake into its heart and there is nothing I can do to stop her." He drained his glass. He stood up and headed toward the kitchen. "I need another drink. Can I get something for you?"

"Yes, a double Tito's on the rocks with a twist."

"Popcorn?"

"Yes."

As she sat and waited for his return, she decided that Gatsby was thinking too narrowly. It was not a common fault of his—he erred by swinging his grasp or his gaze too wide. Her efforts were usually to reel him in and counsel more restraint. But she noted she had at last come up against one of her husband's true limits. She, on the other hand, felt an overwhelming claustrophobia when imagining herself abiding by his plan: to let the lawyers handle it, and if that failed, wait. No, it was ridiculous to let Shirley keep swinging until she grew tired. Miriam was patient but not foolish.

Gatsby returned with a tray containing the drinks and bowls of popcorn. They both were silent for several minutes.

"So, what's your plan?" said Miriam.

"Moe has contacts on Wall Street that could raise the money based on my track record of the three deals I've sold and the potential of EVG and a few others in my current portfolio. The challenge will be to keep the lid on my current problems so that the virus that Shirley is spreading doesn't reach Wall Street before I can raise the money." He shook his head. "The timing will be critical. I have a lot of those meetings set up already, but it is not a slam dunk."

It was a lot to absorb. Gatsby had never before admitted the issues he was facing in his current business. She struggled to wrap her mind around all this new information and its implications for their marriage and her own wellbeing. Again, the feeling of claustrophobia came over her.

"Okay," said Miriam, "let's say you are successful in raising the hundred million dollars and launch the venture fund. What will you do about the insolvency of the current business?"

"Good question. The plan is to keep the current business going and hope that the new venture fund, which will pay us two million a year in salary and in which I will have a carried interest in twenty percent of all the profits, will be enough of a success to generate sufficient cash flow to pay off all the remaining CPNs."

"And if it doesn't?"

Gatsby drained his vodka and set it hard on the table so that Miriam jumped. "Then I'm toast. I'll have to file personal bankruptcy and everything I've worked for over the past thirty years will go down the drain, my net worth, my reputation, and probably a good portion of my network. It will all be gone."

"And what about me?" said Miriam.

"You will lose the few hundred thousand that you've lent me. But your current investment portfolio with J. P. Morgan will be unaffected. You have more than eight million dollars and you can definitely live happily for the rest of your life, with or without me."

After several minutes, she managed to say, "Well, I'm happy to see that you have a plan—even if it is risky."

He smiled. "That's what they pay me for."

"So, what if Shirley continues her rampage, which I fully expect her to do?"

Gatsby shook his head. "There is nothing I can do."

"Have you consider using Achmed to solve our problem? I think I can track him down."

Gatsby stared at her. "Achmed? You can't be serious."

"I'm deadly serious. Pardon the pun."

"That's insane, Miriam. You don't want to go there."

"I've got a dog in this fight, too. She is destroying my reputation right along with yours. She needs to be stopped and Achmed could make that happen."

"Expunge the idea from your mind. You're falling into her trap. We need to 'leave her to heaven' and get on with the business of saving what we've got. We can't let her continue to divert us and consume valuable time and energy. Our life is already complicated. We don't need more issues to add to our already-long list."

"Great quote from Hamlet," she said. "And if we leave her to heaven, she's likely to drive us to hell. I've got a better quote, from Macbeth: 'If it could be all finished and done with when it's done, then it may as well be done quickly.'" She pushed herself out of the chair. "I'm exhausted. I'm going to bed."

CHAPTER 25

MIRIAM

June 23, 2003

Miriam and Joyce were lying on lounge chairs on the top deck of the Viking riverboat which was currently docked in Passau, Germany. It was the fifth day of their Danube cruise that originated in Budapest. They decided to forgo the city tours of churches, markets, and museums in order to soak up some sun and catch up on their sleep.

They had spent two days in Hungary and two days in Austria and were about to embark on the five-day part of the cruise that covered the German ports on the Danube. As they lounged and sipped their wine, they discussed the nine tours they'd taken and the sites they'd seen.

"It's such a jumble," said Joyce. "There is so much to see and so little time available at each place. I'm just glad I don't have to make a report and describe what we've learned. I confess, I'm sick of the churches and the cathedrals."

"Amen," said Miriam. "I've decided to just enjoy the moment and not make any effort to try to remember where we've been and what we saw. It's like good sex. You don't remember the specifics of what you did or what he did, or exactly how it felt. All you remember was that it was great, adequate, or lousy."

"Brilliant," said Joyce. "I love your analogies."

"I never want to disappoint," said Miriam. "Tell me about the woman you're going to visit in Nuremberg."

"Her name is Sally Blake. She was my best friend at Middlebury College and both of us were members of the same sorority. She's a lesbian and never married. She teaches English at Erlangen University which is located fifteen miles from Nuremberg. She's been in Germany since we graduated, twenty-plus years ago. She is outgoing and is totally European. You'll love her."

"Why did she come to Germany?"

"Shortly after we graduated, she went on a grand tour of Europe. During the tour she attended a lesbian retreat and fell in love. She finished the tour, and rather than return to the States and look for a job, she decided to move in with her lover. Unfortunately, the relationship collapsed after nine months. But by that time, she was hooked on Germany and its culture, and she decided to stay and make her life here."

Miriam sat up and turned toward Joyce. "Are you toying with the prospect of some extracurricular action?"

Joyce had a quizzical expression. "Come again?" she said. Then she understood and laughed. "Miriam, I assure you, I'm an old-fashioned girl—monogamous and straight as a broomstick. I'm just not into women, even those whom I love and admire.

"I just thought I'd ask. I hope I didn't offend you."

"Hell, no," said Joyce. "Nothing you can or might say to me could offend me. But now that you've raised the topic, what about you? Might not a romantic affair during this trip help even the score with Gatsby?"

"I can't say that the thought hasn't crossed my mind."

"Well," said Joyce.

"Let's just say, it's a distinct possibility."

Five days later the ship arrived in Nuremberg. Sally Burke was there to greet them when they disembarked. Sally was as tall and lissome as a willow. She had a dark complexion, wore her dark black hair in a bun, and wore no makeup. They all went out to lunch at Albrecht Durer Stube, one of the best restaurants in Nuremberg. Along with an aura of calmness and steadiness, Sally had a jovial personality. Miriam immediately understood how easy it would be to become her close friend.

Sally invited Miriam to stay at her home for a few days so she could show her Nuremberg and the surrounding areas like Firth, Bromberg, and Neuschwanstein Castle. Miriam said she appreciated the offer but frankly she was tired of touring, and she was anxious to get to Geneva so she could rest and shop. Then they all walked over to the taxi stand and said their goodbyes.

As Miriam sat in the train hurtling to Geneva, she breathed a sigh of relief she had shed Joyce and Sally and could devote her attention to the task that had propelled her to Europe—to find Achmed Khordroy.

All she knew about Achmed's whereabouts was what he told her just before the gendarmes broke into his condominium on Saint Martin. While they were dressing in the bedroom and the gendarmes were pounding on the front door, he told her that the French government had labeled him an "undesirable" and expelled him from the island. They were going to march him to an airplane, place him onboard, and fly him to whatever destination he chose. He had not made a final decision, but he was leaning toward one of the French-speaking cantons in Switzerland. He had lived in Switzerland several years ago and believed they would give him a residence permit. Just then, the gendarmes broke the door down, ran into the bedroom, handcuffed him and led him out of his condo. That was the last time she'd seen him.

The only way she was going to be able to locate him was through a contract bridge club. Ahmed was addicted to the game. He was a Life Master and earned a modest living gambling. He'd never move anywhere that wasn't in the proximity of a bridge club.

Her research revealed that there were five of them located around the northern half of Lake Geneva. The one on the western tip of the lake was a few minutes from the hotel where she would be staying. The most eastern one was about a two-hour drive from her hotel; three lay in between. She had an 8x10 photograph of Achmed and herself. She had hired a car and driver and tomorrow planned to visit each of the five bridge clubs and talk with the respective managers about her quest, using the photograph both to identify Achmed and show she was a close friend.

If her strategy was successful and she located Achmed she would, notwithstanding Gatsby's objection, attempt to persuade Achmed to handle Shirley. She hated to deceive Gatsby, and certainly wouldn't have stood for it if the deception had worked the other way around, but she had no choice. To improve the odds of Gatsby's success with the GVF, Shirley had to be neutralized, and Achmed was the only person she knew who could do it.

The train pulled into the Main Geneva Station. She took a taxi to the Grand Hotel Kempinski, which was located on the lake. She chose a room on the tenth floor to guarantee a great view.

After the bellman left the room, Miriam undressed and took a long, hot shower. Then she put on the terrycloth robe and ordered dinner from the room service menu. After dinner, she checked her watch. It was 9 a.m. in Philadelphia. She punched Gatsby's number into her cell phone. Gatsby answered after two rings.

"Hi, hon," he said. "Where are you?"

"I'm in a gorgeous suite in the Grand Hotel Kempinski, enjoying a fabulous view of Lake Geneva.

"Wonderful. How was the cruise?"

"The ship and the crew were great, the food acceptable, and the tours exhausting."

"Did you learn anything good?" said Gatsby.

"Yes, that I hate touring."

"And Joyce?"

"She found her passion. She's been talking to Moe about taking a Rhine Cruise." She paused. "How's it going there?"

"Colin, Everett, and I have been refining the private placement memorandum. I'm leaving for New York tomorrow to test the water. Wish me luck."

"You have it," said Miriam. "Any rumblings from Shirley?"

"Shit, yes. She had run-ins with both Colin and Everett. She threw a glass of water in Everett's face when she cursed him out for being my CPA."

"And Colin?" said Miriam.

"She wrote him a note stating she could no longer volunteer at the concerts because he's representing me."

"She'll never stop," said Miriam.

"We've talked about this, Miriam. We must adhere to our plan and not let her distract us."

There was a long pause in the conversation. Miriam felt the words in her throat and was gripped by the sheer power of habit. She and Gatsby loved each other. They trusted each other. It was an unaccustomed feeling to leave a blank in the conversation where she would have normally told him everything. This lie of omission would take an effort she wasn't sure she could match.

Gatsby said, "Miriam, are you still there?"

"Yes," said Miriam. "I need to get off the phone. It's been a long day and I'm bushed. Good luck in New York."

"Good night sweetheart. I love you. I'm counting the days until our rendezvous."

Miriam plugged her phone into the charger. She took one last look at the lake. "Achmed Khordroy, where are you?"

CHAPTER 26

MIRIAM

June 29, 2003

The driver arrived at the hotel at nine o'clock sharp. Miriam was in the lobby waiting for him. After the driver introduced himself and inquired about the schedule for the day, she said the first destination was the Bridge Club des Bruges. "It's less than ten minutes away on the Avenue Jules-Crosnier. I have a meeting at nine thirty, so we can head over there now."

They pulled up to the entrance of a several-story office building. Miriam asked the driver to wait in the car. She entered the building, approached the security desk and asked for the location of the Club des Bruges.

"Down the hall and to the left," he said with a definite English accent. "The game doesn't start until ten."

She followed the directions of the security officer and entered a large room that contained approximately twenty to thirty bridge tables and accompanying chairs. At the center of the long wall was the manager's station consisting of three desks, several filing cabinets and storage units which probably housed the cards, bid boxes and scoring sheets.

She approached the apparent manager and said, "Monsieur Vallons?"

He nodded and stood.

"I'm Miriam Brooks. We talked last night."

"*Je suis enchanté de faire votre connaissance.*"

"Thank you," said Miriam. "Can we sit at a table?"

"Certainly." When they were seated at the bridge table, she removed the photograph from her briefcase and placed it in front of him. "This is Achmed Khordroy and me in 1998 on Saint Martin Island. We were neighbors and friends. He moved away later that year to one of the French-speaking cantons. Unfortunately, he did not send me his new address. Achmed is a Life Master, and bridge is a large portion of his life. I am certain he is living in a place that is a short drive to one or more bridge clubs. That's how I hope to find him and reconnect with him."

Vallons picked up the photo and studied Achmed's face. He shook his head. "Neither his face nor his name is familiar. He does not play at this club."

Miriam felt her stomach drop. "Do you have any suggestions?" she said. "There are four other clubs in cities along the lake. The farthest, in Monthey, is about a two-hour drive. You have time to visit all four of the clubs today and inquire whether their managers recognize your friend. Since he a Life Master, the manager will know whether he competes at the club."

He stood and walked over to the bank of filing cabinets, opened a drawer, and extracted a sheet of paper. He returned to the table and offered it to Miriam. "Here is a list of all the clubs in the French-speaking cantons, along with the names of the managers, their phone numbers and club addresses. The cities are all accessible from Highways A1 and A9. Your driver will not have any problem locating them."

Miriam stood up and, took the sheet, and said, "Thank you, Monsieur Vallons."

"You're welcome and good luck."

Miriam walked back to her car, gave the sheet to her driver, and asked him to take her to the next bridge club.

"That would be the one called Nyon. It is about a half hour's drive."

"That's fine," said Miriam. She leaned back in the seat and closed her eyes. She was still optimistic. But what if she could not locate Achmed? Well, then the Gatsby's leave-her-to-heaven strategy would become operative by default. At least Miriam would have the satisfaction of having tried harder than Gatsby to eliminate Shirley from their lives.

On the other hand, if she did find Achmed and he agreed to take on the assignment, did she expect to feel any guilt or remorse when she received word that Shirley had disappeared without a trace? She didn't think she would but figured she couldn't know for sure. As of now, she felt absolutely no compunction over arranging for Shirley's death. There would be no peace until she was out of their lives for good.

The Club de Nyon was smaller than the Bridge de Bruges. Fortunately, there was no game in progress. She approached the manager and addressed him, stating that M. Vallons had recommended she contact him. She repeated her story, but the manager of the Club de Nyon did not recognize Achmed's name or face, and seemed skeptical that someone would travel across the world to conduct such a search in person. She returned to the car and asked the driver to head to Lausanne, the next club on the list, hoping that the manager wouldn't put the others on their guard.

The Lausanne Club was large, on the order of the Bridge de Bruges in Geneva, and a game was in progress. The manager was engaged in a conversation, so Miriam stood back until he was free. Then she approached, stated M. Vallons in Geneva had recommended she contact him, not mentioning the skeptical second manager. She repeated her story and displayed the photograph again.

The manager smiled. "Achmed has competed in several tournaments we've hosted. But he is not a regular. I believe he lives southeast of the lake. I understand he plays regularly at the Club de Bridge Monthey. It's about a forty-five-minute drive from here. If you see him, please give him my regards and tell him we miss him."

It took all the self-control Miriam could muster not to jump up in the air and yell. She thanked the manager profusely and literally ran back to the car. She instructed the driver to head to the Monthey club.

As they drove southeast on the way to Monthey, Miriam could hardly contain her glee. She was certain she would locate Achmed. Now the only hurdle that remained was convincing him to take on the assignment. For now, the search was satisfying for its own sake, and she gave no further thought to the gravity of its ultimate purpose.

When she arrived at the Club de Bridge Monthey, all the tables were occupied, and a game was in progress. She approached the manager, introduced herself and asked him whether Achmed Khordroy was playing tonight. He nodded and pointed to a table located along the wall. She looked over the four occupants of the table, all of whom were men. The faces of two of them were not visible from her vantage point. She waited until the hand was over. Two stood up and began to move to the next table. And then she saw him. She called his name and walked as rapidly and gracefully toward him as she could, given she really wanted to break into a run.

He turned toward her and when he recognized her his face broke into a huge smile. He opened his arms and she fell into them.

"*Ma cherie!*" he said. "*Quelle surprise!*"

She started to cry. "I was scared to death that I wouldn't find you."

He disentangled himself from her arms and said, "I'm going to be tied up here until nine p.m. Is Gatsby with you?"

"He's in New York on business."

"That's helpful," he said. "Where are you staying?"

"Grand Hotel Kempinski in Geneva."

"I'll be there by eleven tomorrow," said Achmed.

"Wonderful," said Miriam, "and bring along a bag. We have a lot of ground to cover."

"*D'accord.*" Then he kissed her on both cheeks and moved on to the next table.

The following morning, slightly after eleven, Achmed called her room from the hotel lobby. She provided her room number. While she was talking to him, she slipped off the terrycloth robe she was wearing so that the surprise of her body, she hoped, would give her the upper hand.

He knocked on the door. As Miriam opened the door, she grabbed Achmed by the shirt and pulled him and his bag into the room. She wrapped her arms around his neck and her legs around his hips. She broke lip contact just long enough to say, "I'm anxious for today's activities to begin."

"*Mais bien sûr*," he said, and lifted her up and carried her over to the bed.

And so, they resumed the affair that had been interrupted by the Saint Martin gendarmes five years earlier.

At around three, they ordered a late lunch from room service, and by four they had resumed their lovemaking until they both fell asleep. Miriam awoke first. She took a shower and then ordered a carafe of martinis and smoked-salmon appetizers. She noticed that Achmed was stirring so she got back into bed and cuddled up to him.

When he was awake, she said, "How do you feel?"

He laughed. "Like a teenage boy after his first sexual experience with a sexy older woman."

"You're no slouch, either," said Miriam. "And that says a lot coming from the wife of Philadelphia's number one Casanova."

"I'm fortunate that you and Gatsby have an arrangement."

"He takes advantage of it a lot more than I do. There are just not many guys in our circle that do it for me."

"Well," said Achmed, "I'm doubly fortunate that you've saved all this energy for me." He paused. "What's your schedule?"

"I'm in Geneva tomorrow. On the next day, Gatsby arrives, and I'll meet him at the airport in the afternoon." Miriam kissed him, and looked deep into his eyes, "I had a second motive for coming to Geneva and tracking you down. Let's just say, I'm in desperate need of your professional services."

Achmed laughed. "And I thought you had gone to all that trouble and expense for the sole purpose of resuscitating our affair."

"That, too," said Miriam. "Are you still in business?"

"Yes," he said. "Bridge doesn't pay well, so I need to supplement from time to time. I assume that is what you're talking about."

"Definitely," said Miriam.

"Then," said Achmed, "I suggest we put on our business clothes, discuss your requirement over the martinis and smoked salmon, and take in this fine day from the balcony." He jumped out of bed and headed to the bathroom.

When they were both dressed and seated at the round table that held their plates and martini glasses, Achmed said, "Now I'm ready to hear about your project."

Miriam took out a photo of Shirley and over the next half hour, related the whole saga in detail, including how her actions and antics had affected Gatsby's business and how they could affect it in the future.

"I understand your problem," said Achmed. "How does Gatsby feel about it?"

"He feels helpless. He's talked to her, threatened her, pleaded with her. All to no avail. He's resigned himself to have to deal with the blowback."

"Does Gatsby know what you're planning?"

"No, and unlike this affair, he would not approve of it if he knew anything about it. I do not intend to share any aspect of it with him."

"I see," said Achmed.

"Shirley is going to be on Saint Martin the week of November 23 and will be staying in our timeshare condo. I'd like her to disappear that week."

"That's convenient," said Achmed.

"I was sure you'd find it so," said Miriam.

"Will she be staying alone?"

"I don't know."

"If she has companions, there is a possibility of collateral damage."

Miriam raised her eyebrows, pretty sure she'd caught his meaning.

"Yes," he confirmed, "if the companion interferes with our operation, it may be necessary to have him or her disappear also, so as not to compromise our security. Also, if there is more than one companion, it may be necessary to abort the operation."

Miriam sighed. She was unprepared for the possibility that by ordering Shirley's murder she would be inadvertently ordering the murder of an innocent bystander. *Collateral damage*. What a euphemistic way of putting it.

"Well?" said Achmed.

"You do what you have to do to get Shirley to disappear without a trace."

"This deal is going to cost you $75,000. How are you going to pay for it?"

Miriam took off her earrings and handed them to Achmed. "If you have them appraised, I am certain they will more than cover your fee." She scrounged around on the desk and handed him a hotel envelope to carry the earrings.

Achmed put the earrings in the envelope, sealed it, and put in his jacket pocket and zipped the pocket closed. He drained his martini. He checked his watch, it was already 10 p.m.

"Let's go get a late dinner. There is a great bistro about a five-minute walk from here."

~~~~~~

During dinner they talked about their lives and history on Saint Martin from the early 1990s until Achmed's expulsion. How their affair emerged from the French lessons that Miriam and several other residents of their condo association took from him; then the fishing trips, beach parties, scuba diving excursions and bridge parties. That was their Saint Martin experience. As they talked, laughed, and mused, Miriam recalled how much she'd loved Achmed and how difficult it had been to maintain the affair in the compact Saint Martin environment.

After Achmed asked for the check, he said, "I have a game tomorrow morning in Monthey that will go until noon. I'm going to leave tomorrow at six. After the game I'll have your earrings appraised and give some thought to your project and how it might be accomplished. By the time I get back to your hotel, which will be around six in the evening, I'll have made my decision and we can discuss it."

"That will be fine," said Miriam. "Can you stay overnight?"

"Of course," said Achmed, "assuming you're not angry with me if I turn you down."

She grabbed his left hand, squeezed it, and looked directly at him. "I would be disappointed, but it will not affect how much I love you."
~~~~~~

He leaned over and kissed her. *"C'est bon."*

When Miriam turned out the light that night and cuddled up to Achmed, she felt relaxed and free of anxiety. The reunion could not have gone better. It certainly had boosted her ego to know she could still satisfy her ex-lover after a five-year hiatus. As for the Shirley problem, she had done everything she could do. She hoped Achmed would take the assignment, but she was mentally and emotionally prepared for him to decline. If he did, she would have no alternative but to accept Gatsby's approach.

The next morning, Achmed left the hotel at sunup as planned. When Miriam arose, she had breakfast in her room, got dressed and left the hotel around 10:30 to shop so she would have some clothes to show Gatsby and provide some confirmation she spent most of her time in Geneva relaxing and shopping. When she returned to the hotel, there was a note from Achmed. He expected to arrive around eight and requested she order dinner from room service along with martinis and a bottle of Beaujolais.

When he arrived, he kissed her, threw his jacket on the bed, reached for a martini and said, "Let's talk."

Miriam said, "Dinner will arrive in about twenty minutes."

"Bien."

They sat down at the table inside the room, at Achmed's request. Even though the balcony was located far enough from the next room to be private, Miriam felt tentatively hopeful that his extra discretion meant he was bringing good news.

She lifted her martini and said, "To us."

Ahmed clinked the glasses and said, *"A votre santé."* When he'd placed his glass on the table, he lowered his voice. "I had the earrings appraised and they are adequate to cover our fee. But this deal has a lot of complications. One, I am well-known on Saint Martin and if I'm recognized, the gendarmes would cause me no end of grief. Two, Shirley may not be staying alone. She could have one or more companions. My associate and I will be able to handle two people. If there are more, we would have to abort. In that case I would return $25,000 to you."

"So, you'll do it?" said Shirley.

"We'll try. But for the reasons I just enumerated, success is not guaranteed. Also, you realize that in the event Shirley has one companion, he or she is likely to share the same fate. Do you understand?"

Miriam pondered the question. She was surprised at how uncomfortable she was with the possibility of what Achmed had referred to as collateral damage. It was enough she wanted to cancel the whole proposition and admit she, like Gatsby, had limits. But, she thought, be rational. If she was willing to murder Shirley, how was one life worth any less or any more than another? There was something monstrous about the plan no matter what—and she'd already been comfortable enough with it she hunted down Achmed in the first place.

She said, "I understand." Then she stood up from the table, grabbed Achmed's hand and led him to the bed. "Let seal the deal."

CHAPTER 27

JERRY

June 30, 2003

The sun was just beginning to set as Jerry emerged from the subway exit at 5th Avenue and East 69th Street. The day had been especially warm, and he had felt uncharacteristically lethargic.

They had spent the weekend at their cottage in the Catskills. The weekend had been packed with dinner parties, hiking, fly fishing, picnics—and a visit to the emergency room when Alli was bitten by a snake. Jerry had been exhausted when they'd arrived home late last night, and he still didn't have a clue as to how he managed to get up and make an 8 a.m. meeting. He could not help feeling some nostalgia for the old days—pre-Helen, pre-kids, and pre-mortgage, when it was just him and Chelsey, his beloved Golden Retriever. The weekend had been fun, relaxing, full of great food and great wine. Unfortunately, great sex was never on the agenda anymore. He and Helen barely had either the time, energy, or privacy to rub elbows let alone anything else. The song that kept going through his head all weekend was, *"Those were the days my friend, we thought they'd never end..."*

As he walked along Central Park toward his apartment on East 69th, he caught himself in a reverie. He realized that Chelsey, the last vestige of his pre-Helen life, was almost fourteen, and when she was gone, that prior life would be only a memory. There were times he felt he would do anything to recapture that life. But on reflection he realized he could not give up either Helen or his boys.

But he wasn't happy. He was perpetually tired, bored, and frustrated over the situational celibacy. The same old litany: *I'm tired, the kids were out of control today, Chelsey was sick and threw up all over the living room, I have a headache, I have my period…*

He greeted the doorman of the apartment house, said hi to one of his neighbors who'd entered the building at the same time and took the elevator to the twelfth floor. As he turned the key in the lock of the apartment, he heard Chelsey's signature bark (dog for "He's home!") followed by the yells and screams of Alli and Josh as they raced each other to the door to see who could be the first to greet him. He pushed open the door and was immediately surrounded by his two boys and Chelsey, all imploring him for attention. He bent down, and the boys engulfed him in their arms as Chelsea licked his face.

Helen yelled, "Hi," from the kitchen. "Chelsey's been at the front door since three o'clock. I think she's feeling some anxiety over the separation after four days of togetherness."

Jerry closed the front door, set down his briefcase, and sat on the floor patting Chelsey and hugging his two boys. He felt a surge of guilt over his prior misgivings about his marriage and his life. No more time for ruminating. He was happy and this is what he'd wanted.

He lifted Alli in his arms, and with Chelsea and Josh trailing behind, he walked into the kitchen to greet Helen, who was at the stove stirring dinner. The smell of garlic, hoisin, and other spices emanated from a large frying pan.

"I'm trying a new chicken stir-fry recipe."

"Smells great," he said. Holding Alli in his right arm, he used his left hand to turn Helen's face toward his and kissed her. "I missed you," he said.

"Me too, but I need to keep stirring. I don't want it to burn."

She turned back to the stove.

"I'm going to fix myself a drink. Want anything?"

"No, I'm fine. Dinner in thirty minutes. Will you feed the dog?"

"Sure." He carried Alli into the spacious family room as Josh and Chelsey followed. He set Alli on the large sectional. "Josh, sit next to your brother. Daddy needs to fix his drink and then he'll give you his full attention."

"Hurry, Dad," said Alli, "don't linger."

"Yeah, don't linger," said Josh.

Jerry stopped in his tracks and turned back to his sons. "When did you learn that?"

"Today," said Josh. "Mrs. Rantz scolded me for lingering at recess. I taught the word to Alli."

Jerry smiled at his sons. "I'm impressed. I'll only be a minute and then you can both tell me about your day. Linger all you want."

Later, while they were eating dinner, Jerry casually mentioned that Gatsby was in town and he was meeting him for lunch. Helen did not respond immediately, and for a moment, she seemed poised to dig further. But then she took a bite of the stir-fry and said, "I think this needs something. It's too bland." She stood and walked toward the refrigerator and took out a bottle of chipotle chili sauce. She brought it back to the table and handed it to Jerry.

"Here, try this." Jerry shook several drops over his stir-fry and mixed it up and tasted it. "That's it," he said, and handed the bottle to Helen. As Helen shook the sauce into her plate she said, "Did he tell you why he wanted to see you?"

"No, he didn't. He said he was in town for a few days and he wanted to get together to schmooze. I asked Birney and Jeff to join us—you remember that Birney was the connection to Moe Shultz and then to Gatsby."

Helen tasted her stir-fry. "Good. I'll add this to my recipe. Oh shit! Alli, you spilled your milk!"

Jerry had not been entirely truthful with Helen. He knew how much Helen despised Gatsby and he did not want to give her any excuse for haranguing him. In fact, Gatsby had been straightforward with Jerry about his problem. He was trying to raise one hundred million dollars for a new venture capital fund, and he wanted to explore whether Jerry and his boss Birney could help him. Jerry had explained that the only financing he and Birney ever worked on was specific to mergers and acquisitions; but Jeff's firm, Goldman Sachs, routinely raised private placement money and did IPOs, so he might be able to help. He would have told all this to Helen had she asked, but when she returned to the table and said nothing more about it, he assumed she didn't want to know.

~~~~~

Jerry had arranged for them to all meet for lunch at Fraunces Tavern on Pearl Street in the Financial District. Now they were seated at a table enjoying the exotic beers for which Fraunces was renowned. Birney asked Gatsby how Moe was and whether he'd seen him recently.

Gatsby laughed. "I talk to him every day. He agreed to serve as CEO for one of the deals that I'm promoting and raised a lot of money for, some of which is Moe's. Jerry reviewed and evaluated the situation back in February. Moe was reluctant to take it on—and he's not comfortable with that role, so he calls me constantly."

"Why did he do it?" said Birney.

"Because I twisted his arm. Moe's got a big stake in the deal and the CEO he replaced—per Jerry's recommendation—was underwhelming. I'm searching for a permanent hire for the job." He turned to Jeff. "Jerry told me that you saw action in Vietnam."

"Guilty as charged," said Jeff.

"I was in the army four years. But I had a pretty cushy job in intelligence. I never got near the action."

"You were fortunate. There is no glory in being shot at, especially for a worthless cause."

Gatsby abruptly turned to Jerry and suggested they get started, as he had to leave in forty-five minutes for a meeting with a banker.

Jerry took charge but suggested that Gatsby explain to Birney and Jeff exactly what his objectives were. In between giving the waiter their food orders, Gatsby quickly related the key parts of his CV, ending with
~~~~~

his last ten years as an independent consultant and money-finder for startups.

"I've raised money for and consulted with seventeen firms during the last ten years. Three turned out to be successful investments, one returned its capital, four failed, and I'm currently involved in nine. The payoffs of my options in the three that were successful plus consulting income, when the firms can afford to pay it, have provided my family a decent lifestyle. But it's basically working for wages. Constantly having to raise money for individual deals from individual investors is hard work; I can't afford the staff to vet deals properly and my income fluctuates between starvation and luxury—which is hard on a marriage. My objective is to do what I've been doing, but instead of operating in a retail environment for wages, I want to operate in the wholesale environment of a venture capital fund where my income is steady, and I have a significant upside."

Jeff looked at his watch. "Tell us about the three successes, and the nine deals you're currently involved with—highlights only. Say two minutes per company, and then you can send us the paperwork when you get back to Philadelphia."

"Okay," said Gatsby, "here you go," and he launched into a description of the twelve companies. He had a knack for being clear, cogent and interesting. As he was completing his exposition he glanced at his watch and said, "I'm already running late. I need to leave for my next meeting."

Jerry, Jeff, and Birney all stood up. Gatsby said, "I appreciate your giving me the time to pitch my project," and he proceeded to shake everybody's hand and take his leave.

Jerry said, "The three of us will talk about this and see if we're able to help. I'll email you."

"That will be great," said Gatsby, "take care," and he quickly left.

When Gatsby was gone, Jerry asked Jeff and Birney whether they had time to debrief. They both nodded. "So, what do you think?" said Jerry.

"Moe thinks the guy walks on water," said Birney.

"Who's Moe?" asked Jeff.

"Moe Shultz, one of Philadelphia's billionaires," said Birney, "prominent philanthropist, and car dealership mogul. He inherited significant money and leveraged it into his current fortune. A lot of buildings, galleries, and monuments carry the Shultz name. He met Gatsby in the eighties when they were both at Wharton and has invested in several of his deals."

Jeff took a large swallow of beer and turned to Jerry. "You met Gatsby early in the year, didn't you? Wasn't he in some charity event with Eddie Griffin?"

"More or less," said Jerry. "At Moe's request, Birney sent me to Philadelphia to meet with Gatsby and evaluate a private placement memo for EVG, the deal he mentioned. The basketball thing was a few months later. He's got it all: the money, the charisma, the beautiful wife… He's dynamic enough to pull this thing off, I think."

"And I think we collectively could raise the money," said Jeff, "assuming we can adequately vet him. That part is not going to be easy."

"I don't think that will be a problem," said Birney. "Moe probably knows almost everyone who has worked or is working with him and I'm sure he'll help."

Jeff went to the bar and returned with another round. "Here's what I suggest. First, we vet Gatsby so we can vouch for his experience, competence, and integrity. Second, we review the draft of the private placement memorandum that Gatsby's attorneys prepared and ensure it will pass muster with the bankers and investors we plan to show it to. Third, we fill a room with enough prospects to raise one hundred million and give Gatsby the platform to sell his deal. We charge the fund $50,000 for a retainer and out-of-pocket expenses plus one percent of what we raise, and we split the proceeds between our two firms."

"How many prospects should we invite to the presentation?" Birney asked.

"I'd shoot for fifty," said Jerry. "Gatsby wants to get the deal done before Christmas, so it would be helpful to create a potentially large demand for shares. Incidentally, Gatsby told me he believes he can raise between five and ten million from his current investor pool. He said partners in Goldman and KKR have invested in one of his deals."

"Great," said Jeff. "Get me the names of any Wall Street partners who have invested in any of his deals, including the failures. I need to make sure that any negative information that is on the Street is not sufficient to undermine this project. And I'll work on the auditorium and the date of the presentation. I'll have one of my colleagues develop a prospect list. Jerry, I assume that you'll handle the vetting?"

"Sure," said Jerry. "Also, I suggest that all three of us be involved in reviewing the private placement memorandum."

"Good idea," said Jeff.

"Definitely," said Birney.

"Jerry," said Jeff, "could you draft the email to Gatsby and run in by us for comments?"

"Sure," said Jerry. "You'll have it by the end of the day."

CHAPTER 28

GATSBY

July 3, 2003

As Gatsby emerged from the secure area of the Geneva Airport, Miriam rushed to him with a huge bouquet of roses and threw her arms around him. He let go of his rollaway and reciprocated.

"Holy Christ, did I miss you," he said. "It's been way too long."

"I know. I'm so happy to be in your arms. I'm suffering from acute arousal. Let's go straight to the hotel."

He kissed her and pressed his hips into her body. "Absolutely. Let's go."

During the taxi drive to the Hotel Kempinski, Gatsby said, "Did you enjoy your time in Switzerland?"

"Yes. Our hotel is fabulous. It's right on the lake. I spent my time reading, eating, and shopping and breathing that famous air. I'm fully recovered from the Danube cruise."

"You've had quite a trip," said Gatsby. "Any problems?"

"Just the usual challenges when you're making travel arrangements during a trip." She leaned over and put her left hand over his hand. "But I lost the diamond earrings that you gave me on our fifth anniversary. I was devastated, but I resolved not to let it ruin my trip."

Gatsby glanced toward her briefly. "Where did you lose them?"

"I had them on the cruise. When I got to the hotel in Geneva, I thought I remembered putting them in the room safe, but when I went to get them, they weren't there. I just have no idea. I know they were expensive."

"Very," said Gatsby. "But they're well-insured. Shit happens. Don't fret over it. I'll call the insurance company when we get back to the States and file a claim."

"You're not upset?"

"Come on, Miriam. You know me better than that." He leaned over and kissed her.

They arrived at the hotel. After Gatsby had paid the driver, Miriam grabbed Gatsby's free hand and looked into his eyes. "The wine is in the refrigerator, the fire is on, the bed is made. Let's go pick up where we left off."

CHAPTER 29

JERRY

July 14, 2003

Jerry had previously sent an email to Gatsby confirming that Goldman Sachs and Bricker and Weldon would consider raising the $100 million to capitalize the Gatsby Venture Fund, subject to the completion of their due diligence. Now, Birney, Jeff, and Jerry met in the familiar, almost homey conference room of Bricker and Weldon. The conference table was littered with piles of paper. All three of them read documents and made notes. Birney looked at his watch.

"Okay," said Birney, "I think we need to accomplish the following items before the weekend so we can get them back to Frye and make sure we are all reading from the same page of the musical score." He picked up a yellow pad and read them off.

"Jerry will brief us on the results of his vetting of Gatsby.

"Then," continued Birney, "we all need to review the operating agreement for the Gatsby Venture Fund. I've looked it over and it needs to be beefed up with respect to the operational and financial reports, the composition of the advisory board, and the procedures for calling an advisory board meeting. I suggest the three of us read it a like a love letter, make our comments and then we'll all review them and formulate the response to Frye. Agreed?"

Jerry said, "Fine."

Jeff nodded. "We need to set the location and date of the investor meeting and prepare the invitation list. I think fifty invitees will be adequate. If we can't raise $100 million with fifty, we won't be able to raise it with five times as many."

"I agree," said Jerry. "How about each of us generates twenty-five names and then we'll get together and review and select. I suggest we use the rest of the morning to review the results of my vetting of Gatsby."

Jerry grabbed a group of documents and went to the front of the room where there was a whiteboard. "I'm going to present some of the details of my investigation, answer any questions you have and then present my overall summary and recommendation. First, we discussed Gatsby's CV when we all met for lunch. He currently has nine deals in the oven; five are promising and would be candidates for an investment by the Gatsby Venture Fund."

"I assume Gatsby already has stakes in these companies?" said Birney.

"No doubt," said Jerry.

"I suggest we create a separate paragraph in the operating agreement to address the potential conflicts that can arise if he wants to put fund money in any of the nine companies."

"Absolutely."

"He is active in Republican politics. His CV indicates he's held almost twenty-five positions as a member or officer of a committee. Look at page 2. But that's not all—he also lists over thirty nonprofits he's been involved with. Look at page 3. Now it's evident that both his political and nonprofit activities have provided access to large pools of investors and business opportunities. But the sheer volume raises the question as to how he carves out time for them and still can attend to business, find time for his family, and indulge his passion for scrub basketball. The guy can't possibly sleep more than four hours a night."

Birney and Jeff reviewed the three-page CV. "I've probably looked at 10,000 resumes in the last twenty years," said Birney, "and I've never seen one like this. Is it real?"

"Well," said Jerry, as he shuffled through the papers, "the interviews appear to support it. I interviewed eleven individuals who know him.

The names were provided by Moe. Eight are CEOs, entrepreneurs, and executives. There is one general, one MD, and one basketball friend. They've known Gatsby an aggregate of 105 years. They all vouch for his integrity. One made the point he has been in the public eye so long that if there were any skeletons in his closet they would already have been revealed."

"What were the comments regarding his strengths and weaknesses?" said Jeff.

"Only a couple commented on weaknesses. They said his reporting was weak, and he does not have strong operational skills—which is no surprise, as he is primarily a dealmaker. As for his strengths, most of the interviewees were rhapsodic. He's a quick study, has good judgment, has the contacts and skills, isn't prone to leap at a sexy story, knows how to build a business, creates value… It goes on and on."

Jeff shook his head and smiled. "Seems just too good to be true."

"Exactly," said Jerry. "But I have no idea how to go about disproving it." They both turned to Birney. "What do you think? What else can we do to vet him?"

Birney sat quietly, thinking through all the options. Finally, he said, "I think we go with what we've got. Maybe we're all so jaded we can't recognize a gift-horse when it presents itself. And you, Jeff?" said Birney. "Do you have reservations?"

"None that I can articulate. He is too slick, too polished for my taste. I admit, I'm chronically cautious. I'm still back in 'Nam looking at a crowd of apparently innocent civilians wondering when one of them is going to pull a grenade out of their rucksack. Notwithstanding my gut, I'll vote to go forward."

"I'm in also," said Birney. "It's unanimous, and the Gatsby Venture Fund is off and running. Let's reassemble at 2 p.m. and work on the operating agreement."

CHAPTER 30

GATSBY

While Jerry, Jeff and Birney were concluding their meeting in New York, Kyle Rowan was in Harrisburg, speaking into the microphone of a tape recorder.

"My name is Kyle Rowan, securities compliance officer. Present with me is Mr. Christopher Gatsby Brooks and Nathan Mitchell, chief of enforcement. We are here pursuant to the investigation of Mr. Brooks' convertible promissory notes. Mr. Brooks, do you acknowledge that this meeting is being recorded?"

Gatsby responded. "Yes, I do."

"Also, Mr. Brooks," I want to confirm that although you're entitled to have your attorney participate in this meeting, you've decided to represent yourself. Is that correct?"

Gatsby responded, "Yes, it is."

"And, Mr. Brooks, I want to confirm that you've provided a notebook which contains copies of all the convertible promissory notes that have been sold by you since you first started selling convertible promissory notes. Is that correct?"

Gatsby responded, "Yes, it is."

"I guess, basically, the purpose of our meeting today is to just get some information about all these transactions. You gave us a whole notebook and there are a lot of transactions—so Nathan and I need some background on them."

Rowan picked up a large three-ring binder and gave it to Gatsby. "Mr. Brooks, I'm handing you a notebook, which is a copy of the book you gave us, supplemented by a spreadsheet that summarizes all the notes that have been issued, including the ones that have been paid off, and the ones that are still outstanding. In summary, the spreadsheet shows that you've been selling these notes for approximately ten years and have assigned options in fifteen different companies to various investors. Our calculations show that as of the end of last month, the aggregate principal of the notes is $5.65 million, and the accrued and unpaid interest is $860,000. Does our analysis agree with your understanding, Mr. Brooks?"

Gatsby responded, "Yes, it does."

"Okay," said Kyle, "let's move to the specifics of the companies that you are currently sponsoring. Can you go through them, one by one, giving us the history of the company, a description of its products, services and characteristics of its customer base, the current capitalization, the sales, and profits, if any, some of the major investors and what the current prospects are? That will give us a framework to continue the discussion."

Gatsby smiled and felt almost comfortable in his suit and tie. He had anticipated what their line of questioning would be, and he was prepared. He opened his briefcase and pulled out a thick sheaf of paper and handed it to Kyle. "I thought that you would be asking about the companies I am sponsoring, so I prepared a spreadsheet and backup documentation." He sat back in his chair and waited while Kyle and Nathan pored over the document. As they turned the pages, they whispered back and forth.

"Well," said Kyle, "I appreciate your providing this information. It will take as a while to digest it, but let's just dig right in. We're particularly interested in those companies which have not had a liquidity event and the CPNs are outstanding. Is that okay with you, Mr. Brooks?"

"Fine," said Gatsby.

"Tell me about Philadelphia Medical Systems."

"Philadelphia Medical Systems is obviously located in Philly. Its shareholders are accredited investors in the Pennsylvania. The company is trying to solve one of the Holy Grails of medicine—how to determine accurately, inexpensively, and noninvasively how much blood the heart is pumping beat-to-beat to the rest of the body. The largest reimbursement category in the federal Medicaid/Medicare system is related to congestive heart failure. It's a twenty-billion-dollar problem. There are about five million people in the United States who have been diagnosed with congestive heart failure and at least another half a million join the pool each year. Typically, these people are on pacemakers, beta-blockers, and various other drug therapies that are designed to relax the heart and get more blood to circulate through the body. But if the patient fails to respond, he or she winds up in the hospital either in intensive care or surgery while the docs try to figure out what to do to stabilize the heart." He paused, savoring the chasm that divided his expertise from the DoBS bureaucrats. He could tell they were following, but just barely.

"You don't mind if I get up and move around, do you?"

Kyle looked at Nathan, who nodded. "Make yourself comfortable."

"Thanks," said Gatsby. He stood, walked eight steps and then turned and came back to the table. "Having an accurate method of measuring blood flow is so important. As of now the most accurate measurement is achieved with a catheter that needs to be installed in the right ventricle of the heart. It's dangerous when the patient is in critical condition, and it's expensive." He sat down. "The technology Philadelphia Medical Systems is developing is based on microwave technology. The current device looks like an old hairdryer our moms used when we were growing up."

"This is a medical measuring device?" said Kyle.

"It's a diagnostic tool. And we have to take it through an FDA approval process—but it's a less formidable challenge than what you need to do to get a new drug approved."

"What's the status of the company?" said Nathan.

"The company is doing well in terms of developing its technology and pursuing its intellectual property activities, and this could be a wonderful story for Philadelphia and the Perelman School of Medicine at the University of Pennsylvania, which is doing some of the clinical work."

"When was the company started?" said Kyle.

"Within the past two years."

"Do you currently have patents?"

"We have an exclusive license from the patent holder."

"Who is the CEO?" asked Tatum.

"He is an Israeli, Moshe Stein. He got his PhD from Harvard. The details of the officers and directors are included in the notebook I provided."

"So, what is the probability that this company will have a liquidity event in the next year or so that would result in the conversion of the corresponding CPNs?" said Nathan.

"I think it's pretty damn good," said Gatsby. "Currently there are about forty cardiovascular drugs going through the regulatory approval process, and as of now, the technology that is used to measure blood flow uses ultrasound, and the tests cost $700 each and take about forty-five minutes to do. We expect that the cost of a test using our electromagnetic technology will eventually come in at $25. That makes us a very attractive target for an acquisition. I mean, the markets are huge. We're talking about the potential for billions of dollars in sales every year if somebody achieves this breakthrough—and we think we have it within our grasp. There is just an enormous number of companies and individuals both on Wall Street and in the industrial community that will want this technology."

"You're pretty high on Philadelphia Medical Systems being successful."

"Absolutely," said Gatsby.

Kyle turned to Nathan. "Do you have any further questions about Philadelphia Medical?"

"No," said Nathan.

"Well, then let's move on. Mr. Brooks, tell me about EVG."

Three hours later, having exhausted all his and Nathan's questions about the nine companies that Gatsby was currently sponsoring, Kyle turned to Nathan and sighed. He closed the notebook and looking directly at Gatsby.

"I guess what we want to get into, uh…next, would be… Can you just give us a little background on these convertible promissory notes? I mean they go back many years, and, uh…" He rubbed his eyes. They were all feeling fatigued, but for some reason, he refused to grant a break. "Mr. Brooks, I'll be honest with you. Neither Nathan nor I have ever seen anything like this in the way of…you know, this type of debt instrument, if you want to call it that. So, give us some information about how it came about—I mean this format. Is it something that you created? Is it something you got from an attorney? Do you understand what I'm getting at?"

Gatsby shifted in his seat and pushed his chair back slightly to escape Kyle's stare. If only he had a moment to splash his face and collect himself, he could summon his energy again. He placed his notebook on the table and took a sip of water. "Sure. That's fine," he said.

"A number of years ago I, uh, had a friend who was in some financial difficulty. I had a high regard for him and his family. He had a serious medical problem that was going to be with him for many years. He had followed some of the things that I had done, companies I'd helped, like the ones we've been discussing." He moved his gaze from Nathan to Kyle. "He asked me from time to time if he could invest in one or more of these projects that I was involved with. And I told him that would not be possible because he was not a 'qualified investor' per the Pennsylvania securities laws. He didn't understand what the term meant or how it applied to him, so I explained that Pennsylvania required that investors who want to invest in risky startups must have a net worth more than $1 million or have earned income more than $200,000 per year or $300,00 per year when combined with a spouse in each of the prior two years and an expectation of the same in the current year. Well, he was extremely disappointed because we both knew he was not 'qualified,' but he literally begged me to see if there was a way he could get involved."

Gatsby paused and drained his water glass. It almost refreshed him, a little.

"So, what happened then?" said Nathan.

"Well," said Gatsby, "it so happened that at that time I had a lot of work and was short of cash, so I went to a lawyer in Philly and I asked if there was any way we could structure something that would allow me to help my friend who wanted to become involved in one of my projects so he would be protected on the downside. In return for his helping me, by lending me money, I'd give him the opportunity to participate in the upside of one of these ventures, but I would be the guarantor of the note, so he'd have absolutely no exposure if the company was not successful. That's what I asked my attorney."

"And what did the attorney recommend?" asked Kyle.

"He drafted the note form that I used in that transaction and virtually all subsequent transactions," said Gatsby. He explained the mechanism of the CPN, which he'd already been through a dozen times. When he'd finished, he stood and walked to the end of the conference table with his empty water glass, filled it, took a large gulp, and filled it again, and carried it back to his chair and sat down.

"So," said Kyle, "do you recall when this occurred?"

"It was sometime in the late 1980s," said Gatsby. "That's the date of the notice that my attorney sent to the department advising you or your predecessors we were going to take advantage of the limited offering exemption of the statute."

"I searched my files," said Kyle, "but I couldn't find anything other than the letter. Wasn't there supposed to be an attachment?"

"I only have copies of the letters in my files," said Gatsby. "I assume that the attachment was the form of the note."

"I understand," said Kyle.

"Was it your understanding, Mr. Brooks," said Nathan, "that this was something that had to be renewed annually, or was it a one-time event, that you would file, and it would remain good from that point forward?"

"Frankly," said Gatsby, "I have no idea. I just had my attorney handle it."

"Sure, we understand," said Nathan. "Were these all term notes or were they indefinite in duration—to be called by the holder at his or her option?"

"There is a definite term, typically three to five years. But there is a provision that the note could be extended at their option or mine." Gatsby got up and moved to the water pitcher, filled his glass, and walked back to his seat.

Can you describe generally what types of disclosure you gave to whoever was going to be involved in a CPN? What was said? There're obviously many companies that you're involved in, so did the person come to you and ask to be involved in a specific company?"

"That was usually the case," said Gatsby.

"Okay," said Kyle. "They heard about a company that you were already involved in before and they came to you and said, 'I'd like to be involved in this one, too.' And you said, 'Well, you're not qualified, or you're not accredited, or whatever, but there's another way I might be able to help you out.' I mean, can you just give me a generalization on how a transaction might work?"

"Well," said Gatsby, "there's an expression of interest on the part of some of these people and either they weren't qualified, or I just told them I didn't think they ought to put their money at risk because I didn't think it was...I mean, these are friends of mine."

"Okay. But what I mean is, what did they know about the company before you took their money and you issued them a CPN. Did they. I mean...did you give them—"

Gatsby interrupted, raising his voice from the soft monotone he had been using in previous responses. "They're making their judgment based on their relationship with me. They weren't getting an option to own shares of stock in AT&T. They're looking for a return hopefully greater than that which they could get by putting the money in a money market account."

"These people weren't even given a business plan for the company for which they were receiving an option?" asked Nathan.

"In some cases, yes, but that did not occur in all cases."

"Well," continued Nathan, "were they given a Gatsby & Associates business plan, or something that shows your financial solvency, your wherewithal to repay the note?"

"No," said Gatsby.

"I see," said Nathan. "you say that the folks who came to you may not have been accredited. I gather that several were—from reviewing the names on your list. I mean this list includes some of Philadelphia's most prominent and wealthy citizens."

"I've been fortunate," said Gatsby.

"In these instances, did they approach you because they knew your work, or did you seek them out, saying, for example, 'I've got something I think would be a good opportunity for you?'"

"It worked both ways," said Gatsby.

"It's getting late," said Kyle. "How much more time do you need, Nathan?"

"I just have a few more questions." He turned back to Gatsby. "Do you know which or how many of your investors were accredited?"

"Not exactly."

"Okay, and have you ever received complaints from any of the people to whom you issued CPNs?"

"No one, other than Shirley, has ever complained," he said, his voice rising again.

"And, in those cases when you paid off the notes prior to their due date, what reasons were given by the holder of the CPN?"

"They varied. The most prominent one was that a member of the family became seriously ill and they needed the money for medical expenses. That happened in three or four instances."

"And you repaid the note promptly, Mr. Brooks."

"Absolutely—the principal and all the accumulated interest."

"Thank you, Mr. Brooks." Nathan looked over to Kyle and said. "I think we're done."

"Great," said Kyle. He stood and shook Gatsby's hand. "Thanks for coming, Mr. Brooks. I'll call you if we need to set up another meeting."

As he was driving back to Philadelphia, and Gatsby replayed the scene in his head, he tried to identify exchanges in which he might have done better, been more articulate, or more concise. After fifteen minutes of this exercise, he concluded he did the best that could be done under the circumstances. They would not hang him for any of the answers he'd provided in this disposition. Unfortunately, he could not be as positive about the answers he would be providing after the inevitable next deposition.

~~~~~~

When Gatsby returned to his office, there was a message that George McKnight needed to see him ASAP. He complied immediately and found George sitting behind his desk waiting for him. He pointed to the chair in front of the desk and steepled his fingers.

"Shirley's going to be a much larger problem for you than I anticipated. She sent a package of several hundred pages to one of my wife's Assistant US Attorneys. The package was also sent to the Criminal Division of the IRS, the Securities and Exchange Commission, and the Pennsylvania Department of Banking and Securities and the Pennsylvania Attorney General. I've seen the package. All I can say it is a doozy."

"What could she possibly say about me that would take hundreds of pages?"

McKnight opened a folder and began to read in a flat voice, as if he were reading a menu. "The first section, consisting of six pages, enumerates the various crimes for which you should be prosecuted, and supports these allegations by approximately one hundred and fifty citations of meetings with various individuals, companies, and CPN investors. The package includes over one hundred exhibits. The crimes are conversion, embezzlement, breach of fiduciary duty, fraud, conspiracy, mail and
~~~~~~

wire fraud, and tax fraud. Oh, and the package includes a rather good color picture of you. Sort of a 'Meet the Criminal' touch."

Gatsby shook his head. "Holy shit."

"My sentiments exactly."

"What kind of nut-job is she?" said Gatsby.

"A dangerous nut-job," said McKnight. "She's invested hundreds of hours in preparing the package, meeting with various people, performing research on you and the various companies you sponsored. She is obsessed with you."

"I'm not flattered." He stood and paced around the room. "It's obvious she is responsible for bringing on the DoBS investigation. What is the likelihood of your wife's office initiating an investigation?"

"Slim to none," said McKnight. "They think she is certifiable. I expect that the SEC and IRS will come to the same conclusions. They get a lot of crank letters, and this will be just one more. Your problem will be the DoBS. This is their turf, and they will be quite thorough—and they will have Shirley to keep them on target and efficient."

"Well, then, I better get busy," said Gatsby, "and get the Gatsby Venture Fund launched."

"Absolutely. That is your only way out. If you can beat the Department's issuing a cease-and-desist, your stealth strategy just might be successful." George lifted his huge frame out of the chair, came around the desk and put his arm around Gatsby's shoulder. "Courage," he said, "and good luck."

CHAPTER 31

GATSBY

The following morning Gatsby floated into Frye's office and plopped into the chair in front of his desk.

"Did you see Jerry Bascomb's email?" said Gatsby.

"I did. Congratulations. You may have just hit the trifecta. I checked into both Birney and Jeff, and they represent two prestigious investment banks, and they certainly know how to raise money. Their financial proposal is reasonable—in fact, it looks to me like a teaser rate to set the stage for future business with you. Are you going to be able to give us the $25,000 retainer to finalize the private placement memorandum?"

"You can get started. I'll get you a check by Thursday."

"How did the meeting go with the State?" said Frye.

"No problems yet," said Gatsby. "I think I can stall them for a month."

"Good," said Frye. "With luck, we can put off their cease-and-desist order until the spring or summer of next year while you focus on raising the money." He leaned back in his chair, drawing his face into a grave expression that seemed a hair too studied for Gatsby's taste. "I've been thinking about the PPM for several days," Frye continued, "and looked deeply into the Pennsylvania securities laws with respect to the required disclosures. I don't see any way to finesse the DoBS's CPN investigation. We just have to disclose it."

Gatsby straightened up from his slouch as if he'd been suddenly awakened from a deep sleep.

"What are you saying?"

"We're going to have to disclose the State's investigation of your CPNs in the private placement memo we distribute to the prospective investors. There is no way around it."

Gatsby stood up and walked to the office door and shut it. Then he returned to the front of Frye's desk. He placed his hands on the desk and leaned over so that his face was about eighteen inches away from Frye's. "Now you listen to me. This is a one-hundred-million-dollar deal that is my lifeline out of an existential threat to my reputation and financial security. If the DoBS investigation is disclosed in the PPM, this deal is dead—and so am I. If the Gatsby Venture Fund gets off the ground and is successful, no one will give a fuck about the DoBS's cease-and-desist order."

"And" said Frye, "if the GVF is not a success, our firm will probably be sued."

"So what?" said Gatsby. "I'm sure your firm carries *beaucoup* insurance. Besides, I didn't do anything wrong. I drafted the note on the advice of a securities attorney; we notified this DoBS in 1990 we were invoking the limited-distribution exemption of the Pennsylvania statutes in selling the CPNs; the Department did not respond and took no action. You're supposed to be a smart lawyer. Figure out your defense if they come after your firm. This issue is non-negotiable. Make up your mind. If you will not prepare the PPM that I need, I've got to find myself a new lawyer."

Frye sat quietly and didn't respond. Finally, he stood, walked from behind his desk, put his arm on Gatsby's shoulder and said, "You've made some good points. I'll think about it and let you know tomorrow." Then he escorted Gatsby out of his office.

CHAPTER 32

GATSBY

One month later, August 14, 2003

The auditorium in the Goldman Sachs offices at 200 West Street was packed. Jeff's superior promotion skills had yielded an audience of almost seventy-five bankers, money managers and private investors to hear the Gatsby team's pitch. Gatsby smiled to himself as he looked over the crowd. Although this was a new venue for him, pitching to a large, well-heeled room of Masters of the Universe was his talent. As far as he was concerned, the financing of the Gatsby Venture Fund was a done deal. And as for the two nagging problems of the State investigation of the CPNs and the growing pressure of some CPN holders to be paid—well, like Scarlett O'Hara in *Gone with the Wind*, he'd worry about them tomorrow.

Jerry, Moe, and the three CEOs of Gatsby's most promising companies had met with Jerry, Jeff, and Birney the previous day. Jeff had ensured that all the attendees had received Private Placement Memorandums and was hopeful they would review them prior to the presentation so that many of the concerns and questions could be addressed in the public setting.

In addition, since the most significant thing that Gatsby had to sell was his CV plus the support and validations that Jerry had assembled in the vetting process, they decided to include Gatsby's credentials and

Jerry's vetting results in the package, meaning that when Gatsby took the stage, the bankers would already know quite a bit about him.

They had agreed to try to keep the meeting to under two hours.

At precisely 10 a.m., Birney called the meeting to order, expressed his appreciation to the bankers for taking time away from their busy schedules to attend the presentation, and expressed the hope that several of them would find the investment attractive. He referred the bankers to the outline of the presentation, an agenda that includes pitches from Gatsby, Moe Shultz, and the three CEOs. He introduced Moe first.

Moe moved to the podium, and smiling, looked around the room to make eye contact with several of the bankers. In a firm, commanding voice, Moe said, "First, I'm going to tell you some things about myself that are not included in my resume, then I'll tell you about my relationship with Gatsby, and then I'll tell you why I've taken the time to come to New York from my home in Philadelphia to tell you personally why I think the Gatsby Venture Fund is an excellent investment.

"I was fortunate to have wealthy parents, and when they passed away, I inherited several million dollars. During the last twenty-five years, I've built that inheritance to approximately five billion dollars, primarily through investments in auto dealerships and high technology companies. The investments originated from problem loans at First Interstate Bank and Wells Fargo when Gatsby managed their workout departments. During those years, he analyzed hundreds of problem companies and frequently alerted me to ones he believed had excellent potential. I bought several of them either out of bankruptcy or through negotiation with the bank and grew them into multi-million-dollar enterprises. Therefore, when he decided to leave the bank, I helped him get started in his new venture. I have enormous confidence in Gatsby's ability to build the Gatsby Venture Fund into a major player in the VC field, and therefore I am going to be its first major investor to the tune of $5 million. Thank you for listening to me."

Moe left the podium and took his seat along the wall, next to Gatsby.

Gatsby approached the podium. In his most stentorian voice he said, "I am honored that so many distinguished bankers, money managers, and investors have chosen to invest two hours of their precious time to hear about our new fund, the Gatsby Venture Fund. I'll keep my remarks brief to maximize the time that the three entrepreneurs who have accompanied me on this trip can explain the potential of the ventures they are driving."

He paused, surveyed the room again to ensure he had everyone's attention. In that moment between his call for silence and the crowd's compliance, there was a free fall of fear: he would be ignored, nobody cared, or worse, they would snicker among themselves at his plea and go on talking.

Time stretched out.

Twelve years ago, Gatsby had stood before a less prestigious audience who also held his fate in their hands—the creditors of the technology company he had purchased.

The company had historically generated sales of about ten million dollars a year. The founders had turned the business over to their sons who had mismanaged it straight into the ground. It had been in Gatsby's workout portfolio at the bank, so he was familiar with it. He believed it had excellent growth prospects. So, he looted his 401k fund and his daughter's college fund to scrape up the money to buy the bank's position. He knew at the time he should have insisted on an audit of its books, but there simply was no money or time left to accomplish it. He had said his prayers and forged ahead, feeling that same gap of uncertainty.

The transaction closed. Days later, two of his top engineers quit and were hired by competitors. Sales plummeted. Within the first six months the company's cash flow dried up so much that keeping the doors open and continuing to meet payroll meant stretching payables to ninety days and missing payroll tax deposits.

When the "demand for payment" notices began to arrive, Gatsby retained a consultant to review the company's operations and make a recommendation. The consultant immediately discovered that half of the company's product lines were operating at a loss and that the company's inventory had been overstated by $600,000 at the time of the closing. He recommended that Gatsby immediately sell off the losing product lines for "whatever he could get" and negotiate with his creditors to pay the debt over time.

That's when Gatsby, his consultant by his side, had met with Moe and pitched him on making an investment big enough to float the ship again. Moe agreed to not just invest money, but to vouch for Gatsby's plan with his creditors. In that moment, the free fall of fear slowed. He just needed to convince his employees he wasn't a dirtbag.

And three weeks later, Gatsby was in the company's lunchroom prepared to address a sullen and suspicious audience, many of whom had been deceived and cajoled into continuing to ship to the company even though they were not being paid. He fully recognized that this meeting was his personal Waterloo. If the creditors bought his proposal, he just might pull off a turnaround. If they didn't buy in, he was toast. His daughter wouldn't go to college, and he would be worse than broke because his IRS obligations would not be dischargeable in bankruptcy. Before he stood and made his way to the podium, he'd closed his eyes and uttered a short prayer for the faith of the people before him.

And as it had then, the room began to grow quiet. They wanted to hear what he had to say. He felt his confidence returning.

"As everyone in this room knows," he said, "not every new venture is successful—and I've experienced my share of enterprises that I was certain would succeed, only to see them crash and burn for all the reasons we are all familiar with. Management doesn't measure up to their resumes, a market dislocation occurs, the company is unable to maintain profitable selling prices, a vendor ships a defective product that results in many warranty claims and undermines the reservoir of customer goodwill. However, I've worked with companies that developed products and services that did not previously exist prior to my getting involved with them. I have been successful several times, due in large measure to my ability to analyze complex business concepts and make good decisions about people. These successes have made many people very rich. I've done well, but not nearly as well as I would have done had I achieved these successes in a venture-fund venue. That's why

I want to launch the Gatsby Venture Fund. I hope that many of you will see it is in your best interest to join me.

"Now I'd like to introduce you to the three entrepreneurs who will brief you on their respective companies. The companies are described in the handouts that you were provided."

He introduced three of the CEOs who had traveled with him; and each of the CEOs was allotted fifteen minutes to talk about the status of their respective companies, their potential, challenges, and prospects. After the CEOs' presentations, Jeff took over the meeting and fielded questions from the floor.

There was not a single moment of silence during the question-and-answer session. Jeff allowed it to continue for fifteen minutes beyond the allotted time. Then he announced that the meeting had concluded, refreshments would be served, and the Gatsby team would be available to meet privately with attendees. By any measurement, it was a success.

Chapter 33

GATSBY

Two weeks later, Wednesday, August 27, 2003

"Can we take a break?" said Gatsby. "I really need to use the restroom."

"Certainly," said Kyle. "We're off the tape. You remember where it is?"

Gatsby nodded and walked out the door of the conference room, fleeing his second deposition. Upon entering the restroom, he immediately headed toward a urinal. After relieving himself, he moved to the sink and doused his face with water. He turned that water faucet to the cold position, cupped his hand under the spout and drank a mouthful and gargled. He removed several paper towels from the dispenser and wiped his face. He checked his teeth, then combed his hair. He remained considering the mirror for another minute. *Another fucking Waterloo. Fortunately, the skill level of these bureaucrats is way below those of my creditors or the bankers. Thank God.*

He put on his most sincere face and said to his image in the mirror, "Courage!" Then he left the restroom and walked back to the conference room where Kyle and Nathan were waiting.

Kyle spoke into the tape recorder. "We're back in session on the Christopher Brooks CPN issue. Prior to the break I asked Mr. Brooks to explain how and when some of the notes that have been outstanding for some periods are repaid. Mr. Brooks?"

"Well, they leave it in there because (a) if the company is still operating, they believe the option is valuable and (b) if the company has failed, they enjoy the interest rate."

"Okay. And no one has asked to be repaid except for the people that have been paid, except for Shirley?"

"Shirley has not bought a convertible promissory note."

"Are you certain?" said Kyle. "My understanding was she owned one that included an option on EVG stock."

"If Shirley stated that to you, she was mistaken. She made a $25,000 investment in EVG and owns EVG stock. Check your spreadsheet listing the owners of the CPNs."

Kyle looked toward Nathan who was already reviewing the spreadsheet. Nathan looked up from the spreadsheet, shook his head, and said, "Gatsby's correct. Her name does not appear."

Kyle seemed confused. "Then what was the basis for her complaint?"

"I never talked to her about it," said Gatsby. "I presumed she was complaining about the fact she introduced me to several investors who purchased CPNs."

"Okay," said Kyle, "Let's move on. Before you issued the notes or got involved in these transactions, did you ever provide people with financial statements or anything that showed your financial ability to pay people back?"

Without changing his expression or exhibiting any discomfort, he said, "I've never been asked for one."

"And" said Nathan, "in the event the companies for which these folks hold options don't perform, they have, in effect, invested in you. Do you have any financial statements for the years during which you issued CPNs that would show us that you had the ability to repay the aggregate of the notes outstanding?"

This was the nexus of the interview. This is where the rubber met the road. His key vulnerability. Struggling to maintain his voice even and casual, he said, "I've always discharged all my financial obligations. I am not indebted to any financial institution. I'm proud of that."

"Well," said Kyle, "the way you've described your business history suggests success, so you may very well be able to pay back the five million that's outstanding. However, we would be remiss if we didn't ask you to convince us. That is a key part of our investigation."

"Oh, I understand that," said Gatsby.

"I can't imagine that in light of the complex and sophisticated business that you are in, Mr. Brooks, that you don't have the financial information, and annual statements that you need to keep score," said Nathan. "Your business cannot be managed on the back of an envelope."

"Of course, I have a financial statement," said Gatsby, replying with a measured indignation, "I'm simply trying to understand the level of your inquiry. Let's be blunt. If I sell a note that I don't have the ability to repay, then I've engaged in a fraudulent transaction. I've never done that, and I know of no one who has ever filed a complaint over my failure to repay a note. Do either of you?"

"No, we do not," said Kyle, "but you hit the nail on the head in your statement that if, at the time the notes were issued, you didn't have the wherewithal to pay people back, or the prospect that your business would generate the cash flow that could pay the notes as they came due—that would be a fraudulent transaction, and that is something we need to resolve in our investigation."

Gatsby took a deep breath and put on his most agreeable face. "Be straight with me, guys. Has someone told you that I've been engaged in fraudulent activity?"

"Mr. Brooks, please," said Nathan, "no one is accusing you of anything, and how your selling of convertible promissory notes came to our attention is confidential. But it has, and as the securities watchdog for the State, we're obligated to investigate."

"I understand," said Gatsby. "However, I need to be reassured that when I provide my financial information, it will not be subject to a public disclosure request such that it is made public or gets in the hands of people who frankly don't have my best interests at heart."

"We completely understand your concern," said Nathan. "It is legitimate. We can receive material in confidence and hold it in confidence. If the newspaper calls and asks whether we have an open file on specific subjects, we will have to disclose the fact we had opened a file. But if we have something that is held in confidence we would say, 'We have material that was given to us in confidence,' and we would have the obligation to have this office defend the confidentially in a legal proceeding."

"That's great," said Gatsby. "I just needed to get that issue clarified."

"Okay," said Kyle, "then you're going to get us some financial statements for the periods during which you issued CPNs? The main periods we're interested in are the last seven years, 1995 through 2002."

"I'll have my assistant and my accountant work on the project. I'll be on vacation through the week after Labor Day, and I should be able to give you a firm date by September 8."

"Excellent," said Kyle. "We'll look forward to your call."

Gatsby rose and extended his hand to Kyle and then to Nathan. "Thanks for being so understanding."

"No problem," said Nathan. "And *bon voyage*."

~~~~~~

The following morning Gatsby was in Frye's office briefing him on the interview with Rowan and Mitchell. When he had finished, Frye leaned back in his chair, cogitated for a few minutes, and then sat up.

"I'm sure you realize, Gatsby, they have already decided to issue a cease-and-desist order and whatever information they request, and you provide will only be used to justify their action."

"I agree. No question about it."

"What do you want me to do?" said Frye.

"Assuming we can get the Gatsby Venture Fund launched in the fall, I'll need another eighteen months to develop some positive results, so I can withstand the blowback when the inevitable order becomes public. Your job, Mr. Colin Frye, is to advise the DoBS that you represent me and to launch a Stalingrad defense that would make General Zhukov
~~~~~~

proud. You'll employ the tactics of obfuscation, delay, unavailability, complexity, and misunderstanding. You need to come out of this being viewed by Kyle and Nathan as the most frustrating, difficult attorney with whom they have ever dealt while avoiding any hint that you are intentionally delaying their investigation. Do you get my gist?"

"It won't be easy, and it will be expensive. These guys are tenacious."

"I know, but I have total confidence in your being able to pull it off. Your experience in the US Attorney's office in Manhattan exposed you to every defense tactic in the book."

Frye smiled. "Okay, I'll send Kyle a letter informing him that you've retained me, ask him to draft a specific document request, and set up a time to meet with him and review it."

"Great," said Gatsby. "Let the games begin!"

CHAPTER 34

GATSBY

Monday, September 8, 2003

Gatsby, tanned and preened, entered his office suite.

"Cissy! How did your Labor Day bash go?"

"It was exhausting. I worked like a scullery maid for four days. Do you have any ideas for outsourcing these family reunions? They're killing me."

Gatsby laughed. "You just had too many kids."

"Don't I know it. If I had any idea it was going to be this hard, I would not have married a Catholic. Anyway, I won't burden you with my troubles. Incidentally, Jerry called. He'd like you to call him this morning."

Curious, he sat down at his desk, pulled out his Blackberry and called Jerry.

"How was your holiday, my friend?"

"Hectic," said Jerry. "I'm happy to be back at work. What about yours?"

"We were in Ixtapa for a week. It was hot—but beautiful. The water was fabulous. What's up?"

"Just wanted to say congratulations: we're oversubscribed. We expect to have all the money in by the end of next week I suggest that you plan on an October 1 launch date."

"Incredible! You guys are miracle workers."

"It wasn't us. You, Moe, and your team did a magnificent job at the presentation. Stock up on the champagne. Raising a hundred million dollars is worth a celebration."

"I think we'll do a Christmas party. Will you and Helen come down for it?"

"Absolutely."

"Thanks, Jerry—and thank your brother and Birney."

Jerry kept the back-patting short, however, and Gatsby heard the leafing of the man's ever-present yellow legal pad in the background. "Listen, you're going to need a strong number two to help you vet and price deals, someone with excellent credentials and venture capital experience. Jeff and I are compiling a prospect list. We'll do the initial screening over the next month, and I'll send you our shortlist for your review. I'll come out to participate in the interviewing process and then you can make your decision."

"That's great, Jerry. I appreciate all the help you can give me in that department."

Another flip of a page in the background. "The candidates will probably be associates in existing venture capital companies and we'll have to offer the candidate an attractive deal with a partnership to pry them out of their present deal and motivate them to move to Philadelphia. Their compensation will come out of your 2-percent/20-percent compensation package. So, you need to be thinking about that."

"I understand."

"Okay. Gotta go. Enjoy the moment. After all, you have won the lottery."

Gatsby sat at his desk for several minutes working to absorb the full impact of what had just occurred. The first and most critical part of the plan to extract himself from the CPN quagmire had come to fruition. He had a guarantee of almost $2 million a year income for the next several years with a chance to make a lot more from his carried interest. He had brought it off—against all odds and the efforts of Shirley Frazier to destroy him. He poured a generous three ounces from a bottle of

Tito's into a tumbler and threw in a few ice cubes. He went back to his desk and buzzed Cissy.

"Bring in a tablet and join me in a celebratory drink. What do you say?"

She appeared in the doorway just as he was signing a check. "What are we celebrating?"

"The birth of the Gatsby Venture Fund. They raised the money. All hundred million of it. Want a drink?"

She was smiling, but her answer was crisp. "I better not. I'd be useless the rest of the day, and I imagine that you are going to fill up my plate."

"I am. So, I'll drink alone." He gulped down about half the contents of the tumbler. "That felt really good. Cissy, we plan on launching the fund on the first of October. I want to have a Christmas party to celebrate. Try for the week of the fifteenth of December. Find a date where we can get a room and a decent five- or six-piece band, and then make the first stab at the guest list. Miriam and I will edit it. Assume about 150 to 200 people. Any questions?"

"Not now. I just want to say congratulations, Gatsby. I'm happy for you and Miriam."

"Thank you, Cissy. You've certainly contributed to whatever success I've achieved. I appreciate your loyalty and dedication. Please arrange a conference call with Moe, Frye, and Hawking. I want to share the good news with them."

Cissy turned and started to leave Gatsby's office. She stopped and turned around to face him. "I do have one request. Shirley's invited me to go with her on her trip to Saint Martin, which as you know is the week of Thanksgiving. Can I take Monday, Tuesday, and Wednesday of that week as vacation days so I can go with her? I will have the rest of September and all of October to organize the party and do whatever planning you need done for the fund."

Gatsby absorbed the mention of Shirley's name without blinking, tore the check from his checkbook, and got up from his desk. "You can certainly take the time off, and we will not count it as vacation time." He came around to the other side of the desk and handed her the

$5,000 gift. "This is as good a time as any to give you your bonus for all your efforts on the Gatsby Venture Fund. I hope you and Shirley have a fantastic Thanksgiving vacation on Saint Martin."

Gatsby's enthusiasm as he handed the check to Cissy and hugged her indicated he did not have a hint of a suspicion she would experience anything other than good times on the island of St. Martin.

CHAPTER 35

HELEN

One Month Later

At three p.m. on October 4 Jerry picked up Helga, their house/child/pet-sitter and brought her to the apartment. The boys and Chelsey were all excited to see her and were almost dismissive of Helen's and Jerry's effort to engage them in the bustle of leaving for the airport. Helen admonished the boys to behave and listen to Helga, and Jerry nuzzled Chelsey, who licked his face. He and Helen rolled their suitcases out of the apartment and into the elevator.

At the airport bar, Jerry said, "How do you feel?"

"Apprehensive."

"Why?"

"I just hate leaving Alli and Josh and going so far away."

"You have confidence in Helga, don't you?"

She started to tear up. She took a tissue from her purse and dabbed her eyes.

Jerry took her hand in his. "Helen, you have to decide whether you can get on that plane without anxiety or guilt over leaving Alli and Josh with Helga." He looked at his watch. "We have an hour and a half until boarding starts. You need to decide by then. I'm going to leave you alone to sort this out. You may want to call them and talk to them for a few minutes if you think that will help. I'll be back in an hour and fifteen minutes and you'll either accompany me to the gate or I'll tell the airline attendant we've decided not to go, and they'll retrieve our bags."

He stood, turned, and walked away from the table. It was one of those times when he didn't know if she'd trust he actually meant it—he wasn't putting her in emotional thumbscrews. He needed to take this trip, but he also couldn't stand to see her cry. If she said they had to stay, they'd figure out another plan. God knew what, but they would.

When he came back to the table, his drink was waiting and hers was empty, and she seemed surprised he'd been gone so long. Twenty minutes later, they both boarded the aircraft and settled into their business-class seats.

The ten-hour flight to Tel Aviv was uneventful. They exchanged few words. Jerry read a novel on his Kindle. Helen watched a movie and slept. At approximately 5:30 p.m. Israeli time, the aircraft began its descent. Several passengers moved to the windows to view the city, shoreline, and setting sun. The panorama of the Tel Aviv skyline was turning to various shades of gold, and the horizon was a dusty gold.

After passing through a surprisingly relaxed immigration interview, baggage claim, and customs, they entered the public area and immediately saw Ze'vie at the escalator. Jerry waved, as he and Helen negotiated their way through the throngs of people. Ze'vie shook Jerry's hand and hugged Helen.

"Welcome to Israel. Did you have a pleasant flight?"

Helen was ebullient, her eyes glistening. Her demeanor had changed 180 degrees from the dour, reticent woman who had reluctantly boarded the flight in New York. "I'm thrilled to be here and so appreciative of your taking the time to squire us around. The view of Tel Aviv from the air was breathtaking!"

"It is my pleasure!" said Ze'vie. "My car is just a short walk. We'll go directly to Netanya. I've made reservations at the Davina, one of our best restaurants. You will love the view. It will remind you of California."

Ze'vie led them to his Lexus SUV and opened the front passenger door for Helen. Jerry loaded the luggage in the rear compartment and climbed into the back seat. From Ben Gurion Airport, Netanya was a quick, half-hour's drive north.

The Davina restaurant was located on the beach, and as Ze'vie promised, it had a magnificent view of the Mediterranean. Ze'vie suggested a bottle of Israeli white wine, hummus, shrimp, and chips while they enjoyed the lingering summer sunset and discussed the schedule for the next few days. Sated and satisfied with the plan, they went next to his home in the hills of Netanya. It had an outstanding ocean view. Ze'vie led Jerry and Helen into a spacious guest suite consisting of a large bedroom with a king size bed, large TV, desk, small refrigerator, treadmill, sleeper sofa, large modern bathroom, and walk-in closet.

"Wow said Jerry. It'd be easy to camp out here for a month."

"That's the idea," said Ze'vie. "I frequently have to provide accommodations for guests who need to avoid hotels."

The meaning of what he was saying sunk in, momentarily stopping the usual gush of pleasantries. To Jerry's mild alarm, Helen gave him an unruffled smile and said, "Of course."

"You guys must be exhausted. Why don't you relax for the evening? Let's meet for breakfast at around nine and then we'll tour the northern coast and visit some interesting sites. Sleep well."

~ ~ ~ ~ ~

After breakfast, Ze'vie said, "I've arranged for a private tour of Caesarea, Haifa, and Akko—basically the northern coast region. The tour guide is scheduled to pick us up in a half hour. We'll be back here by about dinnertime. The food will be brought in, so we'll have plenty of time to relax and talk about what you'll be seeing during the rest of your trip. Sound good?"

As they left Netanya and turned on to the main highway toward Caesarea. Helen was caught up in the adventure of being immersed in history, and she peppered the guide with appreciative questions. She felt happy and positive, and every trace of the anxiety she had experienced over leaving Alli and Josh was gone. It was the sensation of being exactly where she belonged, doing exactly what needed to be done.

"Our first stop," said the guide, "will be Caesarea, the city built by Herod the Great in 22 BC in honor of Emperor Augustus."

"Augustus—Julius Caesar's nephew who defeated Marc Anthony and Cleopatra at the battle of Phillipe, correct?" said Helen.

"You certainly know your Roman history," said Ze'vie.

"Not at all," said Helen, "I know my Shakespeare."

After touring the Crusader ruins that dated from 1100 AD, they moved on to the Roman amphitheater which was the site of mass executions. They ate lunch at the Don Caesarean Hotel then drove to Haifa, a port city with a two-thousand-year history. From the top of Mount Carmel, they could view the port, the Bahai World Center—which cascaded down the mountain, and the buildings of the high-tech center. Ze'vie commented that after Tel Aviv, Haifa was the most cosmopolitan city in Israel, and it had a stable Arab and Jewish population.

They continued north to Akko. The guide described its rich history which reached back to the Phoenicians. It was conquered and occupied by the Greeks, Romans, Arabs, Crusaders, Ottoman Turks, Napoleon, the British, and finally the Israelis, among others. Helen admitted she was ignorant of the richness of the history around her, both of its extraordinary detail and the oceans of blood that had been shed on the vistas around them.

As they drove south back to Netanya and viewed the setting sun on their right, Ze'vie asked Helen if she had enjoyed the tour.

She thought for a minute, and said, "I feel as though I was invited to a luxurious banquet, and only allowed to eat a few morsels of food from a limited number of dishes, and then whisked out the door, still hungry. There is so much to see—it's just frustrating."

The tour guide laughed. "Brilliant metaphor."

Ze'vie said, "That is exactly the way we want you to feel—hungry for more so you'll return to Israel and be able to sample many more dishes."

As they entered Ze'vie's home around 7 p.m., Helen said, "I'm bushed. I need a nap."

"Me, too," said Jerry. "This touring business is exhausting."

Ze'vie smiled. "Hey, you just scratched the surface. Look at this as training for your five-day private tour of the entire country. I'll call and put off dinner until eight, so you'll have some time to relax." Jerry and Helen both shuffled off to the bedroom and Ze'vie poured himself a whiskey and soda and turned on the television. When they returned to the dining room an hour later, the table was set, and a woman was in the kitchen mixing a salad.

"Helen, Jerry, I'd like to introduce you to Talisha. She works at the Marrakesh Restaurant, one of Netanya's finest. She will be serving us this evening. Please tell my friends what is on the menu tonight."

She was a short, pragmatic-looking woman whose life's work seemed entirely fulfilled by the culinary offerings around her. "Thank you so much, Ze'vie. I will be serving you salmon, a tangier of lamb, plums, and apricots, alongside potatoes, artichokes, and a salad. For dessert, I will be baking you a chocolate soufflé. We also have both red and white wine."

After dinner they moved to the family room. Helen settled back into the couch with her Irish coffee and caught the rattle and clank of Talisha washing the dishes, cleaning the kitchen, and loading all of her containers, trays, dishes, and hot plates back into the van. Jerry and Ze'vie were reviewing the itinerary of their forthcoming private car tour of Israel conducted by Ze'vie's colleague, Itzak. She stirred the whipped cream on her drink and listened to Jerry's deferential, appreciative murmurs of acknowledgement as Ze'vie described the highlights of the tour. She smiled. There was nothing in the world that this man didn't already know.

At 8:00 a.m. on Friday, Jerry and Helen met Ze'vie's colleague Itzak at their hotel and they had breakfast. When the dishes were cleared away, Helen arranged her notes, guidebooks, and articles on the table.

"You've obviously put in a lot of hours of preparation Helen," said Itzak. "I'm not used to this."

"Jerry laughed. "Ze'vie told us you were the best guide in Israel, and Helen intends to squeeze you for every bit of information you possess. So be prepared."

"Ignore him," said Helen. "This is the first major trip we've taken in a long time, and I just want to make the most of it."

"No problem," said Itzak. "This will be fun!"

During the next two hours Helen and Itzak discussed all the options for locations, monuments, excavation sites, etc. consistent with her objectives and would fit into the five days they had available. By ten thirty they had agreed on an itinerary.

Itzak said he was going back to his office to make the necessary hotel and tour reservation, ensure everything worked, type out the itineraries so they would each have a copy, and then pick them up at 12:30 to begin their tour of Jerusalem.

Itzak drove to the parking area near the Jaffa Gate. They entered the Old City and walked through the maze the made up the four sections of the city: the Armenian, Muslim, Jewish, and Christian quarters. Itzak pointed out and described those landmarks most important in Jewish and Christian history. The streets were crowded, and it was difficult to hear even a person right next to you. Consequently, Helen walked close to Itzak and Jerry walked a few paces behind. Since Jerry would not hear a word that Itzak was saying he focused on absorbing the sounds, smells, and sights of the Old City: a hodgepodge of humanity wearing colorful scarves patterned skirts and shirts, crosses, menorahs, beads, and jewelry; markets teaming with carpets, leather goods, food of every variety, and innumerable peddlers hawking pastries, juices, guidebooks, tours, accommodations, and whatever else a tourist or resident might need.

When they were in the Christian Quarter, they walked along the Via Dolorosa, the path allegedly walked by Jesus on his way toward the site of his crucifixion. Jerry stuck close to Itzak as he identified and explained the importance of each of the Stations of the Cross. After they toured the last ones—in the Church of the Holy Sepulcher—Itzak suggested they have dinner. Since it was Friday night, the Jewish Sabbath would begin at sunset and it would be an optimal time to see the Western Wall, as the students from the yeshivas congregate and dance to celebrate the start of the Sabbath.

They arrived above the Wall shortly after six o'clock. The rabbis were lining up the youths in their respective yeshivas. A crowd already stood there, men on one side and women on the other, a low fence between them—and a massive security checkpoint guarding them.

While Jerry and Itzak watched the square from above, Helen heading down the stairs toward the security queue.

"Where are you going?" said Jerry.

Helen turned. "To the Wall to pray."

After making her way through the scanners, armed guards, and outer crowd, she entered the woman's area slowly making her way to the Wall. She weaved her way through the groups of women sitting on chairs, reading, and nodding, apparently praying. When she got to the Wall, she rubbed her hands on the huge stones that had stood there for 3,000 years. She bent her head for several minutes, her forehead against the wall. Then she reached into her purse and withdrew a piece of paper, folded it, and inserted it between the stones.

Itzak had also been watching her. He said, "It's a tradition. People write out their prayers and hopes and insert it in the cracks between the stones believing that by leaving it at this holiest of sites, it will come to pass."

When Helen at last returned from her excursion to the Wall, she was wiping her eyes and face with a tissue. "You've been crying?" said Jerry.

"Yes, but I feel wonderful. It's an incredible experience. I've read about how praying at the Wall affects people, but frankly I was not expecting such an emotional high."

"It's a custom," said Itzak. He turned to Jerry. "Are you going to do it?"

Jerry laughed. "I'm an incredibly lucky man, Itzak. I have everything I ever wanted. I don't need to pray."

The next day they toured the Galilee area including the cities of Nazareth where Jesus spent his youth; and Tiberias, to see the Tomb of Maimonides, a twelfth-century Jewish scholar, philosopher, jurist, and physician. And then the Sea of Galilee, where several Apostles plied their trade as fishermen.

On the fourth day they traveled south to the Fortress of Mossad in the southern Judean desert inland from the Dead Sea. The fortress was originally a palace built by the Jewish King Herod in the first century BC. They took the tram up to the entrance, which was 1,300 feet aboveground. Itzak led them on a tour of the ruins and explained the storerooms, bathhouses, mosaics, and artifacts. Then he, Helen, and Itzak went to one of the three-hundred-and-sixty-degree observation points and as they looked out on the vistas. Itzak told them the history of the fortress.

During the Jewish revolt against the Romans in 70 AD, about a thousand Jewish rebels and their families fled to the fortress and occupied it. When the Romans marched down from Jerusalem three years later, and it was evident that the Romans would overrun the fortress, the Jews executed their respective family members and then committed suicide. When the Romans eventually built the ramp that allowed them to invade the fortress, all they discovered were ruins and corpses.

Itzak pointed out the route that the Romans marched. He left Helen and Jerry to make a telephone call. Jerry and Helen continued to stare at the route and the surrounding desert. Jerry put his arm around Helen and felt her body shake. He turned and looked at her face and saw she was crying.

"What is the matter, hon?" he said.

She did not reply. She shook her head from side to side.

Jerry enveloped her in his arms and held her tight. "Why are you crying? This event occurred two millennia ago."

She wiggled out of his arms and pulled a tissue from her purse. She dabbed her eyes and blew her nose. After several minutes she said, "Intellectually I know that. But standing here and imagining the Roman legions moving through the desert, I can feel the terror and impending doom that the Jews must have felt. It's horrible."

A few minutes later Itzak beckoned to them. "It's time to get the tram down to the parking lot."

As they were driving to Tel Aviv where they would spend the last day of their tour, Itzak asked them what they thought about Israel. Before Jerry could answer, Helen said, "I love this place. The sights, the people, the history." She took Jerry's hand and squeezed it. She leaned over and kissed him.

"What about you, Jerry?" said Itzak. "Do you share Helen's enthusiasm?"

He looked at Helen and smiled. "She speaks for the both of us. We've had a wonderful trip and I'm certainly looking forward to tomorrow and Tel Aviv."

That evening, they were on the balcony of their bedroom sipping their respective glasses of wine and enjoying the view of Tel Aviv and the ocean beyond. Jerry turned to Helen and said, "You know, I haven't seen you this consistently ebullient, emotional, and enthusiastic since we first dated—and that was almost ten years ago."

Helen laughed. "I know. I feel like a kid in the candy shop who knows her time is limited so she stuffs her face as quickly as she can swallow. Jerry, I confess that I am constantly fighting the urge to keep from jumping up and yelling, 'Yippee!' I haven't felt like this since I went to Paris in my twenties." She grabbed his free hand in her two hands and squeezed. "I hope I'm not embarrassing you."

Jerry smiled and leaned over and kissed her. "Not at all. I wanted you to have a good time and I'm delighted that I've succeeded."

CHAPTER 36

GATSBY

On Saturday, December 20, Gatsby hosted a Christmas party in the main ballroom of the Bellevue Hotel to celebrate the launching of the Gatsby Venture Fund. In attendance was an especially glittering crowd, flush with money and the diamond-edge facets of real power: Moe and Joyce, Miriam, Colin Frye, his wife Ami, the US Attorney for the Eastern District of Pennsylvania and her husband, George McKnight. There was Everett Hawking, Bill Dewyne's widow, Ono, Alicia, Jerry, Helen, and several executives and their wives from various companies that Gatsby was sponsoring and who would likely receive a windfall from the GVF.

Being able to schedule the Gatsby launch party at the Bellevue Hotel during the Christmas season was a stroke of luck—which did not surprise Gatsby, to whom good luck was a matter of course. The large ballroom, which easily accommodated the approximately 200 guests, was slathered with all the usual Christmas accouterments. But to emphasize the purpose of the celebration, these were supplemented by oversize hundred-dollar bills, posters showing the history of the Dow Jones average for the past ten years, large photos of Allan Greenspan, Warren Buffet, and other gurus. It was evident to everyone attending, that while Gatsby was celebrating the Christmas season, he was also celebrating his opportunity to make everyone even richer.

Notwithstanding the pall that had initially hovered over the room because of the recent disappearance of Shirley and Cissy, the mood generally improved. With Miriam in tow, Gatsby visited each table and exchanged quips with the guests. Although Gatsby was ebullient, Miriam was uncharacteristically quiet and appeared distracted. The crowd blamed the holiday season. It was such a stressful time of year for everyone, after all.

After dinner, the guests distributed themselves among the small tables that had been set up in an adjoining room so they could enjoy dessert and after-dinner drinks in a more casual venue. Jerry and Helen gravitated to Moe and Joyce's table. While they were chatting and enjoying Courvoisier, Jerry asked Moe if he knew where Shirley and Cissy were.

Moe looked surprised. "You obviously haven't heard. They disappeared and are presumed dead. It occurred in November over Thanksgiving, on Saint Martin while they were staying at Gatsby's timeshare."

Helen made a startled, "Oh!"

Moe nodded. "The investigation was conducted by the French police on Saint Martin. They concluded that a pleasure yacht from another island berthed at the dock of the condo complex at night—somewhere on the bay at Oyster Pond. One or two men made their way to the condo, gained entrance…" He faltered a bit, seeing Jerry's look of horror.

"Go on, what happened?" asked Helen.

"He…" Moe shrugged. "Well, at the least, he, or they, probably killed Shirley and Cissy, carried the bodies back to the yacht, weighted them, and threw them into the ocean. No evidence has washed ashore. The condo had been ransacked and several small items were missing. The police did not discover any fingerprints. There were no clues."

"How horrible!" exclaimed Helen.

"Gatsby was broken up about it. As you know, Shirley was a colleague and close friend and he had given her a week at the timeshare as a gift along with the business-class ticket to get there. And Cissy had been his Girl Friday for years." He shook his head. "I haven't followed the investigation. I'd be amazed if they ever discover who did it, let alone arrest them."

Glumly, Jerry asked, "Have you met Gatsby's new partner, Hannah van Bladel?"

Moe perked up, seizing on the subject. "Yes, I met her when she came to Philly for the interview. Pretty impressive credentials. Ex-McKinsey consultant with a Stanford MBA and a PhD in molecular biology. How did Gatsby get her to leave her Silicon Valley VC firm?" His laugh was a bit forced, but they were all eager to move on from the bad news.

"It was easy," said Jerry. "She wanted a partnership and she wanted to move to Philadelphia. Gatsby provided both. She will be a huge asset. Gatsby will have to get used to not operating as a one-man band."

"He'll do fine," said Moe. "The guy is infinitely adaptable. This is his big chance to move up from the scrub leagues. He won't fuck it up."

~~~~~~

By 12:30 a.m., most of the guests had left: Jerry and Helen to their room, Miriam and Joyce to their homes in a cab, and Gatsby had his keys out on the table, promising to drive Moe to his home near Rittenhouse Square in a minute. But they had not quite called it quits. Gatsby was looking at a new company to buy, and Moe kept them both from rising by asking polite questions. Yet he didn't seem all that interested in the answers.

Moe drained his glass. "I'm glad we have this time alone, Gatsby. I need to talk to you about something that I'm sure both of us will find unpleasant."

Gatsby, who had way too much to drink, raised his eyebrows. "How in the hell can there be anything unpleasant!" And having said that, he drained his Courvoisier and motioned to the bartender for a refill.

Moe leaned over the table and gently took Gatsby's hand. "Look at me, Gatsby. This is important. Yesterday, Joyce told me that Miriam confided in her she thinks that you are involved with that new assistant of yours. Hannah. She said several friends that have reported seeing
~~~~~~

you both around town. I'm not making any accusations—I'm merely reporting what Joyce told me."

Gatsby, suddenly alert, grimaced. "That's bullshit, Moe. Hannah, Frye, Hawking, and I have been working night and day to get the GVF launched. When Hannah and I have worked late, of course I've taken her out for a drink or dinner. There is nothing there. I don't have the time or energy for that kind of thing right now. I'm focused. Believe me, there is absolutely nothing to it." He glanced over his shoulder to check on the bartender. "But thanks for making me aware of the problem— I'll try to be more circumspect."

Moe sighed. "I want to believe you, Gatsby, and for now I will. I've made a $5 million bet on you, and you need to know that if it turns out that you are having an affair with Hannah you will create a huge problem for Joyce—and for me. A huge problem! You can't afford to be distracted. Just, be careful!"

He stood, picked up his coat from the adjacent chair. "Time to call it a night. Let's return to the bosoms of our spouses. And put those keys in your pocket. We're getting a cab."

CHAPTER 37

JERRY

September 19, 2004

The GVF had been operating for almost one year. Jerry, Jeff, and Birney comprised the GVF advisory board and provided oversight on the part of the investors. And as one of the minds that steered the fund, Jerry decided to go to meet with Gatsby and Hannah to review the investments they'd made as well as some promising fruits they might pick before the end of the year. It was supposed to be a two-day trip that would put Jerry back in his office by Tuesday, in time for a Friday deadline on another project.

He traveled to Philadelphia on Sunday and passed the time on the train reading the Saturday edition of the *Wall Street Journal*. In a BBC interview, UN Secretary-General Kofi Annan described the invasion of Iraq by the US-led coalition as a violation of the UN Charter. The article went on to discuss the history of the Iraq war and growing dissatisfaction among American voters. The reporter predicted that the decision to invade Iraq would be a major issue in the forthcoming election in November. Jerry shook his head and muttered, "Shit, a huge, unforced error." When the train arrived in Philadelphia, he took a cab to the Bellevue, checked in, and immediately went to bed.

Jerry was seated at a window table overlooking Broad Street, people watching, when Hannah approached the table. She was tall for a woman, athletic, and Scandinavian. He stood and extended his hand to greet her.

"It's so good to see you again," said Hannah.

"Likewise," said Jerry. "Let's order while we wait for Gatsby to get here."

"He sent me to keep you company. We're to meet him at his office after breakfast. Everett will also be there."

After they placed their orders, Jerry leaned into the table and said, "When we last met during your interview, we were on such a tight schedule than I didn't have the opportunity to get more insight into your background and the story behind your move to venture capital. I understood from our interview that you were working toward a career in medical research?"

She smiled, mustering the full force of her thirty-two perfect, ultra-bright-white teeth. Frankly, the smile reminded him of a younger Helen. "I can understand why you'd be curious. A certified nerd prepares for a career in medical research and succumbs to the financial lure of venture capital. A great theme for the novel that I'll write someday—me, along with half of my classmates who chose industry over poverty."

"You read my mind," said Jerry.

The waitress placed their breakfasts on the table and black coffee for both. Hannah sprinkled a sweetener over her oatmeal, tasted a spoonful, and took a sip of coffee.

"I'll give you the CliffsNotes version. My father was a professor at the University of Ghent in 1960. My mother, a Californian, attend UCLA and by the time she graduated she was fluent in French, Italian, and German. She got a job in the State Department, took some classes at the University of Ghent, and met and married my father. The one thing they agreed on was that I needed to speak at least as many languages as they did."

"A high bar," said Jerry. "Please take a breath and eat your breakfast before it gets cold."

"Right." She picked up her spoon and ate some oatmeal, took a sip of coffee, and continued. "With such ambitious parents, I thought I was destined to cure cancer. I earned the equivalent of a master's degree in chemistry, and then I got my PhD in microbiology. That was in 1990. I was ready to throw myself into my new career and get to work. But my dad had other plans for me—and since he had paid out a significant portion of his net worth for my education, he had a vote."

"What did he want you to do?" said Jerry.

"My dad had gotten an MBA at Stanford after earning his PhD because he wanted to understand how business drives the economy that provides the paychecks for the academics who live in their ivory towers. He had found that education enormously helpful in his career. He didn't want me to be just another cog in a university wheel, with no sense of how to exercise some power over my fate. I couldn't refute his argument, so I enrolled in Stanford and started in the spring of 1991."

"And you graduated—" Jerry looked down at his notes.

"Three years later. It opened my eyes and modulated my nerdiness. I was no longer sure that I wanted to bury myself in a research lab for the rest of my life, searching for cures. I joined McKinsey to study business all around the world. I became their go-to person for biotech clients and racked up a lot of frequent flier miles in the process." She gave him a one-shouldered shrug, a gesture at odds with a look of slight embarrassment. "In short, greed won out. I'm not as altruistic as I thought. The end."

Jerry laughed. "How the hell would we have gotten through college without CliffsNotes?"

"We wouldn't have." She picked up her spoon and ate the rest of her oatmeal.

"By my informal count, you've got to be working at least sixty hours a week with Gatsby. You don't want to burn out."

"I'm a long way from that."

Jerry asked for the check. As he was signing the credit card, he said, as if an afterthought, "Since you've interned with one of the most prestigious VC firms in the valley, how does Gatsby compare with the VC managing partners you've worked with?"

"That's easy," said Hannah. "He's at the top of that gene pool. He can do it all. He has a talent for sensing what deals have the potential to be successful, and if the deal pencils out, he has the wit and charisma to seduce the entrepreneur to throw his lot in with the GVF. And if the deal comes to fruition, he has the contacts to ensure that the board is properly staffed. He's amazing."

Jerry smiled, not quite prepared to believe that such glowing admiration was entirely professional—though to be fair, he'd seen Gatsby inspire the same intensity in Moe and a roomful of stuffed shirts. "I am happy to hear that." Jerry pushed his chair back, stood, and said, "Let's go meet with your amazing counterpart."

Philadelphia was enjoying an Indian summer, so Jerry suggested they walk the six-tenths of a mile to Gatsby's office. The meeting convened in Gatsby's office at 9:30 a.m. In attendance were Jerry, Hannah, Everett Hawking, and Gatsby himself. Hannah distributed the report she'd prepared which summarized the status of all the investments made from the inception of the GVF.

After several minutes to allow the participants to thumb through the report, Hannah took the floor. "We've invested approximately $42 million in ten deals. For this presentation I've separated them into three groups: 'Promising,' in which there are seven firms, 'Uncertain,' in which there are two, and 'Struggling,' in which there is one. I created the categories and explained my rationale to Gatsby and Everett, and they agreed. What you have here is our collective judgment of the status of the portfolio."

"Let's start with the bottom of the barrel," said Jerry. Why is Philadelphia Medical struggling? I see that the GVF has invested over two million."

"Right," said Hannah. "The company has not been able to raise money from other sources since we made our investment early in the year. The management of Philadelphia Medical entered into a license agreement with another firm, and while the GVF may receive some revenue in the future, the amount and timing of the revenue are speculative."

Hannah, Gatsby, and Everett reviewed the status and prospects of each of the nine investments the GVF had made and provided their rationale for the valuation they expected to assign to each of the investments for the annual report. It felt like a productive day.

That evening, Jerry sat in the bar of the Bellevue nursing a double Jameson on the rocks. He wanted to share his elation over his meeting with Gatsby, Hannah, and Everett. But since it was already late by polite standards, he'd keep it to himself until tomorrow morning. All the uncertainties, anxieties, and second-guessing about the vision, strategy, and competence of the GVF team had been put to rest. Of the $42 million that had been invested in the ten deals, thirty-five million of capital was in seven promising companies, two of which were preparing for initial public offerings. One of the companies was likely to be sold within the next three months. The prospective market value of GVF's investments in these three companies was more than $120 million. If everything stayed on track, these three investments would return the entire investment of the limited partners; subsequent returns would be pure profit. Moreover, the GVF team had been prudent in investing the GVF's assets, ensuring that the GVF was secured. If Philadelphia Medical had to be liquidated, which seemed likely, at least the GVF would recover at least twenty percent of its investment.

Jerry realized that when he reported back to Birney and Jeff tomorrow, he would have to keep a tight rein on his enthusiasm and avoid falling into the trap of overpromising. The venture capital business was notoriously uncertain, and Dame Fortune tended to turn malevolent when one least expected it.

CHAPTER 38

GATSBY

Friday, October 8, 2004

After saying good morning to Kathy, his new assistant, Gatsby headed to his office. Kathy called out to him, "Peter phoned twice this morning. He asked me to have you get in touch with him as soon as you get in."

Gatsby stopped halfway through his office doorway. "Which Peter—the golfer or the logger?"

"The golfer," said Kathy.

"Thanks," said Gatsby. "Call him back and tell him I'll call him at 11:30. And don't disturb me. I'm not taking any calls."

He continued into his office, shut the door behind him, and turned on the television to CNN. Moe had called him to tell him about the terrorist attack on the Taba Hilton in the Sinai by Palestinian terrorists. The targets of the attack were Israeli tourists, twelve of whom were killed. The Palestinians had driven a truck into the lobby of the Taba Hilton and exploded it causing ten floors to collapse. In addition to those killed, 159 people were injured.

He turned to the bar, poured two ounces of Vodka Absolut into a glass, tossed in a few ice cubes, flopped into his desk chair, and watched the news. As the rabbis picked up the body parts, tears ran down his face. This particular carnage brought back memories of what he'd seen when he'd been tasked with inspecting villages that had been attacked by Viet Cong. He knew he should turn off the damn television set before he vomited.

He picked up the desk phone punched in the golfer's number, took a deep breath, and pasted a smile on his face.

"Peter?"

"Hi, Gatsby. Thanks for getting back to me so quickly."

"No problem. Hey, I owe you a celebratory drink. What a fantastic win in the Hartford."

"Thanks. The stars finally aligned."

"You're having an incredible year," Gatsby said.

"It looks as though it will be my best. Everett calculated the third-quarter tax deposits I need to make. I am already late—and they're huge. My only source of operating cash is your convertible promissory note. I need you to pay it off by next Thursday so that I can get it posted before Monday."

Gatsby began to perspire. He moved the phone to his left hand. His throat went dry.

He lifted himself out of the chair and began to pace.

"Gatsby! Are you there?"

"Sorry, Peter, I was just processing."

"Look Gatsby, I know it's short notice. I only got the bad news from Everett on Monday. Frankly, I'm not used to such big numbers. It caught me off-guard. I am under the gun. Can you do it? Can I pick up a check by Thursday?"

Gatsby took a deep breath. "I'll get back to you in an hour."

"Thanks, Gatsby," said Peter. "I appreciate it."

Gatsby hung up the phone, leaned back in his chair and closed his eyes. Five minutes later he opened his office door and said, "Kathy, drop whatever you're doing and get me the following five numbers. The Gatsby Associates cash balance, the GVF cash balance, the accounts payable for Gatsby Associates and GVF, and the management fees we're entitled to through the balance of the year."

Twenty minutes later Kathy came into Gatsby's office and placed a single sheet of paper on his desk. "I think this is everything you want."

He quickly scanned the paper. He took his calculator out of the desk drawer and punched a few numbers. Without looking up from the calculator, he said, "Kathy, prepare a payoff check for Peter in the amount of $267,300. Write a check out of GVF to Gatsby Associates of $333,000 to cover the September and October management fees we're entitled to, and deposit that check this afternoon—and call Peter and tell him can pick up his check on Thursday at 9 a.m."

After Kathy left his office, he again leaned back in his chair, closed his eyes, and muttered, "One bullet at a time. Just dodge one bullet at a time."

During the fall, the pressure from CPN holders had begun to grow. After Gatsby informed his CPN investors it was unlikely that the investment in Philadelphia Medical would provide much of a return, the calls increased. Gatsby offered to swap options he owned in other companies—ones that the GVF had invested in—for the options of the companies that failed or were on the rocks. Several investors agreed to the exchange, but not all. For those who did not agree, Gatsby negotiated payment plans, dipping into the $166,000 a month he was receiving from GVF. He realized he never factored into his projections the demands that the CPN investors would make, once they knew he had such a huge income and access to millions of dollars of GVF assets. He couldn't blame them for leveraging him. He'd bought peace for a while—but the likely collapse of two of the other CPN companies, ones that GVF did not invest in, would probably occur within the next two months. More pressure, more bullets.

~~~~~

Shortly after Thanksgiving Gatsby received a call from Jerry. He wanted a progress report on the status of the GVF's promising investments, and the progress, if any, on the uncertain ones. Gatsby kept his cool and relied on the facts, which he didn't need to inflate in order to give Jerry what amounted to a clean bill of health.
~~~~~

Forty-five minutes later, after they had discussed both the investments and the prospects, Jerry said, "Who are you going to hire to do the tax returns and the year-end financial report?"

"I planned to hire KPMG. Hawking and I have already discussed it."

"Don't you use KPMG for your own stuff?"

"Yeah. They're good."

"Well," said Jerry, "the GVF auditors need to be independent from you personally and Gatsby Associates. We need to avoid any appearance of any conflict of interest."

Gatsby clenched his jaw once, viciously, and then forced his face back into a relaxed expression so it would match his neutral tone. "I see," he said.

"And who did you plan to use to prepare the financial information that the CPAs will be auditing?"

"I planned on having Kathy work with Hawking."

"Does Kathy have an accounting background?" said Jerry.

"She's a bookkeeper," said Gatsby.

"Well, Gatsby, the investors need to have confidence in the information that is provided to the GVF's auditors, and they must know that the GVF's auditors are independent. You need to hire an accountant who is competent to maintain the GVF's books and records and prepare the GVF's year-end financial statement so it can be audited by a CPA. I am more than happy to help you recruit an accountant and interview CPA firms."

Gatsby did not respond immediately. As Jerry had spoken, Gatsby had heard a conciliatory note enter the man's voice, almost a patronizing one—as though Jerry already knew he was asking for too much.

"I understand, Jerry. Let me think about it and I'll get back to you." He slammed down the phone. He sat for several minutes and then punched out Colin Frye's direct number. Frye was in his office. Gatsby told Frye about his conversation with Jerry regarding the apparent five-alarm necessity of the GVF hiring an accountant and moving to a new CPA, in Jerry's words, "to avoid the appearance of a conflict of interest."

"You sound angry," said Frye.

"I'm fucking furious! This is my fund! It has my name on it. I call the shots."

"Okay, I'll review the operating agreement and call you back."

"Thanks," said Gatsby.

Kathy buzzed Gatsby on the intercom. Gatsby picked up the phone. "While you were talking with Jerry, Liz Rosenblatt called. She wants you to call her back."

"Liz Rosenblatt?"

"You know, Moe's attorney."

Gatsby shook his head in stupefaction. "I haven't talked with her in years. Did she say what she wanted?"

Kathy said she didn't and read off the woman's number. Gatsby stared at the phone trying to figure out why in the hell Moe would have his attorney call him rather than just call himself. It did not make sense, and because it did not make sense, he suspected she was not calling to convey good news. He put two ice cubes in a glass and covered them with vodka. He took a large swallow and called the number.

She answered on the first ring.

"Liz? Gatsby. How the hell are you? It's been ages since we last talked."

"I'm just fine, Gatsby. Just older, with more aches and pains. Moe has kept me up to speed on the Gatsby Venture Fund. He is so optimistic over your prospects."

"Well, Moe's a good part of the reason the GVF is a reality. His presentation to the bankers in New York was right out of *Atlas Shrugged*. It was masterful."

"We're all rooting for you, Gatsby."

"Thanks, I need all the cheerleading I can get. What is it that you wanted to talk to me about?"

As she began to respond, Gatsby detected from her carefully crafted language she was extremely uncomfortable carrying out her assignment. "Moe asked me to help him facilitate his desire to have you repay several of his CPNs containing options that have become worthless. Because of his large investment in GVF and his close personal relationship with you he wants to avoid personal involvement in a situation which might become contentious."

Gatsby felt his pulse rate rising. "Why the hell would Moe think that asking me to repay some promissory notes could become contentious?"

"I have no idea," said Liz. "Those were his words, not mine."

Gatsby doodled on the yellow pad on his desk. "What specifically is Moe requesting?"

"I've analyzed all of the CPNs that Moe holds. There are eleven notes aggregating $1,650,000 in principal. Accrued interest through the end of this month is approximately $839,000. The CPNs supported by Philadelphia Medical, and National Physicians Associates, both of which have failed, account for $1,250,000 in principal and $635,000 of accrued interest. Moe would like those paid off before the end of the year."

Gatsby broke the pencil he had been doodling with and threw the pieces across the room. He realized that his level of fury and fear precluded any reasoned and effective response. He managed to say, "I understand, Liz. Send me your analysis and I'll see what I can do."

"That will be fine, Gatsby. You'll get back to me within a week?"

"Absolutely! Take care." He waited to hear the click confirming that Liz had hung up, then he threw the phone against the wall and yelled "*Et tu Brute*! Fuck!"

Kathy opened the door. "What happened?"

"Close the door and leave me alone."

Moe could not have hurt him more if he had thrust a dagger through his toga. He felt an anger attack coming on that could easily morph into uncontrolled fury. He was devastated that Moe would sic his junkyard-dog lawyer on him. Moe! A friend who tells everyone he loves me as he would a brother! That quisling, that Judas, that Benedict Arnold! He looked out the window, fuming so hard that his breath made a cloud on the glass.

It was still overcast, and the weather report promised rain. Although the conditions were not conducive to trudging around downtown, he was afraid if he didn't leave the office and get some air and exercise, he would explode. He grabbed his coat, umbrella, and cell phone, and as he left, he instructed Kathy to check whether his desk phone still operated, call building maintenance and ask them to repair the wall, and to expect him back in a couple of hours.

Gatsby exited his office building and was immediately shocked by a cold gust. He decided to walk the two blocks to the Continental Midtown and have a couple of drinks. He was counting on the liquor to dissipate the anger so he could talk to Frye.

~~~~~

A half hour later, at 3:30 with one martini down and one on the way, he called Frye's office and confirmed a meeting with him at 4:30 p.m. As he waited for the second martini he tried to calculate the amount of money he would have to come up with if all the CPNs demanded repayment; but he could not keep the number straight in his mind.

He pulled a notebook and a pen from his jacket and started to compose a schedule:

Moe: $1,885,000

Other CPNs of failed/failing companies to be paid by end of year ~$600,000

Remaining CPNs?

Total CPN obligation?

He couldn't remember all the numbers. But writing the numbers and looking at them on his notepad virtually eliminated his anger over Moe's demand. It was counterproductive. He had bigger problems. He was facing a demand of over $2.5 million with absolutely no way to pay it.

Gatsby stared at his notes and reviewed the recent conversations he had with CPN investors, including the ones he'd paid, like Peter's and the ones who didn't give him any slack and wanted to be paid back over the next ninety days. And of course, there were the owners of CPNs that held options that were now worthless but who hadn't gotten around to calling yet.
~~~~~

There was no collateral for a bank loan; Moe was a dry hole; and Miriam had already said no. Because of the time it would take for the various other options to monetize, the only source of money to pay off outstanding CPNs was his income from the Gatsby Venture Fund, which was inadequate. He was no longer able to dance around the problem. He needed to have a plan, and for that, he needed to get a firm hold on the numbers. He had to talk to Everett.

He pulled out his cell and called Everett's direct number.

"It's Gatsby. I'm two blocks from your office. Can you spare fifteen minutes?"

Five minutes later, he was in Everett's office. He related the substance of his conversation with Moe's attorney and the various other investors who'd requested repayment.

"I thought I was in the black, but there is no way I can cope with Moe's demand."

Hawking studied the CPN analysis he had done for Frye. "It's been almost a year and a half since I prepared this schedule. Bring me up to date on what's been paid." He slid the sheet across the conference table to Gatsby along with a pen. "Put a check mark next to the paid CPNs along with the date on which they were paid."

Gatsby obeyed, all the while feeling like he was barely passing a pop quiz. He slid the schedule back to Hawking who did a quick analysis and wrote $7,350,000 on a notepad and passed the pad over to Gatsby.

"That is the balance of the CPN obligation through the end of 2004, assigning zero value to the underlying options."

Gatsby stared at the number for a full half of a minute and all he could muster was: "Shit." He felt his heartbeat in his brain. He was sweating under his coat.

"What is the prospect of any of the options being monetized in the next six months?" said Hawking.

"Out of the nine deals in the forecast, two have crashed. Of the seven remaining, all are viable, but only one, Advanced Catheters, looks like it will start to monetize in six months—but the money won't come in until the end of next year."

"Let's see what the effect would be under that assumption. What's your estimate of the stock price versus the option price?"

"The stock price should exceed the option price by at least four dollars a share."

Hawking reviewed the CPN schedule, identified the notes supported by options on Advanced Catheter, and made several calculations. "The monetizing options should extinguish $300,000 of debt and produce $150,000 for you."

The heartbeat in his head grew faster. He could hear it hissing in his ears. "That still leaves $6,900,000, not counting the roughly $500,000 of additional accrued interest."

"It will be less than that," said Hawking.

"Not by much. I still have a $7-something-million problem."

"Agreed," said Hawking. "Do you have a plan to address it?"

Gatsby pushed aside his panic and invited ideas to struggle through. He waited. Nothing. He was totally blank.

He lifted himself out of the chair. "Thanks for meeting with me on such short notice. I need to run."

Hawking escorted Gatsby to the lobby. He put his hand on Gatsby's shoulder and said, "Good luck."

Gatsby turned, smiled at Hawking, and said, "I'm counting on it." He left Hawking's building and walked the three blocks to Frye's office.

Seated with Frye, Gatsby said, "I didn't expect that curveball from Jerry."

"I've reviewed the GVF operating agreement which all the investors signed and have also reviewed some of the major LLC-related appellate opinions. I am comfortable advising you on the issues raised in your conversation with Jerry."

"What are my options?"

"Well, one option is to tell him to go fuck himself!"

Gatsby laughed, but part of him wanted to choke Frye. "Are you serious?"

"Yes, but don't take my suggestion literally. I mean that you don't need to do anything he suggests if you have other equally viable alternatives that you would prefer."

"I don't quite understand," said Gatsby.

"According to Pennsylvania LLC law, as the duly elected manager of an LLC, you have all the authority to manage the LLC as you wish, provided you are not in breach of the operating agreement and are not in violation of your fiduciary duty to the members. You have an advisory board consisting of Jerry, Jeff, and Birney—but as members of a limited liability corporation, they have no authority to compel you to do anything. In fact, to preserve their limited liability situation, they cannot command you to do anything. Moreover, if they are successful in browbeating you to do something that you don't think is in the best interest in the GVF, but you do it to keep peace, and then the action you took results in a loss to the GVF, the fact that the advisory board wanted you to take the action is no defense to a claim against you. In short, you are the king, and you need not listen to either nobles or commoners. Understand?"

"I think so," said Gatsby. "What if I'm unsure whether I have the authority to take some action or not take an action?"

"You ask me for an opinion on an issue. If I give you an opinion and if you rely on that opinion, you are golden; you have a complete defense against any member who might make a claim against you because the issue resulted in a loss to the GVF. And, on this specific matter, Jerry's requesting that you hire a different CPA. I don't even need to give you an opinion because hiring a CPA is a management decision, and Jerry cannot interfere with your management decisions."

"Wow," said Gatsby, "that's great. So legally I'm okay if I tell Jerry, 'Thanks for the advice, but I'd prefer to keep KPMG.'"

"Sure," said Frye, "you can do that." He emphasized the *can*.

"I detect a note of skepticism in your voice. You're not absolutely sold on my retaining KPMG as the GVF's auditor?"

"Frankly, Gatsby," he said, "I think it is in your best interest to retain a different CPA firm, but not for the reasons Jerry presented."

"But why?"

"Hawking knows too much about your personal life and your business life prior to the Gatsby Venture Fund, including the details of your CPN business." He leaned into the table and held Gatsby's gaze, seeming to press the value of his advice deeper into his best client. "You can satisfy the concerns of your advisory board by doing what is in your best interest. Think about it. You have a few weeks before you need to make a decision."

Gatsby suddenly understood where Frye was heading. There could be a situation where he might want to do something as manager of GVF which would not be possible if the GVF auditor was knowledgeable about his personal situation, Gatsby Associates, or his CPN business.

He smiled at Frye.

"You are fucking brilliant. I completely understand," said Gatsby, "and I agree."

CHAPTER 39

GATSBY

Three weeks later, December 24, 10 a.m.

Gatsby stood at the window of his office on the fiftieth floor of the Mellon Bank Center, the third-tallest building in the city and looked out over the river, the east side of the city, and Western New Jersey. He never tired of the view—it was vast and beautiful. He looked over City Hall Tower with its thirty-seven-foot statute of William Penn; the Delaware River and his home at the Residences at Dockside; the Ben Franklin Bridge that connected Philadelphia to Camden.

His office's mesmerizing view was a key to his success. A potential client, visiting for the first time, was inevitably awed by the view and their host's implied power and prestige. And when he would take his potential client to the Pyramid Club, two floors above, its spectacular three-hundred-and-sixty-degree views often turned the prospect into a client.

He had told Miriam he needed to go into the office today to have undisturbed quiet time to figure out a vexing problem. If she only knew just how vexing it was. The CPN gambit had run its course. The repayment demands coupled with the Pennsylvania Department of Banking and Securities investigation had gone from a migraine to a tricky brain tumor. It was also cutting into the time and effort he needed to devote to the GVF—which was his best opportunity for

234

creating wealth for himself and Miriam. The CPN documents included a "call" provision so he could demand that noteholders either convert their options immediately or surrender their notes and accept payment for the principal and accumulated interest. Puff—the problem would be solved in a month. All he needed was about eight million dollars and then, to use Frye's expression, he'd be golden. Like operating on a brain tumor, it was easier said than done.

If he borrowed the money from the GVF and notified the investors immediately, they would probably demand he return the money, threaten to sue, and would probably terminate him for breaching the operating agreement. He'd be worse off. He'd have no job and no income. If he borrowed the money from the GVF and didn't notify the investors he had done so, his appropriation would be disclosed in the next audit. The investors would demand he repay it immediately and terminate him for breaching the operating agreement. Again, he'd wind up with no job and no income. The only advantage of concealing the loan was he would have a year before the 2005 audit, by which time he might have earned some carried interest compensation, which might allow him to pay back some of the money. He was aware he was using the words *if, might*, and *maybe*. Speculation upon speculation.

He picked up his pen and wrote, "Facts Regarding CPN Payoff Alternatives" at the top of the page.

Fact #1: Required Funds: $8 million to pay of all CPN investors.

Fact #2: The only credible source for that amount of money is in the accounts of the Gatsby Venture Fund.

Fact #3: There are three ways that I can accomplish the transfer of $8 million from the GVF accounts to the Gatsby Associates accounts so it will be available to pay CPNs.

1. I could request a loan from GVF—which would require me to petition the investors; or

2. I could simply borrow it, write out a note paying a market rate of interest, and confront Jerry with a fait accompli.

3. I could borrow it and conceal the fact I've borrowed it.

Gatsby looked at the sheet of paper and sighed. He walked over to his wall unit and filled a tumbler with Tito's. He took a long swig and then tore off the top sheet of the pad, placed it on the side of the desk and wrote at the top of the new sheet, "Page 2: Options/Probable Results."

A. Ask to borrow the money. Likely result: questions raised about the veracity of information I previously provided and would probably result in my termination.

B. Borrow the money, but don't tell and don't conceal. Merely insert a note in the file. Likely result: same as above, just four months later.

C. Borrow the money but conceal. Likely result: same as above, plus possible indictment; but provides one year to earn enough carried interest to prevent either indictment or termination.

D. File bankruptcy and extinguish CPN problem. Likely result: Miriam will leave, CPN investors will complain to the Pennsylvania AG or the US Attorney about previous disclosures, Jerry will be shocked (but at least won't be alienated by my taking the GVF's money and concealing it). Maybe could preserve my situation at GVF.

Gatsby stared at page 2 and then looked over page 1. He held his head in his hands. He knew he needed someone to talk with—but who would want to hear he was considering embezzling over $8 million from the Gatsby Venture Fund? He could talk with Miriam—his wife couldn't be forced to testify against him—so there would be no legal risk in talking with her. The real question was, would there be a benefit?

What the hell, he thought. She'd have to do. He carefully folded the two sheets of paper placed them in his jacket pocket and left the office.

~ ~ ~ ~ ~ ~

On the morning of December 26, Gatsby made bloody marys and sat down with Miriam on their living room couch. He noticed that the bright sunlight was falling on her face, so he closed the shutters slightly. They both had a bit of a hangover from the festivities the night before.

"Is that better?"

"Much."

He took the two sheets of paper he had created on Christmas Eve and forced himself to start talking. He summarized several CPN-related events that had occurred during the last week. Then he presented the information on Page 1, Facts, and Page 2, Options/Results.

"The only options that have any possibility of delivering salvation either create a real risk of indictment or require that I file a Chapter 7 bankruptcy—which we discussed after my meeting with George McKnight."

"Wasn't that the mea culpa strategy George suggested?" said Miriam.

"Yes. But we are in a much better position. I'm managing a hundred-million-dollar fund, earning two million a year, and have an excellent prospect to earn more."

Miriam looked deep into the bloody mary, took a sip, and wiped her lip with a Kleenex. Her hand shook a little, and this was the first sign she was boiling inside. "You're assuming Jerry and crew will keep you on. Did you think this through? Do you think they love you so much they won't fire you in five seconds?" She balled up the tissue in her fist. "I don't think so, Gatsby. You're dreaming. The blowback that Jerry, Jeff, and Birney would get when they tell the GVF investors that the manager who was supposed to be Philly's premier venture capitalist has just filed Chapter 7 and stiffed many of the city's most outstanding citizens to the tune of eight million dollars…" She shook her head once, hard. "It will be a tsunami."

Gatsby drained his bloody mary. "I agree, it's a risk."

"It's a huge risk, Gatsby. Forget that option. It's suicide!"

"So," said Gatsby, "that leaves the embezzlement option and hope for the best."

"Absolutely not!" said Miriam. "You don't have to take that risk."

Exasperated, Gatsby stood and paced around the living room until the temptation of walking out and slamming the door vanished, and he was calmer. Then he returned to the chair beside Miriam. "Honey, you're not listening. There are no other options."

"Get it from Moe," she said.

"You're not being serious," said Gatsby. "I told you that Moe wants me to pay him almost two million dollars. He wanted it by the end of the year, and I talked him into giving me another sixty days, until the end of February—which is equally impossible. Why would you expect him to give me a red cent?"

She seemed calmer. "Come on, Captain Gatsby. You were in army intelligence. This is just another operation. You know Moe better than anyone else, and I'm sure you know about skeletons in his closet. Get creative. And do it soon before your CPN house of cards collapses."

Miriam stood up, placed the bloody mary on the end table, and bent down over him. She said, "Squeeze his balls if you have to, threaten to cut off his prick if you have to—but get him to cough up all the money that will guarantee we get out of this mess—I suggest ten million." She rested one knee between his legs and gave him a tentative kiss that grew warmer when he accepted it, relieved. When she pulled away, she gave him a smile that was one part truce, one part warning. "Now, get your ass back to the office and don't come home until you have a plan."

~~~~~

Later that afternoon, Gatsby entered his empty office building. He rode up the elevator to his floor, headed straight to the bar and made himself a strong vodka and tonic. Then he sat down at his desk, leaned back in his chair, and thought carefully about Miriam's command.

To motivate Moe, he needed to identify the leverage that would pressure Moe into loaning him up to $10 million. He tried to recall all the trips he'd taken with Moe over the years. He went over to the file cabinet and dug out his old calendars and started turning pages. He called Miriam and he asked her if she recalled when Moe got married and when he and Joyce had their first girl.

"I think I can figure it out from my old calendars. I'll call you back in a half hour."

He returned to turning pages in his calendars and started writing a list of the dates and places where he and Moe traveled and partied.
~~~~~

There were at least three trips that could cause Moe major grief. It all depended on whether he was single or married at the time.

He closed his eyes and allowed his mind to drift. He thought back over decades of risks, all the times luck had dangled his potential humiliation in front of his eyes like a promise. In those moments, he'd kept control over himself. He'd always found his way out. But this time, it was like he kept finding more dead ends.

He said, ever so softly, "Come on, Lord, give this poor sinner a break."

The phone rang. Miriam.

"He and Joyce were married on October 15, 1994, and Stephanie was born on November 20, 1996." As Miriam was talking to him, Gatsby scanned the list of dates and a huge grin engulfed his face. He took his pen and circled the date, November 24, 1996. He sat back down in his chair and took out an eight-inch Cuban cigar and lit it.

After approximately a half hour having thoroughly enjoyed the cigar while thinking through the details of the meeting he anticipated having with Moe, he closed the office and headed home.

It was just past ten p.m.

He undressed in the bathroom and then slid into bed next to Miriam. He fondled her until she awoke. Before she could say anything, he said, "I've solved our problem. Celebrate?" and she turned toward him.

~ ~ ~ ~ ~

The next morning, Gatsby arrived at his office just after 8 a.m.

He went into his office and called Moe's direct number. Moe's assistant answered, and when he asked for Moe, she hesitated.

Gatsby said, "Look, Mary, I know that Moe is avoiding me. But you tell him he'd better call me back or he will be in a world of hurt. And tell him I am not bluffing!"

Moe eventually called him back and after some small talk, Gatsby said he wanted to meet him in the steam room of the Bellevue's fitness center at midnight.

"You must be kidding."

"No, I'm serious. I don't trust you, Moe. I need to talk with you, and I need to ensure that you are not wearing a wire."

"I am disappointed in you, Gatsby. I always regarded you as one of—if not my closest—friends."

"The feeling was mutual, Moe, until you instructed your lawyer to call me and put the squeeze on me. Just be there. Tonight. I'm renting a room, and if anyone at the hotel inquires, you are my guest. If you don't show, I guarantee you there will be a story about you in the *Inquirer* that will make you very unhappy."

CHAPTER 40

GATSBY

At 12:15 a.m., Gatsby pushed open the door to the men's steam room of the Bellevue's fitness center. He wore nothing but a towel draped around his neck. He stood still for a minute, attempting to locate Moe in the banks of steam. Someone was sitting in the corner on the middle step. He moved in that direction and saw it was Moe. He walked over and extended his hand. Moe stood and clasped Gatsby's hand as Gatsby climbed up to his level.

"It's been a while, Moe. You never call me."

"My lawyers thought it would be best. I wanted to, Gatsby, honestly. But they said no."

"Moe, Moe, please don't bullshit me. It's insulting. Nobody tells you what to do."

Moe tugged his towel tightly around his waist.

"And you don't need to hide your cock under that towel. I've seen your cock many times."

Moe smiled faintly. "Why all this mystery? A secret meeting in a steam room at midnight. Did you filch this scenario from a John le Carré novel?"

"It's simple, Moe. I can't run the risk that some assistant US Attorney would convince you to wear a wire and dig the hole that I'm in even deeper. This venue keeps us both honest."

"Okay, I get it," said Moe. "I hope that you don't have any romantic intentions toward me." He laughed nervously, aware that the joke wasn't the least bit funny.

"Just business. Your shark attorney called me to demand that I repay almost $2 million. I'm getting calls from a lot of my investors. Apparently, the word is out that I'm sitting on a pile of money, and they all want me to pay up. There is a run on the Gatsby Bank, and you know better than anyone that I'm not in any position to dole out millions of dollars. I'm living on my income from GVF and praying that either some of the CPN options monetize soon or that my GVF carried income account starts to build. Unfortunately, the good Lord hasn't paid much attention to my pleas."

Moe started to laugh but caught himself just as the pump turned on and fresh steam began filling the room. "Yeah, you're in an expensive condo, on the water, and drive a Jaguar, have millions in CPN debt, and assume that the Lord will provide? Now that's what I call a fantasy."

"Don't act stupid, Moe. I bought the condo and car when I was liquid. I don't have any money. You know everything about me." He pointed to his crotch. "Including the size, shape, and color of my dick. There is no need for us to bullshit each other."

"So where do you expect to get the several million dollars you committed to paying the investors, including me? How the hell are you going to lay your hands on that kind of cash?"

Gatsby smiled. He moved closer to Moe so that their butts were touching. He placed his right hand on Moe's shoulder and put enough pressure on it so that Moe turned his head to look directly at Gatsby.

"You're not going to molest me, are you?" said Moe, a rigid grin on his face.

"I'm not into men," said Gatsby.

"I didn't think so," said Moe. "So why this touching and closeness?"

"I'm just showing you how much I value your friendship and how much I appreciate the fact you're going to loan me the ten million dollars I need to pay off all my CPNs, including yours. I'm going to secure that note with my GVF carried interest account." Gatsby smiled and pushed his body harder against Moe.

Moe's eyes widened. He tried to move away from Gatsby, but Gatsby tightened his grip on Moe's right shoulder and continued to look directly at him.

"Why the hell should I give you ten million? For what? It's your problem, Gatsby. I've given you plenty of money that has turned to crap. No. Not another cent, farthing, shekel, or drachma."

"I was hoping you'd see things my way," said Gatsby. "You know, a friendship that goes back to graduate school days, plenty of good times together. 'A friend in need is a friend indeed,' and I am certainly a friend in need. Right? So maybe I need to take a different tack. Rather than beseeching, I'll try persuading." Gatsby loosened his grip on Moe's right shoulder and grabbed Moe around the neck as if to choke him and brought his mouth close to Moe's left ear; and simultaneously, with his left hand, reached under Moe's towel, and grabbed his testicles and squeezed.

Moe screamed. He gasped a choked, desperate breath against the pressure around his neck.

"Gatsby, that hurts!" He was coughing and writhing to get away from the pain. "Stop! Please stop!"

Gatsby released the pressure on Moe's testicles and then spoke softly directly into Moe's ear. "Do you remember when we traveled to Las Brises in Acapulco, and partied with two whores, snorted cocaine, and got drunk?" Gatsby applied pressure and Moe screamed again.

"That's bullshit, Gatsby. You bedded down with two whores, snorted cocaine, and got drunk. I went back to our unit and went to sleep."

Gatsby released the pressure. "I know that Moe, but that won't help you. You told Joyce we were going to Pebble Beach to celebrate Stephanie's birth and play golf. When I tell her that you lied to her and did not go to Pebble Beach but joined me on a trip Acapulco—and then she'll believe anything I tell her, specifically that you were partying with whores while she was nursing baby Stephanie." Gatsby re-applied pressure and Moe screamed.

"You're blackmailing me! Stop! Oh, please, stop!"

Gatsby released the pressure but still maintained a firm hold on Moe's testicles. "Good for you Moe, you finally got my gist. If you don't agree to give me the ten million in the next ten seconds, I will squeeze your balls until you pass out. Then I'll deliver the letter that I've prepared to Joyce and tell her where she can find you. You have ten seconds. Nine. Eight. Seven…"

"All right," said Moe. "I'll do it. Just let me go."

Gatsby released his grip on Moe's testicles and took his right arm from around Moe's neck. Moe slumped against the wall; his eyes closed.

Gatsby watched him for ten minutes and said, "Time to go, Moe. Here, let me help you."

Moe let Gatsby help him down from the top step and lead him into the dressing room. Moe sat down on the bench in front of his locker and held his head in his hands. Gatsby left him there and went over his own locker and got dressed.

When Gatsby was dressed and ready to leave, he walked back to Moe, who hadn't moved. He had only managed to put on his underwear and socks. "I'll have Frye prepare the note and security agreement tomorrow and have it to you by Friday morning. I want the check in my office by Monday. Also, just remember, if there is any hiccup in completing this deal, my letter will go to Joyce—and, at a minimum, you'll be looking at a $50-million prenup problem in addition to the breakup of your happy home."

Moe raised his head and looked at Gatsby. His eyes were half-closed.

"There won't be any problem," he said. And then lowered his head.

PART IV

CHAPTER 41

GATSBY

January 3, 2005

A week later, Gatsby entered the foyer of his office at 9 a.m. sharp. He asked Kathy to set up a conference call with Frye and Hawking as soon as they were both available. He estimated that the call would require fifteen to twenty minutes of their time. Hannah was due in the office by 9:30.

"Tell her I need to chat with her," said Gatsby. Then he disappeared into his office with coffee and the *Wall Street Journal*. Kathy buzzed him shortly thereafter and said the meeting with Frye and Hawking was on for 10. He felt good. No, he felt downright expansive. When Hannah came into his office, he chatted with her about her Jackson Hole vacation with her husband and then invited her into the conference room.

"I envy you. I would have preferred your vacation to what I've been doing—which was scut work. The good news is that I solved some pressing problems." He leaned into the table and gave her his most sincere smile. "First, I want to thank you for everything you did last year. Your performance was outstanding, and it will show in the report we'll send the investors. I'm giving you a $25,000-a-year raise effective the beginning of the year. Congratulations."

Slightly blushing, she started to stammer a thank you.

"You're worth a lot more. But I can't afford any more until a few more of our deals monetize. Keep up the great work. The second thing is I need you to clear the decks so that you can draft the annual report to the investors. I expect to have the financials and K-1s from Ernst and Young by mid-February and I want to be able to send out the report with the K-1s in early March. Can you give me a draft in a week to ten days?"

"Absolutely."

"Great." He stood and walked around the desk and shook her hand using both of his. Kathy buzzed him. He picked up the phone as Hannah left the conference room. "They're on the phone."

"Everett, Colin?" said Gatsby.

"We're here," said Frye.

"Thanks for being available on such short notice. I think we're now able to put all this CPN bullshit behind us. I negotiated a five-year, ten-million-dollar loan secured by my carried interest in the GVF."

"That is fantastic," said Everett.

"I agree," said Colin. "You've pulled off a miracle."

"Thanks," said Gatsby. "Colin, I want you to draft the letter to all investors that are holding CPNs and exercise the call provision, which gives them thirty days to either agree to accept full payment and surrender their options or surrender the note and retain the options. I'd appreciate your working with Everett to track the transactions, so he can present me a list of checks I need to issue. I'll also need to know what options to reserve for the investors who have decided to retain their options. Will that work for you guys?"

"I don't see any problem," said Frye.

"I agree," said Everett. "What you've accomplished is amazing. You've avoided a huge train wreck. I've had several sleepless nights worrying about how we were going to deal with the CPN debt. I'm relieved."

Gatsby's feeling of expansiveness seemed to embrace his whole world. "As are we all, my friends."

CHAPTER 42

GATSBY

Five months later, Friday, May 13, 2005

As Gatsby was ushered into Colin Frye's office, he was surprised to see Everett Hawking and Frye's partner, Art Fallon, sitting at the conference table. He pulled out a chair next to Hawking, and looked over to Frye and said, "What's up? Kathy said you needed to see me immediately."

"Guilty as charged," said Frye. "We've got a serious problem with the Department of Securities. Nathan called me yesterday and said they were getting close to completing their investigation and they needed the personal financial statements we said we were working on. He was polite yet blunt. He implied that their office was under a lot of pressure to wind up the investigation."

"Maybe," said Art, "it's time to tell them that all the investors have either been paid in full or have surrendered their notes and retained their options."

Frye shook his head. "We'll do that, but I doubt it will stop their investigation. Learning that you have been able to pay off all the investors who did not want to retain their options would undercut their hypothesis that you are running a Ponzi scheme—but it would have no effect on their position that you were not licensed to sell securities and the securities you sold should have been registered." He seemed to realize how negative he sounded. "But don't worry, I'll tell them when I meet with them to give them the financial statement. I'll make the argument that since the outstanding CPNs have either been paid off or surrendered, their investigation is moot."

Gatsby turned to Everett and said, "What do you think? You know these guys."

"I've been out of this for a while," said Everett. "Please refresh my memory. When did they start the investigation?"

"I don't have an exact date; but it was probably a month or so before Gatsby's first interview," said Frye. "Middle of July 2003. Then a second one in September of the same year."

"I can see why they're anxious," said Everett. "They've been at this for two years."

"Colin, you've done a great job," said Gatsby. "I needed every day of the time you bought."

"Have we given them everything they've asked for?" said Hawking.

"Everything except the seven years of financial statements—which we don't have and can't possibly create," said Frye.

"Have we told them that?" said Hawking.

Frye shook his head. "All we've said is we're working on them."

"To whom does Kyle report?" said Hawking.

"Bill Schenck, the secretary of banking," said Frye.

"Do any of you have a relationship with him?"

"I think George McKnight may," said Gatsby. "He's mentioned his name a few times."

"Good," said Frye, "I suggest that I meet with Kyle and Nathan to deliver Gatsby's current financial statement and tell him that this is the best we can do, and then tell him that all the outstanding notes have either been paid off or surrendered, and I'll offer to provide the proof if he wants it. And then I'll make the argument that their investigation is moot and issuing a cease-and-desist order would not accomplish anything other than sully Gatsby's reputation. After the meeting, I'll brief McKnight and find out whether he feels it's worthwhile to approach Schenck. Frankly, based on what I know about Schenck's reputation, I'm not optimistic."

"Everett, what do you think?" said Frye.

"I can't add anything. It's a Hail Mary, but it's all we've got. They'll probably wind up their investigation within a month and then send us a proposed cease-and-desist order and a proposed fine and ask us to agree to it."

"And then?" said Gatsby, looking toward Frye.

"We negotiate the lowest number we can on the fine, and only admit that you sold the notes, and you didn't have a license. And we tell them we will issue a press release after the order is published and request they refrain from commenting if they receive inquiries. They'll publish the order; the *Inquirer* will pick it up and will include the information in our press release in their article. It's likely that some of your investors will see it and you'll be confronted by the GVF advisory board."

"Shit," said Gatsby, "and then what do I do?"

"You do what you always do," said Frye. "You put your golden tongue into high gear, and you charm their socks off and point to the performance of the GVF. It's extremely unlikely that your advisory board will do anything that might impair the performance of their golden goose. You'll be fine," said Frye. Everett and Art laughed. Gatsby tried to catch the humor, but the thought of the bad publicity made him nauseated.

As Gatsby stood up and prepared to leave, he smiled past his queasiness. "You guys can't imagine how great it feels to know that you all have such confidence in me."

~~~~~

When he returned to his office, he immediately placed a call to Moe. He and Moe had not spoken since the steam room incident just after Christmas. So, he could hardly contain his surprise when Moe answered the phone, and despite caller ID, sounded happy to hear from him.

"Hello, Gatsby. It's been a while."
~~~~~

"I didn't think that you would want to talk to me after our—our altercation."

Moe laughed. "Altercation! There is a euphemism if ever I've heard one. Somehow that word fails to describe the situation that I experienced on December 26. So why are you calling me?"

"Frankly, Moe, because I have no choice."

"It's my sincere hope that you're not calling to try to extract more money."

"Let me put your mind at rest, Moe. I don't need or want any more money from you. The reason I'm calling is because the value of our investment in the Gatsby Venture Fund is in jeopardy."

There was silence on Moe's end of the line. "Moe?"

"Yeah. So, what's the problem now?"

"The DoBS is planning to issue a cease-and-desist order against me within the next two weeks. The order will bar me from selling convertible promissory notes, or similar instruments, and levy a fine against me in the range of $10,000 to $50,000."

"But you're not selling CPNs anymore—and you've paid off or converted all the CPNs previously issued."

"Right. But the DoBS doesn't care about that. Their thinking is that I've violated the statute by selling CPNs without a license and the CPNs should have been registered."

"So why should the order jeopardize the Gatsby Venture Fund?"

"Because when Jerry, Jeff, and Birney see it, they will immediately investigate whether we knew that there was a DoBS investigation when we issued our private placement memorandum, which we did, and if there was one in progress, why we didn't disclose it in the PPM."

"You didn't disclose it?" said Moe.

"I talked to you about it. Frye wanted to disclose the investigation and I said it would kill the deal. The New York investor pool would dry up overnight."

Moe did not immediately respond. Then he said, "Yeah, I recall the conversation and I agreed with you. What do you want me to do?"

"I want you to send the cease-and-desist order to the advisory board when it's issued and respond to any questions they raise. Then I want you to meet with Sam Mason of the *Inquirer*, explain my CPN business, and tell him that you purchased so many millions of CPNs. Tell him that no one who bought a CPN ever complained to any government entity, and all the CPNs have been paid off or the options have been exercised. Stress the fact no one who purchased a CPN has ever lost any money."

"That's assuming you pay off the ten million dollars you extracted from me."

Gatsby wanted to scream at Moe and call him a shithead. But he controlled himself and said quietly, "I think that is a prudent assumption, Moe, but I wouldn't disclose it either to Sam Mason or the members of the advisory board as it would undermine their opinion of your objectivity and independence."

"Loosen up, Gatsby. I was joking. Anything else?"

"No, that's it, I appreciate your doing the heavy lifting."

There was a long silence on Moe's end of the line. Finally, he said, "Between my direct investment in the Gatsby Venture Fund and the ten million you extracted from me, which is secured indirectly by Gatsby Fund assets, I have fifteen million at risk. I'd be a fool to allow my anger and my bottomless disappointment in you to interfere with doing whatever is necessary to protect my investment. *Capisce?* Give my regards to Miriam, and so long."

CHAPTER 43

JERRY

Ten days later

Jerry checked his emails when he returned from lunch. He opened an email from Moe with a link to the *Inquirer* website. Moe's email was cryptic: "Please read the attached and call me."

Jerry read an article announcing that the Pennsylvania Department of Banking and Securities had issued a cease-and-desist order, which stated Christopher "Gatsby" Brooks was precluded from selling convertible promissory notes in the future and was being fined $5,000 for his prior sales of unregistered securities. It contained Gatsby's statement he had relied on the advice of an attorney he could sell his convertible promissory notes (CPNs) pursuant to exemptions from the Pennsylvania securities law. He further stated all the CPNs had either been paid off or surrendered so the notes were no longer in existence.

Jerry forwarded Moe's email to Birney and Jeff with a note he would call Moe and report back. He called Moe's direct number.

"Hi, Moe, what's the story behind this cease-and-desist order?"

As Jerry had feared, Moe's answer was rehearsed.

"Here is the short version, Jerry. Starting about twelve years ago, Gatsby would occasionally borrow money from sophisticated investors, offering an eight percent interest rate and an option for shares that had been awarded to him in a startup company with which he was working. He called the debt he sold convertible promissory notes…"

Jerry scribbled notes, but he already smelled the familiar stink of a crisis being managed. After a few minutes, Moe wrapped up. "Frankly, Jerry, I'm just as surprised as you are because I've never heard that anyone had made a complaint to the regulators."

"Do you know how many dollars' worth of notes he's sold and what is currently outstanding?"

"I don't have any idea about the total notes he's sold, either in number or amount. I do know what is outstanding."

"And how much is that?" said Jerry, bracing himself.

"Zero. He gave the investors the option of receiving cash for their notes or surrendering them and keeping the options."

"When did he do that?"

"Shortly after the first of the year."

"I see," said Jerry. "Do you have a copy of the cease-and-desist order?"

"No," said Moe, "but I'll get it and email it to you."

"Do you know when the investigation was initiated?"

"No idea. I know that Gatsby and Shirley had a falling out over Gatsby's selling the CPNs; that was about the time that Bill Dewyne died. She may have filed a complaint around that time. She was quite agitated about it. But I'm only speculating."

"Do you have a recent financial statement for Gatsby?"

"No. I've never gotten one from him."

That statement caught Jerry's attention. But then again, Moe's net worth conferred on him the freedom to conduct business any way he wanted.

"Is there anything else I can do for you, Jerry, in addition to getting you the order?"

Oh no, Jerry wanted to say, you've already dumped plenty on my lap for the day. "You've been very helpful. I'll look for the order this afternoon."

Moe's email with the order attached arrived at 2 p.m. Jerry forwarded it to Birney and Jeff and suggested they conference in the morning. By that time, he'd already combed through the origination file for the Gatsby Venture Fund and searched the internet for whatever information was available on the cease-and-desist order. The stink of crisis only grew stronger.

~ ~ ~ ~ ~

They convened in Birney's office shortly after 9 a.m. the next morning. Jerry distributed copies of the financial information that Gatsby had presented during their due diligence investigation prior to the launch of the Gatsby Venture Fund.

"I'm going to briefly summarize the facts that I've learned from the documents, my conversation with Moe, and research on the internet. The cease-and-desist order alleges that starting approximately twelve years ago, Gatsby began selling convertible promissory notes based on an opinion from a Philadelphia securities attorney, who said he did not need to register in the State of Pennsylvania." He outlined the CPN scheme and concluded, "Moe advised me he had personally purchased about a million and a half of these notes, hit big on three companies and was not aware of anyone having complained to the DoBS—which is why there was no earlier investigation. In any case, the State concluded that Gatsby did not have the right to sell the notes, and without admitting or denying the allegation, Gatsby agreed to stop selling CPNs and pay a $5,000 fine."

Jerry studied the crossed arms and furrowed brows that faced him across the table. "I know," he said. "It stinks to me, too. Moe also told me that at the beginning of this year, Gatsby exercised the call provision in the notes and forced the investors to either accept payment on their notes or surrender them and retain the options. He swept his CPNs out of existence."

"What does all this have to do with the Gatsby Venture Fund?" said Birney.

"The cease-and-desist order has no effect on the operation of the Gatsby Venture Fund. The GVF is a Pennsylvania LLC and all the appropriate papers have been filed. But the cease-and-desist order raises two issues that reflect on the veracity and completeness of the information Gatsby's team gave us. First, if the start of the DoBS investigation predated the originating of the Gatsby Venture Fund, that investigation should have been disclosed. If we decide that this is a material fact, we can certainly discover when the Department opened their file. Equally troubling is the fact Gatsby did not show any of his CPN debt on the financial statements he provided to us. I can only conclude that the omission was intentional."

"The sonofabitch," exclaimed Birney as he brought his fist down on his desk. "He gave us fraudulent financials?"

"No doubt about it," said Jerry, relieved to put his suspicion into words.

"How come Moe didn't tell us about the CPNs?" said Jeff.

"In a way, he did," said Jerry. "He told us he did several deals with Gatsby and made some serious money, all of which is true. We were the idiots who didn't ask him for details."

"Don't you think we should determine when they started the investigation?" said Jeff. "It could be material."

"I think it depends on what we decide to do about this, if anything," said Jerry.

"Do you have a recommendation?" said Birney.

"I do," said Jerry. He looked from Birney to Jeff. "I stayed up all night thinking about this situation and how to address it. So here goes. Gatsby may be a sonofabitch, but in the words of the inimitable Richard Nixon, he is our sonofabitch. The Gatsby Venture Fund has been operating for almost two years and is generating a cash-on-cash return of approximately 40 percent. Hannah is forecasting that the return will improve next year when EVG goes public. Most VC firms would walk on their grandmother's grave for these kinds of returns. Gatsby may be a fraudster, but he is a genius in the VC business. My recommendation is we do nothing, put up with the stink, and keep it from tainting the fund's reputation."

"Shouldn't we notify the investors?" said Birney. "We are the advisory board. Isn't that one of our responsibilities?"

"The advisory board doesn't have any operational or reporting responsibility to the investors. We could ask Gatsby to call a meeting of the members to advise them of his fraud. But that would be beyond insane. Our charge is to protect the interests of the members, and I believe that by doing everything we can do to keep this matter under the radar, we will be discharging our responsibilities. Also," continued Jerry, "in the event anyone finds out about the order and contacts us, we can just state it has no effect on the operations of the Gatsby Venture Fund, period."

"I agree," said Jeff, "we have to be careful. We can't afford a hint of a suspicion that Gatsby is anything but righteous. His deal flow would dry up and GVF would tank. We need to bury this to the extent we can."

"I'm on board," said Birney. "As they say in Oklahoma, 'You've gotta dance with the one who brung you.'"

CHAPTER 44

GATSBY

Two years later, July 9, 2007

Gatsby traveled to New York to brief the full advisory board of the Gatsby Venture Fund on the projected financial results through the fall of 2007. During the meeting, which took place in the Bricker and Weldon conference room, Gatsby presented a summary of the GVF's performance from inception and forecasted the fund's projected total performance at liquidation—which he estimated could be accomplished by the end of 2008. Jeff, Jerry, and Birney were busy reviewing the documents.

"To summarize," said Gatsby, "when we distribute the next $50 million in March, the partners will have received $130 million—the return of their investment plus a $30 million profit. All the capital except for $2 million has been invested, and we are projecting that at the GVF's termination in 2008, the partners will have realized an additional $60 to $80 million. Our best estimate is that the fund will have generated between 115 and 125 percent." He then distributed another spreadsheet. "This is a report by Thompson Venture Economics on the performance of Venture Capital Funds by vintage year. The GVF vintage year is 2003. The maximum return achieved by the fifty-three funds surveyed is 39.5 percent and the pooled average is minus-six percent."

Gatsby sat back in his seat to allow the information he'd presented to sink in.

"And these projections are a net of all expenses of the fund, including your carried interest?" said Birney.

"Absolutely," said Gatsby.

"I knew we were doing well," said Jerry. "I never dreamed we were doing this well! You and Hannah are to be congratulated."

"I'll echo that," said Jeff.

All Birney could do is shake his head and mutter, "Amazing."

"Gatsby, you've made the three of us heroes," said Jerry. "I expect that our names will appear on more invitation lists."

"Thanks," said Gatsby. "It's been a helluva ride and the three of you have been a great help."

Birney walked over to the liquor cabinet, removed four glasses, and poured aged Jameson into each glass. "It may be a bit early, but this calls for a drink." He distributed the glasses and went back to his chair. "To Gatsby, who managed to exceed all of our expectations. Thank you."

"To Gatsby," said Jeff and Jerry simultaneously. All four drained their glasses.

"You're very kind," said Gatsby. "As we bask in the Jameson glow, I'd like to share my thoughts for the future."

"Shoot," said Jerry.

"I think that my value to the GVF is approaching the point of diminishing returns. The GVF is on course to liquidate within the next three years. Since the GVF is fully invested, our focus is on harvesting the fruits of these investments and winding down the operations to make final distributions to the members. Hannah is fully capable of handling many of the tasks that will need to be accomplished—like monitoring the performance of the companies, participating in the company board meetings, and ensuring we are moving in the right direction.

"I am currently exploring the feasibility of launching a new fund, the Gatsby Hedge Fund, that will invest and trade in late-stage investments and pre-IPO securities of technology companies. It will be capitalized at $1 billion. If I'm successful in raising the money and can launch the

Gatsby Hedge Fund, I would like to reduce my involvement in the day-to-day operations of GVF and increase Hannah's salary. I've talked with her, and she's excited about the prospect of more responsibility."

"What's the time frame?" said Birney.

"I plan to start testing the waters this month. I hope the performance of the GVF will create motivation for many of our investors to place another, larger, bet on me. Hawking, Frye, and Hannah are helping me with the feasibility study."

"Fascinating," said Birney.

"Let us know what you find out," said Jerry. "We're all impressed with Hannah and I'm confident that the GVF will not suffer. The three of us will caucus during the next few days and let you know if we see any issues that you'll have to address."

"Perfect," said Gatsby. "And now, gentlemen, I'll take my leave. I have a meeting at Bear Stearns."

CHAPTER 45

GATSBY

Monday, March 17, 2008

The Gatsby Hedge Fund (GHF), launched in the fall of 2007, had been operating for six months. The success of its predecessor, the Gatsby Venture Fund, was on target to achieve 125 percent cash-on-cash return for the partners, a return of three times that of its best performing peer. Buoyed by that performance, Gatsby and Hannah had no problems raising a billion dollars for the new hedge fund.

The GHF easily found its first investments in firms that had announced their intention to file IPOs. It purchased shares from early investors in those firms who wanted to limit their risks. For the first six months, ending March 2008 the fund was already projecting a 25 percent profit.

Gatsby was riding high. His income finally exceeded the cost of his lifestyle. In Philadelphia, he was a rock star, admired by his investors, appreciated by the charities he supported, and courted by the strategists, analysts, surrogates, and officeholders in the Republican Party. The backbiting and backstabbing had stopped. For the first time during his career in business, he was universally admired, and he felt he had achieved the greatness he longed for. It had been a slog—but he was elated to have made it.

At 10 a.m., Gatsby bounded into his office suite.

"My, you're tanned," said Kathy.

"I spent a lot of time in the water, snorkeling. The weather was great, the kids had a good time. It was perfect."

"Where did you go?"

"Iberostar in Playa del Carmen, Mexico. Great for families."

"Welcome back. Your mail is on your desk along with your messages. When can you meet with Hannah?"

Gatsby looked at his watch. "Tell her that I'll meet with her at 11 a.m."

As Gatsby sipped his coffee, he went through his mail and returned telephone calls. When he completed the mail and the calls, he leaned back in his chair and put his feet up on the desk and opened the *Wall Street Journal*. His eyes immediately zeroed in on the front page: *J.P. Morgan buys Bear in Fire Sale, As Fed Widens Credit to Avert Crisis*. Stunned, Gatsby sat upright in his chair and read the article slowly, forcing himself to comprehend the implications.

There were several additional stories in the paper, and he read one after the other. At one point he felt he was reading a novel, one that grabbed his attention and forced him to turn pages.

But the story about Bear Stearns was true. Distilled to its essentials, the *Wall Street Journal* reported that Bear Stearns, the seventh highest-ranked investment bank in the world, which was founded in 1923 and went public in 1985, had been swallowed by J. P. Morgan. As recently as Monday, it had 15,000 employees with twenty-eight offices around the world, a market capitalization of $3.5 billion, and $18 billion in cash.

Starting on Monday, March 11, a rumor had circulated in the financial community that Bear did not have the liquidity to meet its obligations. Thereafter, Bear was buffeted by lenders demanding repayment, and its normal financing sources refused to accept its collateral. By Thursday night, March 13, Bear's cash position was depleted to the extent that it would not have been able to open on Friday but for the US government guaranteeing a short loan advanced by J. P. Morgan. Faced with the alternative of a bankruptcy filing, or a sale to J. P. Morgan for two dollars a share, or about $236 million, Bear's management chose the sale.

When he had read every article in the paper related to Bear Stearns, he sat back in his chair and tried to comprehend the significance of the event. It just didn't make sense. He knew many of the executives who managed Bear. The retired chairman, Ace Greenberg, was a friend, and an investor in both the Gatsby Venture Fund and in the Gatsby Hedge Fund—as were several other Bear executives.

He buzzed Hannah and asked her to come into his office. When she appeared, he knew by her expression she had already heard the news—probably days ago, while he was on vacation.

"I followed the story all week on the cable news stations. It is mind-boggling."

"I've been in the business world for forty years," said Gatsby, "and I've never seen this before."

"It's rare," said Hannah.

"Do you know what triggered the run in Bear's case?"

"I don't, but I'm sure that your buddies would know, especially the ones at Bear and Goldman Sachs. You should talk with them."

"I will," said Gatsby. Of course, he would. He wanted to talk more, to process his shock, but he didn't like the feeling of being the last person to have heard the news. He forced himself to shrug it off. "How about you bring me up to date on the miracles you performed while I was basking in the sun in Playa del Carmen?" he said, brightly.

After meeting with Hannah, Gatsby asked Kathy to get him lunch at the Continental Midtown. He turned on the computer and put the term "Collapse of Bear Sterns" in his search engine and proceeded to read and take notes on every relevant post. By 4:30 p.m. he was bleary-eyed, exhausted, and thoroughly depressed. Notwithstanding everything he read, he still could not understand how billions in market value and eighty-five years of successful operations could vanish over a four-day period. He simply could not get his mind around the calamity that had consumed Bear. This was the first time since he started the Gatsby Venture Fund that his self-confidence began to ebb. And he was shaken. He decided to pack it in for the day, go home, and get plastered.

~~~~~~

The next morning, he called Kathy from home and asked her to set up individual meetings with Jeff Bascomb at Goldman Sachs and Ace Greenberg at Bear. "A lunch or dinner meeting is fine. I'll take a late train on Wednesday. Get me into the Plaza and book my return on Friday afternoon."

Gatsby arrived on a Penn Station in the later afternoon on Wednesday took a cab to the Plaza, checked into his room, and went downstairs for dinner. He was back in his room by 8:30 p.m., physically and emotionally exhausted. The failure of Bear Stearns had affected him, and when he finally found a name for what he was feeling, it was fear.

If Bear Stearns could be brought down over a four-day period, why not the Gatsby Hedge Fund?

As he lay on the plush mattress, his head propped up by three down pillows, he stared at the news. The commentator was talking about the drama that was playing out between Bear Stearns, J. P. Morgan, the Fed, and Hank Paulson. The markets were reacting. His head was spinning. He had never addressed these kinds of issues. He knew how to find investors, find promising tech companies, fold them together, nurture the resulting brew, and often help create a profitable business that made its investors and managers richer. What the hell did he know about mortgage-backed securities, credit default swaps, Alt-A loans, credit insurance? Nothing. He was like Sargent Shultz, the German prison guard in *Hogan's Heroes*: HE KNEW NOTHING. Yet all these securities and the people who sold them, bought them, and held on to them would have a major effect on his life.

He knew his limitations. And he knew that his skills did not include figuring out how all this financial chaos would affect the billion-dollar hedge fund in which he had invested five million dollars of his own money and a reputation that had taken took him thirty years to establish.

Tomorrow's meetings were critical. He had to get the information he needed from Ace and Jeff. He had no other options. He got out of bed, went into the bathroom, and took a double dose of sleeping pills.
~~~~~~

~~~~~~

The next morning found him in a dark mood. He could not walk into Goldman with a sad-sack attitude. He checked his watch and headed outdoors. The temperature was mild, and the sun was bright and warm. He had time for a walk in Central Park. He crossed the street and circumnavigated the lower part of the park, crossing it through Bethesda Terrace. The street vendors and musicians were already out in force. He was feeling better.

An hour later he entered the Goldman Sachs building and took the elevator to the reception area to wait for Jeff. In a few minutes, he found himself escorted to an office on the southeast corner of the building, one that looked out at the Hudson River. Jeff Bascomb was in the doorway, and he enthusiastically shook Gatsby's hand.

"Welcome to New York. Please sit down." He motioned to a table in the corner. "Congratulations on the pending wind-down of the Gatsby Venture Fund. I understand the final distribution is scheduled for the end of the year. That huge return is incredible for the crappy venture capital environment we've had. You and Hannah should be proud of what you've accomplished."

"A lot of the credit is due to Hannah. I was lucky to have found her. She has been a terrific number two. We all owe her a lot."

"I know, Gatsby. But you are the genius that put it all together. How is the hedge fund?"

"So far, so good. The audited reports should be out in two to three weeks."

"Great," said Jeff. He sat back in his chair. "Kathy said you wanted to see me to talk about the current Wall Street environment."

"Kathy is diplomatic. What I wanted to talk about is this." He opened his briefcase and placed the March 17 issue of the *Wall Street Journal* announcing the purchase of Bear Stearns by J. P. Morgan at two dollars a share. "To put it crudely, we provincials in Philadelphia, a mere hundred miles away, have a hard time understanding how, within the period of a week, an eighty-five-year-old company, with 15,000 employees,
~~~~~~

twenty-eight offices, that was trading for $93 a share a month before, could be swallowed up for two bucks a share and effectively disappear. For us, it's equivalent to the disappearance of the Twin Towers in less than two hours. The reason I'm here is because I know I'm not smart enough to understand it, so I came back to the mecca of investment banking to seek an explanation."

The smile on Jeff's face had faded. He stood and walked over to the window with the view of the Hudson and Ground Zero, where the Twin Towers once stood. He looked at the view for a full minute. Then he turned to Gatsby and said, "I'm hungry, and I assume you'd like something to eat and drink. How about some coffee and French pastries?"

"That would be fine," said Gatsby. "Regular black coffee."

Jeff headed to his office door. "I'll only be a few minutes. There's plenty of stuff to read in the magazine rack." He pointed to the location of the rack and left the office.

Annoyed, Gatsby walked over to the magazine rack, chose the current issue of the *Economist*, and returned to his chair, flipping through the pages to see if the magazine had any information about Bear Stearns. It was like everything else in the world. It was irrelevant, and the guy capable of answering his questions was out playing coffee boy.

Jeff returned in fifteen minutes with his assistant. They were carrying coffee, cups and saucers, silverware and a large plate of French croissants and pastries. The assistant set the table for three persons, poured coffee for Gatsby and Jeff, and then withdrew from the office.

Gatsby looked quizzically at the extra place setting.

"I'm going to respond to your question in accordance with the Goldman party line—the presentation we would make to a client in response to the question that you asked. Then, I've arranged for a member of my group, George Smythe, to join us. I'll introduce you, and then I'll leave you with him for reasons that will become apparent. He's been with the firm for about three years and is the key salesman on our derivatives desk. He is analytical and has a good understanding of the exotic securities that have upended the financial market. He has a reputation for being an iconoclast, but, in the words of the radio commentator Paul Harvey, he'll tell you 'the rest of the story.' My only request is that in the event you share what he tells you with others, you will not reveal the source of the information. Do you agree?"

"Of course," said Gatsby, a bit nonplused.

"Okay," said Jeff. "Here you go. Bear Stearns's problems, which led to its implosion, were largely self-inflicted. Although it had a stellar reputation for being a feisty competitor and racked up years of uninterrupted profits, it had serious management problems and weak leadership. Hence, the serious decline in its reputation and loss of confidence among its lenders and counterparties.

"Two hedge funds had collected $1.6 billion from individual investors' pension funds and other nonprofits but were heavily invested in risky derivatives related to the mortgage market. The two Bear Stearns fund managers were inexperienced and incompetent. The funds were over-leveraged and inadequately hedged. When the housing market started to crater last year, the funds imploded and filed bankruptcy. When the bankruptcy documents were filed, it was revealed that Bear Stearns had made enormous profits from managing and trading with the funds, and the two managers had milked the funds for millions of dollars. The investors lost their entire investment.

"In early November, the *Journal* published a story about Bear Stearns. It revealed that during the ten-day hedge fund crisis—the worst in the firm's history—many of the key executives of the company appeared to be distracted and did no appreciate the magnitude of the crisis the company was facing.

"So, that contributed to a general unease about Bear's liquidity and discouraged lenders from taking Bear's paper as collateral on new transactions. Lenders demanded repayment—all of which led to the run on Bear. It's a damn shame that so many of the employees who'd worked there for years and had their pensions invested in Bear stock have seen their retirement vanish. A damn shame."

Gatsby drank his hot coffee in gulps. He was cold, and somehow, it was only making the cold knot in his stomach worse.

"It's still shocking."

There was a knock on the door. A man with a shaved head, wearing a blue blazer and tan slacks, entered the office.

"George Smythe," said Jeff. "Let's sit down for a few minutes and chat." He filled their cups—Gatsby had drained his. "I've told George our history, Gatsby, and he knows why you're here. George worked for J. P. Morgan on their derivatives sales desk from 1998 through 2005 when he joined Goldman. He's worked on derivatives since he's been here."

Gatsby rose and shook hands with Jeff. "Thanks, Jeff. I appreciate your taking the time to help me understand what happened. And give my regards to your brother."

"Will do, Gatsby. Keep up the great work with the hedge fund."

When Jeff was safely out of the room, Gatsby turned to George. "What is it that you are going to tell me that Jeff doesn't want to hear?"

"Jeff has heard it before. Since what I'm going to tell you deviates from the Goldman party line, he doesn't want to hear it in your presence."

"I see," said Gatsby. "So why did Bear implode?"

"For all the reasons Jeff enumerated, plus one important one he did not want to talk about. Bear failed because one-third of their assets were invested in collateralized debt obligations, CDOs created from residential mortgages. Warren Buffet has referred to these types of securities as 'financial weapons of mass destruction,' which is fairly accurate. They are bundles of home mortgages, like the one that you have on your home, that are structured and sold by an investment bank to offer above-market rates of interest to eager buyers and provide huge fee income to the investment banks for structuring them.

"As long as the housing market was expanding, everything was fine. But when the homeowners began to miss mortgage payments, and the values of houses declined, and homeowners found it was in their best interest to abandon their homes because there was no equity there, the individual mortgages went into default. As the default rates increased in 2007, the market no longer knew how to value or price CDOs. The financial chain that linked the US households that paid the mortgages with the CDO investors who purchased the bundle of mortgages was so long and complex that even experts, such as me, could not predict how the defaults in the mortgages would affect the CDOs at the other end of the chain. The rating agencies lowered their valuations of the CDOs, and the accountants insisted that the CDOs be written down to 'market value.' But because of the high and increasing rates of defaults in the housing market, no one wanted to buy CDOs. So, the investment banks discovered they were impossible to sell without offering a huge discount—and without having comparable sales, they were impossible to value."

Gatsby's head spun with confusion. "I think I understand why the CDOs were created and why an investor would buy them. But I thought that many of them were rated triple-A."

"Ah, yes," said George, "there's the rub. The original CDOs designed by J. P. Morgan when I was there bundled commercial loans, not mortgages. CDOs created out of commercial loans are far less risky because the investment bank can accurately verify the credit and because the bundle of loans is not correlated."

"What do you mean by 'not correlated.'"

"It means that if your bundle consists of loans to different industries, located all over the country, the probability that the default of any single loan would presage the default of another is extremely low. Except in the case of a recession that grips the entire country, each industry essentially marches to the tune of its own drummer. When I was at J. P. Morgan, we did a couple of mortgage backed CDOs, but we were uncomfortable doing them and never pursued the mortgage market. The CDO was just not suitable for that market because of the lack of information about the individual debtors and the fact all the loans come from a single industry—and worse, may come from a single area of the country."

"How many dollars' worth of CDOs have been issued?"

"About two trillion worldwide."

Gatsby shook his head. "What is the solution to the problem, George? I mean, what is going to happen to these investment banks that have billions of dollars of CDOs on their balance sheet and they can't sell them? Do you expect that other investment banks will fail?"

"Definitely—unless they arrange a sale or accomplish a huge restructuring prior to the day that their bank experiences a run. Bear Stearns was the canary in the coal mine. Lehman has a huge inventory of this crap. If they don't merge, they fail, and so will Merrill Lynch."

"What about Goldman?"

"Goldman has only twelve percent of its assets in CDOs, has a lot more cash, and isn't as leveraged. Plus, we have a secret weapon."

"What's that?" said Gatsby.

"Hank Paulson. Do you think that the Secretary of the Treasury will let his alma mater fail?"

Gatsby smiled. "No, I don't. Goldman Sachs is golden." He stood. "George, you've been an enormous help, as has Jeff. Can I have your card—and do you mind if I call you with some follow-up questions?"

George pulled out a card and handed it to Gatsby. "Call me any time. I must say, I don't envy you. Managing a hedge fund is always a risky proposition. The current environment multiplies the risk—significantly."

"Why so?" said Gatsby.

"I suggest you spend some time in the library and refresh your memory on how the economy reacted to the Russian default, the bursting of the dot-com bubble, the Enron/ WorldCom accounting scandals... The current CDO problem is worse than any of those because of the large number of CDOs that have been produced and the fact they have migrated all over the world. It is ugly —and it will get uglier."

~ ~ ~ ~ ~

Gatsby exited the building on Williams Street and walked north to Delmonico's restaurant. It was almost noon. Although he was not particularly hungry, he needed a quiet place to sit, have a drink, and sort out his thoughts. It was a lot to take in. But one thing was clear. He could not have chosen a worse time to have created a hedge fund.

He entered Delmonico's and told the hostess he wanted to sit in the bar. He found a seat and ordered a bloody mary, spicy. He had three and a half hours before his meeting with Ace. He had a hard time imagining what Ace could possibly add to what he's already learned. It was already clear to him what options he had. He could either hunker down, manage the hedge fund, and hope he survived the recession that was sure to come. Or he could voluntarily liquidate a substantial part of the fund, return the capital to the investors, and explain his reasoning. His income would be reduced, but he could recover a large portion of his five-million-dollar investment and would reduce the losses the fund would incur when the recession hit. At least his reputation would be preserved.

After talking with Jeff and George, he no longer had the confidence to pull off a second miracle in the middle of a financial crisis and recession. He finished his drink, paid the bartender, caught a taxi back to his room.

At exactly four o'clock his phone woke him up. It was Ace Greenberg announcing he was in the lobby. "Order me a martini," he said. "I'll meet you in the bar in fifteen."

He quickly dressed, took the elevator down to the main floor and found Ace sitting at a table near the window. His first reaction was shock. Although it had only been a year since he'd last met with Ace, the man looked at least five years older. He put on his most ingratiating smile and said, "Ace, I am so happy that you could arrange to see me."

Ace seemed to have to exert a lot of effort to stand. "It's good to see you, Gatsby. You are a sight for a couple of very sore eyes." Gatsby saw that there were tears in his eyes.

"I know," said Gatsby. "Last week had to have been tough on you."

"You don't know the half of it. It was by far the worst week of my life—worse than when I was diagnosed with cancer many years ago. It was god-awful."

Gatsby lifted his glass and said, "Here's to better times." Ace lifted his glass. "It would take another Holocaust to make them worse."

"Ace," said Gatsby, leaning into the table, "I've read all the articles and I spent a couple of hours at Goldman with Jeff Bascomb. But I'd like to get your insight. Why did this happen? Were there things anyone could have done to prevent the calamity?"

Ace looked down into his drink. Tears started to slide down his face. He pulled a handkerchief from the inside pocket of his coat and dabbed his eyes. Gatsby was afraid he was going to collapse.

Finally, he was able to speak. "It happened because senior management, including myself, was unable to come to grips with the severity of the problems we faced. Our big problem, along with every other investment bank, was the amount of CDO crap we had on our balance sheet. It was impossible to value and more impossible to sell for anywhere near what we had into it. We needed to focus the company on solving that problem—whatever it would take. Unfortunately, we did not do that, Instead, starting in mid-2007, we, senior management, either allowed or participated in one fiasco after another, all of which ruined our stellar reputation, depressed the stock, and provided grist for the rumor mill that resulted in the run that forced us to sell ourselves to Morgan for a pittance."

"After Standard and Poor cut our rating from stable to negative and said the failure of the two hedge funds had 'damaged our reputation,' we arranged an investor conference call, to reassure the public. But we simply could not formulate a believable scenario that might envision a happy ending to the crisis.

Gatsby did not respond. Ace was giving him access to Bear Stearns dirty laundry.

Ace drained his glass. "I talked with other members of the board. We all wrung our hands. We changed CEOs at the end of the year; but there wasn't much the new guy could do, other than rearrange the deck chairs of our *Titanic*. There were no honors in the last hands we played before the run started. We were merely prey, a delectable dinner for the vultures who descended on us two weeks ago."

Ace looked so forlorn, so devastated. If Gatsby did not know that Ace was worth millions and made million-dollar donations to charity, he would think he was looking at someone who was old and broke.

"Why are you taking this so hard, Ace? You've got plenty of money, a beautiful wife, and you've licked your cancer. This monkey is off your back. It's time to focus on enjoying the time you have left."

Ace stared into his empty glass.

"Would you like another drink, Ace?"

Ace did not answer. It was as if he had shut out everything external to himself. Gatsby could see he was in pain.

Ace looked up at him, his eyes red, and his face moist. "I've lost that ability, Gatsby—I mean, to enjoy myself. I'm consumed with guilt. It's sapped my energy."

Gatsby was surprised. "Why the hell should you feel guilty, Ace?"

"Because I was the only one in the entire 15,000-person Bear Stearns organization who both recognized that the current senior management did not have the capability of solving our problems, and had the political capital to influence the board to make changes. We should have brought in a turnaround executive to try to save the company. That was the one card I could have played, but I was so incompetent that all I could do was bitch—which, not surprisingly, had no effect in altering the self-destructive course we were on."

"A turnaround executive?"

"Sure. It could not have resulted in a worse outcome and there is a reasonable probability it could have led to a better one. You know, like what Jerry Bascomb did for their family's tech company in the early 1990s. He turned a debacle into a win, and everyone involved, including their bank, came out of the experience with serious money. I heard him make a presentation about it at a meeting of M&A executives a few years ago. He's on your fund's advisory board, isn't he?"

"Yeah," said Gatsby. "He never mentioned it."

"Jerry's not a self-promoter," said Ace. "He wouldn't mention it unless you asked. Anyway, I've started to see a shrink and I'm taking meds, fighting to get myself out of this depression. But even if or when

I do, I'll never forgive myself for not being more assertive and hands-on. I'll always feel guilty for all those loyal employees we left twisting in the wind. That's the worst part of it. Our stock and earnings made the Bear executives filthy rich, but our employees got fucked." He slowly lifted himself out of the chair. "I hope you won't mind, Gatsby, but I need to pass on dinner. I'm not feeling well; I need to go home and climb into bed."

Gatsby stood. "I understand, Ace. Come, I'll walk out with you."

~ ~ ~ ~ ~

As he watched Ace get into a taxi, Gatsby pulled out his cell phone and called Jerry Bascomb's cell number. Jerry answered on the second ring.

"Hi, Gatsby. How the hell are you?"

"I'm good. How are Helen and the boys?"

"Helen is working at a gallery on the East side and the boys are doing great. They're just growing up too fast."

"I'm in New York for a few days. I'm staying at the Plaza. Are you available to join me for breakfast or lunch tomorrow?"

"I can do breakfast. What time?"

CHAPTER 46

JERRY

"I don't like it and I won't eat it!" Eight-year-old Alli was loud and firm about his opinion of the chicken marsala on his plate. To emphasize his point, he threw the silverware and folded his arms. Helen and Jerry had an agreement regarding the administering of discipline when they were both present. Jerry took the even days and Helen the odd days. It was an odd day. She turned to her son, and in a soothing voice said, "But Alli, Josh seems to like it and," gesturing to Jerry, "your dad has almost cleaned his plate Why not give it a try? You just might like it."

"I will not."

Helen took a deep breath. Jerry and Josh continued to eat. "Alli, remember how hungry you were the last time you refused to eat dinner? Are you willing to go hungry this evening?"

Alli shifted in his chair and closed his eyes. He was obviously straining to remember the incident. Suddenly he opened his eyes and unfolded his arms and without making any further comment took up the utensils and began to eat. Helen looked over to Jerry. He gave her a thumbs-up only she could see. Fourteen-year-old Josh was oblivious to the drama.

Later, the children were in the family room watching television. Misty, the black poodle that had succeeded Chelsey, was stretched out on her bed, snoring, and Helen was cleaning up the kitchen. Jerry was making their coffee.

"I got a call from Gatsby this afternoon," he said.

Helen stopped what she was doing and turned toward him. "The not-so-great-Gatsby?"

"He's running a one-billion-dollar hedge fund."

Helen continued washing the pots and knives. "How did he manage to do that?"

"He leveraged the money and reputation he had created from his venture fund and corralled many of the same investors, all of whom made serious money. His new fund is focused on pre-IPO technology companies. I'll bet Moe Shultz is in it."

She turned off the water, wiped her hands on a dishtowel, accepted a cup of coffee from him, which he had poured into her large decorated cup. The two of them sat down at the table.

"So why did he want to talk to you?"

"He's in town and invited me to breakfast."

She took a long drink of her coffee. "You're not going, are you?"

"Why not?" said Jerry. "Frankly I'm intrigued. The guy is unbelievable. He raised a billion dollars."

"The real enigma," said Helen, "is how he managed to stay out of jail."

"Simple answer. Because he made the investors, including us, a lot of money. If the GVF hadn't been such a win there would have been repercussions. Guys who have done a lot less are rotting in prison."

Helen grimaced. "You remember how he hit on me when we went to lunch? He almost got his hand up to my crotch while we were eating."

"I remember. You handled it well. But then again, I wasn't surprised. When we were at Moe's big function, he could not take his eyes off you. You were charming, and for some reason, he mistakenly sensed that you were available."

"So, it was my fault?"

"I didn't say that, Helen. You're a beautiful woman. He is a philanderer."

"You're going to go to breakfast?"

"Of course."

Apparently resigned, she said, "Sure, but don't give him any money."

"Come off it, Helen. You know that I don't make any investments without consulting you. Besides, I know he's not looking for money."

"*Bon!*" said Helen. "Meeting over." She threw the dishtowel onto the counter and stomped in the direction of the family room.

The next morning Jerry left his apartment and walked to the Plaza Hotel. Gatsby was waiting for him in the lobby. Jerry was surprised to find him somewhat thinner, grayer, and a little wan since he last saw him about a year ago. But he had lost none of his charm and smoothness.

They ordered breakfast. Gatsby inquired about Helen, Birney, Alli, and Josh. "I'm not sure that you know that Miriam and I adopted her sister's kids. Two years ago, in August, a Delta commuter flight from Kentucky crashed on takeoff. Miriam's sister and her husband were on it."

Jerry winced. He remembered. The copilot had taken off in the wrong direction.

"So, I'm in the same boat as you, Jerry, we're geriatric fathers. The boys are two pre-teens—great kids, respectful, polite, and good students. But, at sixty-five, I'm having to learn how to be a father all over again, contending with all these cell phones, video games, and mature pre-teen girls."

Jerry was surprised to feel a pang of empathy for Gatsby. It loosened the conversation, and it was a while before he got around to asking about Moe. Gatsby confirmed he was a major investor in the new fund, and like all the other investors, his money was growing.

Jerry nursed his cappuccino. He glanced at his watch and noticed it is almost ten o'clock. They'd been talking for over an hour. Gatsby got up from the table and said, "I need to pee. When I come back, we'll talk business."

When Gatsby returned to the table, he revealed that the only blemish on his current life is that he'd been diagnosed with prostate cancer and was currently undergoing evaluation. He'd been dealing with the problem for a month and was not sure what the doctors were going to recommend. He confessed that for the first time in his life, he'd had to confront his own mortality and the possibility that his health and possible death would prevent him from achieving the results for the hedge fund he promised his investors.

Gatsby took a sip of coffee and leaned into the table. "And then there is this whole Bear Stearns thing…it's shaken me. With all this CDO crap floating all around the world, it's likely that a lot more dominoes are going to fall. I need to restructure my situation to accommodate the fact I may not survive or survive with vastly diminished capability. My main concern is to ensure that if I'm incapacitated or die, the hedge fund will be managed properly so that the investors will not be left high and dry. People are depending on me."

Jerry had been doing a lot of nodding. He empathized with Gatsby's situation and couldn't help picturing himself in a similar position.

Tears had begun to well up in Gatsby's eyes. He wiped them with the napkin. He was silent for several minutes. Suddenly he stood up. "Sorry, I've got to pee again. This fucking cancer."

When he returned to the table he sat down and looked directly into Jerry's eyes and said, "I need an honest, experienced executive to work with me to guarantee that my empire doesn't fall apart even if my body does. I have confidence in you, Jerry—and if you become my partner, you will likely get rich."

Gatsby described his hedge fund business strategy: namely, investing in private securities pre-IPOs and buyouts. He showed him a schedule of the investors. Jerry noted that Gatsby had invested $5 million of the carried interest he earned from the Gatsby Venture Fund and that Moe invested $10 million. Jerry recognized many of the other names as prior investors in the venture fund.

"The compensation structure for the hedge fund is one percent–twenty percent with a $1 billion capitalization. Hannah is a ten-percent general partner. We get $10 million a year to manage it. For the past year, I've kept the operating costs under $7 million, leaving an income of $3 million a year for Hannah and myself. Our carried interest account is currently $8 million."

"Wow," exclaimed Jerry. "As they say, 'You've come a long way, baby.'"

"It's a great business," said Gatsby. "I am offering you a substantial piece of it. If you come on board as a co-manager, I'll make you a forty-percent partner.

"That's generous," said Jerry. "Frankly, I'm overwhelmed. It's an exceptional offer and I am interested. Give me a couple of weeks to think about it and do some due diligence on the fund and talk with Helen. Will that work for you?"

"That will be fine," said Gatsby. "This is one of the most important decisions that I'll make during my life, and I must ensure its correct. An important ingredient in my confidence will be the fact that after you cogitate and discuss this with your family and close advisors, you will make the same commitment to the Gatsby Hedge Fund that I've made. So, take as long as you want."

"Would you need me to move to Philadelphia?"

Gatsby smiled. "Not as long as I stay on the right side of the grass. I'm perfectly comfortable with your operating out of Manhattan with a few commutes a month to Philadelphia."

CHAPTER 47

JERRY

When Jerry returned to his apartment, there was a note from Helen. She was meeting friends for lunch, and they were going to a matinee and would be home for dinner. He immediately called Jeff.

"Are you doing anything today?"

"Naw, I'm catching up on paperwork and vegetating. Why? What's up."

"I just had breakfast with Gatsby. He offered me a partnership in his hedge fund. I'd like to talk to you about it."

"No shit? I met with him two days ago. He flew in from Philadelphia to get our take on the Bear Stearns collapse."

"What did you tell him?"

"I gave him the standard Goldman spiel. Too high a percentage in illiquid mortgages, turmoil in the executive ranks, growing anxiety among their counterparties. After about twenty minutes I turned him over to George Smythe."

"A no-bullshit straight shooter."

"No doubt about that. I'm sure Gatsby got what he came for, even if he didn't like what he heard."

"So, are you free today?"

"Sure. Let's go bowling. We can talk, drink beer, and relieve our frustrations."

"I haven't bowled since I worked for National," said Jerry. "It's been at least twenty-five years."

"I joined a league two months ago. It's good exercise and great fun. And it's a whole new group of people."

"How so?"

"I'd say that at least half of the league are blue-collar guys, plumbers, construction workers, taxi drivers, truck drivers. It gets me out of the Goldman bubble. It's like I'm back in the military. You'll love it."

"Only if you'll let me buy you dinner at a restaurant of your choice."

"No way," said Jeff. "You can't be halfway decadent. We'll eat at the bowling alley."

Jerry wrote a note to Helen he was going bowling and having dinner with Jeff and would be home late.

Two hours later, they were seated in front of their lanes at the Bowlmor, located at Times Square, drinking Coronas, and snacking on chips and guacamole. They had completed two games. Jerry's score was 206 and Jeff's was 420.

"Don't be discouraged. I've been bowling at least twice a week for three months. It's like any other sport. You need to develop muscle memory, and that just takes time. Let's take a break, get something to eat and talk about your meeting with Gatsby."

Jerry turned his head and scanned the tables littered with food and half-finished beer bottles and the floor covered with popcorn and various kinds of food wrappers. "Don't you worry about eating something that comes out of this kitchen? I mean, the place is so seedy."

Jeff laughed. "Your patrician is showing. The food is fine. I usually get the cheeseburger with grilled onions."

"I'll take my chances with a hamburger with grilled onions," said Jerry. Then he related the substance of the meeting and the terms of the offer. When he finished, Jeff whistled.

"He wants you. A minimum salary of $1.2 million a year and an eight percent carried interest on the profits on a billion dollars of capital. What did they earn last year?"

"Twenty-five percent."

"So, add in your salary, and you would have made $6.2 million."

"I did the same analysis," said Jerry.

They sat quietly sipping their beers. "He's been diagnosed with prostate cancer?" said Jeff.

"That's what he says."

"That explains the weight loss."

"You noticed?" said Jerry.

"How can you not notice?" said Jeff. "It makes sense he wants you."

"Because of the cancer?"

"Not just that. His meeting with George Smythe and me probably shook him up."

"Why?" said Jerry.

"Because he recognized that because of all the toxic mortgage securities floating all over the world, the financial markets, and the financial indexes are heading into a shit storm. Bear Stearns was the first domino to fall. Unless Lehman and Merrill merge with big banks, they'll go the way of Bear. This is not the time to be running a hedge fund that invests in illiquid securities. He's probably realized he may not have the chops to run a billion-dollar financial institution and needs support. He's worked with you for five years and obviously respects you. You're his insurance policy for both the market risks and his health risk." He paused and drained his bottle. "I'm going to get another beer. Do you want one?"

"Are we going to play another game?"

"Absolutely."

As Jeff went for another a beer, Jerry speculated that perhaps it was the other way around: the cancer made Gatsby recognize the danger in the market. If an institution could fall, what was one man? He kept his thoughts to himself, though, and when they had completed the game and were drinking their final round of beer, Jeff asked Jerry whether he was close to a decision about becoming Gatsby's partner.

"It's a real puzzle," said Jerry. "I'm not sure I have all the pieces. Gatsby is an enigma. He's smart, charismatic, and motivated. And he has a damn good track record. But then there are these warts, like submitting fraudulent financials and failing to tell us about the State's investigation into his convertible promissory note business. The most amazing aspect of the Gatsby saga is that despite his character and integrity flaws, he has been incredibly successful, and he's a rock star. So, the rest, the flaws—they're mere idiosyncrasies. Everyone that I talk with seems to overlook, discount, or excuse all of Gatsby foibles. They still love the guy—even his first wife, whom he cheated on three weeks after they were married. And there's Moe, who lost several million investing in some of his early deals, and still put $5 million into the Gatsby Venture Fund and put $10 million into the Gatsby Hedge Fund."

"He's like Ronald Reagan," said Jeff. "Made of Teflon. Nothing bad ever seemed to stick to him. Have you ever talked with anyone who is not a Gatsby acolyte?"

"A few," said Jerry. "Some of the Philadelphia investors who were in the Gatsby Venture Fund had made prior investments in his CPN business and said they believed they lost money. But none of them was critical of Gatsby. They were disappointed they lost money, but they didn't blame him. If the market had been stronger and some of the companies he invested in had gone public, and the dot-com wipeout had not ruined the tech market, he would not have had to call in all the CPN debt, nor submit to the State's cease-and-desist order. No one seems to bear him any resentment. And Moe, Frye, and Hawking all have made significant investments in the hedge fund."

"That just leaves Shirley," said Jeff, "and she's probably dead. Have you asked Birney to look into the Gatsby Hedge Fund and see what he can dig up?"

"Good idea. I'll talk to him in the morning. There are still a few things that are gnawing at me."

"That little Saint Martin kidnapping–murder thing?"

Jerry nodded, not rising to Jeff's dark humor. "It was suspiciously convenient, assuming Shirley had filed the complaint about the CPNs with the Pennsylvania Department of Banking and Securities."

"When are you going to talk to Helen?"

"Tonight. I'm not looking forward to it. She detests him."

Jeff shrugged and paid the bill. As they were walking through the restaurant toward the door, he said, "Jerry, in all seriousness, I think that out of an abundance of caution, you should at least look into the police investigation in Saint Martin and see if you there is anything links Gatsby to it, other than the timeshare."

The thought felt heavy. When they were outside the sidewalk, Jerry shook his head. "It was four and a half years ago. I'd have to go there and stay for a few days. I'm not sure it's worth it."

"I am," said Jeff. "You don't know what you'll find out until you can talk with the people who did the investigation. And if you do find out something that leads you to believe that Gatsby may have been involved, that would be dispositive. You're not collecting evidence for a trial."

Jeff has great instincts, thought Jerry, and since I sought his advice, I'd better take it.

"You're right, my brother." He looked at the calendar on his phone. "I'll start working on it tomorrow."

~ ~ ~ ~ ~

He opened the door to his apartment at 10 p.m. and headed to the den. With a highball glass of Jameson, and seated in his favorite chair, he closed his eyes. As he was taking his third sip and feeling drowsy, he sensed a familiar fragrance. Helen took the glass from his hand, set it on the reading table, sat down on his lap, and kissed him. He felt the adrenaline rush. He opened his eyes, put his arms around her and realized she was nude under her silk robe.

"Since the kids are asleep, we can party. Do you think little Jerry is capable?"

"Oh, yes. I'll take a shower and meet you in bed in ten minutes. Less!" He was already getting up. "Wait, where's Misty?"

"Not to worry, I took her out an hour ago, and she's in the bedroom with the boys. There should be no distractions. But first I need to make sure that your confidence in little Jerry is justified." She slid off his lap, unzipped his fly, and worked her hand under his briefs. She looked up at him and smiled. She leaned over and kissed him. "You have ten minutes. I'll get the wine."

Forty-five minutes later, a contented Helen was reading in bed and a contented Jerry lay next to her, dozing. An empty wine glass stood on each night table. Helen put the book on her lap, took off her reading glasses, and nudged him.

He slowly focused. "Sorry. So tired."

"It's okay. Would you like to talk about your breakfast with Gatsby or should we wait until tomorrow?"

He sat up in bed. "I think I'd like to talk about it." He got out of bed. "I'll get the bottle." He headed out of the bedroom. A few minutes later he returned with an open bottle of wine. The errand had cleared his head. He filled the two glasses, placed the wine bottle on his nightstand, and got into bed. He took a sip of wine and turned toward Helen and related Gatsby's proposal.

"There is a high probability that I can earn more than five million a year more than my current income."

She thought about it for several minutes. "I know that you don't want to hear this, but I don't think you should have anything to do with him. He has no integrity. I don't understand why you'd even give this a second thought."

"Honey, he made the pass on you over five years ago. A lot of changes have occurred in those years. He paid off all the CPNs, he managed a venture capital fund that returned a huge amount to the investors in a lousy market. He's made a lot of money for himself and his investors, including us. He's raising two boys—like we are. And he's been diagnosed with prostate cancer. He is not the same man that hit on you in Philadelphia."

"I accept all of that, but integrity is not something that you change like your clothes. It's a part of you. How old was Gatsby in 2003 when he was giving you the due diligence material?"

Jerry did the math. "He was sixty."

"Okay, so at the age of sixty he felt it was acceptable to provide fraudulent financial statements and withhold from his investors the Pennsylvania State's investigation into his business practices. And during the past five years he's suddenly changed into a different person. You buy that?"

"Helen, it isn't that simple. Had he not done what he did, both he and his business would have gone down the tubes. I've worked with many entrepreneurs who have sliced the salami very thin in order to achieve their goals. If they would have failed, they would have gone bankrupt and may have faced criminal charges. The people around them would have lost their money and in some cases, their jobs. One entrepreneur might become a hero in the community, another might face almost the same situation and not be as lucky, see their reputation trashed, and end up in jail. The life of an entrepreneur involves all sorts of risks. Gatsby took the risk of misleading his investors in order to make a deal that would give him a chance for success. You've never experienced that terror of staring in the face of financial ruin. You don't know what it's like. You're being way too judgmental."

Helen took a measured sip of wine. "All right. I understand your argument. But please explain to me why in God's name, when we are doing so well, you're making good money, and our retirement is funded, you would want to disrupt our life to look for gold at the end of some uncertain rainbow?"

"That is a perfectly valid question. The bottom line is that I've been doing the same job and Bricker and Weldon for twenty-eight years, with the only interruption being my stint with National Technology. I do make good money—not great money—and I occasionally have an interesting client. But it's not challenging. It hasn't stirred my passion for many years. The job that Gatsby's offering provides the opportunity for us to get rich, like the hedge fund managers you read about in the

Sunday supplements with their five or six houses all over the world, their yachts, and their private planes staffed with pilots and flight attendants. I'd like a shot at that life. Joining Gatsby could provide the access. At the least we should think about it—and check it out."

Jerry took a breath. Helen had not interrupted him. She had sipped her wine and occasionally shut her eyes so she could focus on what he was saying. Finally, she said, "You surprise me, Jerry. I didn't realize that you've grown so bored with your job. I thought you enjoyed what you do. I mean, you talk about your deals with such enthusiasm. And I had no idea that you had this passion for huge wealth. I mean, we're doing well. When did this all come on? It seems sudden."

"No, not sudden," said Jerry. "It's been building for several years. I realized that I wasn't reading certain articles in the financial media because I didn't want to know how much money the hedge fund managers were making. I was consumed with envy. I wanted what they had. But I could never get it because I came into the financial arena through a different portal. And that probably has had something to do with my discontent."

"Well," said Helen, "you need to know that I am uncomfortable with your getting into bed with Gatsby. It's a Faustian bargain. My bad feelings about Gatsby have never diminished."

"Have you considered," said Jerry, "the possibility they all derive from that lunch when he hit on you? I'm surprised that you're still holding on to it."

She thought for a minute. "You may be right. But I want you to know he made me feel gross. Soiled. And I don't want you to feel that way, either. Anyway, I'm bushed." She put down the wine glass, turned to him and kissed him, turned out the light and was asleep in three minutes.

Jerry continued to sip his wine and reflect on his speech to Helen. It had been the first time he had articulated his dream about becoming a hedge fund manager. He had surprised himself enough he barely gave a thought to her warning.

CHAPTER 48

JERRY

March 24, 2006

Jerry arrived in Phillipsburg on Saint Martin Island at 1 p.m., a Wednesday morning. He rented a car, drove to Marigot, and checked into the Dawn Beach Hotel. He had a snack in the hotel restaurant, and immediately thereafter drove to the gendarme office in Marigot. He asked the clerk on duty whether he might speak to the lead investigator in the case involving the two American women tourists who'd disappeared in November 2003. She left the window for five minutes and returned.

"That would be Monsieur Gaston. Unfortunately, he is no longer at this office. He was transferred back to Paris two years ago."

"Then I'd like to hire someone who is bilingual and could help me review the records and translate witness statements. Also, if the individual will also do the driving, I'll pay an additional fee."

She said she'd send out a notice to her department including the offices in La Savane and Quartier-d'Orleans and call him if someone came forward. Jerry provided the clerk with his contact information in Saint Martin and returned to his hotel.

Later in the day, as Jerry was sunning himself at the pool and nursing a mai tai, he received a call from a woman who spoke with a very thick accent. She had been referred to him by the clerk. She introduced herself as Nadine Le Roux and said she believed she could help him on his project and serve as a driver/guide during his stay. They agreed on a rate of $1,000 a day with a minimum of two days, paid in advance, and he would pay the out-of-pocket expenses. They would start tomorrow morning at 8 a.m. and she would pick him up at the hotel.

The next morning, as Jerry sipped his coffee in the lobby, he noticed a very attractive statuesque blond wearing a form-fitting pink dress enter the lobby and head for the reception desk. She spoke to the attendant who pointed toward Jerry; then she strode over to Jerry and thrust out her hand.

"Bonjour, Monsieur Bascomb. I'm Nadine Le Roux."

Nadine had determined that all the files relating to Shirley's and Cissy's disappearance were at the Marigot gendarmerie. They drove the six kilometers to the station. Nadine talked with the clerk on duty and arranged for them to use an empty office. They moved to the office, and fifteen minutes later, the clerk arrived with a banker's box. Nadine signed the receipt for the box.

She reviewed the contents of the box and arranged the documents in neat piles: photographs, witness statements, gendarme reports, maps, etc. They decided that Nadine would read and translate simultaneously, and Jerry would take notes and interrupt her if he had a question.

During the next three hours Nadine read and translated all the witness statements, the interviews, and the police report. They reviewed the photos of the condo in which Shirley and Cissy had stayed, the interior rooms and the area around the condo. To his eye, there was little amiss. It looked like any of the blandly restful condos he'd stayed in elsewhere in the tropics: anonymous, empty of life. In the first shot, a desk chair was overturned. He had the urge to reach through the picture and right it. He sifted through the others: a plastic shower curtain torn from its rings. A crooked table next to a broken ceramic bowl and a cluster of blackened bananas on the floor. Nothing plainly violent, but a disturbance had run through the rooms. He felt uneasy.

The witness statements revealed that Shirley and Cissy were seen with several different men at Frogs, a restaurant, Dingy Dock, a bar, and Captain Oliver's Marina Restaurant. The men were not recognized by any of the locals or the police. Also, in the evidence box were several newspaper clippings reporting on the disappearance and the investigation. Nadine read and translated the newspaper accounts. By one o'clock they had reviewed all the documents in the evidence box.

The final police report, authored by the detective in charge of the investigation, opined that there were probably two assailants. They probably sailed from another one of the harbors on the island, or from another nearby island, arrived in the middle of the night, tied up in one of the empty slips on the dock behind the condo, and gained entrance to the residence. They probably found both women asleep, disabled them after a minor struggle, took whatever valuables and cash they could find, and carried them back to the boat, and out to sea. Then, they weighted them down and threw them overboard and sailed away. He offered no opinion as to the motive of the assailants, other than robbery. Jerry thought they couldn't have had much that would tempt men who already had a sailboat.

They located the timeshare condos where Shirley and Cissy stayed. The manager agreed to show them the specific unit they occupied. It was a two-story residence with the master bedroom suite on the main floor and a second and third bedroom and bathroom on the second floor. It was neat—completely purged of the disturbance.

By 3 p.m. in the afternoon they had exhausted all the research opportunities. Jerry had not expected to discover anything significant. There was nothing tangible in the accumulated evidence that tied the crime to Gatsby other than the timeshare condo and the ticket for Shirley's round-trip flight to Saint Martin.

Although the day started out to be a little windy, by the time they left the timeshare, the wind has died down and the ambient temperature was 83 degrees. Nadine suggested they take a stroll on the beach, have a drink at the beach bar, and then go to dinner at Papagayos at Club Orient. Jerry said he'd have to go back to his hotel to get his swimsuit. Nadine smiled and said, "No need. The beach is clothing-optional."

Jerry stared at her.

Still smiling, Nadine said, "Come on, you'll enjoy it. The food is great and I'm sure you'll find the scenery stimulating."

They drove to Orient Beach and parked. Nadine jumped out of the car and retrieved two beach towels and sun lotion from her trunk and a fanny pack. She asked Jerry for his credit card and sixty dollars in cash. She put the cash, credit card, keys to the car and her license in her fanny pack. In a wink, she removed all her clothes and was standing opposite him, wearing only her fanny pack. Jerry did not know where to look. Her breasts, her crotch, her thighs, or her bright smile?

"Well, what are you waiting for?" she asked.

Jerry shook his head and said, "Okay, when in Rome, do as the Romans." And he quickly removed all his clothes. She took one of the towels from the hood of the car, and as she handed it to him, she looked directly at his crotch, which had already begun to respond.

"Nice," she said. "Very nice." Then she locked the car.

Jerry wrapped his towel around his hips and Nadine draped her towel around her shoulders and they headed toward the beach.

When they reached the beach, Jerry was startled. He'd been to beaches in France and Spain where many of the women were topless; but this was his first experience at a nude beach where everyone was fully nude, and where a high percentage of the population was attractive.

They sat down at a table in the café. Jerry said, "I'm not sure I can do this, you know, walk on the beach, without embarrassing myself."

"Don't worry about it. If you get an erection, people will merely recognize you for a beginner. You can always sit down and drape the towel over yourself until you go down. No one will be offended."

Later that evening, they had dinner at the Talk of the Town restaurant. After dinner, aroused by the experience of nude beach, and the several hours of staring at Nadine's sensual body, he brought Nadine back to his hotel, and they made love. She slept over and they spent the following day in bed, never leaving the hotel room. Jerry ordered room service for both lunch and dinner.

Nadine drifted. Jerry lay on his back, listening to her breathing. He had offered little resistance as she'd drawn him into his Walpurgisnacht experience. He had spent a day and a half enveloped in the body of a Venus—and what was most surprising, he felt neither guilt nor remorse over having broken his marriage vows. The experience reminded him—as probably no other could—of what his sex life with Helen had been before kids. Sex with Helen prior to Josh had been 10+ sex, the same as with Nadine. Sex with Helen since she first became pregnant with Josh had ranged from about 5, or maybe 6 or 7 when they were on vacation. He had known that the bloom was off the rose, but he hadn't recognized that the rose was wilted.

The deterioration of their sex life was a result of Helen's having decided to go all in as a mother. Their agreement was he would go all in as the breadwinner, and she would pour her time and effort into tending to their kids' every need, every demand, every tantrum. She was continually driving them to parties, training sessions, and soccer practice. And he had gotten so used to being rebuffed on the many instances he tried to initiate sex that he'd given up trying. So sad. Well, he thought, now that I know, I need to do something about it. Then he turned on his side and cuddled up to Nadine.

The next morning, the alarm woke him at 5 a.m. As he shut it off, he saw that Nadine was still asleep. He checked his tickets confirming that his flight was at 8 a.m. He gathered up the clothes he was going to wear and packed everything else in his bag. He showered and dressed in the bathroom. He emerged just before 6 a.m. Nadine was still asleep on her side. He gently rubbed her back until she awoke. She turned to him and smiled.

"I need to go the airport," he said. He kissed her. "Thanks for everything—and I mean everything."

Nadine, still nude, turned and threw her arms around his neck, pulling him to her. "*C'est dommage, mais c'était magnifique!*"

"*D'accord,*" he said. "I called a taxi. We have the room until 1 p.m., so stay as long as you want." He kissed her, turned, and left the room.

CHAPTER 49

JERRY

When his flight touched down at JFK, Jerry took a cab to Jeff's apartment and arrived shortly after 5 p.m. He briefed his brother on his trip to Saint Martin, edited to avoid any mention of Nadine. "If evidence exists that ties Gatsby to Shirley's and Cissy's disappearance, I couldn't find it. Saint Martin was a dry hole!"

Jeff swirled the ice in his glass of tea and made an ambivalent grunt. "Shirley was pursuing a vendetta against Gatsby and could have been a troublesome witness in any hearing or trial. Her disappearance was just too damn convenient."

"I agree," said Jerry, "but, there is no evidence. All we have are suspicions. And there is the fact Cissy also disappeared. What's your explanation for that?"

"Maybe she was just in the wrong place at the wrong time."

They both sat silently. Jerry was working on getting his head around the implications of his trip. Did it reveal anything at all about Gatsby or Shirley or their relationship? What did his tryst with Nadine reveal about the state of his marriage? If push came to shove, would he accept Gatsby's offer, even if it would jeopardize his marriage? Was his marriage worth missing the chance to become a rich and powerful hedge fund manager?

"What are you going to do about the offer?" said Jeff.

The question jolted Jerry out of his reverie. Jerry sat back in his chair and shook his head. "I don't know, Jeff. It would be an easy decision if Helen was supportive."

"Why, what did she say?"

Jerry laughed. "She wanted me to pass from the beginning. I don't think anything that I learned will change her mind." He stood up from Jeff's kitchen table. "I'm going to mull it over for a few days and then have a serious talk with her."

"Little brother," said Jeff, "I can't help you make your decision. But I can give you some advice. You have a great wife, a great marriage, and two beautiful boys, a great job, and a great lifestyle. Listen to your gut and listen to your wife. The Gatsby deal is not the equivalent of money in the bank. A lot of ducks need to line up and stay lined up for his offer to translate into wealth and fame. You've already won the race. You have a beautiful, healthy family and an income in the 98th percentile both of which you can depend on. To paraphrase the Hippocratic Oath—don't fuck up!"

~~~~~~

The following Sunday, Jerry and Helen were enjoying a quiet dinner at Luigi's restaurant in Midtown. They ordered a carafe of Chianti and an antipasto salad to share and listened to the slightly-too-loud recording of Pavarotti singing Puccini arias.

Several days had passed without Helen inquiring or Jerry offering to discuss his trip to Saint Martin. Jerry had found it difficult to segregate the data from his emotions. He'd attempted to call Nadine but discovered that the number she gave him did not work.

The affair with her had changed the way he viewed Helen. Before he boarded that airplane and traveled to Saint Martin, he "saw" Helen as she was fifteen years ago; but that was more a case of desire swamping reality. He wanted to see her as the vivacious, sexy woman from his days at National, when an evening of lovemaking would transport him to the gates of heaven. But it was an illusion, a mirage. That Helen didn't exist anymore. She was gone, just like the fifteen-years-ago version of
~~~~~~

himself. If his marriage to Helen was going to hold, he needed to accept Helen as she was now—as she accepted him—and take care she didn't discover his changed view of her.

He said, "I've finished my due diligence work on the Gatsby Hedge Fund. I know everything I need to know and what I don't know is probably unknowable. It's time to decide."

"Are you finally going to tell me what you learned in Saint Martin?"

"Nothing of significance. There is no evidence that might implicate Gatsby."

They were both silent. They sipped their wine. The room was engulfed with the sound of Pavarotti singing *Nessun Dorma*.

"Jerry, are you absolutely confident that you want to marry Gatsby with whatever warts, known and unknown, he'll bring with him? Are you thinking with your ambition for more, or are you being thoroughly logical? You know, the brain is a—"

"Yes, I know how my brain works. Logically, it's an excellent opportunity. I'm confident that I can handle Gatsby. But Helen, can you reconcile your antipathy toward Gatsby and move on."

"I don't think so. My antipathy derives from what I know about him, and like I said, I don't want you to be as caught-out as I was. He's cheated on his first wife, he's run a Ponzi scheme, he's lied on his documents to you—there's no loyalty except to himself. His enemies are literally dead before their time. Shirley mysteriously disappeared. Bill Dewyne had a fatal heart attack during an argument with Gatsby over Gatsby's sales of convertible promissory notes. He didn't tell you about the State's investigation of the sales of his convertible promissory notes. I don't care how successful the Gatsby Venture Fund was. He just doesn't pass my smell test. But then again I don't have your sudden drive to be really rich."

"How do you know that Bill had his heart attack when he was arguing with Gatsby?"

"I had lunch with Alicia when we went to Philadelphia to celebrate the launch of the Gatsby Venture Fund. She told me that Moe was in the outer office and heard Bill and Gatsby yelling at each other just before it happened."

"I hadn't heard that," said Jerry.

Helen laughed. "See, I have my own sources. Will you please listen to me?"

"Okay, I get that you don't like him and don't trust him. Do you want me to turn down his offer?"

"Are you hearing me at all, Jerry? Would it be better if I asked you, as your wife, to please not do any more business with the guy who tried to cuckold you?"

He felt himself getting angry. "You're the most important person in my life. I want to make you happy."

"But it is inconsistent with your realizing your dream." Under the edge of the table, she kept folding and refolding the edge of her napkin. Her mind was searching for another tack. "We started our family late in life. We owe those kids the best upbringing we can muster—which includes devoting a lot of family time to them. I want to be a great mother and I want you to be a great dad—and that requires both of us to set aside a good deal of stress-free quality time out of our respective days. I don't see how you can do your part if you are running a billion-dollar business and commuting to Philadelphia. It's not like we don't have enough money to ensure a great education for our boys and a comfortable retirement for us. So please don't bullshit me about money.

"This new 'dream' of yours to be dripping with wealth and power is a chimera brought on by your ego. You want to prove that you can do it. I understand. I really do. But I'm not going to allow you to pursue this dream at our expense—Alli's, Josh's, and mine. I want to minimize the stress and complications in our life. Your jumping into bed with Gatsby would guarantee that *my* dream will not be achieved."

Jerry had listened carefully to what she said—although it was difficult to hear. She was struggling to keep her self-control. "You're drawing a line in the sand?" he asked.

The tears were streaming down her face. She grabbed the napkin off her lap and wiped her eyes. But the tears continued to flow. "I'm sorry,

Jerry. Yes, I am drawing a line in the sand. If you choose to be with Gatsby, you will not be with me."

They both sat quietly, neither making a motion, allowing the magnitude of what had just happened to sink it. Finally, Jerry said, "I don't know about you, but I'm uncomfortable with how this conversation has turned out. I think it's best if we table the discussion for a few days, so we can both think it through." Then he motioned to the waiter and requested the check.

CHAPTER 50

JERRY

Two days later, Jerry's train arrived in Philadelphia in the late afternoon. He checked into the Bellevue. Even after dinner, two Jamesons, and some mindless basketball watching on the TV, he simply tossed and turned, trying to squelch the thoughts about the forthcoming meeting with Gatsby.

He finally put on the lamp next to his bed, pulled a legal pad and pencil from his briefcase, and tried to script for the meeting. One hour later he was still working on the first sentence.

He had to start the script by explaining why he had traveled to Philadelphia to see Gatsby. What was the purpose? He pictured Gatsby sitting opposite him, inquisitive and concerned. He suddenly realized that the very fact he was here created an issue.

He got up from his chair and walked to the window. Broad Street was deserted. He looked at his watch. Two forty-five a.m.

The reason he was here and the reason he could not write the script for the meeting was he was afraid to tell Gatsby the truth; namely, he wanted the job, but he couldn't accept it because Helen had given him a gargantuan ultimatum.

Once Gatsby understood his dilemma, Gatsby's opinion of him would sink like a stone thrown into a pond. How the hell had he allowed Helen to put him in this position? He wanted to scream. He had nowhere to go, no one to turn to.

He found it increasingly difficult to keep his eyes open and concentrate. He jotted a few notes on his tablet, called the front desk, and arranged for a wake-up call at six a.m.

The next morning, he jogged on the treadmill for an hour then got himself ready for the meeting downstairs. He asked to be seated next to the window and ordered a cappuccino. He still had no idea what he intended to say to Gatsby other than he needed two more weeks.

When Gatsby arrived, he greeted Jerry warmly. Over Mediterranean scrambles, he told Jerry he had to leave for the airport shortly, as he was flying to Washington to work on McCain's presidential campaign. Gatsby was animated and enthusiastic about the possibility of having the Republican Party control the White House for another four years. He started to talk about the people he planned to meet with in Washington and what his role might be in the campaign.

After the waiter had placed their breakfast dishes on the table, Gatsby said, "Well, Jerry, where are we? I presume you came here to talk about the offer, so let's talk."

Jerry took a sip of his cappuccino and wiped his lips. "Gatsby, I had hoped by this time, I would be accepting your great offer and we would be discussing the nuts and bolts of the transition and the schedule of announcements. I'm still on that path, but I need you to give me another two weeks to clear my decks."

Gatsby drained his double espresso to wash down a fork full of scramble. "The delay is not a problem. But I need to know what is on your decks that you need to clear." He motioned to the waiter to bring another round of drinks. Then he looked directly at Jerry and waited for his response.

Jerry took a deep breath. "Fair enough," he said. "When I told Helen about the offer, I expected her to be elated. I had discussed with her that your offer was a dream come true for our family. But to my surprise, she revealed she had an entirely different scenario in mind for the balance of my working life; namely, that I would scale back my working hours and invest a lot more time in our two boys and in traveling together."

Gatsby smiled and shook his head. "I must say, Jerry, this is a shock. I never anticipated that you'd allow yourself to be pussy-whipped."

Jerry felt a stab of anger. "What do you mean?"

"I mean," said Gatsby, "that if you were in control of your wife and your family, you would have dealt with the problem immediately by telling her, 'That is a nice fantasy, but honey, that is not what I have in mind for the rest of my working life.' Then you would have immediately called me and accepted the offer. In short, you would have seized the day rather than agonize over it."

Gatsby's response pushed Jerry back on his heels. He would never treat Helen like that. But why should Gatsby's response surprise him? Treating women as objects was in a philanderer's DNA.

Gatsby checked his watch. "I really need to go." His expression had morphed to annoyance. "I'm going to resolve your dilemma. I'm withdrawing the offer. Not because I'm upset or irritated. I'm withdrawing the offer because I realize I made a mistake. You simply don't have the skills that I thought you had—so, I'm going to have to solve my problem in a different way. Oh, and I gave my card to the hostess when I came in, so breakfast, including the tip, is covered."

He drank the remains of his espresso and announced he needed to leave for the airport. He got up.

Jerry was disappointed, but not surprised. He knew that this outcome was likely when he made the reservations for the trip. "I'm finished," said Jerry. "I'll walk out with you."

"Whatever you wish," said Gatsby. His expression was hard. They left the restaurant.

By the time they exited the revolving door and were on the pavement, Gatsby's trademark grin was again in place. He shook hands with Jerry and apologized for having to run off.

"I hope you're not angry with me," said Jerry.

"Don't be silly. A man's gotta do what a man's gotta do." Gatsby told the doorman he needed a cab to airport. The doorman signaled a parked taxi, and it quickly pulled up to the curb.

Gatsby moved toward the cab and began to get into it. He hesitated, stepped back on the curb and approached Jerry, who was waiting to wave goodbye. Gatsby, still wearing his grin, took the several steps toward Jerry, ultimately moving into his personal space.

"I expect that since you will be cutting back on your work schedule, you and Helen will be doing a lot of traveling?"

Jerry, startled and uncomfortable over Gatsby closeness, nodded and said, "We hope to."

"I suggest you avoid Saint Martin," he said. "It may be a great place to fuck, but it can also be a dangerous place—you know—with the drug cartels getting active there. Just a friendly suggestion." He turned and quickly got into the cab.

Jerry remained standing, frozen. His throat went dry. He could not swallow his saliva past the lump of fear in his throat.

Chapter 51

GATSBY

As the taxi drove away from the Bellevue, Gatsby took out his cell phone and called Hannah.

"How did the meeting with Jerry go? Did he accept your offer?"

"Not well. I withdrew the offer.

"Christ! What happened?"

"It became clear to me he would not be the right person for the job. But I'll get into it in more detail when I return. What I need you to do is to get together with Colin and work on a draft to the hedge fund investors advising them of a member meeting for some date during the first two weeks of May. The purpose of the meeting is to brief the members on our analysis as to the uncertainties and instabilities that are likely to affect the financial markets during the next several years and have them decide, considering this new reality, whether they would like to reduce their investment."

"Jeez," said Hannah. "When did you decide to do this?"

"I developed it as a backup plan in the event the deal with Jerry didn't work out. The game has changed since we issued the hedge fund PPM. The investors may want to reduce their risk.

"They'll vote on three options: no change; return of $250 million in capital; or return of $500 million in capital. If they decide on a return of $250 million, the management fee will increase to 1.334 percent and carried interest of 20 percent. If they decide on a return of $500 million, the management fee will be 2 percent and carried interest of 20 percent.

"The meat of the notice will be your writeup of the source of the instability and uncertainty in the market created by the inability of the financial industry to accurately value derivatives manifested by the recent collapse of Bear Stearns. We'll have plenty of time to work on this, but I'm anxious for you to get started."

Hannah had not worked with him so long without learning when to avoid an argument. He was confident she'd see the good sense in his proposal after the shock wore off.

"No problem," she said. "And you have a great trip in Washington."

PART V

CHAPTER 52

JERRY

After the confrontation with Gatsby, Jerry immediately called Jeff and arranged to meet with him at his apartment as soon as he arrived in New York.

He and Jeff sat in the family room, and over drinks, he told him about his disaster with Gatsby. Then he filled Jeff in on the part of the trip to Saint Martin he had left out in their previous meeting—his visit to the nude beach with Nadine, the sex afterwards, and the fact he'd not been able to contact her since he returned.

Jeff, the veteran warrior, the brother who knew quite a lot about the dark side of the world, understood the situation immediately.

"You were set up to hire her and she was primed to provide all the services you required, such as driving, translation, assistance in the police department—and to provide services you didn't need, did not anticipate, but were more than willing to accept. She's a classic plant. Gatsby obviously has contacts on Saint Martin, and he was alerted that you were there, and he made sure he knew everything that you did when you were on the island."

Jerry dropped his head into his hands. "Shit."

"But there is some good news in all this," said Jeff. "As a result of your hiring Nadine, Gatsby revealed he had a serious interest in who was investigating Shirley's disappearance."

Jerry looked up. "Is this supposed to make me feel better?"

"I'm not trying to make you feel better, little brother. We're both working on how to get you out of this mess. Does this prove that Gatsby is responsible? No! But does this justify suspicion on our part he might have been involved? Absolutely!"

He paused, took a sip of his vodka, and said, "On the other hand, you just might be overreacting, Perhaps Gatsby was just pissed that you'd gone to Saint Martin to investigate Shirley's disappearance without telling him and he wanted to jerk your chain and make you squirm. Have you considered that?"

"How the hell do I know?" said Jerry, standing up and starting to pace around the room. "He leered at me when he made the comment about Saint Martin being a dangerous place. It creeped me out."

"All right," said Jeff, "let's assume that Gatsby intended to threaten you. When we add what we just learned about Gatsby to what we already know, is it just possible that Gatsby is a psychopath? Even a mediocre lawyer could make a case he is. When I was in Vietnam one of the guys in my platoon, Chau Lee, was a psychopath. His family was a member of a Chinese tong in New York City, the Hip Sing Association. Basically, a mafia—they make their money through gambling, extortion, drugs, robbery, prostitution, that kind of thing. Chau Lee was my platoon's drug dealer. He supplied the marijuana and heroin to the platoon. He was ruthless, unpredictable, and fearless. There was nothing I could do to control him. If I had interfered with his drug business, he would have fragged me in an instant. Besides, he was my best trooper. He always insisted on walking point."

"So?" said Jerry. "Why is that relevant?"

"Here's why. Based on my experience, when dealing with a psychopath, you not only need to match him in ruthlessness—you need to raise him."

"And in the context of the situation we are dealing with, exactly what does that mean?" Jerry was so frustrated he wanted to hit something. "Come on. I don't have time for fucking story hour."

Jeff sat upright in his chair. "Jerry, we may be dealing with some serious shit. I've only had to deal with a true psychopath once in my life—the kid I told you about. My life was always at risk, and I had to be careful. I was able to employ his courage and daring for the benefit of the platoon—but, if I wanted to stay alive, I had to keep my nose out of his business. That's how I coped. You are in a completely different situation and I don't believe I can help you. However, I think we know someone who can—Ze'vie, Birney's uncle in Israel."

"Ze'vie? How can Ze'vie help me?"

"Jerry, you heard him at Birney's dinner party. He was a member of a Kidon Unit. Their mission is to neutralize Palestinian terrorists—practically a job for psychopaths. You and Helen should meet with him and tell him about your Gatsby situation and get his recommendation. If he isn't scheduled to be in the US during the next week, you and Helen should go to Israel and tell him the whole story."

~~~~~

Jerry returned home at 11 p.m. Alli and Josh were in bed. Misty was in the family room asleep in front of the fire and Helen was sitting on the sofa, reading. Jerry went directly to the sofa and leaned over and kissed her. Then he laid down on the floor next to Misty and nuzzled and petted her.

"How did it go?" said Helen.

"He was surprised, disappointed, and angry in that order," said Jerry.

"I can understand the 'surprised and disappointed.' Why the anger?"

"Somehow he found out that I went to Saint Martin and inquired about Shirley's and Cissy's disappearance. The guy has spies everywhere."

Startled, Helen shut her book and looked over to Jerry, who was still nuzzling Misty. "Please leave the dog alone and come over here and talk to me! Why do you believe he knows about your trip to Saint Martin?"

Jerry got off the floor and looked over to Helen. "He as much as admitted it to me. Let me get a drink and we'll talk about it." He turned and headed toward the kitchen. He returned to the family room five minutes later with a Jameson in one hand, a glass of chardonnay in the other and a bowl of nuts in the crook of his arm. He carefully set the
~~~~~

two drinks on the coffee table and then set the bowl of nuts on the table. He collapsed onto the sofa.

"It's been a real long day," he said. He took a long swig of his Jameson. "This is exactly what happened."

Over the next half hour Jerry related in excruciating detail exactly what transpired from the time he arrived in Philadelphia to the time Gatsby got into the taxi and was driven away. He could repeat some parts of the conversations verbatim. Helen asked him several times to clarify and elaborate, which he did willingly.

Helen shouted. "Shit, he threatened you! And me, Alli, and Josh." She stood and started to cry and looked down at Jerry who continued to sit on the sofa. "Goddamn you, Jerry. I told you not to get involved with Gatsby. We don't know what he's capable of. He may have arranged for Shirley's murder. My God! He threatened us!"

She paced around the room, shaking uncontrollably, and continued to curse Gatsby. He intercepted her and tried to take her in his arms. Furious, she turned on him and pounded her fists against his chest. "Damn you! You and your fucking ego have brought a monster into our lives. What are we going to do? Where can we go?"

Jerry squeezed her up against his chest so she would stop hitting him.

"I've talked with Jeff and he has some ideas. It will take a few days to figure out what to do. But you need to calm down. We can solve this problem. You need to trust me."

The look she gave him could have burned through a bank safe. For a moment, he was afraid she could see everything he hadn't told her, afraid she could see his fear.

"Why should I trust you?" she spat. "You created this damn mess."

"Look, I know that you're angry with me, but none of us could possibly see this coming."

She just laughed, a humorless one.

He ignored it. "Just give me a few days to figure this out and formulate a plan."

She sunk against the chair, deflated. "I guess I'll have to. You didn't leave us any other option" She turned away from Jerry and headed toward the bedroom, where he knew he would not be welcome tonight.

~~~~~~

Later that evening Jerry retrieved Ze'vie's three contact numbers. He started with the first number on the slip and was immediately put into voicemail. He left a message. When he called the second number, he heard Ze'vie's voice.

"Shalom, Jerry. It is so good to hear from you. It's been a while."

"It has," said Jerry. "It's been five years since we enjoyed your generous hospitality."

"We had a great time," said Ze'vie.

"The reason I'm calling, Ze'vie, is that Helen and I are grappling with a serious problem. I've talked extensively about it with my brother, who has personally experienced a similar problem when he was in Vietnam. He strongly suggested that you have the professional expertise that may be able to help us work through it."

"I see," said Ze'vie. "I gather from your brevity that this is something you do not feel comfortable discussing over the phone?"

"Correct," said Jerry. "Do you have plans to come to the States in the immediate future? If not, Helen and I can fly to Israel within the week."

"Unfortunately, I have commitments which will keep me in Israel for the next month. Hold on while I check my schedule and see when I can free up some time." After a long silence, he came back on the line. "Will April 15 through April 20 work for you and Helen?"

"I think so. I'll check with Helen and call you back."

"If I don't answer, just leave a message," said Ze'vie. "I'm looking forward to seeing you and your wife again. I just wish the circumstances were more benevolent."

"So do I," said Jerry.
~~~~~~

Chapter 53

JERRY

April 16, 2008

They arrived in Israel on the afternoon of April 16. An hour later, they reached Ze'vie's home in the hills of Netanya. Ze'vie led them to the guest suite.

"I had forgotten just how luxurious your accommodations are," said Helen.

"Please settle in and rest," said Ze'vie. "You've had a long trip. I've arranged to have dinner brought in at 8 p.m. We'll eat and move to the family room to have some brandy and talk about your problem."

At nine o'clock, they were all seated in the plush chairs and sofa in front of the fire. On the coffee table was an ice bucket, glasses, and bottles of Jameson, Courvoisier, and Hennessey. They each poured a drink. Then Jerry opened a manila folder that contained three documents each of which was several pages. He handed one to Ze'vie and one to Helen and retained one for himself.

"To ensure that you get the complete history of the Gatsby saga, I prepared a timeline of all the events that I believe are significant." Turning to Helen he said, "Honey, if you think I've left anything out just chime in."

Over the next hour, with occasional interjections by Helen, Jerry related the Gatsby saga. At certain points in the narrative he described the detailed conversations he had with Gatsby. By the time he reached the part of the story where Gatsby made his threat, he looked over to Helen and saw that her eyes were heavy with fatigue.

"Ze'vie," Jerry said, "let's call it a night. I'll let you review this, and we can resume when we're fresh."

Ze'vie finished jotting down some notes. "Good idea. We accomplished quite a bit this evening. Let's meet again at breakfast."

When Helen and Jerry walked into the dining room the next morning, they found the table covered with pots of coffee, espresso, and tea, and baskets of pastries and croissants. Next to the table was a flip chart. Ze'vie was already at the table.

As Jerry sat down, he asked, "What's the chart for?"

"I reviewed my notes from our discussion last night and summarized all the key facts as I understood them. While you two are eating, I'll review the facts and conjectures, along with the evidence behind them, and you can tell me if something stands out as being significant or surprising." He flipped over the cover of the chart and launched into an analysis that Jerry absorbed with a fresh wave of dread over having gotten them into this mess. He wondered if Ze'vie had guessed that Gatsby also had blackmail material to back up his threat on Jerry, thanks to the affair.

After about fifteen minutes, Jerry spoke up.

"Three of the eleven facts listed are solely based on conjecture—that Nadine was a Gatsby plant, that Gatsby engineered Shirley's and Cissy's disappearance, and three, that Gatsby's parting comment to me after the breakfast in Philadelphia was intended as a threat." He turned to Helen. "Do you agree, hon?"

She scanned the chart again. "I guess so."

Ze'vie spoke up. "Helen, can you think of any evidence that is available to us that would support any of the three facts—which evidence is necessary for you to conclude that your family is being threatened?"

She shook her head. "No, I don't think we have any."

Ze'vie sat down at the table and poured himself an expresso. "Let's talk a little about what options a civilized society has for coping with a known terrorist, or for that matter, any psychopath."

"That's easy," said Jerry. "You either kill them or lock them up forever—like we do in Guantanamo."

"Killing them is an easy solution," said Ze'vie. "Pow! A shot to the head and the problem is solved. But the key question is, on what evidence do you rely to make the determination that the person you're dealing with is a terrorist or a psychopath? In the Kidon Unit that I ran, we did not identify nor vet targets. The targets were given to us, and our job was to track them down and liquidate them. However, the tribunal that did the selecting and vetting ensured our teams were fully briefed on the evidence supporting the fact the target had blood on his or her hands and we would not be executing an innocent civilian. Do you follow me?"

"Completely," said Jerry.

"I guess so," said Helen.

Ze'vie poured another cup of expresso and took a sip. He glanced back to the chart and said, "I agree that this evidence that you've assembled justifies both your suspicions about Gatsby and your fear as to what he might do to harm your family—but I guarantee you that no legally constituted Israeli tribunal would, based on this evidence, target Gatsby for liquidation."

Ze'vie picked up his espresso cup and remained silent, giving Helen and Jerry time for his comments to sink in.

Jerry shook his head. "I understand, and I don't disagree. I remember my courses in criminal law and having the instructor pound in the meaning of the terms 'probable cause,' 'preponderance of the evidence,' 'clear and convincing,' and 'beyond a reasonable doubt.'"

"Helen?" said Zevi. "Do you follow?"

"I'm not a lawyer or a sniper, but yes. You're saying—"

"I don't think we have probable cause," finished Ze'vie.

Jerry felt his heart sink into his stomach. He knew Ze'vie was right. They didn't have enough evidence to arrest Gatsby, let alone execute him.

Ze'vie stood and closed the flip chart. "Let's leave this alone for now. We'll pick it up later this afternoon. Did you have an opportunity to visit Jaffa when you were here five years ago?"

"No," said Helen. "The only parts of the coast we saw were what was included in the tour that you arranged."

"Well, then let's go see Jaffa, which is not only beautiful, but it incorporates almost 3,500 years of history and culture."

~~~~~

As they left Netanya and turned on to the main highway toward Tel Aviv, Helen felt the anxiety begin to ebb. She was excited to be back in Israel, away from her problems and in a different culture. Notwithstanding that fact that they would talk about the Gatsby problem later in the day, it did not have a stranglehold on her. She was happy, although she knew the feeling's season would be brief.

Ze'vie parked at the old port of Jaffa. They strolled down the cobblestone streets and along the quay that was lined with no-frills fish restaurants. During the next two hours they covered about three square miles of the Old City and Helen was able to see the clock tower with its stained-glass windows, the flea market, the excavations of Summit Park, and Kedumim Square and its third century-BC catacombs.

As they entered Ze'vie's home around 4 p.m., Ze'vie asked them whether they were ready to get back to Gatsby. Helen and Jerry looked at each other, then Helen said, "Give us an hour to relax and we'll start at five." She felt the day's ebullience wilting, and she needed time to steel herself for what came next.

An hour later they entered the family room. Ze'vie pointed to the two pizzas, salads, and drinks arrayed on a card table. "I thought we would have a more productive meeting if we didn't have to break for dinner."

"Good idea," said Jerry. "Let's get to work."
~~~~~

"When we adjourned this morning," said Ze'vie, pointing to his chart "we left you in limbo, perpetually looking over your shoulder. I don't think you're satisfied with purgatory."

Helen couldn't have said it better herself.

"Well," continued Ze'vie, "there is something we can do that may move the ball down the field. It will be expensive, but it may be cost-effective for you. Let's look at the chart. Ask yourself what information we would need to have 'probable cause' and 'clear and convincing' evidence. Look at all the facts that do not have 'high-confidence' support. For example, 'Gatsby arranged Shirley's disappearance,' and, 'Nadine was a plant.'"

"Fine," said Helen, "I get it. If we had hard evidence that Gatsby was involved in Shirley's disappearance, that would do it. If we had evidence that Nadine was a plant, that would indicate he was concerned over what Jerry might learn."

"Exactly," said Ze'vie.

"But how the hell do we do that?" said Helen.

"Remember the maxim that came out of the Watergate investigations?" said Ze'vie.

"I remember it vividly. We used to watch the hearings when I was in college," said Jerry.

"We need to follow the money," said Ze'vie. "If Gatsby arranged Shirley's disappearance, and/or hired Nadine, the payments will show up on his bank statements in some form. They could be certified checks to cash, or large withdrawals of cash or wire transfers. The money must come from somewhere. And from what you've told me about Gatsby, I think the probability he would keep large amounts of cash in a home safe or under a mattress is nil."

"That makes sense to me," said Jerry. "But how do we get access to his bank accounts?"

"We can get them. It is just a matter of cost. But first we must clear another hurdle."

"What hurdle?" said Jerry.

"Assume for the moment we're all sitting in this room about a month from now, and we have six years of records from every one of Gatsby's banks, all the months during which he Gatsby saga occurred. And, further, the records reveal suspicious payments of let's say, $50,000 to $100,000 around the time that Shirley and Cissy disappeared, and payments of $10,000 to $20,000 around the time of Jerry's trip to Saint Martin. My question to the two of you is, 'What is your next step? What action, if any, would you vote for?'"

"That's easy," said Helen. "I'd be willing to do whatever it takes, and pay whatever it takes, to take the sonofabitch out of our lives forever."

"You mean," said Ze'vie, "you would be prepared to hire someone to assassinate him?"

"Absolutely," said Helen. "And I wouldn't shed a tear."

"What about you, Jerry?" said Ze'vie. "Would you be willing to hire someone to assassinate Gatsby?"

Helen looked at him. Jerry stared at the chart and fidgeted in his seat.

"Well, Jerry?" said Helen. "Can you answer Ze'vie's question? Would you be willing to kill a psychopath that is threatening your family?"

Finally, Jerry said. "I'm not there yet. I'd have to think about it." He looked down. "I'm sorry, Ze'vie, I can't give you an answer, at least not now."

Helen thought the apology was remarkable, directed as it was toward Ze'vie and not her.

Ze'vie smiled. "Frankly, I'm not surprised. I can't tell you how many meetings I've attended when the highest-ranking political and military authorities couldn't agree on a plan of action—even for despicable terrorists who had murdered many Israeli men, women, and children. It is not an easy decision.

"In Mossad, there are four bureaucracies that are involved when a target is to be liquidated: there are those who do the research to identify the bad-guy gene pool, those who choose the potential targets from the bad-guy gene pool, those who make the decision as to which of the potential targets to liquidate, and those who carry out the operation.' Jerry and Helen, you two, the deciders, need to be confident that Gatsby has blood on his hands. If the evidence can support that conclusion, and I am also persuaded, then I can find you someone who can reliably carry out the operation."

Helen watched her husband as he stared at the flip chart in silence. When he had first talked to Ze'vie about traveling to Israel, he'd told her that Ze'vie would be able to resolve the Gatsby problem. Now that Ze'vie had formulated the strategy, and identified the action steps, Jerry was getting cold feet. She didn't think that if the chips were down, he'd let someone pull the trigger on Gatsby.

Ze'vie broke the uncomfortable silence. "I think we've done as much as we can this evening. Let's regroup at breakfast tomorrow and decide where we go from here. I'm ready to turn in."

Helen stood and said goodnight to Ze'vie. She turned toward their bedroom suite, eager to be out of that room. After a few steps, she stopped and turned around.

"Are you coming, Jerry?"

"I'm not tired. I think I'll stay up for a while and watch the news."

Ze'vie had already gone to his room. Helen stood still for a moment, and then turned and went to bed alone.

CHAPTER 54

JERRY

Jerry awoke at 5:30 a.m. the next morning. Helen was asleep and snoring softly. Continuously reliving the conflict with her, he had tossed all night. Fortunately, Ze'vie's presence had prevented her from screaming at him. They had experienced a few bumps in the road during their eighteen-year relationship—but nothing that had eroded her opinion of him.

He went into the bathroom, showered, and shaved, and quietly dressed. When he left the bedroom, book in hand, she was still sleeping. He went into the family room turned on the TV, muted it, put it on closed-caption mode and watched the BBC broadcasters report the depressing financial news.

Ze'vie came into the family room at 8:30 a.m. "Did you sleep well"?

"No, unfortunately, not well at all," Jerry responded to his polite question.

Ze'vie shook his head, and then without further comment, went about the business of making coffee, espressos, and putting together the tray of croissants, and pastries.

"Do you and Helen like lox and eggs?"

"Love them," said Jerry.

"Good," said Ze'vie, "I'll cook up a batch of lox, eggs, and tomatoes. You and I can eat , and I'll heat them up for Helen when she wakes." Then he busied himself over the stove and the sink.

When Helen entered the dining room at 9 a.m., Ze'vie and Jerry were just finishing breakfast. Ze'vie heated and served her a portion of the meal.

"My favorite dish, Ze'vie," she said, looking genuinely well-rested. "Maybe you have another career as a chef."

"No way," said Ze'vie. "The food would not come out nearly as good if I had to cook it. I relish and protect my amateur status." He paused. "If it's okay with you, I'd like to talk business." They both nodded.

Ze'vie cleared his throat. "I think it's clear to all of us we are at an impasse about the Gatsby matter. There is no purpose in talking about this any further until the two of you can agree on a common goal and a strategy. If you can both get to the point of agreeing that Gatsby's bank records would provide the evidence he paid an assassin and a plant, and you decide you want to neutralize Gatsby, I can help. But since you are a long way from there, I suggest you both put the matter on the back burner and enjoy the rest of your time in Israel." He looked at Helen and then at Jerry. "And by the 'back burner,' I mean you avoid talking about Gatsby until you are back in the States. Does that make sense to you?"

They both nodded. It was clear he was done with the matter and would not suffer their indecision, even if he was too gracious to say so outright.

"Since you have a flight leaving tomorrow evening, I suggest you make reservations for a hotel at the airport and relax until it's time to go. I'll drive you to the hotel when you're packed."

~ ~ ~ ~ ~

The afternoon before their departure from Tel Aviv, Jerry woke alone in the hotel room from a nap. He said Helen's name, but she was gone.

Heart pounding, he called her cell. "Where are you? Is everything okay?"

She sounded relaxed. "I'm just at the pool," she said. He glanced around the room—indeed, her book and bathing suit were gone, and in the background of the call, he heard children shouting. She asked, "Have you checked the minibar?"

"Yes, it's well stocked."

"I'll be up in ten minutes. We need to talk."

When she entered the room, her expression indicated she was on a mission.

"Pour me a white wine while I get dressed."

Jerry went down the hall to fill the ice bucket. He poured two bottles of Absolut from the minibar over a glass of ice for himself and poured the small bottle of chardonnay into a wine glass for Helen. Helen came out of the bathroom and sat down at the table. Jerry handed her the glass of wine and sat down opposite her. He lifted his glass of vodka to make a toast.

"Here is to a safe trip home." Helen did not make any motion to pick up her glass.

Jerry looked at her and said, "What?"

"Jerry, while I was enjoying the wonderful weather and the hotel pool, I realized I could not lose myself in a novel while this Gatsby mess is hanging over us. I kept reviewing it and reviewing it. It's clear I can't depend on you to solve this problem. You may be a great lawyer, a terrific M&A expert, and based on what you did at National, a good turnaround executive—but you are not competent to solve our problem."

Jerry felt the blood rushing to his head. "Now Helen—"

"Please don't interrupt me. You can tell me what's on your mind after I finish saying what I've been rehearsing for the last hour. I'll rephrase. You haven't shown me that you are competent to solve the problem that you created."

Jerry moved to the edge of his chair and leaned forward.

She continued, "I need to take it out of your hands and take ownership of it for the sake of the safety and tranquility of our family. Moreover, since I refuse to return to the black emotional state I was in prior to our leaving for Israel, I'm going to stay in Israel and work with Ze'vie on our Gatsby problem for as long as it takes until it is solved. Your job will be to take care of the kids and Misty. Make the boys comfortable with the idea that their mother is in Israel on business. And arrange to have $250,000 available to transfer into a bank account when I provide you the number."

Jerry shook his head. "You are being overdramatic. I don't see why—"

"Jerry," she said, raising her voice, "listen to me. Our marriage is in crisis. I'm trying to save it. I'm through talking about it. You've heard what I intend to do. If you want to save this marriage, don't fight me— do exactly what I say. I will take a taxi to Ze'vie's where I'll stay for a few nights until I arrange for a longer-term residence. You'll take the flight home tomorrow as scheduled. I'm going to cancel my reservation this afternoon. Do we understand each other?"

Jerry, defeated, could only manage to say, "I'm sorry I disappointed you. I'll do whatever you want."

CHAPTER 55

HELEN

When Helen arrived at Ze'vie's home in the late afternoon, he had already set the table for dinner. "Can I get you a glass of wine?"

"Something a lot stronger," said Helen, collapsing into one of the comfortable family room chairs. "I can't believe I'm doing this."

Ze'vie pulled a bottle of Tito's vodka from his liquor cabinet, poured three ounces into each of two tumblers full of ice, and handed one of them to Helen. "You are what we call in French *la fille dura*, which translates roughly as a tough lady, a prerequisite for a female Kidon agent." He lifted his glass and said, "*À votre santé.*"

"*Je vous souhaite la même chose*," she replied.

After dinner they sat in the family room sipping Hennessey's. Helen said, "Jerry and I have agreed that I will take over the Gatsby portfolio for our family. I am going to remain in Israel as long as it takes us to resolve the Gatsby problem. I will make the decisions and dole out the fees. Jerry is out of the picture."

"Boy," said Ze'vie, "that must have been some hell of a conversation."

"I tried to keep it civil and professional."

"Did you succeed?"

"Partially."

"I don't intend to pry into your personal situation, but I am sure you recognize that the path you've taken would appear bizarre for a presumably happy and handsome couple with two boys, one dog, and plenty of money. I certainly didn't detect the signs of a family crisis during the time the two of you spent with me."

"You're entitled to an explanation, Ze'vie. Because of the events that culminated in Gatsby's threat, and the way Jerry has coped with the situation, I no longer trust him to protect the boys and me. The entire Gatsby problem resulted from Jerry's unrestrained ego and greed. He had plenty of evidence that Gatsby was bad news. I pleaded with him to pass on Gatsby's offer. But he wouldn't listen. I am angry at him for putting us all in this situation, and as I sit here today, I'm not all certain I'll ever get over it." She shrugged. "There, I've shown you our dirty laundry." She sat back in the chair and took a sip of Hennessy. "I'd like to go ahead and get Gatsby's bank records. Have you received the information from your colleague?"

"It will cost $30,000 and could take up to a month—$15,000 up front and $15,000 when the records are in our hands."

"Can you assure me that Gatsby will not know that his bank records were stolen?"

"Mossad does this all the time. Gatsby will not have any suspicion we have retrieved his bank records."

"That's fine. Then let's move forward. Take me to a bank tomorrow morning so I can set up an account. Jerry will transfer $250,000 after I call him and give him the bank information so I will have access to whatever funds we need without getting Jerry involved. I need your help in getting a place to stay. And I need to rent a car. I was thinking about signing up for a couple of courses at one of your colleges to learn something about Jewish history and culture—you know—so I can keep myself busy while we're working the problem."

Ze'vie sat quietly in his chair, stirring his glass of vodka. He smiled at Helen and said, "Helen, if you want my help in resolving the Gatsby problem, you need to accept the fact that by my getting involved, I am assuming responsibility for your personal safety. That includes ensuring that your whereabouts at any given time are not easily traceable, that you don't sign anything, and that you have 24/7 protection. This also includes your passing on to Jerry my advice as to what he should do to ensure the safety of your boys and himself. If the Gatsby issue hangs over your head, your stay in Israel is not going to be a vacation or a study-abroad sabbatical. It's going to be a lot closer to a house arrest. Do you follow me?"

Helen had been so focused on wresting control of the Gatsby matter from Jerry she had not thought through the implications of her decision. She was annoyed at herself and didn't respond right away.

"Helen, you need to be consistent. You've just told me that you are prepared to spend $30,000 to get Gatsby's bank records to determine whether he had anything to do with Shirley's disappearance. Therefore, you must believe that Gatsby may be a psychopath and that the threat he delivered to Jerry should be taken seriously. It follows that you, Jerry, and your boys are at risk. And you should plan, talk, and act accordingly. Do you follow me?"

"I—yes, I know you're right," said Helen.

"All right," said Ze'vie. "I'm going to spell it out for you anyway. You will live here, in the guest suite. My house is a hardened site: bulletproof glass on all the windows, motion detectors, and cameras everywhere. You will take the battery out of your cell phone and no longer use it. I will buy you a bunch of untraceable burner phones that you can use and periodically discard. You will not give a phone number or location to anyone. I will hire your personal security to provide 24/7 protection. Your security will be with you when you are in the house and will drive you wherever you need to go, though going anywhere should be rare. If you need something, your security will arrange to get it and bring it to you. You will not give your real name to anyone. From now on your name in Israel is Rebecca—one name, like Beyoncé or Madonna."

He grinned, and she tried to return it.

"In addition, you need to arrange for your sons to disappear to a safe place—one unknown to Gatsby. Jerry needs to put your dog in a kennel and disappear to some location that is not easily traceable. Perhaps go on a road trip. He will have to pay cash for all services and anything he buys and never give his real name if he stays in a motel. He needs to stop using his cell phone and get burner phones and not use any electronic devices that are traceable to his location. Do you follow me? Are you willing to do all of this? Do you want to sleep on it and we can decide tomorrow?"

By now, Helen accepted she had been naïve. Life was about to get strange.

"I follow you completely, and I am on board. You will not have to worry about me. I will do whatever is necessary to get the Gatsby mess resolved. When you get me the burner phone, I'll tell Jerry he will have to ship the boys off to my sister Sallie, who lives in Kailua, and arrange for them to be homeschooled. And I'll tell Jerry he needs to take a leave of absence from Bricker for a couple of months, use burner phones, and pay everything in cash."

"Okay," said Ze'vie. "Now that we've agreed as to what this strategy entails for you and your family, I'd like you to take a deep breath and consider an alternative theory."

Helen suddenly became more alert. "What kind of alternative?"

Ze'vie stood up. "Let's go into the dining room and take another look at our chart." He turned and headed for the dining room and Helen followed.

He flipped over the cover. "I'm sure by now you're familiar with the chart?"

"More than familiar," said Helen, "I'm sick of it."

Ze'vie chuckled. "I understand. But bear with me. Which one of these events was the one that precipitated the sequence that brought you to Israel and caused you and Jerry to go your separate ways? This is important, so take your time."

Helen fixated on the chart, carefully looking at every line in the light of Ze'vie's question. After several minutes, she said, "Number 11, Gatsby's threat."

"Correct," said Ze'vie. "And who is it that narrated the incident in which the threat was made?"

"Jerry, of course. He was there. He told me exactly what transpired and what Gatsby said to him."

"Right. I agree. And I am confident, having spent time with Jerry, that his legal training and his stellar character guarantee he narrated what happened to the best of his ability. And I assume that what he related to me when we met after you two first arrived agreed with what he related to you after he returned from Saint Martin."

"Exactly," said Helen.

"I have a serious concern that while Jerry's narration of the facts and statements were accurate, according to his perception, his reaction was so acute because it gave him a severe emotional shock. He doesn't strike me as a man who is easily shocked." Helen could tell Ze'vie was being delicate, talking around his point.

"He's not. What are you saying?"

"What set him off was when Gatsby revealed he was aware of Jerry's trip to Saint Martin and probably knew everything Jerry had seen and done when he was on the island. Are you following me?"

"I think so," said Helen. In the back of her mind, something was coming forward. It was barely a shadow, but now it was in motion, she felt it lay at the root of her disgust with her husband. "Why don't you spell it out for me, Ze'vie."

"I believe that Jerry did not tell you the entire story about his trip. Gatsby's threat may have shaken him because, frankly, in my experience, the best way to deliver a threat is to manipulate some vulnerability your target already has. An indiscretion of some nature. We should be prepared for the possibility that Jerry compromised himself in some way."

Helen was silent, she slumped down in her chair. "I don't know what to say."

Between them was the fact the potential plant, Gatsby's flunky in Saint Martin, was female. Also, the fact Jerry had said almost nothing about her to Helen. The fact kept moving forward through her mind, disturbing every jealous inclination she'd ever felt. Tears of anger filled her eyes, which in turn embarrassed her and made her angrier.

"Don't jump to any conclusions," Ze'vie said. "What I've outlined is just a theory. But we need to find out whether this theory holds water."

Ze'vie waited until Helen had composed herself. He said, "We need to sort this out. My recommendation is that you retain me as a consultant. This will establish a fiduciary relationship between us. You will be my client, not Jerry. Therefore, I do not have to tell him anything that I do or learn on your behalf. My fee will be $2,500 a day plus expenses. I'd prefer to do this without any charge, but it would undermine my status as your fiduciary."

Helen was calm and alert. She nodded.

"Incidentally, whenever I leave the house, my colleague Yakov, also ex-Mossad, will stay here with you. Just as a precaution. He charges only $1,000 a day—but he'll also play hours of chess with you."

He checked his watch. "It's almost seven o'clock. I need to run some errands. Yakov will be here in a half hour. You know your way around the house. My library contains many books in English and French. I'm certain you'll find a few of interest. Don't answer the phone. I'll be back in a few hours."

He stood, and said, "Don't think that I don't appreciate how difficult this will be for you. Hopefully we can clear this up within a month or two."

Helen returned to her suite, showered, and changed her clothes. Ze'vie's suite was empty. When she entered the kitchen a man was sitting at the dining table, drinking coffee.

He stood and smiled. He was tall, muscular, and wearing a white T-shirt. "I'm Yakov, a member of your security detail. I will stay with you when Ze'vie isn't here."

She took his hand and smiled. "I already feel safer."

"Ze'vie invited me to stay here because even before he goes to the States, he needs to leave the house frequently. But don't worry, Ms. Bascomb, I don't go on the clock until Ze'vie leaves the house."

"Please call me Helen. The arrangements are acceptable, as long as you play chess with me once a day." She smiled. "Ze'vie tells me that you are quite good."

"I've won a few tournaments. I'll even share some of my secrets."

CHAPTER 56

JERRY

Sunday, April 20, 2008

Jerry's long flight to JFK gave him ample opportunity to reflect on his sorry situation. The Gatsby affair had pushed their relationship into free fall, with no parachute in sight.

Helen's cold blood shocked him. Again, he wondered if she had intuited any hint of his infidelity. It didn't seem likely, however, or necessary: if it were up to her, he thought, she'd kill Gatsby simply for being a self-centered, self-aggrandizing manipulator. In her mind Gatsby was a monster, the cause of her fear and anxiety. They were miles apart on this matter and Jerry did not see any way to break the logjam. Even so, he admitted to himself he felt relieved she had taken the mess off his plate. He did not have to agonize over it anymore.

He arrived at their apartment at 7:00 a.m. The boys and Helga were asleep. Misty came out to greet him and he decided to take her downstairs for a walk. When he returned to the apartment, he poured himself a triple Jameson and took it into his bedroom. He sent a text to Jeff, asking him to meet at 1:00 p.m. at the Starbucks near Jeff's home. He set his alarm for 9:30 a.m. and went to bed.

By the time the alarm went off the next morning, Jeff had confirmed their meeting.

When he entered the kitchen, the boys were eating breakfast. They leaped out of their chairs to hug him and then quickly realized that their mother was missing. Jerry suggested they go into the family room to discuss it.

He told the boys that while they were in Israel, they had met a promising Israeli artist and had the opportunity to see several of his paintings. He had asked Helen whether she was interested in representing him in the US and she had jumped at the opportunity. She decided to stay in Israel to negotiate the details of the arrangement and explore the possibility of representing other Israeli artists. It might take her several weeks to complete her research. This was an excellent opportunity to ease her way back into the gallery business now that both boys were sufficiently independent so she did not have to be a stay-at-home mom.

On his way to meet Jeff, he decided that the discussion with the boys had gone well. He had assured them they would be able to talk with their mother frequently. He had told them to get ready for school and they didn't give him any pushback. And afterward, Helga had agreed to work full time for at least a week until he caught up at work.

Jerry slid into a table opposite Jeff. There were two coffees and a basket of Danish and croissants on the table. Jerry picked up his cup and took a sip.

"How did it go, little brother?"

"Ze'vie's a mensch. He spent virtually every hour with us. He even took us on a tour of Jaffa."

"I wasn't asking if you had fun. Was Ze'vie helpful?"

Jerry hesitated before he responded. "Not as much as I had hoped. After an exhaustive review, we concluded that if we wanted Ze'vie's help we would need to get him more evidence of Gatsby's role in Shirley's and Cissy's disappearance. He suggested looking at the bank records."

They sat in silence, sipping their coffees. Finally, Jeff said, "What are you going to do?"

Jerry shook his head. "I have no idea. Helen has taken over the whole thing. She's staying in Israel until she and Ze'vie solve the problem—one way or another, as she put it."

"Are you serious?" said Jeff. "You left Helen in Israel?"

"That is the way she wanted it. She is upset with me for not having been more aggressive. At one point in our several arguments about the Gatsby situation she called me a 'prissy pussy.'"

"What did you tell the boys?"

Jerry gave him the cover story and shrugged. "You are the only person who knows the truth."

Jeff shook his head. "The whole truth, as it were." Then he leaned across the table and grabbed Jerry's hand and squeezed it. "I feel for you, little brother. You are in a box."

"And the sides are closing in," said Jerry. "Do you think it's worthwhile to see if I could work something out with your tong contact?"

"I tracked down my psychopathic trooper and met with him while you were in Israel. He understands your problem but said they couldn't help. He said killing Gatsby was the only way to resolve the situation, and they are not in that business. Sorry, Jerry."

"Thanks for trying." Jerry slid out of the booth. "I've got to get home to the boys. I hope to drown my sorrows in work—hopefully."

~~~~~

At 7 a.m. the next morning, the phone rang. Josh answered it.

"Mom!" Josh yelled. "Dad, Alli, Mom is on the phone."

Helen spoke with each of the boys for ten minutes, inquiring about school, confirming the cover story, and listening empathetically as they complained about her being away. She said goodbye to Alli and asked him to put Jerry on the line.

"How is it going?" he asked, without much of a greeting.

"So far, so good. How was your flight to New York?"

"Lonely."

"I can appreciate that. I have bank information for you so you can send a wire transfer." She provided the name of the bank, bank routing number, the account number, and the name of the account owner, namely "Rebecca." She told him not to ask any questions.

"Can you arrange to transfer $250,000 today?"
~~~~~

"I'll do that this morning."

"Good. I'm going to give you some specific instructions which come from Ze'vie. I don't want you to question them or debate them. Ze'vie says it is essential that you follow them to the letter. Can I count on you?"

"What do you want me to do?"

"We're going to pull the boys out of school and send them to Salli. I've talked with her, and she is on board. She will arrange for homeschooling while they are staying with her. You get the plane tickets and coordinate with her. Then you need to put Misty in the kennel and take a leave of absence from Bricker for at least a month, maybe two, and then disappear. Take a road trip across the country or whatever. Don't sign anything, don't use your real name, and pay for anything you buy in cash."

"Aren't you being a bit overdramatic? I don't see why this is necessary. I've got two big deals ready to close and—"

Helen raised her voice. "Will you please shut the fuck up? This is not a game. Until we have hard evidence that Gatsby was not involved in Shirley's and Cissy's disappearance, we need to assume he was and the threat he made in Philadelphia needs to be taken seriously. I've talked at length with Ze'vie, and he believes that this is what we must do to ensure the safety of all the members of our family. Now goddammit, just do it! And never call me overdramatic again."

Jerry bit his tongue, took a breath. "All right. I'll follow the instructions."

"This is going to be our last call. When you have disappeared, you cannot use your cell phone. Buy a bunch of burner phones and change them at least once a week. You and I will stay in touch through Jeff. Arrange for him to be available to take a daily call from you. I'm going to call him tonight, so you call him and ask him to be available. That's about it. Any questions?"

After a long silence, Jerry said, "I guess not."

"Do I have your word that you will follow through?"

"Yes, I give you my word."

"Thanks, Jerry. I know this is hard on you. It's hard on me. I'm living under a house-arrest situation to ensure my safety on this end. We'll get through this. Just thank God we have Ze'vie." There was understanding in her voice, but no warmth. "Goodbye."

After Jerry hung up the phone, he focused on the boys, made sure they had a decent breakfast and got them ready for school. Alli tended to dawdle, and to get him out the door in time for the school bus was an immense challenge—especially this morning.

After Helen's call, all Jerry wanted to do was open a fresh bottle of Jameson and get stone drunk. But he kept his feelings in check while the boys were around. He did not want to call Salli until 9 a.m. her time, which was in about five hours. He would have plenty of time to decide how he would disappear enough to satisfy his wife.

After the boys walked out the door, he called United Airlines and made reservations for a direct flight to Honolulu that would depart from Newark at about 8 a.m. on Friday. He wanted to spend two days with the boys since he had no idea when he would see them again. Then he gave in to his urge and poured himself a double Jameson and went into the family room to think through his plan for the next two months. He needed to concoct a story for Birney to justify his need to take a leave of absence.

He called the kennel and arranged to drop off Misty on Friday, after he took the boys to the airport. He opened the pantry door to see how much dog food was there and determined it would not be enough for a two-month stay. He would have to stop at the pet store to buy some more. He called Jeff and told him he needed to talk with him and proposed lunch. Jeff said he was going to be tied up the next two days and suggested Jerry come by his office late Tuesday afternoon.

Jerry decided he would pack for Alli and Josh before he left for the office. He took a long sip of the whiskey and tried to collect his thoughts. He resented the way Helen had treated him and talked to him starting with their conversation at the hotel before his return flight. She intended to call the shots and did not give a damn how he felt about it.

Yet why was he so reluctant to voice his objections and defy her order to disappear? He planned to discuss it with Jeff.

~ ~ ~ ~ ~ ~

Jerry entered Jeff's office at four o'clock on Tuesday.

"Hi, bro," said Jeff. "Want a drink?"

"Sure," said Jerry. "How about a double Absolut on the rocks?"

"You *are* stressed."

"You don't know the half of it. I've got a knot in my stomach the size of a baseball. Frankly, I'm getting tired of Helen pushing me around and making ridiculous demands."

Jeff went to the bar, poured two vodkas over ice, returned to his desk, and gave one of the glasses to Jerry. "What ridiculous demands has she made?"

"That I send the boys to Salli, and I disappear for one to two months."

"I assume that order came from Ze'vie."

"I don't care who it came from, it's ridiculous! I'm going to send the boys to Salli but I'm leaning toward not disappearing. I'm too damn busy. I've got two deals in the pipeline that should close during the next two months. There is no way I can take off."

Jeff leaned back in his chair and sipped his vodka. "Helen called me this morning and gave me the game plan. Under the circumstances, it's perfectly reasonable. Ze'vie does not want to take the risk that any of you would be accessible if Gatsby unleashed the whirlwind. If you don't follow through on Ze'vie's instructions, it would certainly be a passive-aggressive way to put a stake in your marriage. You've already had an affair. You might as well retain a divorce attorney."

Jerry sat up straight in his chair. "Why do you say that?"

"Because this Gatsby mess is currently the most important thing in Helen's life. It's had a huge negative effect on her mental and emotional state. The two of you have managed to find an expert, Ze'vie, who may get you through this unscathed. If you sabotage Ze'vie's plan, Helen will feel that you no longer respect her nor have the best interests of the family at heart and will end the marriage. She already felt that way when you ignored her unease with Gatsby. Listen to me carefully, bro. If you want to save your marriage, this is your last chance."

Jerry slumped in his chair. He took another sip of vodka. He shook his head. "Damn it! I know you're right. It's just so hard to stomach."

"Jerry, stop over-thinking and ruminating about it. Just do it!"

Jerry drained the glass. "What do I tell Birney? What do I tell my staff?"

"Tell Birney that you need some time off to deal with serious family problems. You'll stay in touch as best you can and will come back as soon as possible. That's it. Don't volunteer another word."

"Since I can't call Helen directly, she decided we should use you as a contact. I'll call you daily around nine p.m. Is that okay with you?"

"No problem. I already talked to Helen about it."

"You've been a lot of help, Jeff, especially in keeping my head screwed on."

"Have you decided how you're going to disappear?"

"I'm going fishing."

Jeff walked him to the door of the office. He hugged Jerry. There were tears in his eyes. "Be careful. I'd hate to lose you."

Jerry nodded, but he still couldn't shake the feeling that everyone was overreacting.

<center>~~~~~</center>

When he arrived home, the boys were watching television. Misty came to the door to meet him. "When was the last time Misty went potty?"

"I took her out when I came home from school," said Josh.

Jerry checked his watch, 6:30 p.m. He took the leash down from the back of the pantry door and left the apartment. He returned a half hour later. The boys were still watching television. He fed Misty and then went into the family room to face the conversation he'd wanted to avoid.

"Why did you pack our bags, Dad?" said Alli.

"Let's turn off the television and I'll explain what is going on." He sat down in the chair adjacent to the sofa and said, "Listen to me carefully. I do not want you to share this information with anyone else. It is important that no one knows what I'm going to tell you. Do you understand?"

Both boys nodded and said, "Yes, Dad."

"Okay. There is a very bad man who wants to hurt our family. Your mom and I are working on a plan to stop him. But in the meantime, we need to ensure that you boys are in a safe place where the bad man can't find you. That is why we're going to send you to Aunt Salli's home. I have reservations for you on an early flight Friday morning. It's a direct flight so you will not have to change planes. Aunt Salli will be waiting for you where you walk past security. She is going to arrange for you to continue your schooling for as long as you stay with her."

"How long are we going to be there?" said Josh.

"We don't know. It could be for up to two months."

"Will we be able to boogie board in the surf?" said Alli.

Jerry laughed and leaned over and tousled Alli's hair. "I guarantee that you'll enjoy many hours of boogie boarding."

"Will you and Mom visit us while we're in Hawaii?" said Josh.

"Unfortunately, no," said Jerry. "But both of us will call often so we will stay in close touch. Any other questions?" He waited for a minute to give the boys an opportunity. "No? Okay, just remember, not a word to anyone. I'm going to call your Aunt Salli and give her your flight information. I'll go to your schools on Monday to tell the principals that you will not be attending for up to two months, and I'll get the lesson plans so I can send them to Aunt Salli. I'm going to keep you out of school the next two days so we can all hang out together. What would you like to do?"

"I'd like to go to the Museum of Natural History," said Josh.

"I'd like to go to a baseball game," said Alli.

"Oh, and I'd like to go to the movies to see *Wall-E*," said Josh.

"Me, too!" said Alli.

"And what would you like to do for dinner tonight?"

In unison, both boys shouted, "Pizza!"

"Okay," said Jerry, give me an hour and I'll plan our next two days, and then we'll go out for pizza."

By Thursday night, Jerry and the boys were all drooping. The two days had been a blur of crowds and pizza restaurants and hamburger joints. Their hair and clothes smelled of fresh air from Central Park, and they'd run themselves silly with Misty. And now that the boys were asleep, it was time to pack for a fishing trip.

Chapter 57

JERRY

April 25, 2008

Jerry woke the boys at 4:30 a.m., fed the boys breakfast, was on the road at 5:30 a.m., and arrived at Newark terminal 6 a.m. He checked their baggage at the ticket counter, got their boarding passes and luggage claim forms, and led them to a Starbucks near the start of the security line. He ordered coffee and soft drinks for the boys.

"Josh, you're in charge. Do you have your cell phone? Good. Alli, you listen to Josh. Do not let him out of your sight. Do you have your cell phone in a safe place? Good. Any questions?" Both boys shook their heads. "Okay, then let the games begin."

He led the boys to the start of the security line. "Do you have your boarding passes?"

Both boys said, "Yes."

"Do you know your gate?"

"Eleven," said Josh.

"Great." He hugged and kissed each of the boys and then led them to the start of the security line. Then he found a spot where he could observe the boys' progress, and he realized he'd forgotten to tell them what to do: but they did it anyway, down to putting their phones in a separate plastic bin and having their shoes untied before they got to the scanner. As he lost sight of them in the crowd, tears started to stream down his face, and a feeling of utter loneliness coursed through him.

~ ~ ~ ~ ~

Jerry arrived at Bricker and Weldon and checked Birney's office. Still too early. He went into his office and started packing his large briefcase with the documents relevant to the two projects likely to close during the next two months. When he had completed packing, he pulled a few books off the shelf he had been planning to read. He stuffed one of them into the briefcase and threw the others into a banker's box. By then, Birney was in.

Jerry shut Birney's door behind him and sat in the chair in front of his desk.

"What's up?" said Birney.

"I'll get right to the point. Helen and I are dealing with a serious family problem. There is no way I can address it and maintain my work schedule and obligations to the firm. I'm requesting a leave of absence of up to two months. I will call in every day and stay in touch with you and my staff. I know it's a huge inconvenience, but I have no choice."

Jerry sat back in his chair, relieved to have gotten this issue out in the open.

A concerned look covered Birney's face. "Gee, Jerry, I'm sorry to hear that. Is this a medical issue?"

"Birney, I'd love to share our problem with you. Unfortunately, I can't. But I need your support and understanding."

"I see," said Birney. "Your anxiety is palpable. Take the time off and do stay in touch. You have two big deals on the fast track."

"Don't I know it. This is the worst possible time for me to be out of the office."

"When are you going to tell your staff?"

"A soon as we're done here. I'll be in the office until 2 p.m. Between now and the time I leave, I will have a staff meeting and repeat exactly what I told you."

Birney put his arm around Jerry's shoulder and steered him to the doorway. "Good luck, boychik. I hope things work out for you and Helen."

Jerry left the building at 2 p.m., drove to the two schools, and met with the administrators advising them that Alli and Josh would be out for up to two months, and asked for their respective lesson plans. He stopped at the bank and withdrew $25,000 in a mix of bills. Then he drove to Walmart and paid cash for fifteen prepaid burner phones. He headed to the apartment, stopping at the pet store to buy Misty's food.

When he arrived at his apartment, Helga was there and had walked Misty. Jerry explained that there had been a change in plans, and she would not need to come for perhaps one to two months, but he did not know exactly. He wrote her a check for two months' pay and said he'd be in touch. He put the boy's lesson plans in an envelope and put on plenty of postage. Then he took Misty to the kennel and stopped at the post office to mail the lesson plans to Salli. Everything was ready.

~~~~~~

Jerry's plan was to go to their cabin in Roscoe, New York, and spend his days fly fishing. If he avoided going into the Roscoe stores and restaurants, it would be unlikely he would run into anyone who would recognize him. He planned to stay on the water until four o'clock every day, with only brief timeouts for pit stops or to eat a sandwich. Then he would call the office and address any issues that either Birney or his staff needed to discuss. He would eat at a restaurant in Hancock, twenty-five miles from Roscoe, and call Jeff on his way back to the cabin.

He packed a suitcase with one week's worth of clothes, two boxes of food from the refrigerator and pantry, and several bottles of liquor. Then, almost as an afterthought, he retrieved his previously packed briefcase from the den and put it next to the banker's box he had brought home from the office.

By 6:30 p.m. he'd picked up the route to Roscoe via NY 17. Three and a half hours later, he turned off at Exit 94 onto Old Highway 17 and carefully navigated to their cabin on the outskirts of Roscoe. He
~~~~~~

had stopped for dinner on the road, so it was 10 p.m. by the time he arrived.

The cabin was only one in name. It was 1,800 square feet, had hardwood floors and knotty pine walls throughout, three bedrooms, three bathrooms, a modest kitchen, a great room and a laundry/mud room big enough to store all the fishing gear and water toys. The place was a little dusty but otherwise pristine since their last visit for Helen's birthday almost a year ago.

He connected the icemaker to the water supply, started the furnace, and then unpacked the car, organized his fishing gear, brushed his teeth, set the alarm for early and crawled into bed.

He whispered, "Goodnight, Mrs. Bascomb—wherever you are."

~~~~~

The Beaverkill is the perfect size for fly fishing. Except during the early spring, it is possible to wade the entire stream width—assuming you can avoid the ever-present deep pools. The mountainous topography of the area consists of many peaks that rise to 3,000 to 4,000 feet at about a 30-degree incline, resulting in valleys shaped like a deep V. For much of the length of the river, the steep hillside shoulders right up to the water's edge, leaving only a band of sky, and limiting the views both upstream and downstream. Even on a day where there are many fishermen on the river, it's possible to feel like the only person on Earth.

Jerry walked back to the car, donned his vest and waders, attached his fishing net to his belt, picked up his insect net and walked twenty paces into the river. He placed the insect net perpendicular to the stream and held it in position for ten minutes, took it out and walked back to his car. He took the magnifying glass out of his vest and examined the insects and then opened the fly box and selected several flies that matched. Tied one of them to the tippet of his tackle, put the others in a small plastic box, and placed the box in his vest. In a moment, he was carrying his rod into the river to stalk fish.

What made fly fishing so attractive was that once he placed himself on a spot beside or in the water, identified a likely trout hideout,
~~~~~

determined what they were eating, selected, and tied on the best-matching fly, took hold of his rod and make the first cast, his thoughts about all his problems and anxieties drained out of his mind. All that remained was the task. Were the fish rising? What were they eating? Did he choose the right fly? Was he out of the fishes' line of sight? How many casts should he make before he moved to a new spot? And on and on until he got a bite, battled the fish for some unpredictable period, reeled it in, netted it, inspected its markings, measured it tip to tail, marked the length in the notebook, removed the hook from its mouth, and tossed the trout back into the river to swim another day.

By noon he had caught and released fifteen fish in the range of 12 to 23 inches. He decided to forego lunch and continue moving up the river. By three o'clock he had caught an additional five fish and had moved about a mile upstream from where he had parked the car. He moved back to the bank, removed his waders, and walked along the stream to the car. He was tired and his lower back ached—but he was content.

As of now he was twenty ahead, and no falls, scrapes, or hook punctures. And best of all, he hadn't thought about Gatsby for a microsecond.

He reached the car by 3:30 p.m. He was famished. He poured a cup of coffee from the thermos and ate one of the pastrami sandwiches. Since it was Sunday, there was no need to call the office. He organized his gear so he would be ready to go tomorrow and then drove to Hancock twenty-five miles west on Highway 17. He stopped in a convenience store to pick up a few things he had forgotten to pack and bought the *Wall Street Journal* and the *New York Times*. He decided to have dinner at the River Run Restaurant on Faulkner Street. If he worked at it carefully, he would get back to the cabin by 9 p.m. to call Jeff.

Jerry adhered to the exact same routine every day, except for changing the restaurant where he dined, and whether or not he called his office and talked with Birney and his staff. Occasionally he fished on Willowemoc Creek instead of the Beaverkill.

At night, there was an inevitable pull to steer his thoughts toward reviewing, examining, and ruminating over the events that had driven his relationship with Helen over the cliff. However, he knew he was wasting the mental effort. He ought to just sleep. What was important was if and how their relationship would recover when the Gatsby mess was resolved, and the uncertainties and contingencies associated with those calculations rendered the entire project a fool's errand. Yet they bothered him when his hands were idle, and the clock ticked its way through the wee hours. He had to be prepared for the possibility that Helen, like the beautiful brown trout he had battled for twenty minutes earlier in the day, might already be in the process of slipping the hook.

CHAPTER 58

HELEN

Netanya, Tuesday, April 22, 2008

Helen awoke from a late afternoon nap the day after she had first called Jerry to convey Ze'vie's instructions. Her first inclination was to call him again, but she remembered she couldn't use her cell phone. She fell back into bed and stared at the ceiling trying to wrap her head around the enormity of what she had done. After several minutes of agonizing soul searching, she once again felt comfortable with her decision to remain in Israel.

She got out of bed, and after some time in the bathroom to insure she was presentable, joined Ze'vie in the family room He was watching a BBC documentary.

When the documentary ended Helen said, "Ze'vie, can we talk?"

He shut off the TV. "Of course, what do you want to talk about?"

Helen smiled at him. "I want to talk about you, Ze'vie. I need to know something about what makes you tick, you know, how you got to be an Israeli hero."

Ze'vie laughed. "Can I ask why?"

"Well, notwithstanding that I've arranged things so that my family and I are wholly dependent on you, I don't know a whole lot about you."

Ze'vie was still amused. He stood and pulled his chair over toward her so they would face each other. "My dear Helen, I'm more than happy to answer any question that doesn't require me to divulge state secrets. Shoot!"

"Terrific. Let's start with the G-rated ones. Why did you join Mossad, and why did you choose to become a Kidon Unit commander? How do you feel about the way you spent those, what was it, thirty years?"

"Thirty-five. I joined Mossad because I was asked to. I had unique language skills they needed for an intelligence operation. When the operation was completed, they asked me to stay on. I enjoyed the assignment and felt I could do the job, so I was satisfied."

"What was the assignment?"

"Gathering intelligence in Lebanon."

"What was it about the assignment that was so enjoyable?"

"*Enjoyable* is the wrong word. How about *super-challenging*? I needed to take on a new identity which consisted of a forged passport, a made-up biography, a cover story as to the reason I was traveling, and attire that would allow me to meld into the population. I flew to Beirut via Rome, passed through immigration and customs as my new identity, rented a car, found a hotel room, and spent several days accumulating the information I was assigned to find, and then reversed the process. Slinked away from Beirut and traveled to Israel without leaving a trace."

"Wasn't that dangerous? Weren't you afraid?"

"It was extremely dangerous. You are in a foreign city, surrounded by people who do not wish you well. You are constantly worried that you will respond to a question in a language that your new identity is not supposed to know, or that you will meet someone who recognizes you from a previous identity. The odd hours at which you enter and leave your hotel might arouse suspicion that will bring you in contact with the police, and since your passport is only good for first impressions, your subterfuge would collapse, and you'd wind up in a dungeon. You're always afraid when involved in an operation. The level of fear tends to decrease as the number of operations under your belt increases, but it never totally disappears."

She had read many thrillers by John le Carré in which characters engaged in these kinds of activities, but she had never met or talked to a flesh-and-blood spy—and she was startled. "And you signed up for a career which would require you to perform these kinds of operations frequently?"

"Yes, because the State of Israel needed people with these skills; and there are only a limited number of us who can steal into a foreign country without diplomatic protection, move around in a hostile environment like a shadow, gather intelligence, shoot a target, plant a bomb, overpower an intruder, vanish without leaving any clues, and make our way back home. I demonstrated that I had the potential to be one of these individuals, and so I was trained to be a lethal weapon."

"And you became a Kidon commander?"

"Yes, after several years of performing in successful operations all over the world, Mossad decided that I had the leadership and management skills to run a unit."

"What did that entail?"

"It's a huge job. There are always operations being conceived, planned, simulated, executed, evaluated, and dissected, and as a commander, you need to be involved in every aspect of the process. You lead the team in the field, you direct the operations, you intervene if things go awry, you make sure everyone gets out, and you attempt to clean up any mess left behind. It is a constant commitment. There are no days off, ever."

"What about the other parts of your life—family, lovers, parents, friends?"

"If you take on this kind of responsibility, you are accepting the fact your job trumps everything else. You can have a family, a lover, see your parents, engage with friends, pursue hobbies, but the Kidon Squad and your obligations to the State of Israel come first."

"So, it's like the priesthood. You give the church your life."

Ze'vie's face burst into a huge grin. "That's about it, Helen. I'm afraid I may have told you more than you wanted to know."

"Not at all. It's fascinating. You're fascinating. Have you ever been married?"

"No, I made a decision early that I personally could not do this kind of work if on every assignment I needed to worry about creating a widow and orphans if things didn't go well. There are many Kidon agents who have families. I wasn't willing to take that risk. But to put your mind at rest, my contract with Mossad does not include a celibacy clause. I have had a number of relationships."

Helen laughed. "I am relieved to learn that you have time for yourself. When did you retire?"

"I moved out of operations in 1992, when I was fifty, and had several subsequent assignments in planning and training. I retired from Mossad in 2002 when I was sixty."

"And now you're consulting?"

"Yes, I'm involved in a number of projects in Israel and the US. But I enjoy what I do. My assignments are challenging. I have a lot more time for friends, family, and hobbies."

"And lovers?" said Helen.

"That, too," said Ze'vie. He looked at his watch. "Well, councilor, have I answered the questions to your satisfaction? If so, I'd like permission to go to bed. I have an early meeting in Tel Aviv with a client. If you think of additional questions, I'll be happy to answer them, subject to the usual restrictions, of course."

~~~~~

One week later, when Ze'vie returned to the house, he was lugging a large briefcase. Helen was in the family room playing chess with Yakov. Ze'vie walked over to the table and looked at the chessboard and the pieces that had been won by each side. "Well, Helen, I see that you have been studying my chess books."

She looked up and smiled. "Dr. Johnson said there was nothing like the prospect of a hanging in the morning to focus your mind. The same could be said of the prospect of perpetual house arrest."

Ze'vie showed the briefcase to Helen. "The prospects for an early release are quite good. We have Gatsby's bank records. I'll analyze them tonight and we can discuss them tomorrow."
~~~~~

When Helen came into the dining room the next morning, she found Ze'vie at the table with several piles of documents in front of him. She poured a cup of coffee and sat down at the table.

"Helen," said Ze'vie, "we have here all of the transactions that have been recorded from the eight banks that Gatsby used between January 1, 2003, and May 1, 2008. My colleague is confident he's identified all the banks and has all the records."

"Fantastic," said Helen. "So, what have we learned?"

"We learned that Nadine was indeed a plant. Here is a wire transfer for $10,000 for the account of Nadine Le Roux to Crédit Mutuel, 5 Rue de la République, Marigot. It was sent two days after Jerry arrived on Saint Martin. And here is a photograph of Ms. Le Roux."

Helen was surprised by her reaction to the face of her enemy. Nordic, tall, young, sculpted. Dressed in a sangria-colored V-neck dress that all but forced the eye into her cleavage. In a way, it was exactly what she had prepared herself for. And in a way, it was a relief. Her husband had probably slept with a younger, saucier version of herself—a body that Helen had resigned herself to no longer having, despite all the other gifts of age.

"She is a knockout," she said with a sigh.

Ze'vie smiled. "As they say in America, 'It takes one to know one.'"

Helen laughed. "You are so diplomatic."

"Also, we learned that there does not appear to be any other wire transfers or cash withdrawals in amounts between $10,000 to $100,000, which you would expect to see if someone was paying for a hit. That's not to say he couldn't have compensated the assassin another way, but that is unlikely. There is no evidence that Gatsby did anything other than hire someone to spy on your husband when he was in Saint Martin."

Helen looked at the photo of Nadine. She turned toward Ze'vie. "And to see he was properly entertained during his trip."

Ze'vie nodded. "I suggest we sit on this information for now and discuss it again tomorrow morning. I need to work on another matter the rest of the day." He checked his watch. "Yakov will arrive shortly so that the tournament can continue."

The next morning Ze'vie set up the venerable flip chart and was examining it when Helen entered the room.

"Good morning. Sleep well?"

"No, not well at all. I'm so damn frustrated over what to do about this damn Gatsby mess."

"I understand," said Ze'vie. "But I think that the work we will do over the next hour will bring closure to some of the issues we've been dealing with. Get yourself some coffee and a scone and sit across from the chart."

When Helen returned to the table, Ze'vie launched into his presentation. He pointed to the chart that summarized all the evidence related to the Gatsby threat. "After considering everything we know, I don't see any evidence that Gatsby is responsible for Shirley's and Cissy's disappearance."

"Then why did he threaten Jerry with his comment that it would not be safe for us to visit Saint Martin?"

"How can you be sure that Gatsby's intention was to threaten Jerry? Or even if it was, that the nature of the threat was one of physical violence?"

"Why else would he say it?"

"Maybe it was his way of lashing back after Jerry had exhibited reluctance to accept what Gatsby considered to be an outstanding offer. Maybe he wanted to inform Jerry he knew that Jerry had gone to Saint Martin, had investigated Shirley's disappearance, had hired a lithe and beautiful translator, and had slept with her."

Helen did not respond. She continued to stare at the chart.

"Consider this fact, Helen. Everything we know about the encounter with Gatsby was told to us from Jerry's perspective. Right?"

"You're implying that Jerry is an unreliable narrator, and the threat was conjured up in his mind."

"Jerry may have accurately reported Gatsby's words, but the meaning of whatever words he heard were the product of his emotional state at the time."

"I don't understand," said Helen. Faced with the increasing likelihood of her husband's affair, her mind was a blur of thoughts, and she could barely grasp one before another took its place. She wasn't sure how she'd been so level-headed yesterday looking at the picture of Nadine. Now, it was like she was learning of the affair for the first time all over again.

"I must get personal," Ze'vie said delicately. "You guys have been married for how many years?"

"Fifteen."

"How would you rate your marriage on a scale of zero to ten?"

"Now or pre-Gatsby?"

"Pre-Gatsby."

"That's easy. Between nine and ten. We were a great team. We were happy."

"During the fifteen years that you've been married, have you had sex with anyone but Jerry?"

"Absolutely not."

"During the fifteen years you've been married to Jerry, did you ever have a hint of a suspicion that Jerry was playing around, seeing other women, having one-night stands?"

"No."

"Exactly what I expected. You've both been faithful up until the time Jerry may have slept with Nadine. Correct?"

"I guess so."

"You've spent fifteen years of your life with Jerry, so you can imagine what his emotional reaction might be when he finds himself threatened with embarrassing news?"

She laughed. "I think I'm a pretty good judge of his character."

"Then I want you to imagine what was going through his mind and what his emotional reaction might have been when he had the confrontation with Gatsby. Close your eyes. You're on the sidewalk witnessing the confrontation. After Gatsby makes the statement about avoiding Saint Martin, what is Jerry thinking? What is Jerry feeling? What can you deduce about Jerry from your vantage point on the sidewalk? Take your time visualizing the scene, and then I'll ask you some questions."

Helen closed her eyes. She recalled having done this exercise in a Gestalt therapy session many years before she met Jerry. She was in Paris, trying to keep her first marriage from crashing. It was all so familiar. She realized that Gatsby's comment would have frightened Jerry if he had an affair with Nadine. Gatsby was not happy with him, and Gatsby had seen his dirty laundry. Gatsby, the psychopath, had maneuvered himself into a position of power over Jerry.

"Ready?"

"Go ahead."

"What is Jerry thinking?"

"He's thinking that Gatsby knows he was investigating Shirley's disappearance, and in the process, he met and had a fling with a beautiful French translator. He's thinking that Gatsby knows he is not the Boy Scout he professes to be. He thinks that Gatsby is able to blackmail him, and that Gatsby has the power to threaten his marriage."

"What is Jerry feeling?"

"He feels guilty over betraying his marriage vows, and he feels fear over what action Gatsby might take to ruin his career and marriage."

"So, considering what Jerry is thinking and what Jerry is feeling because of the encounter, how can we expect his to be an accurate account of what occurred? We can't, and it wasn't. I think he catastrophized and saw a threat to the family, whereas Gatsby's intention was to show Jerry he was not as clever as he thought he was and pull him down from his high horse."

"How can you be so certain?"

"I didn't say I was certain. Jerry's being an unreliable narrator is a plausible explanation for what happened. To be certain, I need to go to the States and interview Jeff and Gatsby. Subject to your approval, I'll forge ahead, schedule meetings, and make travel arrangements."

Without any hesitation, Helen said. "Make your arrangements. I have to put this Gatsby matter to bed before I can begin to think about what to do next."

CHAPTER 59

HELEN

May 8, 2008

Helen spent the next day reading and playing chess with Yakov. Occasionally, her mind would wander over to the Gatsby matter, or rather the Gatsby decision.

In the late afternoon, while Yakov was watching television, Helen made herself a vodka and tonic and went out on the patio to watch the sunset and think. Although she had seen many sunsets since she moved into Ze'vie's home, each time she saw one it was an entirely new experience. Today, at twilight, the sky was a palette of orange and purple that grew livid as the sun melted into the water, finally settling into the deep purple wash of a bruise. It was only a few minutes from the time the sun touched the horizon to the time it disappeared, leaving a single bright laceration of light along the horizon.

She sipped her vodka and tonic and looked at the darkening sky. Two major decisions consumed her: what to do about Gatsby, and what to do about Jerry. She was hopeful that when Ze'vie returned, the Gatsby matter would have been resolved.

Jerry and her marriage were a more difficult problem. There was a high probability that Jeff would confirm Ze'vie's assumption that Jerry had slept with Nadine. If confirmed, the fact certainly would complicate the situation. She couldn't just ask Jerry, let him lie to her, and then convince herself to accept the lie. Stuck with the truth, she would want to know whether it was a one-off fling or an indication that Jerry had grown weary of her.

She was attracted to Ze'vie but recognized that the attraction was probably more like Stockholm syndrome than a real crush. And there was too great a gap in their ages and cultures. And she was not sure she was ready to leave Jerry. That would involve so many complications, custody of the boys, where to move, a decision about her career.

Only money would not be a problem. She estimated that her share of the marital estate was between three and five million, and she intended to work. Fortunately, she still had plenty of time to decide about Jerry, the marriage, and what to do with herself—that is, many more sunsets before she had to face what could well be the end of her life with Jerry.

CHAPTER 60

ZE'VIE

May 12, 2008

When Ze'vie arrived at Delmonico's restaurant on Monday, May 12, Jeff was already seated with a martini in front of him. The hostess brought Ze'vie to the booth. Jeff stood to greet Ze'vie and tell him how happy he was to see him again.

Ze'vie slipped into the booth and got straight to business. "As I mentioned to you on the phone, I've been retained by Helen to help sort out this Gatsby problem. She's advised me that Jerry has agreed it is exclusively her responsibility to determine what action to take, if any. Is that also your understanding?"

"It is. Jerry confirmed their understanding several times before and after he disappeared."

"Do you know where Jerry is?"

"He's in the Catskills, fly fishing. They have a cabin in Roscoe."

"Good for him," said Ze'vie. "There is absolutely nothing better than fly fishing to take your mind off your problems. What was the reason that you advised Jerry and Helen to bring their Gatsby problem to me?"

"Jerry talked with me about the offer from Gatsby on three occasions. As you know we both worked with him as members of the GVF advisory board. He was interested in Gatsby's offer to be co-manager of the hedge fund. But Helen was dead set against it. She didn't like Gatsby and didn't trust him for the reasons you know. Jerry wanted to pursue it. So, he called everyone he knew who had a relationship with Gatsby, and he had Birney check out the hedge fund and sought comments on the Gatsby Hedge Fund strategy from an array of bankers in his circle. Everything came back positive.

"I told Jerry that I was leery about his becoming Gatsby's partner and being liable for Gatsby's shenanigans. When we did the Gatsby vetting related to funding the Gatsby Venture Fund, all three of us—Jerry, Birney, and me—found his resumé to be too good to be true. But we couldn't poke holes in it.

"Our suspicions about Gatsby's not being the straight arrow that his vetting promised were confirmed in May of 2005 when the Pennsylvania Department of Banking and Securities issued its cease-and-desist order. That's when we learned he had sold five million dollars of notes he was liable for and had not bothered to include them on the financial statements he submitted to us.

"When Jerry waffled over accepting the hedge fund job, I told him basically that all hunches come from somewhere. I suggested he go to Saint Martin to see if there was any evidence at all in the police files that might implicate Gatsby in Shirley's and Cissy's disappearance."

"How long was he down there?"

"Three days."

"You talked with him when he returned?"

"He came immediately to my office. He told me what he had done, which included having the translator read him all the police reports and witness statements, and newspaper stories, and going to the timeshare where Shirley and Cissy had stayed. A pretty vanilla trip. He said there was no 'there' there."

"What happened then?"

"Jerry tried to persuade Helen that this was a wonderful opportunity for them to make serious money and live the rich life to which he aspired. Helen said she didn't want to take a risk on Gatsby, and besides, they had enough money, and she was more interested in their having quality time to devote to their boys. In short, she gave him an ultimatum: either Gatsby or her.

"Jerry was in a terrible dilemma. He could not bring himself to turn down Gatsby's offer and he didn't want to risk destroying his marriage if he accepted it over Helen's objection. Also, he was angry at Helen for putting him in an untenable position."

"So, what did he do?" said Ze'vie.

"He decided to travel to Philadelphia and meet with Gatsby and over breakfast and plead for more time to persuade Helen to back down. The meeting did not go well. Gatsby was surprised and disappointed that Jerry would allow himself to be 'pussy-whipped,' his words, by his wife and did not have the balls to take control of the situation—namely, accept the offer and to hell with Helen's concerns. He withdrew the offer at the meeting. Jerry followed him out. They said goodbye at the taxi, shook hands, Gatsby made his remark, and then got back into the car."

The waiter arrived to take their order. "This place is known for its steaks," said Jeff.

"Good idea," said Ze'vie. "That's what I'll order." He handed the menu to the waiter. "Jeff, you said you talked with Jerry three times about the Gatsby offer."

"The third time," said Jeff, "was when he came back from Philadelphia—after Gatsby allegedly threatened him. When he arrived at my office, he was apoplectic, frantic. He was so frightened. He was convinced that Gatsby was a psychopath and he engineered Shirley's disappearance.

"I told him about my experience when I had to deal with a trooper who was a member of a Chinese tong and a psychopath. He was one of my best guys, but to stay alive, I gave him a wide berth when it came to his drug business. I told Jerry, based on our experience, Gatsby exhibited many characteristics of a psychopath, and if that was what we were dealing with, I suggested he contact you because of your experience dealing with violent people."

"Do you recall Jerry's exact quote of Gatsby's threat?"

"I think so. It went something like: 'I suggest you avoid Saint Martin. It may be a great place to fuck, but it can also be a dangerous place— you know—with the drug cartels getting active there. Just a friendly suggestion.'"

"That is somewhat different than what Jerry reported to me when he related his encounter."

Jeff smiled. "I presume Helen was present when Jerry described the encounter. And Helen didn't know he slept with Nadine when he was in Saint Martin. He went to the nude beach with her and then they spent almost two days in bed together."

"I'm not surprised," said Ze'vie. "I suspected as much."

"Why?"

"When you spend forty years in Mossad, as I did, you learn a great deal about psychology and how people react under different kinds of stress. I suspect Jerry realized that Gatsby had set him up for blackmail, or at least some psychological thumbscrews. When did Jerry tell you about the affair?"

"When he returned from Philadelphia. He filled in all the details he neglected on his previous visit. Incidentally, how is Helen holding up?"

"I think she's doing better now that she doesn't have to see Jerry daily. Also, I suggested to her that Jerry's emotional reaction to Gatsby's threat could be way overblown. I think the theory, 'Jerry is indeed an unreliable narrator,' is more plausible than the theory, 'Gatsby is a psychopath.' I'll have a better handle on it after I talk with Gatsby."

"When are you meeting with him?"

"Tomorrow afternoon in Philadelphia. I'll meet with Gatsby, stay overnight, and leave for Washington, DC, in the morning. I'm looking forward to meeting him. He has quite a reputation."

The waiter brought their order to the table. As they started to eat, Jeff said, "Ze'vie, do you recall we talked about the Spielberg film during the dinner party at Birney's?"

"Of course. I pointed out the various aspects of the film that were— let's say *deficient*."

"I rented the movie," said Jeff, "and armed with your critique, I saw it is garbage. A political hack-job."

"Oh, Jeff, you are being much too generous to the film."

~ ~ ~ ~ ~

The next day, Ze'vie arrived at Gatsby's office in the Mellon Bank Center at 2 p.m. He told Kathy his name and that Gatsby was expecting him. Gatsby soon emerged from his office with a wide grin and an extended hand.

"Colonel Goldblatt, I'm so happy to meet you. I've cleared my schedule, so we'll have plenty of time. Come into my office and make yourself comfortable."

"Thank you, Mr. Brooks. You can call me Ze'vie."

"That's fair. You can just call me Gatsby."

They entered Gatsby's office and sat in the corner nook that had deep cushioned chairs.

"Can I get you a drink, Ze'vie?"

"Sure, I'll have a vodka and tonic."

"Coming up," said Gatsby. As he was making the drinks he said, "After you phoned and asked to meet with me, I called my friends in the CIA and DIA to see if anyone knew anything about you. I don't need to tell you that you have one hell of a stellar reputation."

"I've got an effective PR firm, Gatsby."

"You were in Mossad for forty years?"

"Almost—just a hack civil servant."

"That is a great cover story, but I don't buy it. I got a copy of *Gideon's Spies* by Gordon Thomas and read it cover-to-cover nonstop. I realized how little I knew about Mossad."

"That is exactly the way Mossad wants to keep it. As low a profile as possible."

Gatsby brought the drinks to the table along with a bowl of pretzels and sat down opposite Ze'vie. "You said you were representing Jerry's wife and you wanted to talk with me about a matter that is causing her a great deal of concern. I can't imagine how I could help her with any matter she would be concerned about. I haven't seen Helen since December 2003. I offered her husband a job this past March. He had such difficulty addressing the personal aspects of accepting the offer that I decided to withdraw it. So, Ze'vie, please enlighten me." He leaned back, relaxed in the chair, and sipped his drink.

Ze'vie opened his briefcase and took out the notes he made in preparation of this meeting. He laid out Jerry's version of the saga. When Ze'vie got to the part about the conversation outside the Bellevue, he looked up from his notes to see Gatsby's reaction. There was no change in Gatsby's facial expression.

Ze'vie then related how Jerry reacted, his meeting with Jeff, Helen's reaction to Jerry's narrative of the sidewalk encounter, and Jeff's recommendation that they go to Israel to meet him.

Gatsby listened without comment, occasionally stirring the ice in his drink. When completed his presentation, Gatsby said, "So exactly what is it that you would like me to do to alleviate this woman's anxiety? If you were not sitting in my office, having spent a couple of thousand dollars on travel, I'd think that this was created out of whole cloth. Talk about making a mountain out of a molehill!" He chuckled at the absurdity. Ze'vie didn't crack a smile.

"Let me give you my point of view of the incident at the Bellevue," Gatsby said. "When Jerry called me to tell me he was going to be in Philly and wanted to meet me, I knew he was not going to accept the job. If he wanted it, he'd have called me on the phone and said, 'Yes, send me the contract.' Also, I knew he went to Saint Martin to investigate Shirley's disappearance. I've had a timeshare on Saint Martin for years. I know a lot of people there. A detective called me to tell me Jerry was at the police station looking for a translator, and she said she was going to recommend Nadine.

"I was angry he went down there to dig into the Shirley and Cissy mess because everyone who knew anything about their disappearance knew that both women had worked for me and that I'd let them use my condo for a week. I viewed Jerry's going there and stirring the pot a total betrayal. I made him a great offer and he repaid me by embarrassing me where I live.

"Realizing that I was angry, I should not have agreed to a meeting. But I went ahead, met him for breakfast, listened to his story, and told him I had made a mistake in offering him the position. The way he addressed the offer revealed he did not have the skill set the job required. I was ready to say goodbye at the table and leave him in the restaurant, but he insisted on trailing out after me like he wanted a pat on the head for wasting my time—and if you know why I offered him the job in the first place, you know that my time has felt especially valuable to me lately."

Ze'vie nodded. He knew about the cancer diagnosis, and Gatsby declined to say more about it.

"I held my anger," Gatsby continued, "until I was about to get into the taxi. Then I lost it. I let him know he wasn't nearly as clever as he thought. It was a childish taunt. I wanted him to know that I knew he had been on Saint Martin, what he was looking for in Saint Martin, and who he was screwing in Saint Martin. I certainly never expected he would assume that I was threatening him and his family and he'd blow the incident up in his mind." Gatsby gave a sharp laugh of disbelief and shook his head. "I'm terribly sorry. I had no idea he would react like this."

"Why would Jerry believe that you might have engineered Shirley's disappearance?"

"I suggest you ask him. Shirley was a colleague; she worked on several of my deals. In appreciation for the great job she did on these projects, I gave her the week in Saint Martin. She seemed to need the rest. She had no personal life outside of work, but we got along famously until she discovered that I was financing my business by selling convertible promissory notes. She decided they must be illegal because they were not registered. Then an absolutely unstable side of her came out—she sent demand letters to my attorney, told everyone she knew who had purchased these notes that I was not good for them and they were illegal. She totally went off the deep end. And when she bumped into my wife in the parking garage of the building in which we both lived, she said I was evil.

"Now she did these things *before* she went to Saint Martin. What was my motive? All the damage to my reputation she could possibly do—she had done."

"Good point, Gatsby. Your only conceivable motive would be revenge, but that motive mostly occurs in novels—not business."

"Do you want another drink, Ze'vie?"

"Sure."

Gatsby went to the bar to make drinks for himself and Ze'vie. When he brought them back to the table he said, "What can I do for your client to relieve her fear?"

"I believe Jerry misinterpreted your parting statement and saw a threat where none was intended. When I tell her about our meeting and my conclusion, I'll ask her whether there is anything she would have you do to resolve the matter for her."

"What is your schedule for the rest of your trip?"

"I'm staying overnight at the Airport Marriot. I have an early flight tomorrow to Washington, DC. I'll be there for a couple of days and then back to Israel."

"Listen, Ze'vie, if you have no plans for the rest of the day, I'd love to take you to dinner and have you meet my wife, Miriam. We'll go two floors up to the Pyramid Club. The food is fabulous, and the three-hundred-and-sixty-degree view of Philadelphia will knock your socks off."

"Sounds good—and I'd love to meet your wife."

~ ~ ~ ~ ~

Ze'vie, Miriam and Gatsby got drinks at the bar, and while Miriam sat there making phone calls and texting, Gatsby steered Ze'vie around the perimeter of the restaurant, pointing out the iconic Philadelphia sites: City Hall, Rittenhouse Square, the Ben Franklin Bridge, the Residences at Dockside where he and Miriam lived, and Camden, New Jersey.

The hostess led them to the window table. The table caught the last rays of sunlight, and a line of tear-shaped rubies around Miriam's neck sent a spray of crimson dots across the tablecloth. They reminded Ze'vie of laser sights.

After they had placed their orders, Gatsby said, "We've had a timeshare on Saint Martin for about ten years, and we had a neighbor, a single guy who boasted he had worked with Mossad. He was a great guest to have at a party. Lots of stories. Unfortunately, he moved to Switzerland several years ago. But you're the first person I've met who worked for Mossad and was in leadership. I'd like to get some insight as to what your work was like."

"I'd be happy to," said Ze'vie. "It's the least I can do to try to repay you for all the time you've spent with me today."

During the next half hour Ze'vie recited his personal history once again, described some missions that were no longer classified, and shared a little of the commonly known Mossad tradecraft. He talked quite a bit about the places he'd traveled during missions and on vacation.

"You mentioned your Mossad friend moved to Switzerland—that's actually one of my favorite places. I never get tired of going there. You simply cannot beat the scenery, the friendliness of the people, the entire storybook aspect of the place..." Ze'vie turned to Miriam, who had maintained a cool politeness with him. "Have you ever had the chance to spend any time there?"

"I've been to Europe several times," she said smoothly, "but never Switzerland."

Gatsby grinned. "Honey, but you have! Remember the Danube cruise with Joyce in 2003? I joined you in Geneva for a holiday after I got done with the venture fund presentation in New York. That is where you lost your diamond earrings."

Ze'vie was looking directly at Miriam and noted the faint splotches that appeared on the ivory skin of her neck and collarbones. He recalled that there were several transactions in Gatsby's 2003 bank records showing small withdrawals originating in Switzerland.

Miriam quickly recovered and smiled at Ze'vie. "Oh, cruises. It's so easy to lose track of where they go—I find them a little boring, to be honest. And, yes, there is a bad memory attached to that trip: I lost a beautiful pair of earrings that Gatsby had given me on our fifth anniversary." And then she talked for five minutes about all the places she saw and things she did during the cruise.

Years of experience in Mossad intelligence had trained Ze'vie to recognize a tell, an unconscious action that betrays an attempted deception. There was something illicit or embarrassing associated with Switzerland that Miriam wanted to suppress or conceal. He would talk with Yakov about it.

Ze'vie motioned to the waiter, and when he came to the table, he gave him his cell phone and asked the waiter to take a few shots of the three of them.

Much later, they left the restaurant and took the elevator down to the parking garage. As they exited the elevator, four black SUVs pulled up. Several agents dressed in yellow-lettered FBI jackets poured out of the cars and surrounded Ze'vie, Gatsby, and Miriam.

One gentleman in a suit held up his credentials. "I am Special Agent Frank Sanderson, and we have warrants to bring Mr. and Mrs. Brooks in for questioning." He looked at Gatsby and Miriam and said, "Will you cooperate and get into the two SUVs that are flashing their lights and come to our offices?"

Gatsby's face had settled into a mask of calm. "I presume you'll tell us what this is all about?"

"Absolutely."

He and Miriam climbed into their respective SUVs, which immediately drove off. Sanderson turned to Ze'vie. "Colonel Goldblatt, would you please accompany me to our offices, so we can take your statement as to why you traveled to Philadelphia and why you've been meeting with Gatsby?"

"I'm certain that my meetings with Gatsby have nothing to do with the reasons you are bringing him and his wife in for questioning."

Anderson smiled. "That's why we need your statement. When we're finished, we'll drive you to wherever you'd like to go."

CHAPTER 61

ZE'VIE

Netanya, May 17, 2008

Ze'vie arrived back in Netanya around midnight on Saturday. Yakov greeted him. Helen was asleep.

"How did it go, boss?" he said.

Ze'vie summarized the meetings for Yakov, lingering a bit on the adventure with the FBI.

"For what it's worth, I am almost certain that Gatsby did not have anything to do with Shirley's and Cissy's disappearance." Ze'vie poured himself and Yakov triple shots of Hennessey. "It's a beautiful night. Let's go on to the patio and celebrate our good fortune." They carried their drinks out onto the patio and sat down.

Ze'vie raised his glass. "*L'chaim,*" he said, "to Helen, Jeff, Jerry and Gatsby, the principal characters in our drama, which is close to ending."

"Why do you say, 'almost certain?' What more is there to do?"

"I have a suspicion as to who ordered the hit on Shirley and who carried it out. I need to confirm it." He told Yakov about Gatsby's comment about having a neighbor at his Saint Martin timeshare who boasted about having worked for Mossad and moved to Switzerland several years ago; he also explained Miriam's tell during their dinner at the Pyramid Club. "I think Miriam decided to solve their Shirley problem using an assassin who had been her neighbor on Saint Martin, and she traveled to Switzerland to locate him. Gatsby revealed she'd 'lost' a pair of expensive earrings there, and having seen the sort of jewelry she wears, I expect they would have been enough to pay for a hit on Shirley. Poor Cissy was just in the wrong place."

"That's a bushel of assumptions," said Yakov.

"Yes, I agree, but it is plausible."

"Plausible, yes, but how do we prove it?"

"Two things. First, you go to Mossad offices tomorrow and see if you can identify the contractor who lived on Saint Martin prior to 2003 and get his picture. Make copies of the picture that I took of Gatsby and Miriam at the Philadelphia Grill, travel to Geneva, and interview the staff and management at the Hotel Kempinski and see if and when the contractor and Gatsby visited Miriam at the hotel."

Yakov shook his head. "It's been five years."

"I realize that, Yakov, but Miriam is a stunning woman, and she is not easily forgotten. It's worth the effort."

"Okay," said Yakov. "I agree it's worth a try. Email me the pictures from your dinner and I'll get on it tomorrow. What's the second bit of evidence you have?"

"What Sanderson told me—the FBI provided us with a stroke of luck related to an old insurance claim. Gatsby had filed a claim for the pair of earrings allegedly lost or stolen in Switzerland while Miriam was there. The insurance company enlisted the help of Interpol, which sent out notices to see if the earrings had turned up. Several years later, they received notice that the earrings had been pawned in Geneva by a resident of Monthey. When the Swiss authorities questioned him, he provided evidence he and Miriam had been intimate, and she had given him the earrings because he was in financial extremis." A slow smile spread across Ze'vie's face, warmed by the Hennessey. "And the Swiss authorities notified the insurance company, who turned the matter over to the FBI as a fraud case."

"And why did the FBI want to talk with you?" said Yakov.

"To confirm that my meetings with Gatsby had nothing to do with the insurance issue."

"That resident of Monthey is probably our contractor."

"No question about it," said Ze'vie. "Let's hope your trip to Geneva is productive."

~~~~~

The following morning, as Ze'vie was enjoying his morning coffee and croissants, Helen came on to the patio, cup in hand, and sat down.

"Good morning, Helen! You look beautiful as usual, and I think this is going to be a glorious day." He sipped his coffee and took a bite of croissant. "The Gatsby matter is resolved. He did not have any role in Shirley and Cissy's disappearance. And his parting remark to Jerry in Philadelphia was not intended as a threat. Do you want me to brief you on all the details?"

She took a stoic sip of black coffee. "Just tell me if Jerry slept with Nadine."

"The short answer: yes. Jeff told me that when Jerry came to his office following his meeting with Gatsby he was agitated and frightened. He told Jeff everything that occurred in Saint Martin, including the affair with Nadine."

"That hurts." Even though her expression barely changed, tears spilled down her face. "I suspected it, but it hurts so much more to hear you confirm it."

"I'm so sorry, Helen."

She wiped her eyes and folded her tears into the napkin, creasing it again and again. After a minute, she cleared her throat and washed away the catch in her voice with another pull of coffee.

"If Gatsby didn't have anything to do with Shirley's disappearance," she said, "do you have any idea who was behind it?"

"I have a suspicion. Yakov is working on it. We should know in a few days if my suspicion is confirmed. Meanwhile, I think you should hang out here until we complete our investigation so when you leave, you know everything that is knowable. But you're no longer confined to quarters, and if you want to go out and around, I'll arrange for a driver. And you're free to tell Jeff he can contact Jerry to end his disappearance."
~~~~~

They sat silently for several minutes, taking in the view of the sea. It was a beautiful warm day. Plenty of birdsong to accompany the exquisite vistas. Ze'vie could sense that absolutely none of it was helping Helen's distress.

"Gatsby appeared to be genuinely remorseful for the grief you've suffered, and he asked me to inquire whether there was anything he could do to make amends."

Helen laughed. She was silent for several minutes and appeared to be reviewing alternatives. "No, there is nothing he needs to do. Just tell him I appreciate the gesture."

He said, "I'll do that. When are you going to talk to Jerry?"

"I'm going to call Jeff today and ask him to tell Jerry that I will meet him in Paris as soon as I'm done here. I intend to work out a trial separation agreement with him, leave the boys with him, and I'm going to see about getting a visa to stay in Israel for a while."

"I feel for you both," said Ze'vie. "He is a fine man. Most women would be ecstatic to have him for a husband. But it sounds like you've thought about this a lot."

"I have," said Helen, "and he is a fine man. But I think our marriage has run out of steam, and it's time to move on before the mutual resentments start to materialize and affect the boys." She drained her mug.

~~~~~

Three days later, while Helen was being chauffeured around Netanya and Tel Aviv, Yakov returned, sporting a broad smile.

"You nailed it, boss. The likely assassin is Achmed Khordroy, a Lebanese Arab who was a contractor in the late 1970s and early 1980s. Mossad cut him loose when he misidentified a target during a mission."

"I remember him," said Ze'vie, with a bump of surprise. "He fucked up big time. The team had to abort the mission when the target was a no-show, which turned out to be a blessing because Achmed had fingered the wrong guy."
~~~~~

"He moved to Saint Martin and lived there for many years. The gendarmes eventually discovered he was not merely a wealthy bridge playing retiree and pressured him to leave the island."

"Where is he now?" said Ze'vie.

"In 2002 he moved to Monthey, a little more than an hour's drive from Geneva. There is a bridge club in the center of town where he apparently spends most of his time."

"What did you learn in Geneva?"

"Several members of the staff identified all three of them—Miriam, Achmed, and Gatsby—mainly because Gatsby is so outgoing, which jogged the staff's memory for the other two. Achmed stayed with Miriam for a few days. Shortly after he left, Gatsby arrived and stayed for several days." He handed Ze'vie a sheet of paper. "Here are the dates."

"So," said Ze'vie. "It occurred exactly as we suspected. Miriam decided to take matters into her own hands and eliminate Shirley, she used the cover of her cruise to get to Switzerland and track down Achmed, her ex-lover, who happened to be an experienced assassin, and used her earrings to pay for the hit. And Cissy got killed, too."

"Do you think Gatsby figured out what Miriam did?"

"I'm certain he put the pieces together after they were questioned."

Yakov *tsk*ed. "Not much of a chance that Achmed and Miriam will ever be charged for murder unless they confessed, then."

"Between slim and none," said Ze'vie. "As far as we are concerned, the Bascomb–Gatsby matter is resolved, and we're content to stop poking at these sleeping dogs. Let's celebrate with a glass of wine."

CHAPTER 62

JERRY

Thursday, May 22, 2008

On Thursday morning, Jerry awoke at his usual time of 6 a.m., donned his fishing clothes and headed out to the Beaverkill. He shook his foggy head and wiped the tears from his eyes. He had not slept well. He was in purgatory, and because it was a purgatory of one, he had no reason to hide it. The fish did not care whether he was depressed. In fact, they probably rejoiced that their adversary was indifferent, haunted, and tortured by the relentless company of his own miserable conscience.

Today was the twenty-first straight day he'd been on the river. He had improved his skills, but it was getting old. Helen would not return while Gatsby walked the face of the earth; and he, a supposed Master of the Financial Universe, was totally impotent. He had absolutely no ability to change the course he was following. The best he could hope for was that disease would overtake Gatsby, a cancer that would pull him out of Jerry's life forever, so that Helen would return. It was a terrible wish, and also ironic: by doing almost nothing, Gatsby had cuckolded him anyway—to use Helen's word. He felt like a character in a Kafka story who was arrested for a crime he didn't understand, tried in a court presided over by the Mad Hatter, and had received a sentence which no one would reveal. Jerry had no way to contact Helen, so he simply had to wait for her to communicate through Jeff. It was agonizing, feeling his conscience trace his failures on his mind over and over, until they gradually took on new dimensions. Those failures dawned on him fresh every hour: Helen had warned him. Jeff had warned him. His ego had deafened him, and he'd gone chasing after money and sex like a dog in heat.

He came off the river at 4:30 and decided to call Jeff.

It was a miracle: Jeff told him he had heard from Helen.

"She said Ze'vie had advised her that Gatsby was no longer a threat to your family and that you could reactivate your cell phone, come home, and go back to work. She also asked me to tell you she wants to meet you in Paris, at the Jules Verne Restaurant in the Eiffel Tower in two weeks. She will call you shortly to confirm the date and time."

"Did she say anything else? Didn't she want to talk with me? What about Gatsby? How did Ze'vie resolve it? Did she say anything about bringing the boys back from Hawaii?"

"No," said Jeff. "The conversation was pretty short. Only that you could end the disappearance act, go back to work and wait for her call."

Stunned, Jerry felt the bile rising in his throat. This felt more like a nightmare than a miracle.

"Bro? Are you there?"

"Yes, I just can't fucking imagine what is in her mind or what she is doing."

"Neither can I," said Jeff, "but you'll find out soon enough when you see her in Paris. I've got a suggestion that might take your mind off your problems. I have two tickets for tomorrow night, Mets versus the Nationals. Interested?"

"Hell yes," said Jerry.

They made their plans, and Jeff signed off: "Be careful, bro. I know this is stressful. Stay tough!"

~~~~~

Jerry drove into Roscoe and had a tasteless final dinner at Casey's Place. After dinner, he drove back to his cabin and packed his car for tomorrow's drive.
~~~~~

He was back at his apartment by 10 a.m. Notwithstanding the fact he craved Misty's company, he decided he would not pick her up until he returned from Paris. Everything was so up in the air. He took a shower, dressed, and went to the office. Several of his team members came by to say hello and tell him they were happy to have him back. At 11:30 he walked over to Birney's office to rip off the Band-Aid.

"Boychik, how are you?"

"I was happy to hear my team say that the EVG merger is set to close."

"Yes," said Birney. "This has been a tough deal. I will be relieved when it's over. Since you are here, does that mean that you and Helen have solved your problem?"

Jerry was not sure how to respond. Before the silence became uncomfortable, he said, "I hope so. Thanks for asking."

Jerry and Jeff got to their seats along the third base line at 6:30 p.m., carrying beers and hot dogs. He washed his first bit of hot dog down with a large gulp of beer.

"I'm going to owe you, Jeff."

"Forget it. It's the least I can do for a suffering little brother."

"Well, I appreciate it."

They both were looking at the field, watching the Mets warm up.

"How was the fishing?"

"Fabulous. When you spend twenty-one straight days on the river, you can't help but improve. By the last week, I had developed the skills to read the water, determine what the trout were eating, stalk the fish, select the right fly, make a competent cast, and catch a fish. What was even more incredible, I could read articles in the Fly Fishing magazines and understand them. It's a great sport—especially if you want to purge your mind of everything else—which I did. You should try it. I'll teach you."

Jeff laughed. "Not my cup of tea. I don't like getting wet." Then he patted Jerry on the shoulder—a sympathetic answer to the emptiness they both heard under Jerry's answer. They were silent for the next several minutes while they ate their hot dogs and drank their beers. Jeff broke the silence.

"Little brother, as much as I hate to say this, you need to prepare yourself for the reality that Helen may not want to resume a life with you."

"You believe that? I mean, she loves those kids, and we have a great relationship."

"I know. I don't want to hurt you, but you are not as objective about Helen as I am. She is a heat-seeking missile. She homes in on alpha males, preferable ones with a military history. Remember, when she was nineteen, she had an affair with our father—or rather, the three stars on his collar. Then she went after me, with my war stories. I don't want to get over my skis on this, but I want you to be prepared for anything she throws at you in Paris.

"And I don't want to imply that there is anything romantic going on between Helen and Ze'vie. It is just that Ze'vie has served as her protector during a crisis point in her life and she probably could not help comparing you to him. Using the criteria we know is ingrained in Helen's personality, you can't compete with a retired colonel, a national hero, to boot. I'm sorry, Jerry. Welcome to the Club of Estranged Husbands."

Jerry was silent. The announcer was reciting the starting lineups for the Mets. As each name was called, the stands erupted. It was no longer possible to speak. Jerry felt the tears dripping down his face. He finished his hot dog, drained his cup of beer, and wiped his hands on the napkin. He put his arms around Jeff and hugged him. Then he sat back in his seat and watched the Mets take the field for the first inning.

CHAPTER 63

JERRY

Friday, May 30, 2008

One week later, Jerry entered the bar at the Jules Verne Restaurant in the Eiffel Tower and asked for a table near the window. He was wearing beige slacks, a blue blazer, and black loafers with tassels. It was the sort of outfit in which he could receive any news: dressy enough for a celebratory dinner, dignified enough to hold him together if he left the restaurant alone. He followed the hostess into the bar and ordered a double Jameson on the rocks.

Approximately fifteen years ago, he had sat in the same bar, sipped the same drink, and experienced virtually the same level of anxiety as he rehearsed the speech he would deliver to Helen after he asked her to marry him, and before she could accept or refuse.

The speech—at its core a confession—would reveal how he had unbeknownst to her betrayed her trust. At that time, he had no idea as to how she would react. She would have been more than justified in walking out of his life then and there. But fortunately for him, she did not. And fifteen years later, on the other side of a great marriage, two wonderful boys, an active social life, and enough money to live well and plan for retirement, he'd opened Pandora's box and allowed the Gatsby mess to spill out. And motivated by greed, he had chosen to wrap both arms around what turned out to be a tar baby. How stupid he still was!

Somehow, he felt whatever Helen had in store for him, it was not going to be simple.

As the liquor rushed to his head, he saw her, the Mona Lisa herself, as she had entered the bar. He rose so quickly he toppled his chair and rushed to her. He threw his arms around her and pressed into every square inch of her body. He started to cry, but managed to blurt out, "God, how I've missed you!"

Helen returned the embrace, kissing him passionately, oblivious to the several bar patrons who were staring at them. "I know," she said. "I missed you, too."

They sustained their embrace for a long time, an eternity, not speaking. Jerry continued to sob. Helen whispered to him they should sit down, and they slowly disentangled from each other, moved to the table, and sat, holding hands. The waiter came over. Helen ordered a house chardonnay.

"You look wonderful," said Jerry. "But you always look wonderful." He lowered his eyes for a moment. "And I know that I look like shit. I've gained twenty pounds, I've stopped exercising, and I drink way too much. I'm not well since you left. Since before, to be honest."

Helen did not respond.

"I miss you and the kids so damn much."

"You've talked with Jeff, haven't you?"

"Every day. He took me to a Mets game last week. One of the unintended consequences of this mess is that Jeff and I have become closer. He has been a huge source of support. He's listened to me rant and rave about how unfair everything is. Occasionally, he reminds me how lucky I am to have a wife who is so brave and resourceful."

The waiter brought Helen's wine and asked whether they planned to have lunch. Jerry shook his head and the waiter retreated.

"How are the kids?" he asked.

Helen lit up. "They're great. They both miss us. But they've adapted. They're both learning how to surf, and Salli's done a great job supervising their schoolwork."

Tears started streaming down Jerry's face again. He wiped his eyes.

"Are you okay?" said Helen.

Jerry shook his head. "I am definitely not. But I'm hoping to recover. I'm anxious to hear about the Gatsby situation. The fact that I'm sitting here tells me it has been resolved. Am I correct? I need to know what happened."

Helen took a sip of her wine, wiped her lips with her napkin. "This is what I can tell you. When I returned to Ze'vie's house after I left you at the hotel, prior to your flight back to New York, he suggested that I retain him as a consultant and establish a fiduciary relationship between himself and me, which I did. On May 12, he traveled to the states and he met with Jeff and Gatsby. When he returned to Israel, he advised me that Gatsby would no longer pose a problem in our lives. He asked whether I wanted to be briefed on the details of his investigation. I declined. I had already learned what I needed to know, and I was satisfied that the matter had been resolved."

Jerry was flummoxed. But he had promised himself to accept whatever she had to say without arguing, lest she see it as evidence he had not changed and was still unwilling to listen to her.

"How much of the $250,000 did you use?"

"I haven't paid all the expenses yet. I'm projecting less than $100,000."

"Well," he said, "since the Gatsby problem has been resolved, I'd like to take you back to New York. Or we can get a flight to Israel, and I can help you pack."

Helen did not respond. She fiddled with her wine glass, and then took a sip of water. It appeared to Jerry she was weighing alternative responses. His mouth became dry, and he felt his throat constricting. He looked directly into Helen's eyes.

"You are coming home, aren't you?"

"It's complicated," she said. Tears began to well up in her eyes. She opened her small Gucci purse, took out a tissue and dabbed them. "It's complicated."

"Explain it to me," said Jerry, a tinge of anger infusing his remark. "You never contacted me during the three weeks we were apart, which you could have done without revealing your whereabouts. And now you can't give me a straight answer as to when you're coming home. What in the hell is going on? Is it you and Ze'vie ?"

He realized he was being too loud. Heads were again starting to turn toward his table, and he noticed that the hostess was moving toward them.

Helen reached over the table and grabbed his hand. "Please, Jerry. Don't make a scene." She stood up and picked up her purse. "Take care of the bill. I'll meet you on the platform and we'll talk." Without waiting for a response Helen headed to the restaurant exit and then to the elevator which would take her up to the platform, nine hundred feet above the ground, and the magnificent views of Paris.

Stunned, Jerry remained sitting at the table, trying to get his mind around this unanticipated turn of events. He motioned to the waiter. A few minutes later the waiter arrived. Jerry handed the waiter his credit card and asked him to close out the check. As the waiter left the table, Jerry gulped down his Jameson. By the time the waiter returned with his card and receipt, Jerry had downed what was left of Helen's wine, too.

Jerry entered the platform. There were not many tourists, so it would not be difficult to locate Helen. He began walking around the tower in a clockwise direction. He felt woozy and was unsteady. She was standing at the rail on the east corner, looking out toward the Louvre and the Tuileries.

As he approached her, he called, "Helen."

She turned and quickly walked toward him. She took his left hand in her right, and said, "Let's walk."

She steered him to the north corner of the platform. They both looked over the Parisian landscape they had both loved and shared many years ago. After several minutes, Helen turned to Jerry and said, "The reason I didn't call you is that I wanted to avoid conflict. I was angry and resentful and had to sort through it all, and then I had to decide what I wanted in light of what had happened in our lives."

Jerry began to respond. Helen stopped him. "Let me first say what I need to say, okay? I'll cut to the chase. I know what you're thinking, so let me immediately disabuse you. Ze'vie and I have not been intimate.

We've had a professional relationship and we've become friends." The trailing edge of this information had a sharpness to it, as if to say, *And shame on you for thinking I'm still a younger version of myself, but only when it suits you.* He wasn't imagining it—she seemed to read his mind and nodded once, minutely.

She continued, "I need some time on my own to assess my life and decide whether I want to stay in our marriage. I'm going to stay in Israel to work it out. I want you to take the boys. I don't want to expose them to the danger and craziness that pervades domestic life there. When you get back to New York, hire a divorce lawyer to draw up a temporary separation agreement which will provide me a monthly stipend. Make it as large as feasible without squeezing yourself. I have complete confidence that you will be fair." She threw her arms around him and hugged him. "I'm sorry, Jerry."

Jerry did not reciprocate. He felt numb, disoriented. He felt obligated to respond, to say something, but for one of the few times in his life, he didn't know what to say. What can you possibly say to someone who just advised you that the life that you've enjoyed for fifteen years and that you had—against all odds—expected to continue, has just ended? Kaput! Over! He shook his head in disbelief.

"I certainly did not expect this."

"Didn't expect it, Jerry," said Helen, "or didn't want it to come true?"

"Didn't want it to come true," he admitted.

She nodded, acknowledging the honesty. They both knew he'd been thinking about this possibility because it was the worst one he could imagine. "I racked my brain for four days trying to figure out a way to break this to you. I didn't want to hurt you, but I knew I would, and I did. Please don't hate me, Jerry."

Jerry knew he was at a critical stage. He needed to decide how to deal with this turd that Helen had put in his pocket. He needed time to think. "Look," he said, "I need a stiff drink—and we should get something to eat. There is a brasserie about ten minutes from here. Let's go there and we can talk some more."

"Okay," said Helen. She took his arm. "You lead the way."

As they began walking to the Au Petit Sud-Ouest, Helen began to say something. Jerry interrupted her.

"Helen, please, let's just walk. We'll talk when we're seated."

"Sure," she said.

The silence gave Jerry the time he needed to think through the situation. He recalled the spreadsheet that Helen had created back when they were dating in 1990, eighteen years ago. It listed all her twenty-seven affairs, starting in junior high school with statistics about the affair and her lover. The last one on the list, to his surprise at the time, was his brother Jeff, who was married to Helen's sister, Salli, and had had two daughters. His father, a general, was also on the list, as were her two previous husbands. He thought that he, number twenty-eight, would be the last one on the list. But it was not to be, and it was his fault.

They were three long blocks from the restaurant. What were his options? He could act the outraged husband, who seeks revenge because of being dumped—but that wasn't him. He wanted Helen to be happy because he loved her—even if she would no longer be his wife. Then, there was the English aristocracy's way of dealing with it: "Tut tut, my dear Mildred. I would have thought you were above this sort of tawdry behavior. Very well, no matter. I will have my solicitor call your solicitor and work out the details." No! He wasn't going to allow aggressive junkyard divorce lawyers contaminate the relationship.

One and a half blocks away.

He had the memories of fifteen years of a very good marriage and the wellbeing of their two boys to protect—as well as his own mental health. He only had one choice. The one that both fit his personality and would minimize the stress of all the characters in the drama: that of the disappointed, loving, and devoted husband who only wanted what was best for his estranged wife and their two boys. He was comfortable with that role. That was who he was. That was who he would continue to be.

They entered Au Petit Sud-Ouest, and he asked Helen to employ her French to request a booth or table with the maximum privacy that was available in the restaurant. The hostess accommodated them, and Jerry gave her a five-euro tip.

When they were seated, the waiter came to the table for their drink order. Jerry smiled at Helen, and said, "What will you have, honey?"

She ordered a glass of Graves. Jerry ordered another double Jameson on the rocks. The waiter recited the specials and left to get their drinks. Jerry asked Helen what she'd like. She replied, "Order me the fish special."

"Do you mind if I take a minute and check my messages?" said Jerry. "I have two deals in the works that need to be followed."

"Not at all," said Helen. "I'll visit the restroom." She got up and headed toward the back of the room.

Jerry checked his emails, voicemails, and texts. The familiar actions calmed him. The waiter came with their drinks. By the time Helen returned to the table he had consumed half of his double Jamison.

"I suggest," he said, "we deal with the nuts and bolts of the new situation and then perhaps we clear the air about how we got to where we are ."

She took a sip of her wine. "Fine."

"Have you figured out how much you want a month?"

"Not exactly. It will be in the range of twelve to fifteen thousand."

"Can you firm up the number in a week or two?"

"Sure," said Helen. "No problem."

"What is your plan for telling the boys and bringing them home?"

"When we're done here, I'm going back to Israel. On Sunday I'm going to Honolulu. I'll stay with Salli for a week to ten days and then I'll bring the boys to New York, and we'll have a family meeting."

Jerry pulled out his phone and accessed his calendar. "You're estimating arriving at the apartment sometime during the third week in June?"

"That's about right. I'll firm up the date in a few days."

"I assume you want the boys to live with me, subject to visitation rights?"

"Definitely," said Helen.

"I'll find a lawyer who can represent the two of us and put him or her to work on the document. If we come across any problems, I'll call you. And I think that takes care of the nuts and bolts. Do you agree?"

"Yes," said Helen. "I think that covers all the bases."

The waiter brought their food and asked whether they wanted another round of drinks. Jerry nodded assent. They began to eat. He had ordered a smoked-salmon salad and a cup of French onion soup. Helen had ordered the trout and a salad. It all seemed so normal.

When they were several minutes into the lunch Jerry said, "So, since we've been married, we both have worked hard to be brutally honest with each other—which is one of the reasons we've had a pretty healthy marriage. I'd like to continue that tradition, so long as we're married, and ask you for full disclosure as to how we came to this current juncture in our lives. Don't tell me anything that will make you uncomfortable. But I would appreciate knowing everything else. Does that make sense to you, Helen?"

"Yes, Jerry," she said with the same crisp formality that had always pervaded discussions like these. "You're entitled to know." Helen picked up her second glass of wine and gulped down half of it. "I owe you an explanation. You're a good man, a good husband, and a great father, and you certainly don't deserve what's happened to you." She reached into her purse and pulled out her cell phone. "I need to call for a taxi to take me to the airport. My flight to Tel Aviv is at 4:30. We don't have a lot of time.

"When I left you to meet Ze'vie, it was because I could not bear to go back to New York with the Gatsby matter unresolved. Prior to our leaving for Israel, I was frantic, depressed, and frightened. I could not go back to that life. I was determined to resolve the situation—assassinate Gatsby if necessary—anything to ensure that our family was safe. I was hugely disappointed in you in that you did not take charge and commit yourself to do what was necessary to protect us. I felt you failed us, and I haven't changed my opinion. You're a good, kind, and loving man, Jerry. But when the chips were down you could not bring yourself to do what was necessary to defend your family.

"When I got to Ze'vie's house, I effectively put our lives in his hands. He called on his Mossad colleagues to provide the protection and surveillance he decided was required. He became my personal CIA and FBI to ensure I was protected from Gatsby's machinations. He did it enthusiastically, and contrary to what I know you are thinking, he did it without any strings or quid pro quos. He was thoroughly professional. He treated our situation as a mission and me as a client. He did not come on to me, make innuendos, make remarks about my looks, or flirt in any way. I respect and admire him. And as much as I tried not to, I began comparing him to you and began questioning whether I wanted to stay married to you. It didn't help that you had an affair and haven't yet admitted as much to me, even though I'm sure you know it wouldn't remain a secret. So, I'm still questioning if I have it in me to trust you."

There was a contrite silence. "Why are you staying in Israel?"

"I'm fascinated by the culture and the people. Their stoicism, optimism, and good nature as they confront the incredible challenges of everyday life. I think I can be happy there." She checked her watch. "I don't know whether or not I'll fit into the Israeli Jewish culture that is so pervasive, but I've decided to take the leap." She shook her head and then grabbed Jerry's hand and looked into his eyes. "I know that I am taking a huge risk. I'm giving up the great life that I've shared with you for an uncertain future. And I'm not going to con myself into thinking that you'll be there to help me pick up the pieces in the event things don't work out. I'm stepping off the edge of a cliff, eyes wide open."

The hostess came to the table to tell Helen that her taxi was outside.

~~~~~

Helen returned to New York with the boys and they all enjoyed a ten-day family reunion prior to Helen's leaving for Tel Aviv. They decided to tell the boys she was going to Israel to pursue studies in Middle Eastern Art and Culture and would be living there for at least two years. They explained the visitation agreements they had previously worked out. During the period of the reunion, Helen and Jerry slept together and resumed their sex life as if the Gatsby matter had never happened.
~~~~~

When Helen left in mid-June, it required every scintilla of Jerry's thespian skill to conceal his grief from his boys. He was upbeat when he talked about the exciting camping and fishing adventures he was planning. But for several days after Helen left, when the boys were asleep, and Jerry was alone in his bedroom, he allowed his pent-up feelings of emptiness and despair emerge and often cried himself to sleep.

When he awoke on the fifth day after Helen's departure, he felt well-rested. He recalled that sometime during the night he dreamed about the Kris Kristofferson's song, "For the Good Times":

> *Don't look so sad. I know it's over But life goes*
> *on and this world keeps on turning Let's just*
> *be glad we had this time to spend together.*
> *There is no need to watch the bridges we're*
> *burning.*

He realized that these lyrics encapsulated the exact philosophy he should adapt to Helen's departure, no matter what the outcome. Fifteen years of a great marriage was a hell of a lot more than many married couples realize. And he had achieved a huge bonus. Two wonderful kids he would have the opportunity to raise and ensure they were well educated and could enjoy all the benefits he could provide.

The pity party was over. He would focus all his efforts on his boys, his job, and shedding the twenty pounds he had acquired since the Gatsby mess began.

CHAPTER 64

JERRY

Friday, September 12, 2008

The Bricker and Weldon conference room was fully populated with company personnel and management of Superior Plastics, a forty-year-old plastics manufacturing firm with sales of $2.5 billion. Jerry was about to enter the conference room to make a presentation when he received a call from Jeff.

"Hi, bro. I need to take a rain check on dinner. I'm with a Goldman contingent on our way to a meeting at the Fed with Geithner and Secretary Paulson, plus people with all the other major Wall Street banks. It's a big deal."

"Is this about Lehman and their losses?"

"Yep. This is a Hail Mary effort by the Fed to keep Lehman from collapsing. Sorry, bro, I don't have any wiggle room on this one. This is going to be a long, long day."

"I understand. No problem. Let's shoot for the day after tomorrow."

"I think that will work. I'll stay in touch."

Jerry had been following the trials of Lehman Brothers. In light of the huge losses they reported, it was the consensus that if Paulson and Geithner did not find a home for Lehman and it had to file bankruptcy, the markets would tank. He estimated that the Dow Jones average would fall by more than ten percent. Jerry felt fortunate to be in the mergers-

and-acquisitions business, where the profit was from fees for service instead of buying and selling in a market that had been contaminated by voodoo assets that couldn't be valued and therefore couldn't be sold.

Jerry called Jeff on the following Sunday morning to see if he could break away from the Lehman problem and come over for dinner.

"I'm off the hook regarding Lehman. I'll tell you about it over a few Courvoisiers."

After dinner, the boys went into the family room to watch television, and Jerry and Jeff went into Jerry's office with two brandy snifters and an unopened bottle of Courvoisier. Jerry poured two generous drinks and they settled into the comfortable leather chairs.

"What happened at the meeting?"

"There will be no bailout by the banks. No one could come up with a way to distribute Lehman's garbage securities and the promising businesses to satisfy all the potential buyers. And Paulson and Geithner were emphatic that there would be no government bailout. Lehman's president, Richard Fuld, said they've been negotiating with both the Bank of America and Barclays for a possible sale. But unlike the Bear Stearns deal, the government is not offering any guarantees."

"No kidding," said Jerry.

"Nope. They're claiming they are drawing the line with this deal. Moral Hazard, you know. Paulson delivered a moving speech about Lehman's taking on so much risk because they assumed that if things got dicey, the Feds would bail them like they did Bear Stearns—so the government has to draw the line somewhere."

"Do you think that's the reason?" said Jerry.

"That probably half the reason."

"What's the other half?"

"Paulson and Fuld hate each other's guts."

"Be that as it may," said Jerry, "nobody is going to buy that sack of shit without huge guarantees from the government. It will tank and take the market with it."

"You're probably right," said Jeff. "But it's no longer my problem." He took a sip of Courvoisier. "I'd like to talk about another issue."

"Okay," said Jerry. "What's on your mind?"

"You are," said Jeff.

"Me? Why me?"

"How long has it been since Helen left for Israel?"

"About three months, give or take."

"And how many dates have you had since Helen left?"

"Dates? You know I'm not dating."

"Right. You're not. Why not? Are you preparing for the priesthood?"

Jerry did not answer. He swirled his brandy. "I've been too busy. I don't have time for women. I don't have the stomach for the dating game." He hesitated. "It just hasn't been that important to me, I guess. I don't know." He drained his glass and immediately filled it and topped off Jeff's. Then Jerry sat back in the chair and allowed Jeff's comments to sink in.

"You're a pretty good therapist," said Jerry.

"And I'm cheap." He drained his glass and sat up in the chair. "I've been tasked with writing up the summary of the Lehman negotiations for senior management. I need to get my ass back to the office." He stood and pointed to Jerry's crotch, "I have a friend who would be happy to pull little Jerry out of the mothballs and take him for a shakedown cruise. She's a banker, recently divorced, and very attractive." He leaned over Jerry and planted a kiss on his cheek. "I'll check her availability and report back. Goodnight, little brother, and thanks for the dinner."

On Monday morning, Jerry got the boys ready for school, and they all went down the elevator to the lobby, where he picked up the *Wall Street Journal*. As they got back into the elevator to go down to the parking levels, Jerry scanned the headline announcing that the 158-year-old investment bank, Lehman Brothers, had filed bankruptcy, listing $639 billion in assets and $619 in liabilities. It was the largest bankruptcy in the history of the United States. Jerry whistled and shook his head.

Josh said, "Why the whistle, Dad?"

"Just my expressing the fact that I read about something important that occurred today." Jerry pushed the elevator button, and the elevator started its descent.

"What happened?"

"A large and important company on Wall Street announced they couldn't pay their bills and they were going to close the business and because they are so big that thousands of other companies and individuals will be hurt."

"Will we be hurt?" said Alli. The elevator stopped at the parking level Jerry had selected.

The doors opened. Jerry laughed and said, "You boys have nothing to worry about. We're going to be just fine."

Jerry drove the boys to their respective schools, and then drove on to his office. He stopped at Starbucks for his coffee and a scone and took the elevator up to his floor. It was just after eight o'clock, so he would have almost an hour to read the paper and make the calls to Europe he had scheduled.

He completed the several stories about the drama leading up to the Lehman filing and was turning his attention to the rest of the national news when his eye caught a two-column-inch story: "Hedge Fund Manager Pleads Guilty of International Insurance Fraud." He read on. The hedge fund manager was none other than Christopher "Gatsby" Brooks, the famous—now infamous—resident of Philadelphia, Pennsylvania.

Jerry felt his heart skip a beat. He closed the newspaper, and went immediately to his desk, turned on the computer, and googled "Gatsby Brooks insurance fraud." And there they were, at least fifty posts describing the circumstances surrounding Gatsby's arrest and prosecution. Jerry began plowing through them.

An hour later, he believed he understood the allegations and the underlying circumstances.

He called Moe later in the day to get his take. When he explained the reason for his call, Moe said he didn't want to talk about it over the phone, but he planned to attend an investor conference later in the month in New York City and would be happy to meet Jerry and share what he knew.

CHAPTER 65

JERRY

Friday, September 26, 3008

Two weeks later, Jerry attended the investment conference in New York that brought investors, hedge funds managers, M&A firms, and financial advisors together. The large ballroom was redolent with the smell of coffee and the more cloying scent of pastries. He spotted Moe approaching a large table.

"It's so good to see you, Jerry." Moe embraced him. "I was delighted that you called me and we could arrange to get together."

"I appreciate your carving some time out of the conference to meet me. Can we go to the bistro or coffee shop for privacy?" said Jerry.

"Sure," said Moe. As they made their way to the café, Jerry reminded himself he would not talk about any aspect of his effort to investigate Gatsby, Helen's abandoning him, her living in Israel, or the likelihood of a divorce and his becoming a single parent of his two boys. Moe had no need to know, and he had no need to tell. He was here exclusively to talk about Gatsby's plea and get Moe's insight.

Gatsby was a cancer that had destroyed his marriage. Not he was beyond reproach. He knew he had screwed up. He and Jeff had talked about it extensively. But he needed to move on with his life. Make a clean break with both Helen and Gatsby. He had to!

When they had ordered breakfast, Moe said, "What's the status of the Gatsby Venture Fund?"

Jerry took out a single sheet of paper from the breast pocket of his jacket, unfolded it and handed it to Moe. "We're done! I expect Hannah to do a final distribution before the end of the year and then shut it down after all the checks clear. The document you're holding is a summary of the fund's performance from inception." He sat back in his chair and waited for Moe to absorb the numbers.

A huge smile enveloped Moe's face. "You are a fucking miracle worker. We're getting all our money back plus a 125-percent return over the five years. Talk about making chicken salad out of chickenshit. Incredible!"

"Gatsby and Hannah are the major reasons for the success; Birney, Jeff, and I helped occasionally with the heavy lifting."

"You're too modest, Jerry. Your Wall Street buddies should be happy," said Moe.

"Nah," said Jerry. "This is chump change for them. I'm not sure any of the Wall Street guys focused on the GVF after Gatsby resigned. The three of us are pleased with the result, that's all that matters. We put our reputations on the line when we sponsored Gatsby and were vindicated by the results. I'm ecstatic to be able to write a Hollywood ending to this script."

"We need to celebrate this with a drink," said Moe. He motioned to the waiter, and asked, "Can you get my colleague and me mimosas?"

"Certainly, sir." By the smile on the kid's face, Moe's cheer was contagious.

As they ate their meals, they chatted about the election, agreeing that the financial meltdown was pretty much the final nail in the coffin for the McCain campaign. The waiter arrived with their mimosas.

Moe raised his glass and said, "To the genius Jerry Bascomb, his lovely wife, Helen, and the two boys." Jerry smiled and clinked glasses with Moe.

When they returned to their breakfasts, Jerry said, "How is the hedge fund doing? I assume that Gatsby pretty much out of the picture."

"He is," said Moe. "Hannah is on her own and doing a fine job. We're still in the black, which under the circumstances is a minor miracle."

"Can we talk about Gatsby?"

"Sure. Shoot."

"Do you know why he contacted me in late March and pitched me so hard to become a partner in the Gatsby Hedge Fund—and was so pissed off at me when I turned him down?"

"That's an easy one. Gatsby and I had lunch and we talked about it when he returned from New York after you guys met. After Bear Stearns collapsed in March, he came here and met with Ace Greenberg and your brother to get their insight on how this could have happened. He was shaken up that a firm like Bear with its long and rich history, and with sixty-plus billion of capital, could disappear in a matter of days. He was not at all heartened by what he learned on that trip. He was told that Bear was just the canary in the coal mine and the financial situation in the US was going to get a lot worse—which certainly turned out to be the case."

"I still don't understand why what he learned would motivate him to hire me."

"Gatsby has enormous respect for you. He thinks you are an outstanding executive, and he trusts you. He realized he did not possess the CEO heft to manage a billion-dollar hedge fund in the financial environment that was anticipated. Also, the cancer scared him. He felt you were his insurance policy. Your rejection of his offer made him feel like he was left to hang, and you know him—he doesn't like to feel helpless. After he withdrew your offer, he decided it was in the best interest of the investors to return half of their investment, and he made Hannah a thirty-percent partner and co-manager. That decision cost him a great deal of money in potential fees, but considering what's happened to the markets, it was a brilliant decision." Moe drained his mimosa.

Jerry did the same and leaned into the table. "What else can you tell me about Gatsby's plea deal? How could he allow himself to get involved in such a mess? It simply doesn't make sense."

"Gatsby has never shared with me any of the background details of the arrest. All I know about it is what's in the newspapers and on the internet. You know they were both taken into custody as they left the Pyramid Club at the Mellon Bank Center where Gatsby has his office."

"But it's Gatsby who's in jail. How did that happen?"

Moe set down his fork and just looked at him, as if the answer were too obvious.

"He took the rap for her?" Jerry said.

"Are you surprised?"

"I guess not," said Jerry. He took a sip of the cold coffee. "How's his health?"

"He had surgery and radiation treatments. When I asked him about it the last time, we talked he said, 'it was iffy,' whatever that means."

"That's a shame," said Jerry. Finally, encouraged by Moe's candor, he asked what was really bothering him. "Shirley's disappearance—I mean, it was so convenient. Do you think he…" Yet in the end, he couldn't bring himself to suggest that Gatsby was a murderer.

Moe's eyes watered. He shook his head. "I have no idea," he said. "I hope not."

After a long silence, Jerry said, "He is certainly an enigma. How he managed to get out of his CPN debt, put off the Pennsylvania Department of Banking and Securities for two years, raise a hundred million dollars using fraudulent personal financial statements, and manage to return all the investor's capital plus $125 million in profits is worthy of a medal."

"Or a novel," said Moe.

Jerry laughed and then mused for a minute. "Moe, despite the grief he's caused me and my family, I can't find it in myself to bear him any resentment."

Moe laughed, "And that has always been the source of Gatsby's greatness."

EPILOGUE

JEFF

Wednesday, January 13, 2009

Jeff Bascomb stood in front of the floor-to-ceiling window in his office and looked out at the view of lower Manhattan. He had enjoyed this view every single day since 1993.

The panorama varied depending on the seasons, and in storms, it sometimes vanished almost completely. And after the attack on the World Trade Center, the scar and the cleanup brought him to tears almost daily for months.

Two years later, when construction of the memorial, the museum, and the new buildings started, the site was always a beehive of activity. Mesmerized by the movement of men and machinery, he experienced the wonder and pride of patriotism, reminiscent of the time he wore a uniform.

He loved his office. And he would miss it when he retired in a couple of years.

He checked his watch. The *Inquirer* reporter would arrive in a half hour to interview him about Gatsby. Although he had been thinking about the interview and the questions the reporter would probably ask, he needed to jot down some notes so he wouldn't ramble.

Forty minutes later, his secretary ushered Sam Mason into his office. Mason was a hulking man with a full head of long gray hair. His suit was rumpled and his tie askew. He shook Jeff's hand and said, "I appreciate your taking the time to talk with me. After Moe turned me down, and I learned that your brother was on an extended vacation, I was at my wits' end. The paper is committed to running the Gatsby retrospective series starting on Friday."

Jeff smiled at him and motioned for him to take a seat near the window so he could enjoy the view. When they were seated, Jeff asked him why he thought Moe turned him down.

"He said he was too broken up over Gatsby's death and he didn't want to talk about it. They'd been friends for over thirty years. He referred me to Jerry and said if Jerry wasn't available, I should talk with you. So, where's Jerry?"

"My brother is reprising Steinbeck's *Travels with Charley* with his black standard poodle. He checks in with me periodically. He is currently in Florida."

"Good for him," said Sam. "How much time can you give me?"

"You have until noon if you need it, but I expect to run out of information before then."

"That's kind of you." Sam reached down and opened his briefcase and removed a small notebook and a tape recorder. "You don't mind if I tape the interview, do you?"

"Not at all."

"Okay, so let's get started. Please tell me about your background and how you came to know Gatsby."

It was a softball question, designed to loosen him up. When Jeff concluded, Sam said, "Jerry has a stellar reputation."

"He certainly does." Jeff laughed. "I'll tell you a family secret. When we were growing up, we were continuously at each other's throats. I used to refer to him as 'the privileged little fucker.' My dad was a three-star general, a martinet, but he cut Jerry a whole lot of slack—which I resented. But I owe Jerry big time, both for the miracle he pulled off at our company in the early '90s and for his helping me get my job at Goldman Sachs."

Sam had jotted almost nothing. He quickly looked through his notebook. Jeff's secretary came into the office carrying a pot of coffee, cups, plates, and a tray loaded with croissants and muffins. She placed everything on the table, served them, and left. Sam took a bite from the buttered croissant he had selected and sipped his coffee. He put down the cup and the croissant and wiped his fingertips with a napkin.

"Can you summarize your overall thoughts and lasting impressions of Mr. Brooks?"

"I knew you would ask me that question," said Jeff. "Gatsby is a complex character—the vicissitudes of his career, the wide range of opinions that many people I know and respect hold about his character, integrity, personality, and ability… All of that makes it impossible to provide a succinct response. And then I had an epiphany."

"An epiphany," said Sam.

"I'm sure you've read *Moby Dick*?"

"Of course, in high school like everyone else."

"Thinking about Gatsby reminded me of the part of the book where Ishmael, who is about to embark on a whaling expedition with Ahab, is in a conversation with a sea captain who had previously sailed with Ahab." Jeff stood and retrieved the book from his desk and opened it to the page he had previously marked. "He asks the captain to tell him about Ahab, and the captain responds as follows."

I know Captain Ahab well; I've sailed with him as mate years ago; I know what he is—a good man—not a pious, good man, like Bildad, but a swearing good man—something like me—only there's a good deal more of him. Aye, aye, I know he was never very jolly; and I know that on the passage home, he was a little out of his mind for a spell; but it was the sharp shooting pains in his bleeding stump that brought that about, as any one might see. I know, too, that ever since he lost his leg last voyage by that accursed whale, he's been a kind of moody—desperate moody, and savage sometimes; but that will all pass off. And once for all, let me tell thee and assure thee, young man, it's better to sail with a moody good captain than a laughing bad one.

Jeff closed the book and placed it on the table. "I could say something comparable about Gatsby. Despite what many believe, he is no Bernie Madoff. The Gatsby Venture Fund distributed returns of more than a hundred and twenty-five percent. On the other hand, he is no choirboy. Jerry and I witnessed several instances in which be bent the rules to the point that if the Gatsby Venture Fund had failed to deliver good returns, he could have been in serious legal trouble." He paused. "Based on my experience, and many conversations with Jerry, who has had the opportunity to work with hundreds of CEOs, I've found that entrepreneurs can be placed on a continuum depending on their ethical behavior, their risk aversion, and their drive."

Sam leaned forward, scribbling notes. "Please go on."

"Both the promoter of a legitimate business proposition and the con man or Ponzi schemer use the same tools to sell their ideas and separate investors from their money—a *Music Man* personality that projects conviction, the prospect of returns far in excess of market averages, risk of loss that is invariably underestimated, and the scarcity of the investment opportunity.

"For example, since Madoff never invested any of the money he took from investors and generated fabricated statements, he is at the zero-percent end of the continuum. On the other extreme is Steve Jobs, who made Apple into a financial powerhouse delivering new products and great returns year after year. He is at the hundred-percent end of the continuum. But for every Madoff or Jobs there are thousands upon thousands of entrepreneurs who fall between the two on the continuum and the positions they occupy at the end of their careers is not only a result of their business skill but often the result of luck—both good and bad. An entrepreneur promoting a risky business plan might get some lucky breaks, along with adequate financing and competent board members, and succeed. He could approach Steve Jobs' position. Another equally competent, driven, and dedicated entrepreneur may start with a realistic plan that is not over-hyped but be unable to adequately finance it. Then he loses some key employees, occasionally skips payroll tax deposits to buy supplies, and borrows on collateral that is overvalued.

He may eventually be forced to declare bankruptcy, at which time every one of his financial transgressions will become public, subject to legal action. He will end up being placed toward the Madoff end of the continuum."

"Your analysis is good," said Sam. "When I think about the various entrepreneurs in Philly that I've written about over the years, I can place every one of them on your continuum. But where do you place Gatsby?"

Jeff smiled. "That, Mr. Mason, will be your decision."

Sam looked over the list of questions he had prepared and the several pages of notes he'd taken. He looked up at Jeff and made a show of being finished. "I think you covered everything I need for the article. Gatsby certainly was a complex individual."

"Most of the entrepreneurs that I've worked with over the past twenty-five years are. Gatsby was just one of the more flamboyant ones."

Sam stood, opened his weathered briefcase, and shrugged his coat onto his shoulders. He tucked away his notebook and pushed his coffee mug away. He patted his pockets, checked his wallet, and by all measures was on his way out.

"Oh, before I forget…" Sam picked up his briefcase. "It's got me stumped, and maybe you have a thought. Who do you think arranged for the disappearance of Shirley and Cissy?"

Jeff noticed the tape recorder still on the table, and the red light was on.

Jeff chuckled. "Fortunately, in the words of a good friend who devoted his life and career to Israel, 'I don't know, and I don't need to know.' But, if you discover the identities of the guilty parties, it might garner you a Pulitzer."

The End